CRUEL
IS THE
LIGHT

This book contains fictional depictions of self-harm. The intention of these scenes is to establish an ancient ritual that is part of this alternate historical world.

Text copyright © 2025 by Sophie Clark
Jacket art copyright © 2025 by Mona Finden
Map copyright © 2025 by Virginia Allyn

All rights reserved. Published in the United States by Alfred A. Knopf, an imprint of Random House Children's Books, a division of Penguin Random House LLC, New York. Originally published by Penguin Random House UK, London, and Penguin Random House Australia, Sydney, in 2025.

Knopf, Borzoi Books, and the colophon are registered trademarks of Penguin Random House LLC.

Visit us on the Web! GetUnderlined.com

Educators and librarians, for a variety of teaching tools, visit us at RHTeachersLibrarians.com

Library of Congress Cataloging-in-Publication Data
Names: Clark, Sophie, author.
Title: Cruel is the light / by Sophie Clark.
Description: First edition. | New York : Alfred A. Knopf, 2025. | "A Borzoi Book." | Audience term: Teenagers | Audience: Ages 12 and up. | Audience: Grades 7–9. | Summary: When high-ranking exorcist Selene and mysterious soldier Jules form an alliance despite their forbidden attraction, they uncover a terrible conspiracy about the centuries-old war between demons and the Vatican.
Identifiers: LCCN 2024024522 (print) | LCCN 2024024523 (ebook) | ISBN 978-0-593-81072-9 (hardcover) | ISBN 978-0-593-81074-3 (ebook)
Subjects: CYAC: Imaginary wars and battles—Fiction. | Demonology—Fiction. | Vatican City—Fiction. | Fantasy. | Romance stories. | LCGFT: Fantasy fiction. | Romance fiction. | Novels.
Classification: LCC PZ7.1.C5824 Cr 2025 (print) | LCC PZ7.1.C5824 (ebook) | DDC [Fic]—dc23

The text of this book is set in 11-point Adobe Garamond.

Printed in the United States of America
10 9 8 7 6 5 4 3 2 1
First American Edition

The authorized representative in the EU for product safety and compliance is Penguin Random House Ireland, Morrison Chambers, 32 Nassau Street, Dublin D02 YH68, Ireland, https://eu-contact.penguin.ie.

Random House Children's Books supports the First Amendment and celebrates the right to read.

Penguin Random House values and supports copyright. Copyright fuels creativity, encourages diverse voices, promotes free speech, and creates a vibrant culture. Thank you for buying an authorized edition of this book and for complying with copyright laws by not reproducing, scanning, or distributing any part of it in any form without permission. You are supporting writers and allowing Penguin Random House to continue to publish books for every reader. Please note that no part of this book may be used or reproduced in any manner for the purpose of training artificial intelligence technologies or systems.

SOPHIE CLARK

ALFRED A. KNOPF
NEW YORK

For my mother, Amanda—this book would not
exist without you.

You give more than anyone.

And to my very first readers—
thanks for coming along for the ride!

THE ACADEMY

TRAINING COURTYARD

WAR FALCON TOWER

TRAINING YARDS

IMPERIUM BELLUM RESIDENCE

THE FACADE

ACADEMY RESIDENCES

THE OBE[...]

TRASTEVERE

ALLEVA PALAZZO

SPARROW'S JOINT

THE AELIAN BRIDGE

THE HOLY VA[...]

Benedetta was almost clear when broken glass crunched beneath her boot. The demon's head snapped in her direction. Selene raced to intercept as the demon went for Benedetta, but it was impossibly fast even as its skin split at the seams of those fingers. The demon's jaw disengaged as it lunged, tearing its cheeks as it bit out Benedetta's jugular.

No!

Benedetta's body slumped to its knees.

Tumbling forward, Selene aimed and squeezed the trigger. Her bullets shattered a cobweb-draped chandelier as the demon skittered away, making a curious sound. Laughter.

It was *laughing.*

Propelled by cold rage, Selene followed, driving it back. Reaching for the sword slung across her back, she caught the demon the moment it failed to navigate the second chandelier, lopping off its legs at the knee.

An agonized shriek pierced her eardrums and the world rang with pure silence. Across the room, Ambrose pressed his remaining palm to a bleeding ear.

Selene ignored her own pain. "Get out!"

He obeyed as the creature landed scrabbling on the floor.

Selene pinned it with her sword, straddling it to hold down its clawing hands. It bucked its small, powerful body. It could crush a man's skull between two overlong fingers, but her strength was greater. Selene leaned to look into those haunting blue eyes and bared her teeth.

She would make it suffer for Benedetta's life.

It lunged, teeth clicking in front of her face. Selene punched it. Once, twice. It dodged her third, and her fist ruptured stone. Pain popped behind her eyes when she flexed her fingers.

The demon subsided and Selene drew her knife. Best to end this quickly. *An exorcism, then*, she thought, a familiar ache behind her ribs. *Before anyone else dies.*

And so, with the knife she hadn't used to save Ambrose's arm, she carved the symbols.

Devour. Return. Teeth. Burn.

When her blood hit the air, it smoked, coiling and lashing like a viper. The symbols she whittled into bone flared gold, as though filled by molten metal. Her magic could raze a city block if she wanted it to. Perhaps the whole of Rome.

And in *that* breath of misused magic, she'd be worse than dead and a monster in more ways than one.

Her hearing slammed back and her eyesight cleared so evening became a summer afternoon. Only the demon beneath her was shadowy. A writhing supernova of untamed energy. *This* was power.

She could feel everything that moved in the apartment building. Could even feel the skittering heartbeat of a mouse holding still in the walls.

As though time had slowed, she could count every eyelash and freckle on the demon's stolen face as she laid a palm against its forehead. The creature lunged, teeth lengthening. Then it disappeared in a burst of light so intense it could blind.

Blinking the spots away, Selene approached Benedetta. Her blond hair haloed her head, slowly soaking crimson. Horrific, even to the *Macellaia di Roma*. The Butcher of Rome.

"I'm sorry," Selene breathed, closing the healer's eyes.

A draft stirred up dust from the dull parquet floor, caressing Caterina's dark hair over her cheek where silvery scar tissue devoured smooth skin on one side of her face. "That was a Level Four," Caterina said accusingly, setting her shotgun on her shoulder.

Selene waved Caterina off. "I know. I didn't sense it." She

THE HOLY VATICAN EMPIRE:
A HIERARCHY

Exorcist Primus OF THE HOLY VATICAN EMPIRE
The Exorcist Primus is the supreme ruler and spiritual leader of the
Holy Vatican Empire, though he delegates the day-to-day running
of the empire to the two Imperiums in their respective capacities as
Vatican military leader and head of government.

The current Exorcist Primus, His Holiness Alexander II, is af-
flicted with poor health and has relinquished even more of his re-
sponsibilities than usual to the ambitious young Imperium Bellum.

Imperium Bellum | LORD OF WAR
As military head of the Holy Vatican Empire, the Imperium Bellum has near unlimited power in the realm of war. This role is presently occupied by Cesare Alleva, who has accumulated even greater
power as the Exorcist Primus's health wanes. In times of war an
especially impressive Imperium Bellum may be known as the
Shadow of God.

Cesare Alleva is the Shadow of God.

Imperium Politikos | CHANCELLOR OF STATE
A role currently held by exorcist Adriano de Sanctis. In years prior,
the political arm of the empire's power structure was divorced from
the Vatican and the cult of the Deathless God, but in the past half

century it has become exceedingly rare for this position to be filled by anyone other than a Roman exorcist.

The Sovereign EMPRESS OF THE HOLY VATICAN EMPIRE

Ofelia Augustus is the current Empress of the Holy Vatican Empire. As sovereign she fulfills a purely ceremonial role. The Imperial family lost power in the years since the Deathless God made his home in Rome and the Vatican gained influence and control.

EXORCIST FIRST CLASS

The highest class of exorcist in the Vatican. They will be a team leader and afforded the freedom to direct their team as they see fit when not deployed directly by the Imperium Bellum. This class is reserved for those who are capable—or are believed to be capable by their superior—of taking down a Viscount, a Level V demon. Even Exorcists First Class only have an estimated 1 percent chance of surviving a Demon Duke.

EXORCIST SECOND CLASS

To be promoted to Exorcist Second Class, they must be believed capable of killing a Noble—a Level IV demon. In rare cases, they might find a Level V demon an unsurvivable challenge.

EXORCIST THIRD CLASS

Newly graduated exorcists will become Exorcists Third Class upon graduating the Academy—if they do not attain the skills required to meet this class, they will not be allowed to graduate. Exorcists Third Class must be capable of defeating all demons from Levels I to III.

In rare cases, an exorcist will specialize in healing in the same way a brother or sister of medicine might. However, unlike artificers, Exorcist healers have the capacity to access far greater magic and thus are capable of *miracles*. They will never climb the ranks, as they are deemed incapable of killing a Noble—a Level IV demon—which is a requirement of promotion.

Even so, they are *extremely valuable*.

Artificer

There are two classes of artificer: medicine and war.

Medicine

Brothers and sisters of medicine are the Vatican's healers—they are the final stand between Rome and ruin, as they keep the Vatican ranks from being decimated.

War

Brothers and sisters of war choose the martial path and may then select one of four subclasses:

- Gunslinger—warriors specialized in the use of artillery and explosives
- Brawler—a rare subclass, brawlers specialize in close-range and hand-to-hand combat
- Melee—warriors specialized in mid- to close-range combat and utilize swords and other bladed weapons
- Ranged—warriors specialized in ranged attacks, who do not utilize artillery-type weapons

Many exorcists also choose to specialize in one of these classes. This specialization is less vital to their continued survival, as they have their magic to draw upon. Artificers, by contrast, can specialize only once, and craft their chosen weapon during their final year before graduating from the Vatican Academy as accredited artificers.

VATICAN ACADEMY
HANDBOOK: THE DEMONS

LEVEL I DEMONS aka *Curses*
They whisper from the shadows and cause madness. Sometimes they're drawn to exorcists and more powerful demons and are usually destroyed by proximity. They will fade away in the human realm unless they are clever. They have always been here in some form.

LEVEL II DEMONS aka *Ghouls*
Ghouls can temporarily possess carrion birds and dead humans if they are in want of a body because, like Fiends, Ghouls in this world are frequently observed to be more smokelike than physical beings. They are still dangerous and can briefly manifest teeth and claws with which to maim or, indeed, kill.

LEVEL III DEMONS aka *Fiends*
Their bodies are rarely intact in this world and Fiends are frequently observed to be possessed of smokelike forms rather than a physical body, though they are no less dangerous in their ephemeral form. They can possess humans—but their presence is a corrupting force that destroys the host body quickly.

They can be challenging for all levels of artificer and Exorcists Third Class.

Level IV Demons aka *Nobles*

While Nobles can be killed by Exorcists Second Class and above, they are far more dangerous to civilians and Vatican support staff. Though they're not a hazard on a grander scale like Level V and VI demons, Nobles can wreak havoc in a limited area and are considered a severe threat to life.

They can be challenging for Exorcists Second Class.

Level V Demons aka *Viscounts*

Viscounts are the first of the Cataclysm Class demons.

May have access to elemental magic, capable of possessing humans with some consequences, but a successful magical exorcism performed by a Vatican exorcist can result in the human surviving.

They are a threat even to Exorcists First Class.

Level VI Demons aka *Dukes*

Demon Dukes are the most powerful demons. They can easily possess humans and are capable of widespread destruction with their innate command of powerful elemental magic. They can remain undetected for a time when they possess humans, but their magic is too great for human bodies to contain for long. Each one has been named and cataloged by the Vatican.

Only Exorcists First Class have any chance of surviving an encounter.

However, survival is not an eventuality to be expected and the Holy Vatican Empire thanks you for your life and death.

DRAMATIS PERSONAE

JULES LACROIX (*Stigmajka*)—A soldier and corporal in the Vatican Empire's army based in Ostrava, Czechoslovakia. Abandoned as a baby in Saint-Jeannet, France, and raised an orphan in Nice.

SELENE ALLEVA (*Macellaia di Roma* | the Butcher of Rome)— Exorcist Second Class and captain within the Vatican's demon-hunting military arm.

CESARE ALLEVA (*Imperium Bellum* | Lord of War)—The exorcist in command of the Vatican's military, known as the Shadow of God for his influence and power. Uncle and guardian to Selene, he has taken on the duties of Exorcist Primus due to the current Primus's failing health.

KIAN DAUMIER—A constable in the Gendarmerie de Nice, he is Jules's childhood friend and confidant.

SPARROW (*L'occhio della Malavita* | the Eye of the Underworld)— The demon who oversees the Vatican compact that allows Rome's licensed and branded part-demons to live.

VATICAN EXORCISTS

ALEXANDER II, HIS HOLINESS—The ailing Exorcist Primus of Rome.

ADRIANO DE SANCTIS (*Imperium Politikos* | Chancellor of State)— The exorcist in charge of the Vatican's political arm, he was once mentor to Matteo Alleva.

MATTEO ALLEVA (†)—Exorcist and father to Selene, he was earmarked to replace Adriano de Sanctis as Imperium Politikos before he was crucified as a traitor against God.

Eliot D'Alessandro—Exorcist Third Class, childhood friend and fiancé to Selene who was exiled from Rome as a youth.

Benedetta Fiore—Exorcist Third Class, trained in healing and the newest member of Selene's team, known for her kindness.

Florentina Altieri—Exorcist Second Class, classmate and rival from Selene's Academy days, and current second-in-command to Captain Gabriel Notaro.

Gabriel Notaro—Exorcist First Class, Florentina Altieri's commanding officer and a captain within the Vatican's demon-hunting military arm.

Lorena—Exorcist First Class, superior to Vissia and Tobio, deployed to Ostrava.

Tommaso—Exorcist Third Class, first meets Jules on the battlefield in Ostrava.

VATICAN ARTIFICERS

Ambrose Zurzulo—Brother of war, brawler, a new member of Selene's team known for his reckless attitude.

Caterina Altamura—Sister of war, gunslinger, second-in-command to Selene Alleva.

Lucia Scavo—Sister of medicine, cleric, loyal only to Selene and Caterina, and member of Selene's team, known for her sensitivity to demon magic.

Vissia—Sister of war, gunslinger, a member of Lorena's team deployed to Ostrava.

Tobio—Brother of war, melee, a member of Lorena's team deployed to Ostrava.

Chiara—Sister of war, melee, a member of Gabriel and Florentina's team.

HOLY VATICAN EMPIRE & IMPERIAL MILITARY

FARAH BACHELET—Jules's commanding officer, a sergeant in the Vatican Empire's army.

OFELIA AUGUSTUS—Empress of the Holy Vatican Empire, a purely ceremonial role in the years since the holy power of the Vatican gained influence and control.

LADY YAJIN—Trusted adviser and lady-in-waiting to Empress Augustus.

GILBERT—A member of the Empress's security detail.

THE DEMONS

BALIEL—Duke of Briars, the most powerful of the twelve Demon Dukes, he has not been seen in the human world for many years.

THE WEATHER DEMON—A powerful demon summoned to fight in Ostrava.

ANASTASIA ALEXANDROVA ROMANOV—Tsarina of the Caspian Federation and notorious half-demon.

ARIUS—The Uncrowned King, a powerful demon.

VALERIA—Duchess of Razors, the traitor.

THE DEMON UNDERWORLD

GIULIETTA—Part-demon bouncer who sometimes works for Sparrow.

KALINDRA—Part-demon information broker who sometimes works for Sparrow.

CRUEL

IS THE

LIGHT

PROLOGUE

Baliel felt the weight of a world not his own before he had eyes with which to see. It wrapped itself around him, smothering his light. The world was dim. *Night.* He rolled his shoulders experimentally. The skin pulled too tight. Stretching, tearing. The very fibers of the flesh coming undone before his magic sewed it back together over the wings of his shoulder blades. Muscle and tendon too; all tore and healed in moments.

The tarnished glass of a mirror captured an image that Baliel did not recognize. Turning, he surveyed the fragile shell that housed him.

He was still beautiful, his essence carving the bones to better suit his needs. But as it did, he corrupted it.

Even as he watched, the violent blue of his eyes burned the sockets black.

I suppose this will have to do, he thought, curling fingers that were lengthened by his overwhelming essence. The skin over his knuckles split, and his lip curled in distaste. An Elysian like him rarely fit comfortably inside a human shell. With the possible exception of those born with Elysian blood in their veins. At a stretch, even Kairos blood would do.

The humans called them all *demons* just the same.

Cool air slid along his naked limbs as he stepped onto the street and turned toward the stone church built into the mountainside.

He towered head and shoulders above the humans who skittered like rats in the shadows.

Flurries of frozen white danced around him.

Snow, his memory supplied.

He tested the word. Only the ashen scratch at the edges hinted at the breakdown of the vocal cords. This body would not last.

Baliel flicked his fingers, dispelling the flurry, and his magic razed the street. His essence flared, striking the turbulent clouds with a lick of cerulean flame. All that remained of the terraced street were charcoal sticks jutting into the sky like a blackened, burned forest.

Running his eyes over the carnage, Baliel frowned.

He would need to be more careful; this shell barely contained him as it was.

CHAPTER ONE

*G*od created man and demon.
    Demon crucified God.
    Man abandoned God.

And one more tenet only the Vatican knew:

Man harnessed demons' unholy magic.

Selene Alleva ghosted her blade over the faint blue veins of her inner arm, lingering when she found the symbol carved into her bones. *Devour.* She hesitated. Her magic was the enemy, bleeding her with every exorcism. If it was only fear of pain that gave her pause, or some misplaced *principle*, then she could overcome it. Pain no longer frightened her—it had become familiar in the years of her Vatican training.

Dio Immortale, she swore. She'd made mistakes tonight. If she had done one thing differently, she wouldn't be in this predicament now—poised to bleed herself for power as the scent of rot and mold encased her. The metallic tang of blood beneath it all. She should *never* have lowered her guard.

*   *   *

The threat of snow scented the air. Selene shivered, but not because the evening's chill sliced knifelike up her spine. A rank wave of demonic magic ached through her eye teeth and into the depths of her skull.

That was more than one demon.

They tasted like violence. Like a split lip. Vaguely iron and putrid. "Captain Alleva?"

Selene silenced her subordinate with a look. Ambrose Zurzulo was not perceptive enough to feel the tainted magic, and Selene had no patience for his dearth of natural talent. She glanced at the rune-carved metal hugging his hands. *Knuckle-dusters. Honestly.* But he was too infatuated with his own magnificence to notice her disdain.

Why anyone would elect for extreme close-range combat, and willingly let a demon so damn near, she had no clue.

"We're close. Move." She led her team down a shallow flight of stairs, chasing the cold pull of demon magic to a crumbling stucco building at the end of the street. It looked abandoned—but wasn't. Two. No, three. Maybe more. An infestation of this size was not unheard of in the heart of Rome, but it was unusual to find one so close to the Vatican.

She would reward them with steel for their trouble.

Selene skidded to a stop out of sight of the windows, flanked by Ambrose and Benedetta. Both were new to her team, and while Benedetta Fiore had been in Selene's year at the Academy, they'd never been close. It wasn't ideal that today was her first opportunity to see them in action.

Ambrose stretched his fingers, knuckles cracking. "I'll take point," he said, starting to shadowbox.

Not ideal at all.

But she had little say in the matter. Her superiors had spoken, and if the Vatican was anything at all, it was a place of strict hierarchy.

"I think not," Selene said, her voice dangerously soft. "Don't even look a demon in the eye without my say-so." She counted on her fingers. "Obey. Impress me. Survive. In *that* order. Simple enough." *Even for you.*

She pinned Benedetta with her eyes. "Stay close to Zurzulo. He'll protect you."

Ambrose nodded his agreement, and the knot of worry in her chest loosened. Just a bit.

"What about you?" Benedetta asked.

Selene held her gaze. "I'll protect you too."

Benedetta blinked wide-eyed, and smiled a lightbulb smile. "Oh, I know that. I *meant* who's going to protect you?"

Selene didn't think that required an answer.

A tall figure rounded the corner. "O Captain, my Captain," Caterina Altamura drawled, flicking a still-glowing cigarette into the dark. "Relax. The cavalry's here."

Selene finally let a small smile show.

A weapons artificer like Ambrose, Caterina was as skillful as she was insubordinate.

Then a second figure trailed Caterina out of the dark.

Lucia Scavo angled her pointed chin into the breeze, turning her pretty heart-shaped face as though scenting the air. Her sensitivity to demon magic was well known within the Vatican, and Selene trusted Lucia's instincts nearly as much as her own.

Selene extended her senses too. Her power was always with her. In her blood. But it sang louder now in proximity to demons. She glanced at Lucia. "I don't feel anything above a Level Two."

The sister of medicine nodded, her cheeks whipped ruddy by the cold. "And no more than five. All low grade."

The Vatican ranked demons on a six-point scale. Curses and Ghouls frequently broke through nowadays. Low level, low difficulty, but with high potential for collateral damage. Enough to force the Vatican to respond quickly. With extreme prejudice.

Ambrose flipped a hexagonal disc that glimmered in the weak lamplight, and Selene snatched it from the air.

She frowned. "Do you have any idea what this is?"

The brawler pushed his hands into his pockets. "Found it."

"Where?"

He shrugged.

Selene turned it between her fingers, inspecting it. It was stamped with the seal of the Deathless God. A ward coin. One of many hidden within statues around Rome, their powerful magic working together to ward off demons. Which begged the question, why did Ambrose have it?

Lucia's voice broke into her thoughts, sounding uncharacteristically hesitant. "I sense . . . maybe a Fiend?"

Benedetta paled at that, touching her forehead, throat, and the middle of her chest in a quick prayer. As if Selene needed further confirmation Benedetta had no business facing demons in the field.

"Save your prayers," Selene said coldly. "No need to call on God for a Level Three."

Caterina smothered a smile, but Lucia smirked openly.

Ignoring them, Selene slipped the ward coin into her pocket and turned to the building. The chipped stucco facade appeared more orange than pink in the glow of the streetlamps, but Selene was more focused on the presences beyond. They throbbed weakly, like butterflies in her fist. Soon she'd crush them just as easily.

Despite that confidence, unease coiled in her rib cage. Something felt off.

Caterina sliced her thumb and pressed it against the seal on her rifle. Bright threads of power raced along the gun's six barrels, as her blood unlocked its full potential.

The five of them parted ways, silently sweeping the apartments on the ground floor before climbing the stairs to the next. Selene shadowed Ambrose and Benedetta, keeping them in her line of sight. She didn't need to tell Caterina and Lucia what to do—they'd climbed the ranks two years ahead of her at the Academy and had been an effective team far longer than she'd been their commander. She respected their prowess. But she didn't trust the other two.

She'd fought tooth and nail against having Benedetta on this mission, but, no. *Two healers*, they'd said. And so she obeyed her directive.

A smoky, vaguely reptilian Curse demon trickled from the shadows, stretching toward Ambrose. Level One. Selene cut through it before Ambrose even noticed, flicking clinging shadows off her blade. She turned in the center of the room and then sheathed her sword.

Behind her came a clang as a Ghoul scrabbled its way out of a disused dumbwaiter, grinning rows of serrated teeth in a horrible wide mouth. Level Two. Distinguishable by the fact that she felt barely a ripple of power from it. It had made its home in a corpse on the wrong side of decomposing, corrupting it with its magic. Benedetta shrank back, but Ambrose strode forward. His eyes gleamed with the fire of a subordinate desperate to prove his mettle.

Selene flung an arm out to stop him. "Wait!"

But Ambrose crowed a battle cry and wound up for a punch that would take the demon's head off its shoulders.

The demon was deceptively fast. It opened its terrible maw, swallowing Ambrose's arm to the elbow. His scream ricocheted around inside her ribs.

"Captain!" Ambrose pleaded, his arm and those damned knuckle-dusters buried in the demon's gullet. Time slowed as she watched his eyes—black now from blown pupils and desperation. *Save me*, they said. *Save me, please.*

The arm was salvageable. His stupidity—*terminal*.

In a blink she had her knife poised over skin and bone—the cutting edge above the symbol for *devour*. She hesitated. Triggering her magic would devour another piece of her soul. If she wasn't careful, soon she'd have nothing left. Cold fingers caressed her spine at the unwelcome thought. She moved the blade away from her skin.

Sorry, Ambrose.

Even a single drop of her magic was worth more than a limb. And so she sacrificed his arm on the altar of her ambition. There were other, far more powerful demons to kill, and she didn't know how much soul she had left.

She flipped the knife and sheathed it, then drew the gun at her thigh in the same sinuous movement. Ambrose's eyes widened as Selene chose, as she did so often, to fight and condemn with hot metal and blade. Her first bullet detached his arm at the shoulder. Selene strode closer, firing shot after shot until the demon went still. As she nudged it with her boot, her nose wrinkled in distaste. Deader than dead. Still not dead enough.

Selene toyed with the idea of shooting it again.

Instead, she turned on her heel, blinking blood from her lashes. Benedetta knelt beside Ambrose, applying a tourniquet to his arm.

As Ambrose whimpered piteously, Selene thought about the

final unspoken tenet of their religion. *Man harnessed demons' unholy magic.*

A secret. Though perhaps not their most dangerous. One known only to the select few who graduated from the Vatican's elite military academy. Demons had given them the means of fighting back. Unwillingly. Bitterly, perhaps.

At his continued whimpering, Selene indicated the brawler. "Silence him."

Biting her lower lip, Benedetta touched his forehead with two fingers. His pain drained away. Silent now, Ambrose glared at Selene over Benedetta's shoulder, hatred replacing agony.

Selene crouched in front of him. "We'll get you another arm. One made of steel this time, like your little knuckle-dusters."

Benedetta redirected her attention to the demon. Pushing her wispy blond hair beneath her habit, she withdrew vials to collect blood and humors. She hesitated over the mess Selene had made of the demon's skull before delicately extracting a tooth for later analysis.

Selene extended her senses as she circled the room, open to the slightest stirring of demon magic. Nothing. Satisfied, she followed the hum of voices down the hallway as Caterina and Lucia compared notes on their kills. She stepped into the doorway just in time to see Caterina level her secondary weapon, a shotgun, and blast a demon across the room. The bullet flared on impact.

As the imprint of the demon faded, she felt another.

Pivoting, she searched the dark corners. Somewhere nearby another demon waited. It plucked at her senses like a spider playing the threads of its own web—gleaning information from her. More than she was getting from it. Selene hissed, drawing her handgun. Too slow. A demon smashed through the lead-light transom window over the door on the other side of the hall. It had crawled into the body of a small girl. Bright doll-blue eyes glinted prettily through a fall of dark hair. Its elbows bent the wrong way as it skittered across the ceiling, disappearing into the hallway's gloom.

A Level Four.

Caterina and Lucia were supposed to have cleared that end, but had evidently fucked it up. And *she* had lowered her guard. How had she not sensed a *Noble*? Plunging through milky spiderwebs, she arrived in the main room a split second after the demon. Borne by the essence of a child, it would burn out quickly. When its power started to wane, it would seek another body to consume from within. *Parasite.*

It already had Benedetta cornered.

Selene met the child's blue eyes. *No, damn it all, don't lose focus. The child's gone.* The reminder rang hollow.

Projecting calm, Selene twitched a finger. *Go.*

Benedetta eased toward the closest doorway.

"Well, hello," Selene said conversationally.

"Exorcist," the creature hissed, tongue curling across its dead cheek.

She had to keep the demon's attention on her. "I'm impressed you managed to penetrate this far into Rome undetected. Quite a feat. You must be powerful indeed."

The demon preened. "More powerful with you. I shall enjoy possessing your body. My every whim will be at our fingertips." It curled its backward-jointed fingers, skin and tendons snapping.

Selene nodded sagely. "Ah, yes. I too appreciate that mental imagery."

The demon blinked double-lidded eyes, head tipping. "You do?"

Her brow inched higher. The Noble was a literalist, then.

turned to Lucia, whose white habit was now splattered with gore. "And neither did *you*. I thought you were meant to be good at this."

Lucia shrugged. "We all make mistakes."

Selene jabbed her finger to where Benedetta's body lay. "Tell *her* that."

Caterina stepped between them. "She said sorry."

"She did *not*," Selene drawled, circling the room. "And I shouldn't need to point out that Lucia wasn't the only one who made mistakes tonight."

Caterina's jaw worked but she didn't argue.

"The next regional assignment will be all yours. You two can get out of Rome for a while. Enjoy the *quiet*."

Distantly Ave Maria, one of the Vatican's six bells, rang out a fraction of a second ahead of the others. Angling her wrist, Selene glanced at her watch. *Late. Damn.*

Pivoting on her heel, she left them to the cleanup, her expression melting from angry to contemplative.

If she alone had made that mistake . . . well, that was one thing. But Lucia had also miscalculated the enemy's strength and numbers. Unusual, because she was the most perceptive in all the Vatican. It made Selene's stomach coil. *Unusual* was never good when it came to demons.

Unusual meant something had changed.

And death was sure to follow.

CHAPTER TWO

A newspaper broadsheet tumbled over the frozen mud of the battlefield, a dark silhouette against the blood-smeared horizon. Jules Lacroix blinked. No, not blood. Blood never remained that aggressive shade for long. That particular vibrancy was just the rising sun. Jules let out a long breath. The endless night was almost done. *Praise the Deathless God.*

The broadsheet caught against a coil of barbed wire, fluttering in the wind. As though unwilling to be rid of imminent death just yet, Jules stood brushing ice off his shoulders. *What news from Rome?*

Eyeing the tattered broadsheet, Jules pulled himself over the edge of the trench, scrabbling in the mud to reach it. Ignoring tired shouts, he grabbed the newspaper and slid back to safety just as gunfire ate up the mud. He grinned, sliding down the wall as his legs collapsed beneath him.

Someone kicked his boot. "Crazy motherfucker."

Yeah, and? Jules smoothed the broadsheet over his knees, smearing mud and printing ink.

Most of the soldiers in the trench with him were new, so green they still had the puppy fat of youth. Still remembered the taste of croissants, the scent of snow untainted by gunpowder and blood, remembered what it was like to close their eyes without seeing death painted on the backs of their eyelids. He didn't know any of them by name. Not one. And he wouldn't bother learning either. Not when they'd only die like all the rest.

Jules drank in the large type of the headline: ROME CRIES BLOOD. He smirked slightly, knowing the headline wasn't about the war. *Their* blood didn't count. No doubt some exorcist had left a trail of carnage again. It happened a lot. Demons didn't go down easy. He knew that better than most.

The most powerful demons could kill a regiment single-handed. The ones who played with fire or wind, or spoke to the wild things. The ones who controlled ice. Jules could count on one hand the number of times a demon like that had been within even a hundred miles. Otherwise he wouldn't be breathing.

With shaking fingers Jules withdrew a tin of slender black cigarettes and put one between his lips, but the matches were damp and wouldn't strike. "Shit."

He squinted at the date. January 6. He turned nineteen today. It was four years to the day since the orphanage in Nice had given him the steel-capped boot an hour before dawn. He'd been only fifteen. That auspicious age when French boys with no family and fewer prospects were shipped off to war.

Matron had dragged him out by his ear. "Out with you, little thorn. Fifteen today and a man in all ways but the ones that count! Now you can change that last, at least."

And so he had.

He put away his cigarette tin, eyes roaming the page.

Gazette de France

ROME CRIES BLOOD

VIGIL FOR THE LOST AS Vatican contends with a surge of demon activity. The Office of the Exorcist Primus has refused to make a statement about the recent clashes between their exorcists and demons.

News out of the Holy Vatican Empire's great capital is unclear at best, but unofficial word from the Office of the Imperium Bellum is that there is "no cause for alarm."

Uncorroborated reports belie these claims, with eyewitness testimony suggesting greater numbers of low-class demons have been terrorizing Rome in recent weeks, leading to a rising death toll that is as yet unconfirmed.

In light of this, we must ask ourselves, what is to be done? Can Rome survive this adversity? Talks persist of shifting the capital as another exodus sweeps the population . . .

Rome. The Holy Vatican Empire was a ravenous beast devouring all Europe. Now even their proud French newspapers spent ink on constant speculation about the capital, where the Deathless God resided in His steepled churches that had grown jagged and dark, their stone spires edging toward the sky as the exorcists built up their defenses. All to protect their god from the demons who wanted to prove that *Deathless* was not a permanent state of being, only wishful thinking.

He considered dropping the newspaper into the slurry beneath his feet, but thought better of it and tucked it into his pocket instead.

"Jules, get up from there. You're done."

He reached for the rough wooden bar of the trench, the splinters biting his palm proof enough he was alive as he pulled himself nose to nose with his superior. Frost gilded his eyelashes and eyebrows and probably his stubble since yesterday's shave. The cold was inside his bones. Had been for four years, since he began haunting the no-man's land outside Ostrava with the rest of his regiment.

He could barely remember what warmth felt like.

"Sergeant—"

"Corporal Lacroix, that was not a request."

Jules sighed, pushing his hands into his pockets.

"How long since you've slept? How long since you've eaten?"

Jules shook his head, unable to answer either question. "Farah—"

"My name is not an answer, Corporal. You look half dead." The hard line between her brows deepened, and he could see what she was thinking: *More than half.*

Jules pressed his lips together, watching a place behind her ear. She was right. And maybe he should be. Dead with the rest of his regiment.

Farah snapped her fingers in his face, drawing back his wandering mind. Worry worked its way into her eyes, and for the first time he considered that maybe she was right to be concerned. As he followed her back through the trenches toward their main encampment, nestled in the lee of Ostrava's crumbling stone wall, he wavered on his feet. Hunger was not new, far from it, but this hollow ache had settled in beneath his ribs.

Farah caught him, ducking beneath his arm. "Damn it, Lacroix. Starving yourself will not buy us victory."

"Worth a try." He let a small grin tip his lips.

She shook her head, frustration darkening her eyes. Just a few years older than Jules, not even twenty-five, and already silver glinted in the gold at her temples. Unlike him, she'd volunteered for this— trained for this. But still, war ate them all.

"Jules, you need to take care of yourself. You're the last of my original men. Don't make me walk forward alone." Farah looked away, gazing blankly over the frozen mud. After a pause she added in the clipped tone of his superior, "Besides, Rome cannot afford to lose you."

As Farah led Jules along the path farthest from the grimmest of front-line trenches, Jules recognized a few faces. They watched him warily, nodding when he caught their eye. He could be back here too, warmer and drier than the pups at the front.

Lacroix. How many kills? Does that make it a hundred, Lacroix? Two hundred? More?

Jules heard them as though they screamed at him, and looked away. Two hundred demon kills would be admirable for sure, but it was nowhere near the reality. His hands were dark with blood. But the worst part was how intrinsic it felt to him. The strength of his body. The pull of the kill. Being *truly* excellent at something. When it was just him with a blade in his hand, the world became quiet. His choices simple.

Live or die.

Fight or die.

Kill or die.

And he was good at it. Sometimes he hated how good.

Absently Jules tugged at his sleeve. Countless pale scars twined in neat rows past his elbows. He felt eyes on him and adjusted his shirt cuff lower, hiding . . .

The ozone scent of distant lightning made his nose itch. Jules tipped his head, closing his eyes for a moment. A storm thickened the air, making it almost crackle with intent. The blood red of predawn had diluted into a weak piss yellow, and when Jules narrowed his eyes against the rising sun, he could see storm clouds gathering nearly out of sight.

He almost slammed into Farah, tugging again at his sleeve.

"Inside." She held open the canvas door of her tent, not missing his gesture.

"Farah—"

"Sergeant Bachelet."

Jules rolled his eyes and ducked under her arm, ignoring the whistles that abruptly ceased when Farah cut the offending parties a sharp look. Dropping the door and lending them some semblance of privacy, she set a kettle on to boil.

"Take those off. I intend to burn them. They reek worse than a dead demon's asshole."

"You want me naked that bad, Farah? This is the last shirt I have."

"No, it's not." She indicated her pallet bed and a neat stack of clothes—fresh elements of his usual uniform. "A shipment came in from Rome. I made sure to get you some."

Jules lifted a brow. "The Vatican managed to spare us some funds, huh?"

"Apparently, there's an exorcist in Rome running about nearly nude."

"Poor thing. No seasonal winter wardrobe. It must be rough."

"Terribly."

"Just the silver spoon they were born with clacking between their teeth."

"Careful. You almost sound bitter."

He laughed, tension easing from his shoulders. "I know what they do for us." He lifted up the shirt, rubbing his thumb over the Vatican seal pressed into each button. "But is it really so important we die branded as Vatican property?"

Farah's lips quirked as she spooned coffee grounds into a filter, but she was too loyal to agree with more than her eyes.

The Vatican, where the cult of the Deathless God had crawled inside the bones of whatever came before, and the epicenter of the centuries-old assault by demons against God.

Whether you were a soldier in the mud, or an exorcist in Rome, you knew that two hundred years ago, God had intervened to defend the holy city and its people. With smoke blackening the sky and flames devouring the city, He had stepped forth in human form to fight for them. In a titanic battle at the heart of the old Vatican City, a demon had impaled Him, but not before God had delivered a killing blow of His own.

And so the Vatican had been chosen by God as the place His body would rest for eternity in a forever Deathless state.

Or so the dogma claimed.

The thick canvas walls billowed and an icy draft bit at his ankles. It wasn't getting any warmer, so Jules pulled his shirt over his head to wash in the lukewarm water of her basin.

Jules felt Farah at his shoulder as she stepped up behind him. Rolling up her sleeves with the weight of ritual, she held her wrist against his, baring her kill scars.

He smiled at her reflection in the small mirror and angled his forearm so she could see his new row of marks. She read the silvery scars in his skin like words in a forgotten language. A language of their own making—telling the stories of demons he'd killed in each of the longer downward strokes.

Farah's expression darkened. "So many," she said, meaning the horizontal lines that marked their dead.

For every demon he killed, they lost two or three of their own. Sometimes more.

Only he and Farah were left of those who marked kills in their flesh. Jules wasn't sure how it started. All he knew was he couldn't stop.

The luxuriant scent of coffee filled the tent, but Jules could still smell the promise of a violent storm. He pushed open the tent flap, crossing his arms over his bare chest as he leaned a shoulder against the post, staring over the tent city toward the forest. The front line stretched for a thousand miles in both directions. Maybe more. He didn't really know. He was just a soldier. Beyond the trees, gathering clouds darkened the horizon.

Farah handed him a mug and he took it, his brows furrowing. "What is it?" she asked.

"I smell lightning."

Farah arched a brow. "Are you a dog?"

He gave her an unamused look and she laughed.

Jules set down his untouched mug so he could yank on his shirt, his fingers clumsy as he transferred his metal collar buttons from the old—truly reeking, Farah was right about that—to the new. Unease twisted in his belly as he pulled on his jacket. The night had been quiet. He'd stayed awake throughout, waiting for an attack, but none had come. This disquiet was probably just the residual effects of exhaustion and starvation . . . And yet, he couldn't relax.

"Jules, eat something. That's an order."

"Something's not right—"

"Sit *down*—"

The downpour roared like a monsoon, rain pelting their tent. Surprised shouts came from outside at the sudden, drenching rain. Tipping his head back, Jules stared at the tent roof, waiting. The hairs on his nape prickled at electricity in the air. "This isn't right."

Farah nodded grimly, reaching for her gun belt. Jules grabbed his sword, pulling it from its scabbard to count the sigils on the flat side. Vatican-forged, it would only survive fifty kills. One sigil for every ten, he had three sigils remaining. The other two, burned and blackened, marked his sword half spent.

It would have to do.

The Caspian Federation's demon horde had arrived.

CHAPTER THREE

W hen Selene hit the street, it was full dark. Flakes of snow alighted on her shoulders, melting instantly. She wiped one off her nose with her sleeve as she marched toward the buttery gold light of gas lanterns along the main road.

"Selene Alleva."

Selene's lip curled. Lowering her hand, she met Florentina's eyes.

There were many choice things she could say about Florentina Altieri, but at the heart of it she was *competition*. They had been in the same year at the Academy, and Florentina never let her win easily. Now she managed to lounge against a filigreed pole in such a way that she looked both utterly relaxed and also ready to disembowel someone. Her wheaten ponytail draped over her shoulder, rivaling her uniform's gold buttons in brightness. Flanking her were a pair of artificers Selene didn't know.

"*Florentina*, you actually graduated?"

Florentina laughed, a sound devoid of any humor. "You should know. You were there."

"I must have forgotten," Selene said flatly. "Too busy being first in class."

"Captain, *please*." Lucia's distinct whine interrupted Florentina's next words. "Don't send me to the regions. I'll be so bored. I *hate* being bored." Florentina's dark eyes lit with interest.

Of course Lucia wouldn't take her punishment quietly. Selene rubbed a finger between crumpled brows. Her mistake. "We will discuss this later."

Caterina shadowed Lucia, adjusting her rifle over her shoulder. "This whining will be all I hear for weeks." Seeing Florentina, Caterina straightened her shoulders and took her place at Selene's right hand. "I'm sorry, Lieutenant Altieri, you've arrived too late for the fight."

"We got *five* demons." Lucia wiggled five fingers. "Which happens to be five more than you've killed this week."

"It's only Tuesday. Give me time." Florentina let her eyes trail over them. "And where's the rest of your team?"

Selene bit the inside of her mouth. "Florentina, we're done here. You were *too slow*."

Florentina's expression flattened and she pushed away from the lamppost. At the edge of the circle of light, she paused. "Five demons, you said. What kind?"

Caterina raised one shoulder, but Lucia, ever the callous little thing, said, "It was a Noble that killed Benedetta."

A Noble. A Level Four demon. How had she *missed* it? Surprise flickered across Florentina's face. "And the rest?"

"A handful of lower demons," Selene replied. "Ghouls mostly."

Lucia stretched so her spine arched. "And a Fiend."

"Enough." Selene massaged her temple. "Florentina can read the report."

Laughing, Florentina gave a mock salute. "You know how much I love your reports, Selene, so full of sparkling wit and vivid detail." She yawned hugely. "Just thinking about it makes me excited."

There was a flash.

Selene raised a hand, squinting against a second flashbulb pop. *Reporter.*

He lowered the camera, his eyes searching their faces eagerly. "What happened here tonight, *Macellaia*?"

"Get him out of here," Florentina snapped, stepping between the reporter and Selene.

The bandages that had wrapped Florentina's arms coiled to the cobblestones, exposing the tender flesh of her inner arms and the rows of sigils tattooed in pale metallic ink between wrist and elbow. Of course, Florentina guarded her hard-earned symbols jealously.

"Did I hear correctly that you've suffered casualties? Who died, Captain Alleva?" the reporter asked, voice sharp with interest. He smelled a story the same way she smelled demons. "Was it Benedetta Fiore? Of the Fiore exorcists?"

How had he slipped through their perimeter?

One of Florentina's artificers relieved him of his camera, lifting the strap over his head while the other took him unyieldingly by the elbow, steering him away. He twisted, looking over his shoulder at Selene. "Do you have any words for her family?"

Florentina scoffed, waving him off.

She had ten symbols on each arm now but Selene refused to be impressed.

Unlike artificers, who were limited to one weapon, exorcist magic was infinitely adaptable. With mastery their magic could be woven into a complex working like the notes in a symphony. Each note a symbol. Each symbol a word. Some exorcists knew only a few words of power—enough to weave an exorcism and not much more. Others were like Florentina, who constantly added to her repertoire—inking sigils into skin.

None were like Selene, who had hers carved into her bones.

She allowed herself a moment of self-indulgent bitterness.

Florentina needed only to lightly score the symbols on her arms in order to release her magic. Whereas Selene's magic was tethered to her bones. An exorcist triggered the symbols they intended to use and wove them into an intention—limited only by the number of words they could master.

And how far you could push the limits of your body.

With feline languidness Florentina rebound her forearms with the bandages, concealing her tattoos once more. Twenty symbols. *Twenty* words of power. And if Selene knew anything at all about her competition, Florentina knew how to use them.

"I guess I'll head back." Tucking her hands into her pockets, Florentina melted into the night.

Seamlessly resuming their earlier conversation, Caterina turned to Selene. "Lucia made a mistake tonight," Caterina said, low enough not to be overheard. "She knows that. She's sorry."

"I am. *So* sorry. Please, Selene."

Selene considered letting it slide. They were excellent hunters, and their city needed them. The Vatican had branches across the map—from Edinburgh to Marrakech to Shanghai—but they were small units, adept at dispelling curses and managing the illegal trade of demon magic. And sometimes, however rarely, lower-level demons needed to be dispelled. But the vast majority of demon attacks happened within Rome. Their talents *would* be more useful within city limits, but Caterina and Lucia sorely needed a lesson on the dangers of complacency.

"Report my decision to the field office upon your return. And enjoy your secondment . . . After today I'm certain neither of you are prepared to face another Noble."

Maybe they'll learn rather than die.

Selene moved from the dark streets, lit only by gas lamps and a few candles on windowsills, to a busier boulevard, where orange lights flickered faintly overhead. Yet again demonic power had knocked out their electricity.

Here, Romans strolled, unafraid of night or cold or demon. Laughter spilled from an aperitivo bar. Tempting, if she hadn't just lost a subordinate. Or if she cared a little less.

News of another death would already be spreading through the city. It was cruel that Benedetta would just become a statistic. The citizens would mourn—of course they would—but Rome had never really known her.

Selene pulled up the hood of her black coat, but the sword crossing her back was a brand. As she passed through the late market—through wafting steam scented with roasted chestnuts, sweet apples, and toffee—ordinary Romans fell away from her, giving her space. Whether it was a sign of fear or respect, the result was the same. Selene ignored the whispers as though she was deaf to them, her face a pitiless mask, just as they'd expect from one such as her.

There goes the Butcher of Rome.

She could never be sure whether they called her *Butcher* because of the demons she slaughtered or the bodies she left in her wake.

Vatican bodies. Other exorcists. Her father.

And now Benedetta, another to her tally.

Dio . . . perhaps she should have ordered her to stay back? *No.*

Artificers might typically be weaker than exorcists—their magic was borrowed only briefly—but far be it from her to ever underestimate them. She'd grown up idolizing hunters like Caterina who wielded their artificed weapons like an extension of their own body.

Her fingertips brushed the Alleva family crest on the hilt of her sword. It had been forged by her father and so she had never had to forge her own. *Praise the Deathless God.* Wielding her own body as a weapon was taxing enough.

Breath puffing in the cold air, Selene sighed. She'd lost her edge tonight. Let down her guard and paid for it with her own lifeblood. Not a mistake she could afford to repeat. Despite disciplining Caterina and Lucia, the fault was hers. *She* was their commanding officer.

A burgundy tram whispered past and she ran to leap up its steps before the doors snapped shut. The world seemed closer than usual. The metallic clanking of the tram changing tracks, and the electric hum of the lights, were almost claustrophobic in her heightened state. The earlier use of her magic seemed to leach a piece of her into everything now. Sinking into the cobbles flying beneath the tram, the rails under the wheels, and the flesh of those around her. Into their breath and blood.

The other passengers in the tram gave her a wide berth. *Vedi Vaticano nero, addio tuo amante*, a popular saying coined in Rome, roughly translated to: see Vatican black, farewell your lover.

Exorcists were not exactly *feared* but were rightly considered dangerous. That they only appeared where demons already were, and not the other way around, was considered inconsequential.

One man, with the glazed eyes of a drunkard and dressed well enough to be a young aristocrat playing with trouble, leaned in to speak quietly to the girl draped languorously between him and another man.

Trouble, Selene assumed.

"That, my lovely, is Selene Alleva."

As the girl twisted to look, she pulled the second man's shirt, revealing to Selene's exorcist eye a brand across his back, reflected in the tram window.

He watched her with a lidded gaze as the inebriated youth lowered his voice further. "The Imperium Bellum's protégée."

The girl drew in a soft gasp.

Pride flickered in Selene's chest at the words.

Some two hundred years had passed since full political power shifted to the Vatican, where it rested uneasily between the Imperiums—the Imperium Bellum, Lord of War, and the Imperium Politikos, Chancellor of State—leaving Empress Augustus naught but a figurehead, a tiger made toothless by the holy power that rested within the Vatican's walls. And ruling over all, the Exorcist Primus, whose word was law.

Selene reveled in her body's near-intolerable hypervigilance. In the mixed-up euphoria of it, even the pain of her wounds felt sublime. St. Peter's dome came into view as the tram trundled around a corner. Lit with russet-gold tones, it shone high above the city skyline. Leaping off the tram, she glanced at her watch as she crossed St. Peter's Square.

Fifteen minutes late.

Cesare Alleva, Imperium Bellum to the rest of Rome, was not the sort of man to be kept waiting. With no time to change out of her bloodstained gear, she set her shoulders and strode toward the Vatican dining hall, tightening her leather armguard to stem the flow of blood. Her vision briefly dulled as agony rolled through her in a deep ache.

"God fucking damn it," she hissed between her teeth.

The checkerboard marble amplified the click of her shiny boots.

Either side of her, subordinates shrank away, pressing their backs to the walls and their fists to their hearts in ardent salute. No doubt news had spread of another fallen body. Selene inclined her chin at the few she knew by name.

At least her white button-down shirt had survived the initial blood spray. It remained unstained, the gold chains linking its double-breasted buttons untarnished by gore.

"Captain Alleva, the Imperium's gone ahead to the *Cor Cordium*."

Her jaw tightened. "When?"

"Moments ago."

She could catch him.

Desperate to intercept Cesare before he reached the chamber at the heart of the Vatican, she ran.

Artificers and exorcists moved aside for her. Even ignoring the difference in uniform, they were easy enough to tell apart. Artificers were always accompanied by their weapon—typically something obscenely large, like Caterina's rifle—and exorcists had their tattoos.

The Vatican bells echoed through the halls.

Her uncle, the Imperium Bellum, cut an impressive figure. When she saw him ahead, she slowed. His shadow stretched ahead of him, taking up space. The Shadow of God, they called him. A title spoken in whispers.

Hearing her footsteps, he paused.

Tonight his hair was messy. He was relaxed, then. Otherwise it would be slicked back, displaying the barest glint of silver at his temples. But as she approached, something about his posture made her ill at ease. Cesare wasn't entirely off duty.

Then again, when was he ever?

His voice rolled across the marble like distant thunder. "The Butcher of Rome finally favors me with her presence." The hard cut of his jaw made it difficult to tell if he was being serious, but the slightest twitch at the edge of his lips betrayed the way he bit back a smile.

"Apologies, Imperium, I was waylaid." Selene pressed her fist to her chest.

His eyes snagged on her armguards. "You used your magic?"

She nodded, crushing a grimace.

After eight years in the role, Cesare was still frequently considered the *new* Imperium Bellum. His predecessor had held the role for almost sixty years before his death, and to many Cesare was seen as something of an upstart. An impression not improved by his relative youth, not even thirty at the time of his appointment. But he was the only Imperium Bellum Selene had ever known.

His expression darkened. "I see."

"It was already on the brink of death," she said simply.

The exorcism had not used much of her power. But now her veins were flooded with unused magic, tempting her to wield it.

"Power is dangerous as well as heady." Cesare rested a palm against an ornate double door. "You need to be more careful. Remember?"

She averted her eyes from the lacquered board that sealed the doors permanently closed. Of course she did. On her first attempt to harness her magic, Cesare had been inside that vaulted room with her as her magic lashed out wildly, stripping priceless friezes from the walls and corroding stone.

The stolen blood being pumped through her body was a double-edged sword.

It had begun as a destructive thing, but now the damage was invisible. It took place inside her veins.

Cesare knew the facts of her predicament, but he would never understand. Not really.

Shoving away her bitterness, she considered it from his perspective. He was right to be disappointed. She'd let a demon goad her into using too much of her magic. *Pathetic.* Unlike other exorcists, unlike even Cesare, when *she* shed blood for magic, it smoked when it hit the air—acrid black, writhing with the violence of a headless snake. That was the power in her blood. A blessing *and* a curse. She was one of the most powerful exorcists in the order, but each time she used her magic her life trickled away.

In fact, it was worse. If it was only her life, she could live with it. The glory of a short life appealed to her, burning bright before flashing out of existence, but it wasn't only her *life* at stake. It was her *soul*. More than once, Selene had been present when an older exorcist pushed their magic to its limit, and witnessed the corruption that spread through them, unleashing the beast within. She'd *seen* it. She never wanted to *be* it.

She would die first.

Cesare lifted her chin with the backs of his fingers. His expression softened. "I don't want to be the one to have to put you down, Selene. Not you, too."

She drew a steady breath and flicked her eyes up to his. "I know. I promise I'm careful."

He was somber, somewhere inside his own head, and a weight like a stone settled into her stomach.

"What is it?" she asked, afraid of the answer. "*Really.*"

Selene had heard whispers Cesare now spoke for the ailing Exorcist Primus of Rome. In practice, that made him the most powerful man in the city—and the world. When she'd asked him if it was true, "His Holiness the Exorcist Primus has had quite a few good ideas lately, no?" was all Cesare had said, a hidden smile at the corner of his mouth.

"I'm conflicted. On the one hand, you're my most powerful exorcist. On the other, I am afraid of you overextending. We've all seen what happens when an exorcist pushes beyond their limits . . ." His eyes pinned her with more ferocity than affection. "I've lost too many good exorcists, Selene. I can't bear the thought of losing you."

"Nobody wants that, uncle." She held his eyes, unflinching. "But you said you were conflicted? My magic can't be all that's bothering you."

His lips tightened into a reluctant smile. She fell into step beside him.

The Basilica's echoing halls were quiet given the late hour, though the Vatican never truly slept. They didn't have the luxury of switching off. They were the guardians of Rome, and Rome was under attack.

"I have a job for you," Cesare said. "I suspect it'll test your limits in a way they have not been tested here in Rome."

"You're sending me away?" Selene asked sharply.

"Not as such. But I must ask you to forgive me. All this time I've put you in a position where you constantly risk having to use your magic, and now I'm asking you to do just that."

"I don't mind."

"You don't care that your uncle is a hypocrite?"

Selene shifted, and again her gloved thumb ghosted over the Alleva family crest on her sword hilt. "Tell me more, then I'll decide."

In fact, she was surprised he hadn't done more than allude to it already.

It was unusual for there to be any lapse between their becoming aware of demonic activity and the Vatican's reaction to it. Usually a team would be deployed within minutes.

Cesare chuckled, amused. "Very well."

When he was done, silence stretched between them. *An hour ago, a village was destroyed close to Nice*, he had said. *We suspect a demon.*

And it would be dangerous.

"You know what this means," Selene murmured.

Cesare jerked his chin in acknowledgment.

A high-level demon. Powerful beyond anything the local branch was capable of fending off. In the heart of Rome powerful wards prevented them from being entirely overrun—though they couldn't stop the demons entirely. Except for the Vatican, which had been warded to keep away even the highest-ranked demons, there were always places demons slipped through. Nice was not so lucky.

Selene frowned, raising her glove to pull it tighter on her aching fingers. They were broken beneath the supple leather, but nobody else needed to know that. Her body would heal soon enough with the blood in her veins. A secret the Vatican held tighter than any other was the source of their stolen power; stolen from the lifeblood of demons condemned to die. The thought of it brought to mind the metallic tang on her tongue. Trickling hot down her throat.

Her hands curled into fists, the splintered bones grinding.

Cesare angled his head toward her slightly, catching the sound of her weakness with his keen senses. Selene was grateful he said nothing of it.

"Do you know who we have in France at the moment?" she asked.

Cesare shook his head and rubbed his jaw with a calloused thumb. "No. And it doesn't matter. You'll be taking lead." They approached the *Cor Cordium*, and, rounding the corner, the enormous doors of the Crucifixion Room loomed up ahead. "I'll put in a call to the Nice office and have someone meet you."

She nodded distractedly, keeping her face turned so she wouldn't have to see the doors.

"I should go," she blurted, her words tumbling over each other. "Prepare for—"

But she was too late.

His reply was swallowed by yawning silence. It rolled from beyond the studded doors as the guards swung them soundlessly open. Selene turned her head, catching a pale glimmer at the far end of the dark room. She wrenched her gaze away. She hadn't seen a thing. She *refused* to see.

Selene turned her wrist to look at her watch. The hands seemed to bend against the movement of time, as though every second she stood this close to the Vatican's heart, time itself slowed.

"I really must—"

"Pray with me." It was not a request.

Selene bit the inside of her mouth.

Cesare watched her strangely, and belatedly she realized his demand had the ring of words repeated. Unable to refuse, she trailed him into the *Cor Cordium*. The Vatican's heart of hearts.

The Deathless God towered over them, crucified on the great beams of the cathedral that had burned around Him. Selene pressed her fingertips to her forehead, blocking Him from sight for a moment, before she touched her breastbone and sank to her knees on the marble.

When her eyes settled on His face, tears slipped down her cheeks. He was beautiful, His hair an inky spill across his forehead. His head bent forward, hanging heavily. Dark lashes cast crescents against His cheeks. For a moment she let herself believe He was sleeping. Then her traitorous gaze tracked the length of the great spear that pierced Him through, pinning Him to the obsidian pillar along His spine. Lustrous blood dripped down the spear to the floor, where a pool of liquid gold filled the center of the room.

"*Dio Immortale*," she murmured.

But she was not faithful.

None of them were.

The Vatican was splitting at its stony seams with heathens who had killed their god. If not by driving the spear deep, then by choosing not to pull it free.

And we revel in His eternal death.

After kissing her fingertips, Selene dipped her fingers into the pool of golden blood and drew a rune on her forehead with the edge of her thumbnail.

God's blood was still warm.

CHAPTER FOUR

A sigil burned out on Jules's blade as he sliced down a demon. "This isn't a natural storm," he shouted to Farah as a streak of red lightning split the dark.

Even though it was nearing noon, all but the faintest hint of daylight was swallowed by the tumultuous clouds. Savage rain churned up the battlefield mud, making every step a challenge.

Farah wiped cold rain from her eyes.

He joined her, cleaning his sword on his pants. "Must be a powerful demon."

"Very good, grunt." An exorcist loomed out of the downpour, taut muscles visible beneath his saturated uniform. Surprise flickered over Farah's face at his sudden appearance. His eyes roved over them, finally settling on Farah after reading her lapels. "Abandon the trenches. The fight's shifting to the city. Hold them off while Ostrava is evacuated."

Jules didn't bother asking if the Vatican would be fighting alongside them. They were not fodder. Not like Jules and the rest.

"Tommaso!" Turning at his name, the exorcist left them forgotten.

"Why didn't he go after the weather demon?" Jules shouted over the roar of rain against the bare branches overhead. Few trees had survived the trenches and the bullets. They stood sentinel, reminders of what this place could've been.

Farah tapped her lapel. "He was low-ranked. Not strong enough."

Jules hissed through his teeth. Of course. Why would the Vatican send their best to die alongside them?

"Fall back to Ostrava!"

Their company had retreated to the city limits, where crumbling buildings with blown-out windows like jagged teeth provided scant relief from the slanting rain, and even less from bullets. A war falcon cut through the late afternoon, its angular wings gilded by lightning flashes.

Intent on tying off the bandage around Jules's torso, Farah did not notice the bird.

Wind whipping his unbuttoned shirt, Jules straddled the ridge of the roof and raised his forearm. Talons bit into his skin as the falcon landed, ruffling its feathers against the spattering rain. He slid down the tiles to rejoin Farah, sheltering the falcon from the worst of the elements. With clumsy fingers, she untied the note, reading it with her lip caught between her teeth. "They're sending reinforcements." She shot him a smile.

Reluctantly he smiled back. "Who?"

"Exorcists. Someone who can actually kill that goddamn demon."

His bones went liquid with relief. The relative quiet of the last hour had only made him more worried—indicative of an enemy regrouping for another, stronger assault. One Jules wasn't sure they'd survive. Relieved of its duty, the war falcon chirruped, letting him scratch its feathered throat with a fingertip before it took flight.

As Jules watched it go, he caught movement beyond the last

stand of abandoned buildings. Wiping water from his eyelashes, he squinted against the dark. A forked tongue of lightning lashed from the sky, illuminating the enemy soldiers passing through a copse of towering cypresses. Somehow they were sheltered from wind and rain, and mostly hidden in deep shadow as they approached the city limits. And at their center, a figure in sky blue.

"How close are the reinforcements?" Jules asked, voice carefully neutral.

"Ten minutes out," Farah said, confirming his worst suspicions. They wouldn't last ten minutes.

He dragged on his coat over his unbuttoned shirt. "I'll lead a team to intercept the enemy, hold them off—" Lightning struck one of the watchtowers, setting it ablaze. The weather demon was closing in.

Farah's jaw flexed beneath her skin, the hope of moments ago fading. She nodded. "I'll wait for the exorcists here, then we'll join you. Don't die."

Making his way down a crumbling stairwell, Jules poked his head into grim concrete rooms. Nowhere was dry, and soldiers huddled in the corners to avoid the worst of the wind whistling through blown-out windows. With infinite sadness, Jules tapped a few shoulders, singling out soldiers he knew. "With me."

None of them were veterans of this war—other than him and Farah, few remained—but neither did he choose the pups who'd arrived only the month before. He wasn't a monster. They'd just be fodder.

He recognized the soldiers who'd been here awhile not by name but by the haunted hollows of their eyes. They knew death when they saw it. They saw it in Jules.

Lives trickled through his fingers like sand. As they fought in the streets, holding the attackers back and pushing forward when they could, his soldiers died deaths of insignificance. No battle would be won on their heads alone. Their war against the Caspian Federation was only the most recent iteration of humanity's long fight against demons. *Centuries* of bloodshed. Long enough that their sacrifice was worth nothing at all.

Night was near, made imminent by the dark thunderclouds.

Jules knelt to clean his blade on a fallen comrade's jacket and prized the dead man's sword from his fingers, angling it absently to check the sigils. Only one remained. Better than nothing. He slid the sword through his belt and straightened. "Push on." Few enough remained that he did not need to raise his voice; they stood close enough to hear him breathe. "Stay sharp." Ankle-deep water drowned the cobblestone street.

The shout and clang of battle faded, and despite himself Jules slowed, listening through his ragged breaths. As he rounded the next corner, he faltered. Hundreds of Vatican Empire soldiers had been cut down, their bodies roughly piled into makeshift barricades. Someone started to retch.

"Group up." Jules fingered his blade, angling it so he could see its sigils in the dark. A nervous twitch. Mere inches to his left, a soldier was shot down. His body flung back with the force of the bullet, sliding across the cobbles.

Demons broke through the ranks of Caspian soldiers, grins splitting their cheeks. Beyond the lower-ranked demons, the weather demon, cloaked in pale blue, paid them no mind. It bent its head, conferring with a smaller figure in pristine white that remained unsoiled by the mud coating everyone else.

"Jules!"

He turned.

On the other side of the square, Farah crouched beside a broken wall to avoid being shot. Beside her were figures in black.

The Vatican exorcists with Farah did not hesitate, cutting their way through the approaching soldiers in a lethal flurry, eviscerating demon and Caspian alike. He had never wondered if killing could be beautiful, but as he watched the deadly dance, he knew it could.

Tracer bullets silently sliced the air, ending lives as a female exorcist leveled a handgun, her waist-length plait whipping around her as she twisted in place. Even from a distance, Jules could tell these weapons were far more potent than the generic demon-killing blades the Vatican armed *them* with.

A huge exorcist wielding a pike plunged into the fray, as beside Farah a third readied herself for the fight, drawing the sleeves of her shirt up her forearms so they were bare.

They were saved.

Despite the tumult of battle, Jules heard the soft breath of awe from the soldier beside him. He turned to her, smiling broadly. Her eyes were shadowed by her peaked cap. Uneasy, he reached to grasp her shoulder. Her chin dropped forward and water poured from her eyes and mouth.

A wordless cry was torn out of him as he leaped back, and the drowned soldier collapsed. With ice in his veins, Jules turned to find the weather demon watching him from within its deep hood. All he could see was the glint of pale eyes. Its head cocked, and a light, almost musical voice reached his ears: "Protect the Tsarina."

The ranks of Caspian soldiers and demons closed around the figure in white as the weather demon broke away.

Anastasia Alexandrova Romanov, the Caspian Tsarina, *here*.

Jules's fingers flexed on his sword.

She was the heart of this war. The throbbing blood-gorged heart. With her dead it could end.

Nobody else seemed to have heard the demon's words in the chaos. Jules spun in place, searching for an exorcist. He needed to tell them. This changed everything.

The blue-garbed demon used a length of weathered wood to spin and whirl in the midst of the imperial soldiers, striking them down. In one swift turn, the demon's hood fell back to reveal the face of a beautiful young woman—were it not for the white marbles of her eyes and the way her cheeks split, baring far too many teeth. She flung out a hand, manipulating the elements like an extension of herself.

The Vatican had their own system of classifying demons, a system Jules didn't give a shit to know. What he did know was this: the more human a demon looked, the deadlier. And far more difficult to kill.

Those uncanny eyes settled on Jules with unwavering intensity. The demon cut her way toward him, and wherever she went the tide of battle turned. Tracer bullets cut through the air between them. The demon faltered, head whipping around. Then the handgun-wielding exorcist who had decimated the demons' ranks was cleaved in two by an unnatural bolt of ragged lightning.

With a howl the exorcist with the pike attacked the demon, raining down a flurry of blows. None seemed to land. The air thrummed with power that billowed off the weather demon, tasting of ozone and rain. Then the demon captured the man's face between two delicate hands and crushed his head.

Jules tightened his grip on his sword as he fought his way through water up to his knees. He sliced a Caspian soldier from hip to shoulder and kicked him aside, finding the last living exorcist with his eyes. The ring she wore on her thumb glinted in the dim light, revealing the hidden blade that she dashed against her knuckles. And as she did, Jules felt an incredible swell of power.

In a flash of movement, the exorcist drew an arrow of pure light and released it from her longbow.

The weather demon laughed and plucked the flying shaft from the air. She pivoted, flinging it back at the exorcist upon her captive wind. The arrow pierced the exorcist through, pinning her against the wall. Rain battered the exorcist's upturned face. When the arrow's magic died, she collapsed and did not rise.

Jules staggered, horrified by the swift reversal. In moments, all the Vatican agents had been cut down.

The weather demon spun around, unerringly finding Jules again. From the corner of his eye he saw a glimmer of gold. Farah snatched a fallen sword from the slick cobbles, angling it to check the sigils as she finally stopped beside him. Her expression was grim as she flicked a glance his way. "Get out of here, Lacroix. Tell them we've lost." He barely heard her words as they were whipped away on the wind. At his feet, the weather demon's long shadow darkened the stones.

He tightened his grip on his sword. He wanted to tell Farah to run or hide or drop her sword and fall to her knees—anything to save herself and not him—but it would be futile. That was not Farah.

She roared and charged.

"No!" He moved too, but the wind pressed him back.

The weather demon bent at the knees, sweeping up a broken spear that she used to impale Farah. Only a being of immense strength could have forced the splintered wood through a human rib cage. Then Farah was tossed to the muddy cobbles in a boneless heap, like nothing more than a child's discarded doll, broken and glassy-eyed. And utterly, inescapably dead.

Jules howled, his knuckles whitening around his sword hilt.

The demon came for him next. Survival superseded grief and

he folded beneath the deadly arc of her war staff to get inside her guard. Like a lantern flickering in the dark, his killing instinct awakened. With the promise of a death blow guiding his hand, Jules thrust his sword through her mouth.

The blade fractured as the final sigil burned out, and the sword shattered in his hand, sending shards of useless metal into the rushing water.

Fuck.

A few sharp teeth fell from the demon's mouth, but she was alive. And angry.

Her nails lengthened.

Tossing aside his spent weapon, Jules tumbled back as fingernails like beetle-black shellac raked his skin. He threw himself away in time to save his life—that clear, distant note of agony muffled by adrenaline. Plunging his hand into icy water, he searched for the exorcist's fallen pike. The swirling water clouded with his blood. Cold fingers closing on the metal shaft, Jules pulled it free of the torrent. He turned the pike in a tight arc and the demon's own momentum drove her onto its length, right to his white-knuckle grip.

Keening in pain, the demon disintegrated like ash. But in the moments before she died, he thought he felt the demon *leave*, the unfathomable weight of her presence suddenly no more. Power pulsed from the exorcist weapon, its magical recoil a thousandfold stronger than his army-issue blade.

"*You.*"

He almost thought it was the wind across the now-silent battlefield—the last raging of the unnatural storm—then the Caspian Tsarina stepped through the falling ash, her blue eyes alight with curiosity.

Face framed by the pale ermine lining her cloak, Anastasia Romanov appeared soft and pretty, but Jules wasn't fooled. His heart slammed against his rib cage as he pushed himself up from the mud, his eyes not leaving her. Part demon, the rumors said, with fangs behind those soft lips. His gaze narrowed in on the pulse at her throat, and he gave the pike an experimental twirl.

"You're the killer, the boy with the scars on his arms, the one they call *Stigmajka*."

The word meant nothing to him. *Stigma* sounded Latin. The rest? Probably Caspian, but that was all he knew.

The Tsarina continued, "The empire's toy soldier who always knows where to strike. How many Kairos have you slain, boy?" She spoke with a faint accent.

"Kairos?" Jules repeated.

"Demons," she said with a curl of her lip. "*You* would call them demons. The Holy Vatican Empire, and all those beneath their aegis, have forgotten much."

Not really understanding, Jules shook his head. Besides, he didn't care what they called themselves. "Why do you ask? Does the number even matter?" He reined in his emotions, not wanting her to see how much her recognition troubled him. *The boy with the scars on his arms.* There were a thousand soldiers, ten thousand, *more*. And many of those had scars. But he knew what she meant. Of course he did.

As though reading his mind, Anastasia found the healed marks on his hands. Her eyes darkened. "I knew it was you."

The Tsarina's lilting tone played on his nerves.

On this field of death she was vulnerable. All her protectors gone. He'd end this whole war if he could kill her. It was worth a shot. And certainly better than having a conversation.

Jules twirled the pike toward her throat. "I'm not here to talk."

For a moment the sun slipped from behind a cloud and the world was magnified. Colors brighter. Lines crisper. He could see the end of the war and victory for the Vatican at his hands, as though the world moved in slow motion. He saw the killing stroke—the path his pike would take as it sliced the air—and *knew* he had her, that he'd split her throat.

His body moved, trusting that promise. But Anastasia effortlessly folded away from his strike, impossibly fast and graceful.

Unbalanced, Jules slipped in a patch of icy mud and he fell to one knee.

"Listen." The Tsarina's voice was melodic, striking notes that felt somehow familiar. "How do you always know where to strike to kill?" Her smile was sharp where moments ago she had appeared completely human. Anastasia gestured broadly, encompassing the battlefield. The death. The uncountable small tragedies. "Because you're like me, *Stigmajka*," she whispered.

Jules shook his head, gritting his teeth against the agony of his ribs, ignoring the hot blood he could feel darkening the waistband of his pants as he gained his footing. A glint of blond fluttered in his peripheral vision. Then the sun disappeared behind another bank of clouds and Farah's hair was the last thing that glinted bright in the dull gray world.

He angled the pike at Anastasia's chin. "I may be a killer but I'm *nothing* like you. You could stop all this, *Tsarina*. The war, the bloodshed, the needless *death*."

When she didn't move, he ghosted the serrated blade against her throat. But, curious what she had to say, he held the blow.

She wore the hint of a smile. "*Oh?* You can't do it, can you?"

And she was right. He couldn't move, his own hand foreign to him as he clutched the pike.

Because you're like me, she'd said.

A killer of unprecedented scale . . . ?

Reaching up, she smoothed a fingertip along the blade like she was stroking a kitten. "*Stigmajka*, so adept with the blade. So very deadly. How many scars mark your arms?" She glanced toward Farah, eyes finding the marked hand on her hilt. Her body seemed to flicker, and then she was kneeling over her, ripping aside Farah's sleeve. Where Jules's arms were more silvery scar tissue than unmarked flesh, Farah's arm showed only the occasional pale line.

Stigmajka, he realized then. *Scarred killer.*

He swung the pike, resting it against the back of the Tsarina's bowed neck. But his hand trembled against the staff as she gently smoothed Farah's eyelids closed.

"You think you're like this one here, little killer? Because she scarred herself too? You are not. You're a creature all your own, *Stigmajka*. Now let's be done with this. Kill me. *If you can.*"

Jules's temples throbbed and a headache like none he'd ever known crowded into his skull. He backed away and Anastasia chuckled. Her peal of laughter was obscene on this battlefield among the dead and dismembered. His hands were dark with blood, tacky against the pike shaft and, horrified, he flung it aside. That killing instinct that guided him to the perfect death stroke glimmered out of existence as he backed away.

Anastasia did not pursue him, only turned her head to watch his retreat.

With her words echoing in his ears, he ran.

CHAPTER FIVE

Chill air greeted Selene when she stepped outside. She fought the urge to look back at the Vatican proper. To her right, the Academy building, home for half her life, annexed St. Peter's, mirroring the palaces where His Holiness the Exorcist Primus lived.

Or rather subsisted.

He was dying. In truth, he'd been dying for years.

She jogged down the wide steps, past a returning team of exorcists. Only a few dared glance at her carved-up arm. Fewer still realized what it meant. The difference between their magic and hers was too vast. Too many of them thought she *refused* to use her power for conscientious reasons to realize that tonight she had tapped her magic. Not that she'd enlighten them. It suited her much better this way. She was the Butcher of Rome, always covered in blood. They didn't need to know most of it was hers.

"Exorcist."

Selene's expression twisted to one of dislike even before she turned to the tall man holding a slender cigarette between his fingers and a folded newspaper in his other hand.

He smiled, amused, breathing out a coil of cobalt smoke. "At least pretend to be pleased to see me."

"Sparrow."

"You've already hit the news. Condolences." He tapped the newspaper with his index finger, handing it to her.

She tucked it under her arm without looking.

Shifting in place, Sparrow leaned one shoulder more comfortably against the vast column that shadowed his form. Selene joined him in the deeper dark and tipped her chin to look up at him. One eye pierced the dark, blue and too knowing.

"What is it?" she asked.

"Something. I don't know yet."

She spread her hands, palms up. "Not sure what you want me to do with that."

He sighed, straightening to his full height, and looked down at her. "There's talk in the underground, that's all. Nobody's saying what they've seen. Of course, I can only speak for those still alive."

Selene frowned. "I hadn't heard of any recent deaths."

"It's not yours doing the killing." *This time.* Sparrow left the words unsaid. "All I know is . . . something's stirring." His gaze shifted away, a bar of pale light crossing his scarred and ruined eye. He knew more than he was saying. They called him the Eye of the Underworld for a reason. What was he holding back?

He arched a brow, looking at her blood-soaked sleeve. "This is rare. Usually you aren't the one left bleeding."

Selene pressed her palm to the leather armguard, grimacing. Of all people, why did Sparrow have to be witness to her shame? She tightened the straps again, ignoring the pallor of her bloodless fingers. Why did she need to spill her blood and carve her bones for magic?

Why her and nobody else? It was cruel.

Of course she *knew* why. But the truth of it, nestled deep inside her rib cage, did not lessen the hurt.

She frowned as she walked away. Sparrow rarely sought her out, and never with something as nebulous as this. Presumably he wanted to know what she knew. Was it possible that Sparrow had already heard about a powerful demon somewhere in France?

Again she had that sense that something imperceptible had changed. The world as she knew it had shifted just enough to throw her off balance.

Her earlier thought trickled through her mind. *Unusual* meant something had changed.

This went beyond unusual. *And death is sure to follow.*

Before she passed beneath the colonnade, she turned back to read the inscription through a flurry of her own dark hair: IN HONOREM PRINCIPUM ROMAE EXORCISTAE ROMAE ANNO MCMV POST SAECULUM BELLUM DAEMONIUM CONTRA DEUM ET CIVITATEM.

The vast travertine frieze on the Basilica's portico had said something different once. Words that had been lost to time and insignificance. Selene touched her brow as she turned her back on the words. Words that had carved their way into her bones in no less tangible a way than her knife had earlier. *In honor of the Princes of Rome, the Roman exorcists, in 1905, a century after Demons declared war on God and Humanity.*

And now these same vaunted exorcists walked the knife edge. Few guessed that they existed in that gray area between the shining light of God and the shadows cast by the demons they hunted. The populace saw exorcists as their intermediaries with the divine. What they could never know was that if an exorcist failed to balance his magic, he would himself unleash evil on the world. Sometimes Selene felt dangerously close to that inevitable tipping point.

Frustration dug its teeth into her. How easy it was for others. They could go years without consequence. *Her* magic was a vast and untamed thing that made each use a roll of the dice. Would this be the time she used too much power and burned herself out?

Perhaps.

Absently she caressed the pistol at her thigh. The matched pair had been a graduation gift from her uncle and she was already earning them a reputation. An origin story written in blood. No wonder Rome called her Butcher. All *they* saw was the carnage she left behind.

She considered Cesare's parting words.

As they had crossed through the Vatican gardens, walking in the shadows beneath cypresses and cloud pines lit all in amber, Selene had drawn Ambrose's ward coin from her pocket, rolling it between her fingers. "One of my team found this today."

Cesare turned to her with mild interest, extending his hand. He took his time inspecting it, then raised both brows at her. "You're concerned?"

"Well, yes. Aren't you?"

He chuckled. "I have a lot of things to worry about, but this isn't one of them. A single ward coin?" He shook his head, thumb rubbing the notched edge. "I wonder how long this has been rattling around."

He flipped the coin into a fountain. It turned end over end and landed with a delicate splash between a mosaic mermaid and a hippocampus, winking in the clear water alongside dozens of others.

None quite so valuable as this one.

"Well, that was stupid," she said, exasperated.

He laughed, stopping her with a hand on her elbow before she could stick her boot into the fountain to go and get it. "In a city the size of Rome, one ward coin is insignificant. Also, you may call me stupid, but you will do it with respect."

She rolled her eyes at him, letting him pull her back. "That was very stupid, Imperium."

She fell into step with him as they passed between neat box hedges, his warm chuckle as golden as the lantern light. "Better."

In the end they shared a smile when Selene recounted with deadpan humor how Ambrose had shoved his arm into the demon's razor maw. Ambrose and his silly little ill-advised knuckle-dusters. The hatred that had bled into his eyes wouldn't usually bother her, except it reminded her too much of the rest of Rome. They hated her too. *Her* specifically. Not Captain Alleva, Exorcist Second Class. *Selene* Alleva. And if not hatred, something close to it. But she could live with that, couldn't she? She was a Roman exorcist. Protector of humanity. And sometimes that meant forgoing hers.

Jules swayed on the station platform, feet numb in his boots. The gash across his ribs had stopped bleeding, and with a shaking hand he buttoned the shirt over the bandages that wrapped his torso. The distinct metallic flap of the Solari board drew his attention and he held his breath, waiting for the letters and numbers to settle.

PARIS GARE DU NORD

The last train out of Ostrava was scheduled to arrive in Paris via Prague. If he was lucky, he might be able to change trains in Metz to get to Nice. Either way, the entire journey would take days. But the siren call of home was all his broken mind could grasp right then.

He felt hollowed out. Existed as nothing more than his next step. Nice—*home*—was the one place he might find answers. Though he refused to contemplate what those answers might be.

Because you're like me, Stigmajka.

He slammed his fist against the steam train's green carriage and pressed his forehead to the cold glass. The gentleman inside gave him a startled look, folded his newspaper, and hurried to change seats. Jules choked back his urge to scream.

By the time he stepped off the train in Metz, Jules had lost most identifying aspects of his military uniform. His white shirt was still tucked into his black pants but the chevrons were missing from his collar, and he'd sewed squares of black cloth over every double-breasted coat button imprinted with the Holy Vatican Empire's insignia. Jules had nothing to his name but his boots—well made, military issue—and the folded scrap of newspaper in his back pocket. Though it was yesterday's news, he couldn't bear to throw it away.

ROME CRIES BLOOD. And so they should. Rome might not give a damn for Farah, but they'd suffer for losing Sergeant Bachelet. He flinched from the memory. There'd be time to grieve later.

A poster greeted him at the platform, one corner already curling away from the wall. He slapped his hand over it, tearing it down. *DESERTER* still fluttered in tattered print.

A double row of flyers stretched away from him, wallpapering the station tiles with his face. The official portrait portrayed a solemn Jules in his full dress uniform. Tossing his cigarette, Jules scuffed it out with a boot. He'd thought the confusion of a bloody battle might buy him a few days. Better yet, he'd hoped they'd think he was dead.

Farther along the platform, a portly gendarme in blue pasted up more flyers.

CRUEL IS THE LIGHT

Bloody hell. If only half the passengers on his train to Nice saw them he'd count himself lucky.

Of course they wouldn't just let him go. He was an officer now. The empire's skilled killer. *Stigmajka*, the Tsarina had called him. Scarred killer. Jules took three long strides to the train, leaping for the open door just as the whistle sounded.

The gendarme turned, catching him in the act. Flyers tumbled to the platform as he ran after Jules. "Hey, you! Stop!"

A hand shot out to grab his elbow, yanking him into the safety of the train.

"Ay, boyo, did you steal away just to see me?"

Jules barely had time to register the smooth Marseillais drawl he knew so well before he was shoved into a narrow space with an ornate telephone and the door snapped shut, leaving him alone inside.

"Daumier, did you see someone just now?"

Jules pressed his ear against the door as the train began to inch away from the station.

"I don't think so. I swept the whole train. Nobody that looks like, um, Julian Delacroix?"

"*Jules La—* Never mind." The gendarme sounded impatient, puffing like a winded bull as he trotted alongside the moving train. "We still have hundreds of flyers to post, hurry up and get off."

"Be right there," Kian said cheerily, patting his belt. "Shoot, I think I forgot my baton!"

"Constable Daumier, get off that train right now or I'll have your badge."

"But it's moving so *fast*," Kian said of the trundling train. "God protect me, I've missed my chance!"

Jules pushed the door ajar and rolled his eyes at Kian's theatrics.

Grasping the handhold, Kian swung out to shout back at his

dwindling superior. "See you back in Nice, sir." Wind buffeting his distinctive red hair, he didn't even try to hide his shit-eating grin.

Jules pulled him inside by the collar, dragging him into a hug. "Kian? What the hell are you doing here?"

Even after years apart, Kian had barely changed from the boy he remembered. Jules had spent his entire life at the orphanage, where Matron had taken an immediate dislike to him. Kian, on the other hand, with his hair like flickering candle flame and an infectious smile, had been her favorite. It didn't help that Matron steadfastly refused to believe any mischief could be Kian's fault, instead laying the blame for all of it at Jules's feet.

No wonder Kian liked having him around.

"Not much, as it happens. Just saving your ass as usual."

Kian was dressed in uniform and it took Jules a moment to put the word *constable* together with his troublemaking childhood friend. Snapping the door closed and deadening the train's metallic clanking, Kian lowered his voice. "I tried not to flash your face around too much, but couldn't entirely avoid it. Try not to draw too much attention. Hard for you, I know."

They grinned at each other.

"Reminds me of when we were kids," Jules said. "Remember how you'd always get us into trouble, and I'd end up taking the rap?"

"Nope."

"You don't?"

"*Definitely* not."

"So . . . you're a cop now?" Jules rubbed his grin away with a thumb. "I guess you got so used to Matron polishing your halo, you had to turn being a goody two-shoes into a vocation."

Kian grinned. "We can't all charm our way out of trouble.

Lucky for you I like you a lot more than Matron ever did, so I won't turn you in—"

Jules laughed. "You like me even more than Matron liked you, and that's truly saying something."

"—*unless* you piss me off," Kian continued, as though he hadn't heard him. "Which seems increasingly unlikely." Kian's grin softened to his usual infectious smile and he pushed his hands into his pockets, rocking on his heels. "I guess saving your backside became something of a habit."

Jules widened his eyes. "You saving *me*? One time does not a pattern make."

"Should I tell the train to turn around?"

"Trains don't turn around, Kian."

Expression growing somber, Kian drew a flyer out of his pocket, smoothing it open. "This really true? Are you a deserter, Jules?"

Jules released a shaky breath. "Yeah."

Kian searched his face. "They had you long enough. *Years* longer than Rome deserves." He ripped it up, tucking the shredded poster into his inside pocket.

Kian's words lit warmth in his chest.

"Never thought an idiot like you would last this long, to be honest," Kian continued, not missing a beat. "What, did your face scare the enemy away?"

"Shithead." Jules kind of wanted to punch Kian. Instead, he asked, "What now? Will I make it?"

"No question." Kian set his kepi atop Jules's head—the brim shadowing his eyes—and shrugged off his own jacket, helping Jules put it on. It strained across his shoulders. Jules's pants were military style, similar enough to Kian's police uniform to fool the casual observer. So, fortunately, Kian didn't have to offer up his.

As they walked down the middle of the train, they were greeted by a chorus of "Officers!" and "Won't you join us, Monsieur Policeman?" from a group of pretty girls.

Ah, France.

Jules touched his kepi, nodding at them. "If only, but I'm not paid to enjoy myself, ladies."

"You're not paid at all," Kian muttered, wincing when Jules's elbow dug into his ribs.

Finally they reached the train's last carriage and were all but alone. Jules flicked Kian's shoulder board. "How did *this* happen?"

"Matron put in some extra effort to set me up with a sponsor. Outdid herself, I say. The work ain't half bad."

Jules didn't even feel bitter, too busy feeling boneless with relief that Kian had avoided the draft. He'd spent more than one sleepless night worrying about Kian being sent to war. After another tight hug, Jules looked him over. Taller, maybe a little more flame-haired, but otherwise he was the same as ever. Like nothing had changed.

But it had.

In the four years since they'd seen each other last, Jules had *killed*. He wasn't the same naive boy who'd left their orphanage to fight in a war he didn't understand. It made no difference that he'd had little choice in the matter. He had bared his teeth and charged into war, as though he alone was an answer to the problem. He curled his fingers inside his pockets. They had used scars to mark their skin because blood washed off too easily.

An ache filled his chest. All this time he'd fought like it could fix something that was broken. Even when he barely understood what that was. He'd chosen to fight. Even if it hadn't really been a choice at all, he had fought with the kind of ferocity he thought might make a difference. Now it was his choice *not* to fight.

He hadn't killed the Tsarina when her bent neck was beneath his blade. Even as she accused him of being the killer he was.

But was that all he was?

He didn't know. And he couldn't fight again until he did.

Jules drew his hand from his pocket, staring at his gloved palm. He wouldn't even touch a blade. Not until he knew who he was. He couldn't be Farah's Corporal Lacroix or Kian's childhood friend, because neither of those iterations of him existed anymore. They died on the battlefield under the cold gaze of the Caspian Tsarina.

He was not *Stigmajka* either, because *that* soldier would never be without a killing blade in his hand.

Now he was choosing to walk away. A real choice this time, not one forced upon him.

Jules peeled the thin leather gloves off one hand at a time.

Marked skin taunted him.

He dropped the gloves to the ground so he could see the scars silvering his hands. Silently he swore on the lives he'd taken and the ones he'd avenged that he would not use a weapon again. Not until he could answer the question that had opened like a pit in his heart: *Who is Jules Lacroix?*

Kian's low whistle broke through his thoughts and Jules looked up sharply. Kian's face had blanched, the freckles standing out more than usual as he stared at Jules's skin.

Jules shoved his hands into his pockets. *Don't ask*, he thought. *Please don't ask.* He was no longer the same man Kian remembered. "I need a smoke."

Kian accepted the subject change. "I haven't smoked in a year." He laughed, the sound only slightly strained. "No, wait, longer." He tipped his head back, gazing toward the sky in a gesture Jules knew well, accessing some half-forgotten memory. "Ah, that's right. Not since the packet you left dried up."

Jules blinked. "The one I hid in the clock tower?"

"That's the one."

Jules patted his pocket and pulled out a small tin, opening it up. His fingers found a slender black cigarette.

Kian smiled in admiration, flinging the last door of the final carriage wide. Pausing in the doorway, Jules lit the cigarette with unsteady fingers, cupping his hands around his mouth. Stepping up beside Kian, he handed him the cigarette and stared at the seemingly endless stretch of track. It smelled like snow and the breeze bit his skin, tearing at him with vicious little teeth.

Kian took a drag and passed the cigarette back, falling easily into a familiar pattern. "You're making me nostalgic. I was there yesterday, you know? I go by every week to check on the kiddos."

"How is it?"

The sounds of the train shifted as they entered a tunnel of trees, passing through thick winter woods.

Kian shrugged. "This time of year's always grim. You know how Matron feels about the war. I think she maybe hates it even more than she hates you."

Matron had lost so many children to the war, most of them conscripted right out of the orphanage. She might've lost more than anyone. Pain flared in his chest. "And yet I'm the one who came back," Jules muttered. "Cruel really."

Kian tackled him and aggressively ruffled his hair. "Stop being maudlin. Who gives a damn whether Matron cares that you lived or not? *I'm* over the moon, and I'm the most important person in Nice."

"*Self-appointed* most important person."

"Doesn't make it untrue."

Jules chuckled, shoving him off.

Kian's smile faded. "Are you in trouble?" He patted the pocket where he'd tucked the torn flyer. "More than this, I mean. Something's happened to you." The questions Kian didn't ask were more telling than the ones he did. He didn't ask why Jules deserted, guessing whatever was eating him was behind it. He'd always been sharp; now he missed nothing. Being a constable suited him.

Jules leaned his elbows on the railing, flicking his cigarette away. The wind captured his hair. "I don't know where I'm going anymore."

Kian snorted, unimpressed. "What does that even mean?"

"I mean . . ." Jules sighed. "I guess I want to know where I'm from. Not knowing was all right for a while. Following orders makes it easy, right? There's not a lot of time to second-guess anything when death's waiting."

"Where did this come from?"

"Someone told me something and I need to prove her wrong. Nothing else matters until I do."

"Did a girl say you were bad in bed? Because seriously, boyo, man up. We all hear that sometimes."

Jules shot him a droll look. "No. And, no, we don't."

A ticket collector rapped on the glass and leaned around the door, his red hat threatening to fly off in the rush of air. "Where to?"

"Nice," Kian answered, handing over his ticket as Jules made a show of patting down his jacket. He finished up at the breast pocket embossed with Nice's police seal. Eyeing his uniform, the ticket collector punched Kian's ticket and left without a word.

When they were alone, Kian said, "I don't understand. You're *Jules*. I've known you my whole life. If you're ever confused, I'll tell you who you are."

The Tsarina's words still echoed between his ears, but they were nowhere near as insistent as the question haunting him. *Who is Jules Lacroix?*

He smiled faintly. "You know who I *was*. Since then I've made my entire self-worth about killing. How many demons I killed, whether I could pay them back for the friends I lost—"

"Jules . . ."

He shook his head, about to tell Kian he was fine, but before he could, hot tears streaked down his cheeks. His chest ached, more painful than any battlefield wound, and the words wouldn't come. Kian squeezed his shoulder. When the warmth of Kian's hand soaked into his bones, he let out a shuddering sigh. Kian dropped his hand to his forearm and didn't move it again as Jules began to speak.

"My commanding officer died a few days back. The day I left. Sergeant—" He broke off, his next words softer. "Farah. She was a good one, Kian. You would've liked her." A smile touched his lips. "The world is a worse place without her in it."

They stood quietly for a while, watching the scenery of northeast France disappear behind them. The crisp air wrapped around Jules, a fitting match for the somber mood.

Kian broke the silence. "I can't do anything about Farah, but I might have an idea about your history."

He tucked his hand in his pocket and drew out a fine silver pocket watch. Jules's eyes widened and he leaned closer. Kian used his thumbnail to open it, revealing the crystal face. The inner workings ticked away smoothly inside, gold filigree cogs and gears and a small blue sapphire inset into the tip of the big hand.

"I thought you were a copper now, not a crook."

Kian rolled his eyes, grinning. "I am. This is my inheritance. Damn fine piece, right?"

Jules nodded. "I'll say. But your *what*?"

"Inheritance," Kian explained. "Matron saves whatever came with you as a baby to give you when you age out. Even if it's just a threadbare cloth. Even if it's probably stolen." He tapped his pocket watch, grinning sheepishly.

"Can't believe she gave you a parting gift." Jules made a face. "Actually I *can*. All she ever gave me was a tongue-lashing and a dislocated earlobe."

"Ain't nothing to dislocate in an earlobe."

"Shows what you know. I recall a distinct tearing sensation."

Kian snorted. "So she didn't give you your inheritance?"

Jules arched a brow. "Kian, I was abandoned at birth. I hate to admit it, but Matron probably wasn't just being a cow."

"*Everyone* had a file," Kian insisted. "I saw yours once. Remember when Marcel was a baby? He had whooping cough and Matron sent me to find his birth certificate . . . just in case."

Jules nodded, grimacing. He remembered.

Even though Jules had been barely a day old when they found him on the doorstep, screaming bloody murder as snow piled around him in his bassinet, if Kian said he knew, Jules believed him. On the day he was drafted, Matron had barely let him grab his worn leather boots, let alone lingered long enough to give him his inheritance. Jules felt a stirring of anger toward Matron. It wasn't a new feeling, but this time it felt darker.

He curled his hand into a fist. "I want it."

Kian raised his chin, smirking slightly. "Then let's get it. One last escapade for the road."

The train whistled, as though punctuating his statement.

To Nice.

CHAPTER SIX

The train to Nice left at midnight.

Setting her case on the green-velvet seat, Selene remained standing as the train readied to depart. It was not her first time catching this particular train, but it had been years since she had left the heart of the Holy Vatican Empire.

Once, the regions had been independent of Rome, ruled by their own disparate forms of government. Dysfunctional as they were, warring between themselves, it had seemed to work for them. For the most part. Until God had been crucified.

Then the power of the Vatican had washed the land, cleansing the demons from the earth in the name of God, even as they kept Him insensible within their walls. Protected, from everyone but *them*. Obviously it was the right choice. The only choice, really. Selene didn't question that. But she could still note the irony.

Selene held her sword, the charm on the hilt turning as the pale jade tassel fluttered in a phantom breeze. On one side, the Alleva coat of arms, and that of the Deathless God on the other. Exposing an inch of the black blade, she sliced her thumb and locked it with a bloody thumbprint so nobody but her might ever draw it. Then she tucked it into the leather straps of her case.

On the platform outside, a man with one crutch doubled his pace to make the train. Bandages wrapped his hands and his head. He was missing a leg from the thigh. A veteran of the war sweeping across their northeastern border with the Caspian Federation, just trying to make his way home and unaware of the altered schedule. Steam hissed as the train began to ease along the platform. He wouldn't make it.

Sympathy knifed through her. The Vatican rarely concerned itself with the inconvenience to civilians when they requisitioned trains. It was a vital strategic advantage in their war on two fronts: the battles fought mainly in shadow against demons who got too close to Rome, and the open bloodshed against the Caspian Federation, led by their part-demon Tsarina Anastasia Alexandrova Romanov. A classified secret that had quickly become common knowledge. Now the worst of the gossip rags claimed Anastasia had her horns shaved down each week, her pointed teeth filed smooth and pretty. Nonsense, of course. But disinformation was not their enemy. The Vatican kept their secrets close. The truth even closer.

The shiny steam trains were for the Vatican first and everyone else a distant second.

A whistle pierced the night.

As the engine drew slowly out of the station, steam billowed to engulf the hobbling man. His determined expression didn't waver, even as the train picked up speed. Selene didn't stop to think. She flew from her cabin and ran down the length of the carriage, flinging the last door open. "Hurry! I've got you." She stretched out her gloved fingers.

He could make it. She'd pull him in.

He stowed his crutch under one arm and lunged for her, his bandaged fingers brushing her own. She leaned out, grasping the brass handle with her other hand. Then his expression changed.

"*Macellaia di Roma.*" She saw his mouth form the words before they were torn away by the wind.

He flinched from her grasp and the train parted them.

Dark hair whipped against her cheeks as she clung to the door, staring back into the billowing steam.

"*Signorina?*"

She swung herself inside and closed the door. Hurt lanced through her. Stretching the soft leather taut on her fingers, Selene adjusted her glove and met the conductor's look. He wore an expression she couldn't quite read. Not sympathy, surely. She arched a single brow and he dropped his gaze.

When she returned to her cabin, she didn't need to see her reflection to know her expression was unbroken. Her cheeks whipped ruddy by the cold air and dampened by falling rain, not tears. The Butcher of Rome wasn't wounded so easily.

The sway of the train brought with it a swell of nostalgia not easy to ignore.

The train's tasseled curtains shivered with their quick passage through the smoke-shrouded city. Rome's domes and columns were lit by gold lantern light. The sky broke and rain slashed against the train windows, driving rivulets across the glass.

The last time she left Rome she had been a child wearing white kid gloves detailed with tiny river pearls, a smaller version of her mother's. Selene curled her fingers inside the black calfskin glove that held her shattered hand together. Some things changed, others did not.

She and her twin, Niccolò, had been seven. Only a year later, she began training at the Vatican's military academy. Three years after that her father had been executed for high treason and apostasy.

Leaning her forehead against the glass, she met her reflection. She twisted the knob, dimming the gas lamps in the cabin, but it did little to lessen the bittersweet impression that someone with eyes very like her own stared back. *Niccolò.* When their father died, she'd lost him too.

Selene closed her eyes, but memories played behind her eyelids in an unstoppable reel. It was the sensations she remembered most vividly. The sound of rain falling on St. Peter's Square where the proud obelisk had long ago been moved to make room for the Academy Arena. But that day it had been set up for an execution.

Icy rain dripped off the ends of her hair and trickled down her face in a mockery of tears as she cut through the square dressed in her Academy gear. She hadn't intended to watch her father die. There was no point. No good could come of it. Niccolò would hate her. Their mother would look at her with accusing eyes.

She wore her boots buckled tightly up her calves, as though to distract from the fact that her father would be chained up twice as tight. Or maybe . . . maybe she wanted to remind herself. Who was she to forget?

"There she is." She turned at the familiar voice.

Eliot had an arm around Niccolò, a hand tightly holding his shoulder as though to keep him on his feet. Niccolò's eyes shot up. Amber like the golden light of dawn. Those eyes, identical to her own, struck her motionless.

No, she thought bitterly. *Identical in theory alone.* She was too guarded for her eyes to ever be that wide. Too cynical for them to be that beautiful. Barely eleven and she had already killed. She would never be innocent again.

Niccolò took half a step toward her. "Selene!"

His soul shone from his eyes; hers was naught but a broken thing. Too dull to ignite even a candlewick.

Their family motto was *animas nostras pro populo.* Our souls for the people. But didn't Rome deserve better than her twisted soul?

So it was lucky, really, that the Latin so easily translated the same word a different way. Our *lives* for the people.

That she could give.

When he said her name again, she raised her chin. "Niccolò, Eliot," she greeted them, her words sounding clipped even to her own ears. "I'm sorry."

Niccolò was barely dressed, with one leg of his fawn pants only half tucked into his brown boots, and a forest-green jacket pulled over a poorly buttoned white shirt. He didn't seem to care.

Straightening, she pressed the heels of her shiny black boots together. Looking her over, his eyes widened even further, finally seeing her neat Academy uniform, her polished boots, the fact that she had tamed her dark hair into a sleek Dutch braid down her spine.

"Selene—"

"I swear I'll restore our family's honor—"

"I don't *care* about our honor," Niccolò spat.

A vast dark cloud of realization painted itself across his face, and she had the unique, glorious torture of witnessing his eyes dim as the last innocence of childhood was snatched away. Selene would remember for many years the last moments he looked at her as anything other than a killer.

"What did you do? Selene, *what* did you *do*?"

He always saw her so clearly. Whether it was just him, always uniquely perceptive, or whether it was because he was her twin, Niccolò could always read her like a book.

"*Selene*." His voice broke on her name. "Is this because of you?" She had turned away from him when the sunshine in his eyes broke.

Eliot held Niccolò back, fighting him to the flagstones where he cradled him in his arms. She had walked away with a spine made iron by long training and a vicious determination not to let anyone see her crumble. The watching eyes tracked her progress with obscene interest. The last thing she would ever allow was for *them* to see her cry. She refused to let the vultures pick her bones.

And she had not cried since.

Stepping off the train five hours later, case in hand, Selene inhaled a deep lungful of coal and leather. The scent of journeys. Overhead, the high beams of the Gare de Nice-Ville were illuminated by muted gas lamps and, at the highest point, the graceful glass arches were lit from behind by the flickering pinpricks of stars.

Her eyes roved hungrily over familiar constellations until the steam engine's billowing clouds filled the upper reaches of the station, blocking them from sight. She shook herself. She was a Roman exorcist; homesickness was a luxury she couldn't afford.

Rather than change trains to get to the small village of Saint-Jeannet, Selene had opted for a town car to collect her. Angling her wrist, she checked her watch. It would already be waiting at the north exit. She was quite anticipating the drive to the Alps, despite her antipathy toward the regions.

Or . . . perhaps, rather than the regions themselves, it was the potential of who might be waiting for her outside Rome.

Her fragile smile cracked.

At least there was no chance of meeting her exiled family in a town car.

Selene didn't know where they had fled to when they'd been banished from Rome. They could be anywhere on the continent, but she couldn't help but feel as though they might be around every corner.

It made her feel watched.

The hairs on the back of her neck prickled as she threaded between women in sleek plaid slacks and men wearing slouchy caps and stylish suspenders. Nice was glamorous. Almost as glamorous as Paris and Rome—if you ignored the risk of death by demon. To most, the risk was worth the reward. Rome was the jewel of the Holy Vatican Empire, and exile the only suitable punishment for Roman elites who stepped out of line.

The thought of her own family as traitors made pain throb behind her eyes. Selene winced, massaging her temple with two fingers. A moment delayed, she realized it wasn't tarnished nostalgia making her eyes ache in her skull. An intense wave of demon magic washed over her, dropping her to one knee.

Gasping raggedly, her heart rate spiked.

"*Mademoiselle*, are you well?"

A handful of Niçoises surrounded her. Selene fought a dry heave as an older woman extended a soft, crinkled hand to smooth back her hair. Her gentle shushing became a shriek. She stumbled back, clutching her wrist as her fingers withered to brittle blackened sticks. With dazed horror Selene realized the woman had brushed the rune on her brow. She'd *touched* the blood of God.

"I'm sorry." Selene braced a hand on the wall to gather herself before pushing through the group.

"*Exorciste*." Whispers followed her, drowned by the woman's screams.

A broad-shouldered young man with tousled hair rounded the corner, tossing his cigarette to the tracks below. Her shoulder slammed into his and she pivoted on her heel. It felt like hitting a brick wall. But *Dio*, he had to be the most beautiful creature she'd ever seen.

He caught her elbow as her newspaper fell to the ground.

"Watch it," she snapped.

Hot air caught her hair like a pennant as a train screamed past the platform. Express to the busy port station Nice-Riquier, she supposed. His lips moved, but she couldn't hear him over the train. A flame-haired man grabbed his lapel as the last carriage disappeared.

"C'mon, don't be a bloody idiot. If we do this, we do it tonight."

The young man bent to retrieve her fallen newspaper and Selene's gaze snagged on the insignia of the Nice *gendarmerie* on his pocket. She turned on her heel, striding away before he could offer her the newspaper. If the police found an old woman with magical damage, they might have questions. She wanted to be long gone before they did.

She had no time to waste and a demon to hunt.

Exiting the south entrance, she hunted the demon power along Nice's wide boulevards. Down narrow alleys. In and out of the city's arteries until she came upon the white facade of the Notre-Dame de Nice. The woman's screams still rang in her ears. Clenching her teeth, she dashed across the road and up the steps to hammer the door with her fist.

A doe-eyed nun in starched white eased the enormous door open. Selene nodded in greeting. "Captain Selene Alleva, Exorcist Second Class. A woman has suffered a divine touch in the Gare de Nice-Ville." Ordinary people could be killed by even accidental contact with God's blood. Exorcists were immune to this divine touch. Whether because they were intermediaries between God and man, and their proximity to divinity safeguarded them, or because of the stolen magic in their veins. "Deal with it."

Her skin prickled at each new wave of demonic power.

"Captain Alleva," the nun whispered, dampening her lips as she eased the door an inch wider. "Do you feel that?"

She had no time for this.

"I do." Drawing her gun, Selene turned. She'd done all she could for the woman with the withered fingers. She had other, more urgent concerns.

The power peaked as Selene raced along a tree-lined street and a building burst into flame. She smothered a gasp, ribs constricting under the overwhelming power. Then it stopped, as suddenly as it began. An echoing hollowness followed in its wake.

A loose group of bystanders, dressed warmly against the pre-dawn chill, stared in horror at the licking flames.

Selene grabbed a newspaper boy by the scruff, dragging him closer to the doomed structure and the roaring flames. "What is this building?"

"How do you say—?" The boy stumbled over the Italian. Impatience was an ugly trait, but her jaw creaked as she ground her teeth. "*Archives communales de Nice.* The civil registry building? Many records are kept here."

"Is that all?"

The crowd flinched back as the building caved in—all but Selene and her captive.

She ignored the heat on her cheeks. "Is that all?" she repeated, raising her voice to be heard above the shriek of collapsing structural beams. She gave the boy a rough shake. No, not a *boy*. He was just shy of military age.

"*Et la Bibliothèque Généalogique.*"

Selene loosened her fingers and let him pull away. "*Merci,*" she muttered, a frown crumpling her brows.

The demon—*her* demon—had been here, at the Genealogical Library.

Silent witnesses lined the street, their glassy eyes reflecting the flames.

If demons gained a foothold here, they would destroy this city.

She'd always considered herself a necessary evil in this world. A small cruel cog in the machine that kept demons at bay. And she could live with that if it meant protecting them. Selene thought again of the woman in the station.

Even cleansing fire burned everything it touched.

CHAPTER SEVEN

The palms of the Promenade des Anglais cast shadows over the tracks as the tram trundled parallel to the beach. Standing in the open door, Jules unfolded the newspaper forgotten by the beautiful girl at the station. It was in Italian, but that didn't slow him half as much as the salt-scented breeze that rustled the pages. He lit a cigarette, its ember glow all the light he needed to read by.

L'Eco di Roma

DEATH IN TRASTEVERE

FIRST-YEAR EXORCIST LATEST CASUALTY

By Aurelio Sabatino

VATICAN MORE THAN A match for demons, according to the Office of the Imperium Politikos, Adriano de Sanctis.

A vigil is planned for first-year graduate Exorcist Third Class Benedetta Fiore, who died on duty in Trastevere. The last in a line of Fiore exorcists, her superior, Captain Selene Alleva, reportedly said she "died a hero." This most recent death raises questions about Vatican ability to repopulate the ranks, especially in view of an exodus from the city.

In light of events ongoing, Exorcist Primus Alexander II has been forced to denounce calls to abandon Rome, citing the dogma that Rome is God's chosen resting place.

Most recently this reporter learned that one prominent family has abandoned their palazzo on the Piazza Farnese for locations unknown. Their young son was expected at the Vatican Academy in the coming months.

This is only the latest and most notable Roman family to abandon their city—and their duty.

This reporter has to ask: whatever happened to noblesse oblige?

Kian leaned his chin on Jules's shoulder, reading too. "Noblesse oblige?"

"Privilege entails responsibility," Jules murmured. "*This reporter* sounds pretty sympathetic to the Vatican." He folded the newspaper and dropped it onto the slatted seat for the next person.

After what he'd witnessed in Ostrava, could he really blame anyone for refusing to send their child to the Vatican Academy? Graduating meant a life of significance, yes. But, like as not, it'd be a short one.

He remembered the exorcists. All that training just to die in the mud beside conscript soldiers. What a waste.

The orphanage was plain by most standards, wedged between a fire station and Nice's industrial area. A short clock tower was its most interesting feature.

"Still ugly as fuck."

"You've been gone a day, Kian. What did you expect?" Jules tipped his head to look up. The room of moving gears had been their refuge once. "Is your stash of mags still behind the clock or did the kids finally figure out your hiding spot?"

"They're probably still there." Kian grinned. "You know, Matron put up a celebratory banner when you aged out. It was kind of a big deal." Kian spoke through crumbs as he finished off a croissant.

Jules smirked. "What did it say? Praise the Deathless God, little thorn is gone?"

Kian laughed, though he glanced around nervously at Jules invoking the name of God.

Some people drew a hard line at any discussion of the Deathless God. Superstitious nonsense, Jules thought. But he wouldn't say it. Not when Kian could prosecute an argument drunk and half asleep. Kian always said, "Don't mess with what you don't understand." And maybe he was right.

It was barely five-thirty. They had half an hour to find what they wanted before Matron woke with military discipline at six on the dot.

"Let's go."

"Wait a minute, shouldn't we—?"

Jules emerged from the concealing shadows. "No more waiting."

The promise of what he might find thrummed in his veins. The Tsarina's words taunted him. He'd spent most of his life thinking he was nothing—less than shit on Matron's heel, the little thorn in her side—and too long on the battlefield trying to prove he wasn't. The Tsarina didn't get to take that away.

He found a narrow kitchen window unlatched. At seven feet high, it was just above head height for him. He pulled himself through first and narrowly missed a bowl of soaking potatoes as he dropped to a crouch on the kitchen counter. Copper saucepans and knives glinted on the wall, refracting what little moonlight crept in. With some help from Jules, Kian slipped through next, landing featherlight on the counter beside him.

His grin flashed like cook's favorite cleaver. "Nice."

"Come on," Jules whispered.

A loud sawing sound made them both freeze. Jules's hand twitched for the Vatican blade he no longer carried. Kian made a choking noise. Shooting him an alarmed look, Jules realized he was smothering a laugh.

The sound came again, followed by a snort. It was cook, snoring in her room adjoining the kitchen. She'd caught Jules with his hand in the breadbasket more than once. Beside him, Kian was fighting for his life. Elbowing him none-too-gently, Jules nodded to the door at the far end of the room.

Locked. No surprise.

Before easing the slender tip of a flick knife into the lock, Kian rummaged in his hair and withdrew a long pin.

Jules bent closer to watch. "You're doing it wrong. More jiggling. With the knife, not the pin."

"If you don't quiet down, I'll jiggle this knife in your guts."

Lost in concentration, Kian's tongue poked past his lips. He jiggled the knife and, Jules noted with silent satisfaction, the door clicked open.

Jules patted his shoulder. "Well done, Kian, but *whatever* did you do?" Perhaps not-so-silent satisfaction after all.

Straightening, Kian pressed the knife against his stomach. "I'm not above disemboweling you like a whiskered catfish, friend."

Jules disarmed him effortlessly and flourished the knife in a courtly bow.

Kian's disgruntled look was a reward all its own.

Without exchanging a word they jumped the creaky bottom step, the seventh, and the last two before the landing. At the door to Matron's office, Jules penned the knife in his hand and went to work on the lock—intent on showing Kian how it was done. In return, Kian favored him with a stream-of-consciousness narration.

Jules flicked him an annoyed look. "Yeah, yeah. You got me." His voice was tight, but Kian didn't seem to care. "Grin all you like. This lock's far trickier."

"You say that, boyo, but they look the same to me." Finally, the lock disengaged.

During the day, Matron's office had all the potential to be a large sunny room, but in the dark, filing cabinets loomed ominously and the dusty books lining the bookshelves looked like broken teeth. Jules pulled out a book and dust motes stirred in golden flurries, catching in the bars of orange light that slid through the blinds.

"It's gotta be in here," Kian said, trying one of the drawers. "If I'm wrong, and there ain't nothing, it's no reflection on you. You know that, right?"

Jules nodded jerkily, but he didn't really believe it. "I thought you said everyone has something?"

"I'm a fool. Don't listen to me." Jules's throat was too tight to answer.

Starting from either end, they were about halfway when Jules's fingertips brushed a brown envelope, bound shut with string. He knew before he saw his name that it was his.

Lacroix.

Jules shared a glance with Kian as a churning sense of dread twisted his guts.

He weighed it in one hand. It was light. Half its weight had to come from the thick cardboard envelope. He twirled the envelope between his fingers by its corners, hesitating.

Kian cleared his throat and gave an encouraging nod.

Jules's fingers shook slightly as he unwound the string loop by loop. When he slid the contents onto his waiting palm, he took a moment to identify the object. A circlet made of metal so pale it could be wrought from moonlight, and leaves so detailed—down to the delicate veins—that he might believe they were picked and gilded last night, if somebody told him so. Nestled among the leaves, exquisite workmanship linked tiny perfect thorns curving at irregular intervals. When he tipped his hand, light refracted off the razor edges.

A low scrape interrupted his inspection.

Jules knew the sounds of this place. Knew that one didn't fit.

"What is it?" Kian asked, not looking away from the silver circlet and unaware of Jules's shift in focus. When he didn't answer, Kian snatched the circlet for a closer look, hissing when one of the thorns pricked his skin. He sucked on a fingertip that welled with dark blood.

The sound came again, louder now. This time Kian heard it too. The scream of tearing metal. Jules parted the blinds with a finger, finding the imposing iron gates that fronted the orphanage. The bars with their fleur-de-lis spikes bent inexorably inward, straining against the chain that held them closed.

The chain shattered and the gates ruptured open.

A man stepped through. *No, not a man.* He was taller than anyone Jules had ever seen, with bones that sang of nobility. Eyes of blue fire burned in his skull. He looked like a god, but he was no god.

"*Demon.*"

Back at the Gare de Nice-Ville, Selene put in a direct call to the Vatican. Pressing her forehead to the phone booth's glass window, she waited on Cesare Alleva. The calming instrumental music of the Vatican switchboard set her teeth on edge.

When the line clicked, she didn't wait for Cesare to speak. "Imperium, it was Baliel, Duke of Briars."

Even if she hadn't memorized the major signifiers for each of the twelve demon dukes, she would know who she was dealing with. Reports of wildfires of blue flame and the conflagration she'd witnessed with her own eyes . . . Yes, she knew this demon with his flame magic. Rare enough among demons to be noteworthy. The Vatican texts were clear.

Her uncle's voice was soft on the other end of the line. "Does anyone else know?"

"Of course not."

He was silent a moment. The quiet of serious thinking, not the quiet of gears grinding to a halt or wiring misfiring. It was the sound of *competence*. Selene closed her eyes, praying that Cesare would command her back to the capital. She was already done with the unknown of it. Done waiting for old ghosts. If she ever met Niccolò or their mother again, she'd never walk away unbroken.

"You're the best I've got, Selene. Find him."

"Sir," Selene said as she leaned her forehead against the glass. "He's killed more than three hundred people. He's well above my class—"

"Untrue."

She bit out the pertinent word: "—*publicly*."

His silence was acknowledgment enough. After a few moments, he sighed. "The only reason you're not an Exorcist First Class is because of politics. That doesn't mean I'm going to entrust this to anyone else. I'm stuck here until January fifteenth at the earliest. The *Baie des Démons* festival will be that weekend. I hesitate to cancel it and give the French another reason to curse Rome. If you haven't figured this out by then, I'll join you."

"I see." Selene pinched the bridge of her nose. *Of course.* The timing couldn't be worse.

The festival centered on Nice's waterfront. At the peak of the festival, a great straw demon effigy would be burned on a raft in the middle of the Bay of Demons. Once named the Bay of Angels, the French had renamed it at some point in the chaotic years after a demon tried to slaughter God. She didn't know if it was irony or nihilism.

"Can you do it?" he asked.

"Yes, sir."

Again she thought of the demonic energy that had washed over her when she first stepped off the train. The imprint of it at the still-burning Genealogical Library. It had the unmistakable tang of intense power. But that confirmed nothing about the demon who had destroyed Saint-Jeannet. She mentally shook herself. All she knew for sure was that Baliel was *here.* It could have been another demon that razed Saint-Jeannet—the likelihood of that was infinitesimal, but she still had to know.

She shivered, tightening her coat against the relatively mild night. The Duke of Briars, first and greatest of the twelve known demon dukes.

And the most terrible.

His tells had been cataloged and taught at the Academy, and given almost equal weight as other vital lessons like how to trigger words of power and how to exorcise a demon. At the time, their instructors' rigor had seemed superfluous—nobody had seen a duke in decades—but now she was glad for it.

Her knuckles were white where she held the receiver to her ear.

When Cesare spoke, his voice was utterly calm. He had faith in her. "A support team is en route to you and the head of the Nice headquarters will act as your second until you release him."

She recalled what Cesare had said in Rome, that he had asked the Nice office to have someone meet her when she arrived. But the presence of a demon duke changed everything. Whoever was mediocre enough to climb to the top job in the Nice office would only be a liability.

"I don't need a second."

She heard the rustling of papers. "I take it Eliot D'Alessandro hasn't arrived yet?"

Her brows furrowed, the glass no longer nice and cool against her burning skin. "Excuse me?"

"You need a second."

"I don't *need* a second! And what do you mean, Eliot D'Alessandro?"

"Selene, I'm being called away. Whatever you do, don't tell anyone else the Duke of Briars is vacationing in the French Riviera. We don't need a panic on our hands."

"Yes, sir," she said through gritted teeth.

"Oh . . . and say hello to your fiancé for me." The line went dead.

Selene slammed the handset into the cradle. And a couple more times for good measure.

"Damn it! Damn it *all*."

The phone let out a high-pitched dial tone and she left it alone.

Backing out of the phone booth, she bumped into a tall figure and whirled on him. "How *dare* you eavesdrop—"

"I hope that wasn't about me?"

Dark eyes flicked to the abused telephone handset and back to Selene. She swallowed, inventorying all the ways he'd changed from the slight, pretty boy she'd known to a slight, handsome man. In the intervening years, the roundness of youth had fallen away to reveal the fine aristocratic jaw he'd inherited from his mother. This was, without a doubt, Eliot D'Alessandro.

"Oh, no. No, of course not." She didn't sound convincing, even to her own ears, and saw his expression tighten as the joke became cruel reality.

"Oh."

He stood in the wide military stance trained into them at the Academy, but beneath the uniform she could see her dearest childhood friend. Her *fiancé*.

But the word no longer fit. She was his superior now. "How long have you been here?" she asked.

"In Nice?"

"I . . . Yes." Heat flared in her cheeks and she instantly regretted the question. She didn't want Eliot to know she hadn't bothered to follow his postings. When he'd left Rome, she had been a *child*. Her father newly dead. Her mother gone. Eliot was just one of many losses she'd shouldered that year. But so much time had passed since then, and now Selene wondered how she'd been so complacent.

"Um. This entire time. Since I was exiled."

Silence stretched between them, and not for the first time Selene wondered why their teachers had forced him out, making him watch their world from afar.

The phone handset shrieked again and she heard a little voice. "*Hello . . . hello . . . hello? Vatican switch. Hello?*"

"Excuse me." She smiled, pivoted on her heel, and snatched up the handset. This time when she slammed it down the cradle broke and the phone stopped making any noise at all. Turning back to Eliot, she nodded sagely. "I see. Almost seven years."

"Seven years this June."

Seven years . . . Every memory they shared belonged to two different people. The last time she'd seen him was the day her father died.

"Look, Eliot—"

"Selene, I'd love—"

She cocked her head, panic igniting in her chest. *He'd love.* He'd love what? They were almost eighteen. Was he saying he wanted to marry her?

He smiled. "You go."

She shook her head and waved for him to continue, forgetting her words. All of them.

"Selene—"

"Captain," she interrupted. *Shit.*

He hesitated, reaching to loosen his tie.

She wanted to bury her burning face in her hands.

He took a breath. "Captain Alleva . . . Selene . . . I would love nothing more than to—"

"I'm sorry, Eliot, but that's just not possible."

"—marry you, but—"

"What?"

But?

His face fell. "Oh. I understand."

Wait.

In contrast to his dark hair, Eliot's skin was alabaster. Even in winter, he stood out among the sun-kissed Niçoises. Now his cheeks blotched red, heat creeping to his ears.

"Eliot." He flinched and she grimaced. "Let me say something, then I want you to say *exactly* what you wanted to tell me a moment ago. Agreed?"

His dark gaze flicked up to hers, brows drawing low. "Fine."

"I don't want to marry you."

His eyes widened.

"Your turn," she prompted.

Eliot dampened his lips. "Me neither," he admitted. "In theory I want to marry you, but in practice I'm not ready for that . . ." She saw a complex interplay of expressions cross his face, the tug of his brows and the tightening of his jaw. Once she would have known how to read him.

She laughed. "I know."

He pressed his lips into a cautious smile. A frightened deer to her wolf. "Should I request a transfer?"

Pain lanced through her at his suggestion.

The wind picked up, blowing her hair across her face and she brushed it aside to better see this new, fully grown Eliot. She could still see the boy she knew, but he was almost gone.

Surprising herself, she caught his sleeve, pinching it tight to stop him going. "No."

He met her eyes and she saw home there. Though it was one she no longer recognized.

His lips tipped wryly in a barely-there smile, but his gaze turned sharp and assessing. "Are you sure? You don't need a second, remember?"

Damn. He *had* heard.

"If I have to work with someone I crushed in every class, at least it's you."

The corners of his eyes crinkled in amusement. "Is that so?"

"It is."

"Not *every* class."

"Hm. Not my recollection. I bested everyone, including you."

"Geography?" he mused.

"Truly not even a subject that should be taught at the Academy."

"First aid?"

"Pointless. We have healers for a reason."

He chuckled and an answering laugh bubbled out of her. She'd missed this. Missed *him*. And even though the man in front of her wasn't exactly the same Eliot—this one was something of a stranger to her—she already had the map to his secrets in her pocket.

"When you left Rome, I thought you'd never graduate."

Eliot pressed his lips into a tight smile. "My grandfather still has his fingers all up in the Vatican's business. As a favor to him, Beni Sforza trained me up here. From the stories I coaxed out of him, he owed my grandfather a limb or two from their demon-hunting days. When it was time, he even tracked down a demon with me so I could graduate."

She rocked forward on the balls of her feet, intrigued. "What level?"

"Five." A Viscount. He looked away, a blush dusting his cheekbones. He never had been overproud or driven by ego. But this time he deserved to be. Hunting down a higher-level demon was a status symbol and gave him greater power too.

Her gloves muffled her slow clap in the still night. He covered his face with one hand but couldn't completely hide his grin.

"Incredible," she said earnestly. "How did you find a Viscount?"

"Not easily. Beni had a contact intercepting official telegrams. We arrived in Geneva and killed it a couple of hours before the exorcist deployed from Rome arrived. He was . . ."

"Not pleased?"

"To put it mildly."

She laughed. "Good for you, Eliot. Now they won't be able to ignore you. Oh, my uncle sends his regards."

His expression shifted, lashes lowering to cover his dark eyes. "Your uncle is too kind. I would imagine myself beneath his notice." He withdrew a slim notebook from his pocket and thumbed the pages. "Before I forget, I received a message an hour ago. We analyzed the residue from the demon fire in Saint-Jeannet. It appears as though the demon didn't immediately leave town."

"What do you mean?"

"He . . . he went to the *church*."

Selene frowned, rubbing two fingers between her brows.

Eliot continued. "Even though it was the opposite direction . . . he went to the church first."

She filed the information away. Another reason to visit Saint-Jeannet.

"Even though the Imperium wants you as my second until we find this demon, I know I . . . kind of steamrolled you on the transfer thing. If that's what you really want, given everything . . ." She faltered over the words, then finally spat them out. "Will working for me be a problem for you?"

Eliot shook his head, drawing one of the twin D'Alessandro family swords at his hip. It shone, as wicked sharp as ever. He held it across his palms and bowed at the waist. "Whatever you need of me, I'm yours, Captain."

She trailed her eyes over the sword crossing his hands, taking in the symbols in the metal. It was the D'Alessandro moon blade, traditionally drawn between dusk and dawn. Twin to the sun blade for daytime slaughter. Selene felt him watching her, eyes lingering on her face. But when she looked up he dropped his gaze, a touch of pink coloring his cheeks.

"Good." She smiled. "I'm so pleased."

When he straightened to his full height, she realized how tall he'd become. When they'd last met, Eliot had been precisely her height. And now he looked down at her with an unfamiliar look in his eyes.

"Eliot—" she began, throat closing on his name.

He staggered as a familiar wave of demonic power rolled over them. Selene fought down the impulse to vomit.

Her demon was hungry tonight.

CHAPTER EIGHT

"Demon."

A second pair of eyes slid open beneath the first. And as though the demon heard his whisper all the way from the gate, all four eyes shifted, pinning Jules in place.

"What?" Kian asked, confused, crowding up beside Jules at the window.

"Quiet." Jules slapped a hand over his mouth and wrestled him away from the glass.

"Did you knock your head?" Kian mumbled between his fingers. "We're in Nice, not Rome."

He frowned. Kian was right. A demon walking the streets of Nice was beyond unlikely, but . . . "I know what I saw." The burning truth of it flickered in his guts.

Kian squirmed in his grip. "That hurts," he hissed, pulling away.

Snatching the back of his shirt, Jules propelled Kian toward the door. "We need to get out of h—"

"Don't know your own strength?" The voice was sonorous and low, vibrating in his bones.

Jules looked up at the silhouette filling the doorway. *Too fast*, he thought, a chill crawling sluggishly down his spine.

The demon was beautiful, if utterly terrifying. His elongated bones had stretched his skin. His well-carved biceps, chest, and stomach were powerful, as though carved by a Renaissance sculptor, but his joints had begun to split free, like a seam too tightly sewn.

His eyes were the worst. They were piercing blue in the depths of his skull, but the sclera and surrounding skin were charcoal, with veins of deepest black spiderwebbing outward as the blazing irises seemed to burn him from within.

No, not him. His . . . *body*. The one he'd stolen to walk among them.

Jules stepped in front of Kian, straightening to his full height. He rarely felt small, but he did as the demon bent to pass through the open door.

Already moving, Jules caught Kian's eye, mouthing, *Run!*

Jules knew he was fast, but as he sprang toward the demon, it was as though the world slowed and only the demon kept moving.

The demon's grin was one of straight white teeth that gleamed when he passed through the bars of orange light. Before Jules registered the movement, the demon's enormous fist caught him in the gut and slammed him back against the window. Shatter lines fractured from the point of impact.

Jules groaned. Near the door, Kian faltered. Kian—his brother in all things but blood—took one stumbling step back toward him, and the demon's eyes snapped up. The demon's fingers lengthened into a grotesque bone spear. With one sharp thrust, Kian's body jerked, impaled on wickedly sharp bone.

A wordless sound of rage clawed up his throat as Jules threw himself at the demon. Weaponless, it was suicide. He didn't care. Indistinct lines of attack formed, but no pure killing blow. *No matter.* If he'd survived Ostrava for any reason at all, it was so he could die shredding this demon apart with his bare hands.

Without sparing Jules a glance, the demon caught him by the throat. The demon's long fingers encircled his windpipe, tightening to cut off his breath. Then, with passionless ease, the demon flung him through the window.

Glass shattered and Jules fell.

Pavement cracked beneath his shoulders. His teeth snapped together. Stunned, he lay still as Kian's death played across the backs of his eyelids.

He fought a scream. One that threatened to crack ribs and rupture organs.

Through the pain, he breathed a botanical scent off the breeze. It coiled in the darkness behind his eyes.

Star jasmine. A bite of spice and citrus.

A girl dropped to one knee at his side, two fingers jabbing the pulse point beneath his jaw. His eyes refocused. Her dark hair slid forward, brushing his cheek. Her eyes were trained on the broken window, brows crumpled with rage.

His breath was tangled. Thoughts fuzzy. But he recognized the beautiful girl from the station. Now ephemeral golden marks twined around her wrists and fingers, vanishing beneath her sleeves. Jules blinked and they were gone.

His heart thundered behind his ribs.

"*Sei vivo?*" she gasped, amber eyes widening as she yanked her hand back.

A pulse beat warm beneath her fingertips.

"You're alive?" Selene looked at him in surprise.

She had witnessed the moment the boy was thrown bodily from a third-floor window by the Duke of Briars.

"*Exorciste*," he rasped, pulling away from her touch.

She switched to French. "Yes. What's your name?"

He was silent for a staggeringly long moment. Impatience flared in her chest, but if the halo of red was anything to go by, he had cracked his skull on the stones.

"Jules," he said at last.

"Good." At least he remembered his name. Probably.

She stood, smoothly drawing a knife from her boot, and stepped over him.

Multiple ruptured organs, a broken spine, and possibly some kind of critical brain injury. He wouldn't be going anywhere. If he was lucky, he'd survive until Eliot arrived.

Her breathing was rapid. When the demonic energy had just about flattened them, she'd cut through the early-morning traffic on foot.

The orphanage's large double doors had been decimated. Raising her guard and extending her senses, she took the stairs three at a time.

The cold flicker of her magic licked at the ventricles of her heart, lashing the insides of her ribs in howling answer to the demon. It wanted to be unleashed. She could feel his essence encased in the flesh he'd possessed—it pulsed as though wanting to escape its bounds. A silent scream only she could hear.

Yes, her magic whispered back. *I'll free you.*

A snow-tinged draft rattled the vertical blinds as Selene slid, shadowlike, into the room. The far wall was painted with gore. A body lay crumpled on the floor.

She sensed the demon but didn't see him until he moved.

Stepping out of the dark, he was silhouetted against the smashed window. Her eyes tracked down his body. Her brow edged up. "Was that as you found it, or . . . ?"

CRUEL IS THE LIGHT

"I brought something to the table."

His voice was gravelly, but warm and rich as forest loam. And for a moment Selene thought perhaps she could appreciate this monster. At least two parts of him, anyway. "Impressive."

The demon watched her inscrutably. The sapphire flames of his eyes burned bright in the hollows of his skull. Echoes of power in his rotted shell.

She let him see the glint of the knife in her hand. He smiled indulgently—it was a thistle to a lion.

"I take it I have the pleasure of meeting the Duke of Briars?"

"Call me Baliel." His eyes flared with interest and he bent fractionally at the waist.

"No, thank you."

Circling the room, she slid a gloved fingertip atop a dusty bookshelf. Her hand still ached from being broken the night before, and the cold didn't help. When her body blocked his line of sight, she drew her gun and spun, loosing a round of bullets.

Baliel raised a casual palm and the bullets combusted. Igniting with blue fire, they slowed and melted, dripping to the floor like melted wax.

She swung her knife into one of his four eyes and a hot wash of blood coated her hand.

Baliel laughed.

She averted her gaze from his wide smile as she yanked her knife free and pivoted away, putting as much space between them as she could. Baliel slashed the air where she'd just been with a lance of bone. He was a blur, too fast to dodge.

To stay alive, she'd need to predict his attacks before they landed.

Ducking behind the desk, she used it as cover to shoot him. He dodged all but one that struck his breastbone. Selene followed the bullet, stabbing for his armpit with the knife. He met her half-way, ramming her with his shoulder. Ribs cracked and she wheezed against a sudden tightness in her chest.

She sprang back. Knife poised to carve her sigils, she sliced away her sleeve.

Baliel knew too well what she intended and batted her knife away from her exposed flesh. His smile showed too many teeth.

"Selene!"

Eliot's voice reached her faintly from beyond the shattered window. She ran, leaping to kneel on the sill.

Eliot held her scabbarded sword aloft. It was so close and yet—

Utilizing the distraction, Baliel attempted to punch through her spine. She twisted out of the way but his hand burned a scalding line across her side—skin and clothing blistering from the heat of his flame-coated hand.

She kicked him in the chest and thrust her arm out the window, fingers stretching.

There was a grunt and her sword sailed through the air end over end. Not close enough.

Selene lunged, hanging over the window ledge to catch the strap with a crooked finger.

Baliel's fire warmed her back and she could smell the burning air as he closed in. Catching his attack on the scabbard of her blade, they grappled for a moment before tumbling apart.

She drew her sword.

DEUS IMMORTALIS.

He smiled, eyes trailing over the writing on her blade with the tenderness of a lover. "Now I can stop holding back."

They struck and parried. It was nearer a dance than a fight, they were so well matched. The joy on the demon's face made nausea churn in her gut. He was *enjoying* this. She was just trying to survive.

They broke apart, backing away from each other. The tension between them heightened. Each searching for an opportunity to strike. If she hadn't been watching him so intently, she would never have noticed the shift.

He cocked his head. The joy was gone from his eyes. Only murderous intent remained. "I know your type. You hunt, don't you? Always *hunting*."

"Obviously." Not taking her eyes off him, she wiped a trickle of blood from her brow.

"Even young ones. Even when we're born here, just like you." He rolled his shoulder, watching her with terribly cold eyes.

"Gleefully," she hissed through bared teeth.

Baliel laughed, though it was a joyless sound, and a cold chill caressed her skin.

Selene lifted her sword, questioning whether she dared risk exorcising him. She wasn't sure how much magic would be required to destroy his body and sever the hold he had over it. Given the vastness of his power, it could well be more than she was willing to give.

Selene swallowed.

And then he attacked.

Catching his first blow on her sword, her back hit the wall and the plaster fractured. Baliel gritted his teeth in a silent snarl, and hot lines of blue light wrapped around his throat like burning brands, digging into his flesh with acrid coils of smoke.

Selene stared, horrified. What was happening to him? His neck corded with agony. "Vatican. At the heart—"

Dio. Baliel was fighting to even speak.

She had never seen it, but she recognized the signs from her textbooks. Sometimes powerful demons appeared on the front lines in their war with the Caspian Federation. They were bound through some profane means by Caspia's damned demonologists, who bent them to their will to bolster the war effort. To do so was to first invite a powerful demon into this world. Dangerous even under the best of circumstances.

Baliel was *bound*.

Her mind spun as Baliel tangled his fingers in the burning brands around his throat and stripped them away, dropping them like tattered ribbons. No sooner had he done so than others snapped into being about his neck. It made no sense. If he had been ensnared, why was he here? He should be making his terrible way to the front lines like some angel of death.

Selene was the last person in the Vatican to soften in the face of a demon, but she could feel no flaw in the powerful invocation that bound him. The way it wound around his body and soul, tangled in the threads of his being, he had to be in *agony*. And still he fought. In that moment, she respected him.

Her back was against the wall. "Why fight?" she whispered.

"It's what I do."

The downward pressure from his bone spear against her sword made her tremble with exertion. The plaster behind her back cratered and her sword slipped past him, giving the demon a gaping bloody opening, but he held himself still.

His gaze burned into her. The shadowy darkness spreading from his eyes crackled the skin of his cheeks like broken pottery. "The Vatican." Baliel ground out the words through clenched teeth.

Her heart sank. Not the front lines, then. He was being pulled to Rome.

Again Baliel ripped at the powerful magic that bound his body, ribbon after shredded ribbon of it falling to the floor in ashes. Her fingers tightened on her sword. She had to end him or he'd threaten Rome.

His throat worked, as though he wanted to speak, but no words came. Then his gaze flicked down to her hand, keen eyes recognizing the determination of her grip. She swung for his neck, the blade slicing through the burning brands around his throat as though they were nothing. Baliel folded backward and she missed his flesh. She twisted, swinging her sword in a full arc as though to gut him.

Baliel caught her blade. His expression was no longer tormented—the glimmering bindings around him gone.

Together they smashed through the plaster wall, filling the air with dust. His foot met her chest and she was thrown bodily through the next, bringing down a fall of bricks around her. Vision wavering, Selene pulled herself up by the banister, swaying on the landing as Baliel stepped through the Selene-sized hole in the wall. Baliel shook bricks off his shoulders and straightened to his full height.

With aching muscles and joints she leveled her sword.

Beyond his towering form, a row of doors lined the hall. Children in snow-white nightclothes stood clustered in the open doorways, staring with large innocent eyes at the horror before them. The closest, a young boy no older than seven, dragged a rabbit half his own size by the ears.

She sprang at the demon. His eyes flamed as they collided.

The child screamed, blond curls buffeted as they raged toward him. She wanted to tell him to run. The other children were already scrambling to put distance between themselves and the dervish of heat and blades. She wanted to tell him that he would die if he didn't move. But it was already too late. A maw of despair opened in her chest. She could do nothing more than parry the demon's blows on a collision course with the child.

She pushed the thought aside in the moment between breaths, focusing on the only thing she could influence—the fight. To lose concentration would be to die.

She couldn't save the children. She could barely save herself.

And the Butcher of Rome would leave another body in her wake.

Selene gasped against the pain of her broken bones and planted her foot against a fall of bricks. She raised her sword, one hand splayed against the flat of her blade. A final stand between the demon and the child. But the fight was too fast and she wasn't strong enough. Selene braced herself for the spray of blood.

Instead, everything went terribly still.

She blinked at the strange tableau. It was like waking from a dream. The young man from the pavement—Jules, probably—had one hand flung toward the demon, his other holding the child. Frozen in place, Baliel's spear of bone was barely an inch from splitting Jules's outstretched hand.

Baliel stepped away, almost stumbling, as the bone spear crumbled to reveal long elegant fingers. He sagged as he leaned against the wall. The body seemed to be failing him, its flesh slower to stitch itself together where it tore.

Jules stumbled back, turning his body to protect the child.

"What's happening?" the child whimpered, clutching Jules's shirt in his fists.

"We're alive, you little shit," he answered, voice rasping with disbelief. "We're *alive*."

The child promptly vomited down his shirt.

With an effort of will, Baliel pushed himself up, his four eyes narrowing as he stared at Jules, whose expression twisted in what

Selene assumed was belated terror at having gained the demon's full attention.

Jules set the child down behind himself. "Run, Marcel."

Baliel snarled, a terrible sound like shredding skin and bone. A flick of his fingers released a billow of blue flame and shadow. His essence overwhelmed the bounds of his physical body, withering the flesh of his right hand until there was only bone. Soon not even that. It crept up his bicep, eating away at him.

Jules watched the small child dash away as Baliel's flames exploded outward. He flung both hands toward Baliel, as though to push against the flames.

But they engulfed him.

Selene leaped back, covering her face. Flesh burned away from her arm, leaving it red and raw. She swallowed her pain. Swallowed a whimper before it could spill free. Instead, she carved a quick mark into her scorched flesh to find the bone. She bit her lip, breathing through the agony.

Protezione. Gold flared within the symbol carved into the very quick of her bone.

The word of power washed over her like cool water. Her magic felt less gutting here in Nice. Or perhaps she was so badly wounded that her senses were skewed. It didn't tear through her like wildfire. It lit in her like the steady flame of a candle.

Selene's vision cleared, her magic lending her heightened senses. A billowing shadow built from within her blood, seeping into a skeletal, serpentine form that coiled around her, protecting her from further damage.

Because her magic felt so natural here, she did something inescapably reckless. She pushed it out. *Protezione.* Not just protection for her, but protection for—

Her consciousness faltered. Black crowded in on the edges of her world.

Protection for all of them. From Baliel, from his flames.

In her last moments of consciousness, the walls creaked as the orphanage was devoured by flames from within. Baliel reached for Jules, one enormous hand cupping his head, as though to crush it. Baliel made a terrible choked sound of agony. It was a smoky thing that echoed through his ruined body. Echoing from within his essence. The demon flames licked the walls, spreading with the kind of vigor that would not be stopped. And then Baliel disappeared in ash and fire.

The moment his vivid presence disappeared, his blue flames died too.

Jules stood in the embers. His clothes were burned, but his skin remained unmarked.

"You—" she rasped, coughing ash and smoke. "You're not—"

Hurt.

Then darkness claimed her.

CHAPTER NINE

Jules carried the unconscious exorcist down the stairs. The building was burning. Normal flames this time, not the demon fire that had raged earlier. He tried to shake the memory of those flames. The way they'd wrapped him in a heat so intense they might have consumed his very soul.

The fight flashed through his mind. By the time Jules had found his feet and followed the exorcist into the orphanage, she looked half dead, and the demon not much better. Her power had sung in the thickened atmosphere, slicing the air as she fought. In that moment, he realized the difference between the exorcists he'd seen at the front and this girl—a true Vatican elite. A legend made flesh. Next to her, other exorcists paled like candles beside a halogen lamp.

He gently shifted her as blood trickled down her arm and off her index finger. Beneath the iron tang hid a unique scent, and Jules wondered if it was the vestiges of her magic fresh from her veins.

He thought of the seconds before the demon's body had burned away, destroyed by his own immense power, when a light of recognition lit the demon's cobalt eyes. Then Kian's killer had warned him in a disintegrating voice: *You cannot trust them. The Vatican, and all Rome, are your enemy.* A small smile had touched the demon's lips as he was undone.

Freezing air greeted Jules when he stumbled outside with the exorcist cradled in his arms.

Matron made orderly queues from the chaos and a wave of relief washed over him when he spotted Marcel. Soot-stained and teary-eyed but alive. As Jules watched, Matron knelt to wipe soot off the child's cheeks. Sniffing, he said something that made Matron freeze.

There was no surprise on Matron's face when she stood to find Jules, only a tightening at the corners of her lips.

Adjusting his hand beneath the exorcist's knees, Jules tried not to back away as Matron stormed toward him. "What are you doing back here?" she asked, her voice terribly cold. Cold as the demon's flames burned hot.

Behind her, lights approached the gates. An ambulance drove onto the orphanage grounds while the police and a convoy of black town cars glided to a stop on the street.

His cheeks flared with heat and he pulled the exorcist to his chest like a shield. Madness. She'd probably turn on him too if she were conscious.

What survived of his military uniform hung off his frame in charred rags, and Matron's sharp eyes focused on the hand holding the exorcist's rib cage. Her eyes roved over the marks on his fingers before trailing up his bicep to find the band of thorns that had been carved into his flesh as a babe.

Little thorn.

Nobody else knew where her name for him had come from.

Perhaps even she had forgotten why she first called him that. He'd been the thorn in her side before he could talk.

Her expression twisted. "I asked you a question."

Jules swallowed, taking a half step back. "I . . . We—"

She flinched. "We?"

"Kian and I."

Four years at war meant nothing standing before her now, obediently answering her questions.

"Where is Kian?"

Snow began to fall. Wet and fat, the flakes hissed as they landed on his hot skin. Glancing down at the girl in his arms, concerned, he realized her clothes were smoldering where they touched him, and his hands burned through the rich wool of her Vatican uniform.

He was *burning* her. Yet *his* skin was smooth and unmarked.

It reminded Jules that once, when he and Kian had come back from playing with scraped knees and bloody palms, by the time they stood before Matron only Kian had anything to show for it. No wonder she hated him. Always the instigator, never the victim. He'd always healed so fast. Panic clawed up his throat at the thought. He pushed it away. *No. No, no, no.* The horror of the night was playing tricks with his mind. That had to be it. That was all it was. That and nothing more—

"Where is he?" Matron's trembling voice intruded on his thoughts.

The answer caught in his throat.

A pair of nuns—sisters of medicine by the looks of them—rushed up with a stretcher, the crossed spears of the Deathless God at their throats where long ago nuns might have worn a crucifix. Instead of rosaries and prayers, now they carried guns and magic born of blood. "Out of the way."

Matron turned and scooped up Marcel, though her eyes continued to burn into Jules. He'd need to answer her questions eventually.

A small nun with a pretty elfin face noticed him then. "Lieutenant D'Alessandro, she's over here!"

"Selene!" A man approached with long strides, wearing the polished buttons and black military garb of the exorcists. Twin swords hung at his hip. Unlike the nuns, it was clear he wasn't here to tend the wounded. A spark of panic lit his eyes when they locked on the girl limp in Jules's arms.

At the urging of the nun, Jules gently lowered the exorcist onto a stretcher. Careful not to touch her skin, he cradled the back of her head with what remained of Kian's police jacket.

"Captain Alleva?" the nun said, patting her cheek with the back of her hand. "This is bad, Eliot. I need to get to work."

Eliot pushed the nun's hands aside, leaning over Selene with an expression of such sincere longing Jules was surprised nobody looked away.

Jules tipped his head, looking down at the girl. His fingers flexed and then curled into fists at the sight of the bruises on her neck and exposed collarbone. It was like seeing one of the war falcons with an injured wing—so beautiful and so broken.

"Eliot, we need to move."

He ignored her. "*Selene.*"

Selene Alleva stirred with a soft moan of pain and her eyes opened, flicking between the nun and Eliot before finding Jules, catching his eyes in an amber hold so intense he couldn't move. Then her lashes fluttered closed, sealing all the power of that gaze away.

"Fuck . . ." Eliot dropped his head back to stare at the sky.

Matron's voice came from behind Jules, quieter now. "Where is Kian?"

Such a simple question.

Such a final answer. "Dead."

Everything happened in fits and starts, silence crowding in on him in the seconds between too many things happening at once. Matron's scream broke the quiet and she crumpled to her knees.

Jules squeezed his eyes closed.

A nun medic rushed over with a pile of blankets, moving to cover his shoulders so he wouldn't be standing nearly naked in the snow, but he backed away. She shot him a strange look and turned her attention to Matron, crouching beside her shaking form.

Fluffy snowflakes continued to fall and melt against his skin.

"I have to go," he muttered, mostly to himself, and stepped right into Matron's palm.

She delivered a stinging slap across his face. Her expression flickered between rage and pain as she curled shiny reddened fingers. Scalded, as though by boiling water. "Curse you," she snarled softly. "Kian's life is on your head. Go!"

Jules backed away, raising his hands as Eliot looked up with dark, intelligent eyes, observing the ruckus. He should leave, like Matron said. Put distance between himself and everything that had happened here.

The edges of the world were dark and crowding in.

He wanted to defend himself but he'd never been able to before. Why would he now? And how could he protest his innocence when this time she was right?

Matron picked up a discarded broom and broke it over his back, her expression one of agony and grief. "Go! Go, little thorn!"

He felt Selene's eyes on him again as he crossed the yard.

The sister of medicine bent over Selene. "Please stay still, Captain. You've been badly wounded, but you'll be fine."

But the exorcist ignored the nun, pushing herself onto her elbow with her other arm cradled against her body. It was red-raw and burned to the muscle and her curled fingers showed glimpses of bone. Agony washed all color from her face, but her eyes remained locked on Jules, burning brighter than the yellow lamps edging the tree-lined street. Fear lanced through him as her dry, lovely lips formed words he couldn't hear.

Then the nun pressed two fingers against the exorcist's forehead and Selene slumped back onto the stretcher.

Jules let out a breath, backing away until he was fully out of sight beneath the row of big old trees. He had to leave before they clocked him. His eyes adjusted quickly, and he saw Eliot standing in the shadows.

Without thinking, Jules drifted nearer. Remaining in the deeper dark of the orphanage wall until he could lean his back against a trunk, out of sight, but close enough to hear soft voices.

"No casualties," Eliot said, which showed how much he knew. "Remarkable."

"First Saint-Jeannet, now this? It's weird."

"That's putting it mildly, Altamura."

"And this demon bested *her*, our own *Macellaia di Roma*."

The Butcher of Rome.

Jules *knew* that name.

The most notorious young exorcist to come out of the Academy in Rome. The top student of an entire cohort who were feared and . . . *worshipped* in a kind of unholy union of war heroes and gods.

"*Sì*. This doesn't bode well."

"Get in the ambulance, D'Alessandro!" the small nun shouted from the open doors. She swung the first shut with finality, reaching for the other. "Or I leave you behind."

Eliot swore and took off into the dark.

Jules stilled, waiting for Eliot to pass him and climb into the ambulance. When its taillights disappeared from view, he released a breath. Blue cigarette smoke coiled around him in the dark beneath the elm and a smoke-sweet breath spoke behind his ear. "Hello."

He turned, caught.

The nun who had been speaking with Eliot pinched a cigarette near her lips and watched him, amused. *Altamura*, he recalled. An enormous rifle rested on her shoulder even though she didn't *seem* on the edge of violence. But from the way she held herself that didn't mean much. She was probably always on the edge of violence.

"Sister," he greeted her.

She looked him up and down. "You're positively indecent. Put this on." She extended a black wool coat on a crooked finger.

Jules blinked.

Altamura drew a deep drag of her cigarette and crushed it out against the trunk of the tree, a sharp smile curling her lips as she threw the coat in his face.

He shrugged it on. "Do you want something?"

A line appeared between her brows. She was silent a moment, then finally shook her head as though dismissing a thought. "Don't eavesdrop on Vatican exorcists, boy." She turned away, speaking over the monster of a gun. "That is all. For now."

As he watched her go, Jules turned over what he'd learned. The Butcher of Rome, here in Nice. And the town. He knew that name too . . . Saint-Jeannet, the small village in the French Alps where he'd been born.

Allez! Allez, petite épine!

Selene's eyes snapped open, staring at the ambulance ceiling.

Petite épine. Little thorn. She rubbed a temple, trying to force her sluggish brain into motion. Why did it matter what the matron called him. She bit her lip, hoping the pain would jolt her back into form.

"Captain?" Lucia asked with concern.

Her throat felt tight from smoke inhalation. "Stop the car," Selene husked out.

She forced her tired body to sit, bracing herself for pain. Her arm, however, was perfect once more. Now she had skin where there had been none. Selene shot Lucia a grateful look. Standing, she pressed her hands to the ceiling of the van as the entire convoy pulled over along the Promenade des Anglais. To the side, a rocky beach stretched out of sight, its white pebbles bright in the predawn. Only put to shame by the lonely moon glinting off the ocean.

Lucia scowled at her. "I hadn't finished."

"You've done enough." She rotated her shoulder, wincing. "You've done beautifully. I'm lucky you were here."

"Well." Lucia crossed her arms, satisfaction softening her expression. Then she grinned. "You created your own luck. Literally. Thanks for the assignment, boss."

She ignored that. "What about the boy?"

Lucia frowned. "All the children were fine. Thanks to you."

Selene rolled her knuckles against her temple, grimacing as she tried to remember. "Even the one who was on fire?"

Lucia shifted back. "Uh, hate to break it to you, but *you* were the one on fire."

Selene rolled her eyes. "I'm aware. I recall the excruciating pain. But . . . wasn't there a boy? About my age?"

Lucia shook her head. "The oldest child was fifteen. Are you sure—?"

"Forget it." Selene scowled. He'd slipped through her fingers. But she couldn't quite remember why it mattered. "I need to go to Saint-Jeannet." She braced herself against the ceiling and stood.

"Captain—"

"Now."

"Selene!" Lucia grabbed her arm, teeth gritted against her ire. "Wait."

Selene obliged, brow tipping.

Lucia waved one hand, mumbling something unintelligible. Then, quick as a viper, she plunged a syringe into Selene's bicep with her other. "Okay, now you may go. If you can." She smiled sweetly.

"*Lucia . . .*" Selene wavered, muscles turning to liquid. She collapsed back on the stretcher and the hand reaching for Lucia's throat refused to cooperate.

"Your body will thank me, boss."

Selene finally let her head drop back, her eyes closing under the influence of the drug. "Saint . . ." Was that her slurring like a drunkard? She tried to make her words crisp through sheer force of will. "Saint . . . Saint-Jeannet. I want—"

There was a rustle of movement as someone climbed through from the cab.

"We're on it, Selene. Trust us. *Rest.*"

Eliot. His cool palm rested against her forehead and smoothed back her hair. She tried to open her eyes but they wouldn't obey. She felt a brush of lips against her brow. Even with her eyes closed, she could see Eliot's gentle smile behind her eyelids.

She fought against exhaustion, against the slow creep of warmth through her muscles. But in vain.

"Fine." It came out as a breath.

And at last she let herself sleep.

CHAPTER TEN

T he Vatican beat Jules to the French Alps. Because of course
    they did.

By the time he stepped off the train from Nice—at a station
little more than a platform in a field—it was already fading to winter dark and his path to Saint-Jeannet was blocked by two police
cars parked at an angle on the narrow cliffside road. Police, not so
strange. The Vatican nuns smoking slim pastel cigarettes by the edge,
however, certainly was.

One nun pored over a map spread across the car hood, her knee
propped up to show a stretch of slender leg.

The other, impressively, managed to stand upright despite the
massive gun slung across her back. She tapped her cigarette, turning to blow smoke over her shoulder. Half angel, half warrior, her
face was a mess of scars, but otherwise her brown skin was luminous. *Altamura.*

He instantly recognized the first as the sister of medicine who'd
treated the Butcher of Rome in Nice that morning. *Dieu Immortel,*
he cursed. At least the exorcist he'd first seen at the Gare de Nice-Ville
would be down for the count. She'd almost lost an arm in the fire.

Instead of attempting the road—and testing the nuns—Jules

decided to bypass the checkpoint entirely. Backtracking a few hundred feet, he set his toe in a crevice and began to climb. There was no world in which he wanted to tempt the nun and her beast of a gun.

Nor did he particularly want to give Altamura back her coat.

Jules had stolen a white linen shirt off a back-alley line, which would be enough in the Côte d'Azur's forgiving climate, especially after his time in Ostrava. But without the woollen overcoat the chill would be bitter this high in the Alps.

Once he was fifty feet above the road, Jules edged along the cliff, moving more carefully as he neared the checkpoint below. He made sure to keep the sparse bushes clinging to the steep rock between him and the road. Though he was out of sight, he was very much within their hearing range. But his steps were true.

Then his hand landed on scales. Aghast, he yanked it back to his chest as an asp viper flicked its stubby tail and retreated into a crevice. Sand trickled down the cliff face. Jules froze, rabbitlike. When no shout came, he let out a breath and turned his gaze ahead.

Rounding the bend, he choked on his next breath.

Saint-Jeannet was in ruins.

Nothing was left of the stone buildings but blackened sticks piercing the wintry sky. Only a single stone tower remained, belonging to the old church of Saint-Pierre where he'd been born. Or, at the very least, where he'd been left. Beyond it, the remnants of Saint-Jeannet's medieval castle had been spilled across the valley— ancient chunks of stone visible only as lumps beneath the coating snow.

Jules's heel skidded from beneath him and rocky scree tumbled down the hill.

Grabbing a handful of brittle twigs, he thought for a second that he'd saved himself, but they snapped beneath his grip.

"*Fermati!*" Altamura shouted from below, as Jules scrambled for another handful of bush, trying to pull himself against the shelter of the cliff, but the roots came free of the rocky crevice, sending him into free fall.

He covered his head, rolling and sliding down the length of the steep incline until he slammed onto the road.

"Stop! Vatican!" The same voice, this time in heavily accented French.

Jules didn't stop. He launched himself to his feet and threw himself off the opposite side of the narrow road, tumbling down the scree in an only slightly more controlled fall than before. At least this time his feet were beneath him. He attempted to manage his speed with fistfuls of sad winter shrubbery and rocky handholds.

The ground in front of his feet was chewed up by a force more violent than nature. Splintered shards of stone ricocheted in every direction beneath the heavy-caliber bullets.

"*Stop.*"

Jules skidded to a halt on the steep shale. Turning slowly with his hands up, he tried a smile. "This . . . is me stopping." He looked up to where the nun still stood on the edge of the road.

"*You—*" Recognition lit Altamura's eyes. She leaped from the cliff, landing with a light step, seeming unfazed when limestone cracked beneath her feet from the height. These Vatican monsters were a different species. "Stupid, ignorant trash. Do you want to become red mist, boy?"

"Not really."

Altamura slid down the hill, swinging the rifle onto her back and pulling a long pistol in the same fluid movement, leveling it at him. "You don't sound so sure; maybe we should test it."

"Caterina!" The other nun stumbled down the hill, crashing

into her tall frame. Caterina didn't flinch, subtly shifting her weight so they didn't slide down the rocky slope. Nor did her pistol hand waver.

The sister of medicine gasped, her blue eyes pinning Jules's face. "Thank you. But don't you dare shoot, Caterina! Look how cute he is." Jules turned a sardonic look on the smaller nun. She was at least two heads shorter than him, with the heart-shaped face of a china doll. "Me?" he asked, his lips curling slowly. "If I'm cute, what are you?"

She smiled a wide toothy smile. "Dangerous."

The nun strolled closer and Jules noticed a slit up her thigh, exposing the long sheer stocking that stopped above her knee, threaded with a slender velvet ribbon.

Jules dragged his gaze back up and her eyes crinkled in amusement. "Interesting, um, habit . . . Sister."

"Oh, this? What's piety without utility?"

"Lucia, stop flirting."

"Me?" She gasped, pressing a hand to her chest. "*He's* flirting with *me*."

"Guilty," Jules said with a wink.

Caterina sighed, ratcheting open the magazine to load a few more bullets.

"*Fine*." Lucia rolled her eyes at Jules but her expression hardened. "What are you doing here? Didn't you notice the Vatican barriers? Or were you too busy sneaking along the cliff edge in the dark and snow to notice?"

Jules rubbed the back of his neck, trying to look embarrassed. "Yeah, you know what? It's a funny story—"

"If it's not actually funny, I shoot," Caterina interjected.

He focused on Lucia, switching on his most winning smile. "I always heard this town had the prettiest girls. Turns out the rumors were true."

"Not funny," Caterina said.

"Shh, *shh*." Lucia reached blindly for Caterina's gun hand, pushing it down. "Let him finish."

He glanced toward the village and he couldn't find the words. "What happened here?" His voice was soft, almost plaintive.

"Fire. Arson. Very sad."

Jules scoffed and Caterina's eyes narrowed at his insolence.

He took half a step back. "Since when has the Vatican been stealing work from the local fire authorities?"

Lucia tried to smother her laugh. But not very hard.

"No fire I know can burn stone," Jules added, nodding toward the church in the distance.

Caterina stepped between him and the ruins, her eyes intense on him. "What do you think happened?" she asked, and struck a match on her pistol to light another cigarette. It lit her face, flickering against the perfect structure of her bones and scar tissue. Her eyes were as flat as a snake's as she watched him down the length of her pistol. "Kitten," she added as an afterthought, blowing out a coil of blue smoke.

Jules knew the answer; it was the only reason they were there. "Demon," he replied, not missing a beat.

Caterina's brow edged up in a look of mild surprise. "Good guess for a normie, don't you think, Lucia?"

"I don't know." Lucia tapped her cheek. "What else could burn a town without flames, leaving nothing but the medieval foundations and a lone church tower to reign over it all? Nothing . . . Nothing but a demon, that is."

Her lilting voice made the terrible words strangely lovely as she closed the distance between them, stepping in front of him to clamp a delicate silver cuff around one wrist. He pulled away, but she quickly snapped on the other.

The metal seemed to mold to his skin. When they were both in place, Caterina snapped her fingers and a fine silver chain sprang between them. Jules raised his hands, trying to see the mechanism by which the chain had appeared, and shot Lucia a dirty look.

She shrugged. "Sorry."

Caterina breathed a trail of smoke into the sky as she mused quietly, as though to herself. "*We* know these things. We know about demon fire. We know what happened here . . . But how does he?" She dropped her chin, eyes alight with suspicion.

"I don't know." Lucia lifted her chin, nostrils flaring. "But beyond your cigarettes, my love, I smell demon."

Their stances shifted. They were apex predators and primal fear ignited in his stomach. He threw himself back, his head knocking a sharp rock, his bound wrists restricting his movements. Blood trickled into his eyes, blinding him as he scrambled back. Caterina snatched the rifle from over her shoulder and leveled it at him. Damn, she was fast. She braced herself on the hillside with one long leg, the muscles of her thigh coiling as she prepared to make him red mist.

This time he wouldn't get a warning shot.

He swung around, hands extended. "Wait." He swiped his bloody forehead against his shoulder.

Lucia prowled closer.

He backed away. "Just . . . *wait*."

Caterina smiled, her cigarette burning cherry red and illuminating the planes of her cheeks. She shifted her hold on the trigger, prepared to release a ground-devouring rain of bullets. "Speak fast."

Jules raised bound hands—futile protection if she decided she was done playing. "Sorry. Look, I'm not running." He planted his feet, squinting one eye open to look at them. "I just got a fright." He bunched his hand in his shirt, shaking it slightly. "I *would* smell of demon, sister. I just came from Ostrava."

"Czechoslovakia?"

He nodded and the nuns shared a look.

"I've killed demons and been covered in their blood," he continued. "And I survived by listening to the stories of what they can do. Even if I don't know what's true or what's a lie, I can make a guess of it."

Caterina pursed her lips, nodding thoughtfully. "There *is* a battalion there."

A test.

"More than one," he corrected her.

Caterina's expression tightened. He'd passed her test, but if anything, she seemed even more irritated by the fact of his existence.

"Half of us were decimated," he said. "My superior and entire unit were killed. I'm the last." He turned his face toward Saint-Jeannet. "And I thought I'd see the town where I was born. Weird, right? Being so close to death—" He choked off, as though he couldn't finish the thought. But it was less an act than he liked, his throat tightening at the memory of Kian's death. Of Farah's.

Caterina did not look convinced by his performance. Nor did she lower her rifle.

"Why did you run?" she asked softly, stepping forward to press her gun between his eyes.

A clear voice rang out from the top of the cliff.

Jules shielded his eyes, trying to make out the figure silhouetted against the glare of headlights. She had a presence like metal on his tongue, as though he'd licked bloody steel. A black town car purred, idling at her back.

"*Fermatevi!*" Stop.

The figure skidded down the shale, flinging herself between Jules and the nuns.

"Captain, you're awake. We're in Saint-Jeannet." Lucia flung her arms wide as though her superior might have missed the faintly smoking ruins.

"I know. I'm actually surprised."

"Why? You gave the order."

"I didn't think insubordinates like you would listen."

Selene Alleva, healed and whole once more.

She glanced at him, brow arched. Belatedly, Jules realized he'd spoken aloud, her name decadent on his tongue.

Catching his heel on a rock, Jules stumbled onto his ass, teeth clacking. The Butcher of Rome stepped over his leg, standing between him and Caterina—who gave him a look like her trigger finger might slip.

"He ran. *Twice.*"

"No accounting for taste," Lucia quipped.

Selene ignored them, grabbing Jules by the shirt to haul him to his feet. Her eyes narrowed. "Out of uniform today, *officer*?"

Jules swallowed when his eyes met amber, as cold and hard as stone. He hadn't thought she'd remember their first encounter at Nice-Ville. "About that . . ." Jules began, but when he hesitated, searching for a suitable lie, Lucia straightened to her full—inconsiderable—height, ready to squeal. "I'm not actually a gendarme."

"*And?*"

"And what?"

"Who are you really?" she asked, her voice growing softer. "And why do you turn up everywhere you shouldn't?" Finally releasing him, she spread her hands, indicating the entirety of Saint-Jeannet in a more somber mirror of Lucia earlier. "Rather suspicious, really."

"I'm a soldier."

"You're a long way from the front."

Jules gritted his teeth. This was getting dangerous. "Well, you see. Funny story actually—"

"Not another one," Caterina drawled.

He shot her a wry look. "Not funny ha-ha."

"Neither was the last."

"I mean, this one isn't *supposed* to be funny."

"Enough," Selene snapped, her fingers tapping a rhythm on her elbow. "What is this, a comedy duo? I hate to break it to you, *neither* of you are funny."

"It doesn't sound like you hate breaking it to them," Lucia stage-whispered.

Before Selene could respond, Caterina snapped her fingers. "I just figured out how I know his face."

Selene's brow edged up irritably. "Share it with the whole class, Altamura."

"He's a deserter." With quiet triumph Caterina reached into her inner pocket and pulled out a familiar flyer, folded small.

Selene snatched it.

Caterina and Lucia smirked, sharing a knowing look when she accidentally tore it along the softened crease and had to hold its edges together beside his face. Her eyes flicked from the flyer to Jules and back again.

"Corporal Lacroix?"

"In the flesh."

"All right," Selene mused softly, slowly folding the flyer once more. "Well, I can hardly free you back onto the streets given your desertion. During a time of war, Lacroix, for shame. I suppose I could execute you. There's a lot to be said for getting it over with and done with."

"*Wait—*"

"I really don't have time for a court martial."

"Notoriously onerous procedures," Caterina agreed.

"And boring," Lucia added, poking out her lower lip.

Before Jules could say a word, Selene cut off his protest, raising a finger to silence him. "All right, you've convinced me. I'll stay your execution by"—she angled her wrist, checking her watch—"twelve whole hours."

Neither Lucia nor Caterina showed any emotion at this. For her part, Selene looked bored.

"Twelve hours?" He wondered at his chances if he tried to run for a third time—probably not great.

The Butcher nodded. "I'll give you until we arrive in Rome to convince me that you can be useful."

What did that even mean to a Roman exorcist?

"And I want to believe you won't breathe a word of what truly happened in Nice."

Jules arched a brow. "So no demon?"

"Certainly not. I didn't see one, did you?"

He released a slow breath. "Nope. It was a . . . gas explosion?"

"Starting in the kitchen," Selene agreed with a sharp smile.

"Horrible really. Praise the Deathless God that they experienced no casualties."

"And that the Vatican were so quick to respond, I suppose."

Selene tucked the folded flyer into her pocket. "Oh, no. We were nowhere near Nice when it happened. And now that I think about it, neither were you." She flicked her hand in a silent order and turned for the road.

Caterina grabbed his elbow, propelling him along in her wake. He watched Selene through narrowed eyes as she climbed the shale with sure steps. If he hadn't known to look for it, he never would have noticed her favoring the arm she'd wounded, cradling it against her torso.

A frisson of alarm shot through him. Why had his skin remained unmarred, when Selene, with all her considerable power, had almost lost an arm to the blaze? The thoughts slid their way through his mind before he banished them. Now was not the time. Not feet away from the infamous Butcher of Rome.

All he'd seen told him Selene had earned her reputation. Their entire conversation had been a game, one he'd been losing from the very first move. He never stood a chance.

The town car idled, waiting for them on the road.

He dragged his feet. Caterina shoved him between the shoulder blades, making his heel skid out from under him.

"What do you *want*?" he snapped.

"I want you to come of your own volition or you'll ride in the trunk. I'll leave the decision to you."

"Some choice."

"Don't say I never gave you anything, kitten."

He rolled his eyes, sobering as he caught a final glimpse of the ruined town before they rounded the rocky foot of the cliffs. He glanced at Lucia, who walked beside him with light steps, not seeming to struggle at all on the loose shale. "So there's nothing left of Saint-Jeannet?" he asked quietly.

"Nothing, I'm afraid." Lucia gave him a lingering look. "If you really were here for nostalgia, there's none of that to be had. Only bodies we're struggling to reclaim. Only death."

Selene called over her shoulder. "This never happened either."

Jules sneered at her back. "Of course it didn't. And I was never here. And Saint-Jeannet never existed."

"That's the spirit," she said cheerfully.

CHAPTER ELEVEN

S elene strode into the field office. Glancing up from his notebook, Eliot lifted the nib of his pen off the page before the ink
could bleed. He raised a brow in silent question. *So? What have you
decided?* He still knew her so well.

It had been a short stop in Saint-Jeannet, but it was long enough
for her to confirm that it had been Baliel and his distinctive blue
flames who destroyed the village.

"I'm returning to Rome. I've seen enough here."

"You sure that's wise?"

She considered that. "I saw Baliel's body undone with my own
eyes. That would slow even him down."

"And when he returns?"

She recalled the demon's words. *Vatican. At the heart.*

When he returned, it wouldn't be to Nice. It would be to Rome.
"Nice will be safe."

Eliot twirled his pen around his finger and thumb, watching her with an expression she couldn't read. When had his eyes
become so liquid deep and *knowing*? She felt as though he could
see right through her. He didn't argue; instead he nodded out the
open door, where Jules chatted easily with Lucia and Caterina. Even

handcuffed, he was utterly charming as he won over her subordinates.

"Who is he?" Eliot asked.

Though unmarked by the flames that had burned her so terribly, Jules did have a sooty smudge on his cheek. Still, he was as magnetically handsome as the first time she'd seen him ever so briefly in the Gare de Nice-Ville.

She dragged her eyes off Jules Lacroix. Instead of answering, she said, "Eliot, I have a favor to ask . . ."

They waited at a nearby station. If a single small platform in a field could even be called that. Early crocuses dotted the grass, turning blue faces to the evening sky.

Icy wind whipped Selene's hair against her cheeks and frustration bit at her. She tried not to dwell on the boy who'd turned up like a bad penny at two of the three scenes visited by the demon Baliel. She knew there was something she ought to remember, but it kept slipping through her fingers like sand. What she recalled of the fight had been rent by half-remembered agony. Magic had saved her arm, barely, but it had done little for the pain.

No matter. She didn't need her memories to know there was more to Corporal Jules Lacroix than met the eye.

"Lucia?" She crooked her finger, calling her over. "How badly wounded was he? Did you heal him?"

Lucia shook her head. "It wasn't me."

How had he gone up against the Duke of Briars and walked away with not even a scratch?

"Huh." Selene adjusted her grip on her travel case.

Her arm had finished healing while she slept. Lucia had outdone herself. The flesh was smooth, blending seamlessly with her un-burned shoulder. Still, she felt the cold keenly this close to the Alps, especially the wind's freezing breath on her new skin.

Tightening his wool coat against the chill, Eliot took Lucia's place at Selene's side. He nodded past the woods where pale smoke drifted into the sky. "Train's nearly here." He set down his case and drew a dossier from beneath his elbow. "As you requested."

She thumbed the soft edges of the portfolio's contents.

Curiosity got the best of her when she felt the sharp corner of a photograph. Opening it up, she skimmed Jules's military records in the copper light of the lanterns, drawing out the photo of him as a fifteen-year-old conscript. So very young.

She glanced past Eliot through the flurry of her wind-whipped hair. Jules stood between Caterina and Lucia at the far end of the platform. There was a peal of laughter as Lucia threw her head back at something Jules said, and even Caterina paused her efficient motions to smile, grease streaking her naked fingers as she cleaned and oiled her rifle.

The whistle of the train drew her back. "Thank you," she said belatedly.

Eliot watched Selene with an expression she couldn't read.

Hesitantly he reached up, pushing her hair behind her ear so he could properly see her face. Eliot and his serious dark eyes. Those at least were the same. He dropped his hand when the engine came into view, breathing its smoke into the evening.

Moving to take Jules's elbow, Eliot silently indicated the train easing into the station. A porter smartly whipped open the brass door to the first-class carriage and ushered them inside.

"Are you sure about this, boss?" Caterina asked in a low voice, stopping beside her. "He's a deserter. You can't trust him."

Selene turned the dossier in her hands. "He fought in our army for four years. That kind of dedication doesn't disappear overnight. He won't try anything, Caterina, and even if he does . . ." She trailed off. Let Caterina infer what she would.

The whistle blasted and the train began inching along the platform. "Oh, and—" Selene looked her subordinate up and down. "Altamura, why is the prisoner wearing your coat?"

Taking a few quick steps, Selene leaped onto the step and gripped the handle, calling back to Caterina and Lucia. "I'll be in touch when we arrive in Rome. See if you can't pinpoint Baliel's movements. I want to know everything he did between Saint-Jeannet and *la Bibliothèque Généalogique.* Understand?"

"Boss."

Lucia skipped after the train, waving. Caterina leaned one shoulder against a filigreed lamppost. The light cast her face into extremes.

Selene raised a hand in farewell—just for a moment—then they were out of sight.

The train felt like a living creature as it thundered through the French countryside toward Rome. It was a vastly different experience from Jules's icy journey from Ostrava. Instead of a drafty cargo car, they traveled in luxury. The first-class cabin was warm, scented by rich coffee and walnut-colored leather. The ceiling was vaulted, ribbed with dark wood and painted to look like a spring sky.

They had bid adieu to Caterina and Lucia in Saint-Jeannet. A shame. They were just beginning to warm to him. Now he'd have to start over. He glanced at Selene in the reflection of the train window and grimaced. He didn't fancy his chances.

Her lashes were low, shadowing her eyes as she wrote in sharp little strokes of her pen, crossing *t*'s aggressively and not even bothering with the *i*'s. *Probably a waste of time*, he thought. But when she did her *y*'s, they looped double.

His brows drew together. Not so easy to pin down after all.

Outside the train windows, France sped by. The rocky hills climbing to soaring peaks that made up the French Alps, all of it carpeted in pure white snow.

Without looking up from a leather portfolio bursting with handwritten pages, Selene broke the silence. "Why do you think I brought you with me, Lacroix?"

Her musical Roman accent made his name military hard. Or maybe it was just her lips. Plush and lovely as they were, they were like the rest of her—intolerant of time wasted.

They were presently alone in the spacious cabin—the male exorcist, Eliot, was off doing whatever exorcists did when they weren't strutting about satisfying their savior complexes.

Jules smiled, leaning back in his seat, and laced his fingers behind his head. "How could one such as me expect to know the dark, still waters of your mind, exorcist?"

He saw the dimple in her cheek as she bit the inside of her mouth. *Oh, she was too easy.*

"Don't be evasive."

He smiled easily, showing teeth. "I'm not. I'm genuinely asking a question. So now you're being evasive."

"I am not—" She cut herself off, laughing humorlessly. "*Oh.* Oh, you're the worst."

"I've been reliably informed that I'm the best."

"The best at wha—" She bit off the question, realization dawning. *Damn, so close. Maybe next time.*

Selene leaned forward, drawing a knife from her boot. Face set to neutral, she flipped it between her fingers and used the tip to push against her cuticle. Her voice was soft when she said, "You survived the Battle of Drowning Ostrava—"

"Is that what they're calling it? *Tad* sensationalized."

She continued as though he hadn't spoken. "You survived a demon duke." He tried not to react, his attention sharpening. "And most impressively, you survived Catarina Altamura. Twice. And you plan to die, here, today, on this train?"

He swallowed, throat suddenly dry.

Her expression said, *That's what I thought.* "So why not have a conversation? Answer my questions, without sarcasm or innuendo, and maybe we can reach an accord."

He frowned, thinking of her words. A demon duke. He'd never heard those words in that order before. It almost made the demons sound *civilized*, not something he could have imagined on the front lines. It made him curious. What other secrets was the Vatican hiding?

"You *wanted* to kill me," he reminded her.

"Still sore about that? I changed my mind."

"Oh yes, a twelve-hour stay of execution. So generous."

She rolled her eyes. "Hypersensitive baby."

"It's not hypersensitive to want to survive the day." A muscle feathered in Selene's jaw as her veneer of patience fractured. He noted the way her hand stilled on the knife. "Fine. What did you want to talk about, exorcist?" He tried to spread his hands, but the chains hindered his movement. Jangling the cuffs obnoxiously, he added, "I really hate to break it to you, but if you have to tie them up first, the friendship's probably one-sided."

Taunting the exorcist gave him the same thrill of adrenaline he'd been missing since leaving the front. The exhilaration of facing down death with careless abandon.

Crazy motherfucker, he heard in echo.

Selene sat back, watching him from beneath her lashes. "Get your boots off the seat."

"Make me."

"I promise you don't want me to do that," she said with deadly quiet.

He raised a brow. "I've been on the front lines a long time, lovely. You'd be surprised what I'd do to get a girl's attention."

"Are you trying to provoke me?" Selene battled the urge to grind her teeth.

"Whatever for? I'm terrified of you."

She searched his expression, finding nothing close to terror there. "Not nearly terrified enough. Is this funny to you?"

A crooked smile tempted his lips. "Maybe. I might as well laugh on the way to the gallows."

"Crucifix," she corrected him.

He blanched.

"As a deserter, you'd typically die by firing squad. But Roman law dictates the method of execution within the city limits. We prefer crucifixion. It's kind of symbolic. You can thank the Phoenicians for lending us that. But of course we Romans perfected it." She resumed pushing back her cuticles with the tip of her boot dagger. Downside: having something to do with her hands prevented her strangling him. Upside: it would make stabbing him easier. "So, crucifix, you see? Not gallows."

He stood to pace, thus removing his boots from the tufted leather.

"Thank you," she said.

"Hanging, firing squad . . ." His throat bobbed with a swallow. "*Crucifixion*. It's something of a moot point given I ultimately end up dead."

"You wouldn't say that if you'd ever witnessed a crucifixion, Lacroix."

He strode between the door and window and finally decided to lean—*casually*—against the doorframe. As casually as he could cuffed by metal that had been quenched in the blood of the Deathless God and carved with sacramental symbols for strength and durability—and one particular sigil that would cause intense suffering for any demon trapped within its grip. Unfortunately that one didn't appear to work on him or he'd look far less smug and far more tormented.

A pity.

At least she knew he wasn't a demon.

Selene rubbed two fingers between her brows as if to coax her faded memories to return. There was more to Jules Lacroix than met the eye. She didn't need proof. She knew it to the marrow of her bones.

His throat fluttered. If she listened closely, she could hear his heart thudding. *What is he hiding?* Selene wanted to unwrap him, uncoil his sinew and muscle and skin until she could see to the heart of the issue. Then she might dissect that too.

She slid the knife back into her boot. "Enough games." As though he was a frightened animal, Selene approached Jules carefully, palms up. *See? No dagger.*

He watched her warily.

"In fact, I don't want to kill you. If I did, you wouldn't have survived Saint-Jeannet. Far less paperwork that way. Only a verbal report to my superiors." Winning hearts and minds, not her strong suit.

"Comforting," he said dryly.

"It should be. I loathe paperwork."

And she *loathed* mysteries.

Particularly mysteries in the gorgeous packaging of a young French soldier. She hadn't told Caterina and Lucia what happened at the orphanage or what she suspected—though *suspected* was perhaps too strong a word given she only half remembered most of it—but Caterina would eventually figure out that Selene would never drag a soldier all the way to Rome for court martial if there wasn't more to it than simple desertion.

The clock was already ticking.

But *that* was a future Selene problem.

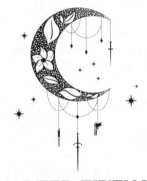

CHAPTER TWELVE

The silence stretching between them was heavy.

Jules wanted to thrash against the elegant handcuffs binding his wrists. Wanted to slam his shoulder against the door like a wild animal to escape. While Selene stood there calmly. So terribly in control.

He wondered if she ever second-guessed herself—or the path she stalked. Had she ever glanced back, wondering where she'd taken a wrong turn? Somehow he doubted it.

"Corporal Lacroix." There was a taut moment before she said his name again, softer this time. "*Lacroix*. I don't intend to kill you, and I promise I won't let anything happen to you in Rome. I need your help."

He scoffed. *I don't intend to kill you*, she'd said. But that didn't mean she *wouldn't*.

Her lips twisted. "You think I'm lying?"

"I *think* you're full of shit. I saw you fight."

"And?" she demanded.

"You really need me to say it? I can't help you if you can't help yourself, exorcist."

Selene's guarded expression softened when she parsed his meaning. She was so far above him. Mythology made flesh. Impossible for him to reach from where he stood with two feet firmly planted in the mud.

He was nothing. An orphan. A soldier.

Stigmajka.

He leaned back against the door, attempting to cross his arms, but his shackles clinked softly in reminder.

As Selene took another step toward him, he resisted the temptation to lean away from her touch. Gliding a finger against his bindings, she released him, and the handcuffs dropped to the floor. Even though he knew she was manipulating him, the tension in his shoulders eased.

She shifted back, but didn't sit. Instead, she leaned against the window so they were facing off. France sped by behind her, there in the fathomless black, pricked by only the rarest lantern light. Selene raised her chin so she could hold his gaze. Those eyes of hers were magnetic, and despite himself he couldn't look away.

"There are many ways you can help me, Lacroix. For starters, I need you to stay close so that you might survive the week. And so that Nice or Rome—or both—will not be razed by the fucking Duke of Briars." He raised a brow. She added, "I would like to avoid that."

Again, this Duke of Briars. He wanted to ask about the demon, but the negotiations weren't over and Jules refused to give her the upper hand again. Instead, he let his words become a lazy drawl. "How is staying close to you meant to do anything other than drive me to drink, exorcist?"

She rolled her eyes. "Honestly? I don't care *what* you do—*staying close* is the only prerequisite." She wasn't telling him something—

a whole host of somethings—but he didn't really have a choice. The shackles had been pure showmanship. He was at her mercy. And she knew it.

As if reading his mind, she added, "Besides, you're still a suspicious person regarding the events in Saint-Jeannet. I can hold you indefinitely for that. So be glad that I don't enjoy spending time in dungeons."

His thoughts snagged on the implication. "How could I have anything to do with that? You *saw* me in Nice."

"Only *after* it happened." She waved an airy hand, dismissing his next words. "I will admit, multiple sources place you with your regiment during a series of decisive battles against the Caspian Federation at the time in question, but for the purposes of this inquiry your involvement remains pertinent so long as I want it to be."

The beat of his own heart sounded terribly loud in the quiet of the cabin. There was only the exorcist, her low voice, and the muffled clickety-clack of the wheels.

"So my desertion is your plausible deniability for arresting me and my presence in Saint-Jeannet is your plausible deniability for taking me to Rome. Why?"

"Because I don't trust you." Her expression flickered, brows tugging together in consternation. "No. I *refuse* to trust you." Her eyes held his, lit deep amber by the gas lanterns.

He believed her. Selene's trust was not something he could earn with charm. The fountain pen rolled off the portfolio as the carriage rocked gently, its nib soaking blue into the tufted leather seat.

Retrieving her pen, Selene tugged the portfolio into her lap and straightened the strewn pages.

War reports written in the same economical hand boasted innumerable intriguing phrases—*prodigious, sole survivor, kill count*—and yet it wasn't enough. None of it explained *him* to her satisfaction.

Selene glanced up at him. "Tell me. Why *were* you in Saint-Jeannet? You had only just arrived back in Nice that morning. Just in time to witness the conflagration of your childhood home, granted. But it seems like a strange choice to me, Lacroix." She tipped her head. "What kind of ghoulish curiosity compelled you to visit the site of such a terrible massacre?"

His wounded expression should have been a victory bell . . . but she didn't feel good about it. Stiffening her spine, she pushed away the softer emotion.

"Massacre?" he asked faintly.

"You saw the town. It was razed."

"I saw the *buildings*, but . . ." He visibly struggled with his words. "But that was the stones. The walls. What about the people?"

Selene tilted her head, confused. After years at war, he couldn't possibly be this naive about death. "What do you mean?"

"What happened to the people?"

"They're dead."

The color drained from his face. "All of them?"

"I don't see—" Selene cut herself off.

The entire village had been burned with holy fire. All that was left were the shadows on the walls. The fallen bicycles, the gutted post office, the empty classroom with no children now or ever again. She continued quietly, selecting her words with care. "I don't see how there could be any survivors. My report to the Vatican listed all five hundred and thirty-five residents of Saint-Jeannet as casualties."

Jules stared at his linked fingers. His hands trembled.

"I'm . . . sorry." It sounded too much like a question.

A hoarse sound escaped his throat. Concerned, she shifted closer. He raised both hands, wiping one eye and then the other with his sleeve. "You appear to be struggling to process sadness, exorcist." There was a twist of bitter amusement to his lips.

Annoyed, Selene replied, "Is this life-threatening or can we continue?"

"I'm fine," he said rather unconvincingly.

Her nose crinkled at the tears on his lashes. "Did you injure yourself? Are you in pain?"

He leveled her with a cold look. "What do you want anyway?"

"I *want* to interrogate you," she snapped.

He barked a laugh. "You want to know about Saint-Jeannet?" He tipped his head against the seat. "I was abandoned in Saint-Jeannet as a baby."

His voice was so quiet she almost missed the words. The answer was not one she'd anticipated. She scrawled this new information into the portfolio.

"You were born there?"

He rubbed long fingers between crumpled brows, battling some painful emotion. Selene had no patience for that. For *sadness*. She didn't intend to give him a chance to feel anything until she finished twisting him around her little finger—even if it meant breaking him first. Saint-Jeannet was a weakness she could exploit. Impatient at his silence, she glanced at him from beneath her lashes. Her heart gave an uncomfortable throb at his look of pain for people he didn't know.

Grief, where she felt nothing at all.

The exorcist was no longer listening to him.

She leafed through her portfolio, eyes a thousand miles away. Finally she eased the cover closed. A twist of dissatisfaction at the corner of her lips. "You were born there?"

He nodded. "I was left on the steps of the church as a newborn babe."

"Église Saint-Pierre?" she confirmed. Something played across her face. When their gazes met, her eyes burned like flame.

Oh. He'd been wrong about her attention being elsewhere. Her focus was all on him now and it felt like gravity.

"What?" His thundering heartbeat blended into the chuff of the steam engine and the clicking of rail joints.

She schooled her expression. "Nothing."

"Liar."

Selene didn't like the accusation one bit. Her eyes pinned Jules in his seat like a mounted moth. And yet she didn't deny it. "Who are you really, Jules Lacroix?"

The question caught him with the force of a bullet. "Me? Nobody. An orphan. A soldier."

"Liar," she shot back, using his own accusation against him.

"I'm not lying," he snarled. *Stigmajka.*

His body moved before he knew what he was doing, long strides eating up the cabin between them. He gripped her chin in his hand, his fingers feeling impossibly rough against her skin.

Her eyes flared with something very close to triumph. Grief and anger swept through him, making him ache to grasp a sword.

Dieu, I really am a monster, aren't I?

"I too want to know who I am."

CHAPTER THIRTEEN

Wounded was no longer the word to describe him. Something dangerous flickered in his eyes as he ran the backs of his fingers along the line of her jaw before holding her chin in an unyielding grip. *This* was what she'd wanted.

Show me your dark side, Jules Lacroix.

"I have no answers for you. But you know what? I wish I knew." His breathing was ragged. "I wish I knew why I was abandoned. I wish I knew by whom. But, more than that, I want to know why, when I was mere moments from unraveling something—any bloody damn thing—about myself, a demon appeared and killed my best friend."

His fingers, warm and strong against her jaw, didn't frighten her—his powerful hands held surprising gentleness—but the shadow across his eyes, like tattered clouds veiling the moon, certainly did.

"Coincidence?" he mused, introspective. "No. There aren't so many coincidences in all the world."

He was *grieving*, not angry. Unexpected pain knifed between her ribs. *Sympathy?*

"And not just any demon; the Duke of Briars," Selene said softly,

CRUEL IS THE LIGHT

studying Jules from close quarters. He had pale green eyes ringed by a golden starburst. "Coincidences like *that* do not happen."

He shook his head, releasing her jaw with none of his earlier gentleness. She whipped her head back, unerringly finding his eyes. If this was his dark side, she could handle it.

"When it comes to demons, any change in the balance is a bad sign," she continued. "If, as I suspect, he continues to track you . . ." His expression tightened. "Well, it's something of a mystery, isn't it?"

"Who is the Duke of Briars?"

"A powerful demon. Quite possibly *the most* powerful demon we have had the misfortune to catalog." She hesitated, considering whether she should tell him more.

The Academy was clandestine with their knowledge, dealing it out gradually over ten years of schooling. All her training told her to bite her tongue, but she ignored it. He deserved to know.

And if this demon really was hunting him, he *needed* to.

"He is one of the Twelve. They have been mythologized, but they are very real. Each a demon of the highest class. Each more powerful by orders of magnitude than demons the next level down. In two hundred years, we have seen each of them once. Each time it leads to tragedy. Each time . . . many people die."

"Like Saint-Jeannet?"

"Worse. Far worse."

His eyes were pale speckled jade, and she could drown in them. But there was darkness in them. Grief and anger and suspicion. What Selene didn't see was fear. Not really. Not as much as she might have expected. He looked away, breaking the moment. Lacroix didn't yet understand. The Baliel at the orphanage, wrapped in a wholly unsuitable body, had been a shadow of the demon she had learned about at the Academy.

"A mystery," Jules said quietly, then sighed, scrubbing fingers through his hair. "If you hadn't abducted me—"

"Excuse me? You're a deserter."

"Kidnapping is still a crime."

She indicated the fallen shackles. "You're *under arrest.*"

He gave a languid shrug, as though that too could be open to interpretation. *Dio*, he was impossible. How had he survived four years of the hardest war in human history with so little respect for authority? She wanted to shake him, but refused to sink to his level.

She took a calming breath. "You were saying?"

"If you hadn't abduct—"

"*After* that," she snapped.

He gave her a look. "I was planning to visit the Genealogical Library to see if there was any hint of a baby born in Saint-Jeannet on that blessed night in January."

Blessed night, indeed. Her sardonic laugh died in her throat. *La Bibliothèque Généalogique.* Another connection.

His attention sharpened. "What?"

"Well . . ." Her mind worked fast and her words came slow. "Even if I hadn't abducted you—"

He looked triumphant at that but didn't interrupt.

"—you would have found it difficult to find anything at Nice's Genealogical Library, I'm afraid."

"Why?"

"Because it burned."

His eyes widened as realization spread across his features.

And dread.

Interesting.

"It's a real shame . . ." she mused, twirling her fountain pen around her thumb experimentally, mirroring Eliot earlier, then pinning it to the page in front of her. "Fun fact: Rome has the greatest libraries in the world."

That suspicious look was back in his eyes. "Good for Rome."

She refused to smile, knowing it would be smug. "If there's anywhere that still had a copy of Nice's genealogical records, it would be the Vatican archives."

"I'm sure they love giving tours. Can I get a military discount?"

"No discount. But I could get you in. If I wanted to."

He narrowed his eyes. "What do I have to do, promise you my firstborn child?"

She crinkled her nose. "Nobody wants that. All I want is your cooperation. You'll do what I say, when I say it. Understand? If it helps, you can pretend I'm your superior and that you're actually a dutiful soldier."

He snorted, but his eyes were thoughtful.

She bit back her smile. "Do we have a deal?"

"Perhaps." He rubbed his jaw, watching her. "Lucia said there were no casualties in Nice, but Kian was at the orphanage with me. I *know* he couldn't have survived. Why the discrepancy?"

Kian, the childhood friend.

Perhaps it would be cruel to give him false hope. So she settled on telling him the facts. "They recovered what they could from the burned wing. Preliminary results have been coming in all day. No human remains have been found so far. Not even a tooth."

His expression did not waver. "Then, in exchange for my cooperation, I have two requests. One, you'll look for Kian, and—"

"I'm the Butcher of Rome; would anyone really believe I'd divert Vatican resources to search for a missing orphan?"

"I don't give a fuck what they think."

"Fine. *Now* do we have a deal?"

"I have a second request. Don't agree until you know what it is, *Bouchère de Rome*."

She spread her hands in a "proceed" gesture, smothering a wince at hearing the pejorative name from him.

"I want more from you than an escort. I want you to *help* me. The library is a start, but I want your word you'll throw your support behind me and we won't stop until I say I'm done."

She bit back a smile. A visit to the library *would* be too easy, wouldn't it?

"Agreed," she said, perhaps too quickly. And she meant it.

She would have agreed to more. Whatever was going on here, he was the only suspected link she had to Baliel since his body had been destroyed. From what Selene knew of Jules, his military history, and his impressive record of killing demons, she could use him. Even if that meant she needed to protect him from other exorcists. How she'd swing that would be the next difficulty. But she'd already set her plan for that in motion.

Then there were Caterina and Lucia, who both knew about Jules and his recent military disgrace. They could prove a problem. She shrugged it off. Her subordinates had a chronic inability to follow any kind of protocol—so they probably wouldn't balk at her writing her own playbook just this once.

"And I refuse to touch a weapon," Jules said softly, breaking into her thoughts.

She looked at him sharply. *That* might prove troublesome.

His stubborn expression set her jaw on edge. She decided not to push. His conviction would soon melt away. Although Jules didn't have the eyes of someone who would bend easily.

"All right," she murmured. "The Vatican will throw its efforts behind finding out what happened to your childhood friend and I'll help you unveil the great secret that is, well, *you*."

After all, that was her goal as well. And perhaps by the time they'd unraveled that enigma, she would know the nature of his connection to Baliel. And if she had to—if her mission's success depended upon it—she would use Jules as bait.

Baliel would cause no more trouble in Nice, she felt sure of that. His destination, like their own, was Rome. Still . . . she couldn't explain that gut instinct to any of her Vatican superiors. Even Cesare would struggle to back her with such an incomplete picture. Nor would he allow any kind of mercy to a deserter.

No matter how strongly she suspected that Jules was an important part of this puzzle, her superiors didn't need to know the reality of the situation. And they *couldn't* know she suspected Baliel was hunting them right back.

"Why did you agree so quickly?" Jules asked.

"I love a good mystery." She leaned forward, lowering her voice. "And if we figure out who you are, maybe this whole thing will unravel before our eyes. If I'm right . . . you won't survive a week without me. If I'm right, the Duke of Briars is on your tail, and I'm the only one who can help."

His eyes clouded and satisfaction coiled in her rib cage, serpentine and luxurious. She had him.

"And more importantly," she added softly, "I'm the only one who cares to."

CHAPTER FOURTEEN

Jules stared out the train window with unseeing eyes. His mind returned again and again to Kian. No matter how proficient he'd become at burying his pain, Kian's death was an open wound. The exorcist, with her underwhelming reassurances, had changed nothing. His heart had given a small skip of hope and promptly shriveled up once more. He propped his feet up on the seat opposite. *Preliminary results, my ass.* Whoever had concocted those hadn't been inside the orphanage with them.

Nobody could have survived that.

Eliot stepped into the cabin. He knocked Jules's boots off the seat and sat facing him, hands loosely linked between his knees as he locked their gazes.

Jules tipped a curious brow.

"Eliot," Selene said in greeting, though she didn't look up from the leather portfolio.

In spite of himself, Jules was beginning to feel a muted curiosity about what she was reading.

Eliot's expression was set to careful neutral as he unhooked the twin blades at his hip, but a line between his brows betrayed him.

Then he set a neat stack of clothes on the seat beside him. "Are you sure about this?" Eliot asked without taking his eyes off Jules.

"Shouldn't I be asking you that?" Selene said, setting aside her portfolio and capping her pen.

By way of answer, Eliot extended the twin blades to Jules. "For you."

Raising both hands, Jules leaned away. "No. I can't." He glanced down at his gloved fingers, curling them. The leather creaked. "I refuse."

And he would refuse until he could confidently answer the question: *Who is Jules Lacroix?* He didn't know. The man he'd been for four years had died on the battlefield beside Farah, with the Tsarina's laughter ringing in his ears. And he'd died again in Nice when Kian did. A more brutal death still.

Selene's eyes flickered with annoyance. "He won't touch a blade. Not even if his life depends on it."

Why were they arming him, for God's sake? Half an hour earlier he'd been in chains. He looked between the swords and Eliot, as though they might bite. "What's this about?"

Eliot made a soft sound of exasperation. "Would you wear them on your hip if I promise you don't have to use them?"

He considered it, then gave a nod.

Selene scoffed as Eliot set the swords on the seat beside him. "I need some air before Nice." She stood suddenly. "Eliot, explain the rest, won't you?"

Eliot's dark eyes followed Selene as she stalked out the door.

"She seems fun." Jules stood, tucking his hands into his pockets as he stared out the window.

Outside, the mountains hurried by in a blur. The glass radiated cold.

"My uniform. My ancestral blades." Eliot indicated the pile of clothing and then waved toward a small monogrammed travel case in the corner. "Given you cannot merely walk into the Vatican as a civilian"—he pinched the bridge of his nose—"*or* as a member of our military, even if you hadn't *already* deserted your post . . . you will impersonate me in Rome while I assist Caterina and Lucia in Nice."

"Impersonate you?"

"Yes. You'll be entering the Vatican as me."

Jules barked a humorless laugh. "We look nothing alike."

"Luckily nobody in Rome has seen me in seven years. A lot can change in that time."

"I don't think even seven years could do this."

Eliot was slight and inches shorter than Jules. All they shared was their dark hair, and even that was marked by more differences than similarities. Where Eliot's was slicked back, military style, and shaved close at the sides, Jules's was a bird's nest. But there was more to their differences than looks. Eliot held himself like a noble. Similar to Selene, but with a reticence Jules could sense but not quite put his finger on.

Eliot's mouth twitched. He sat, leaning back in his seat. "I'll teach you what I can before Nice." He extended the twin blades again.

Theirs was a compact written in steel.

Jules grimaced and pushed his hands into his pockets. They were beautiful weapons, but *that* wasn't the problem.

He didn't want to be a monster.

Eliot sighed. "I know this sounds risky, but I agree with Selene that this is the best way. I wouldn't go along with it if I thought it was more dangerous than going in as yourself. Being me will give you a measure of protection you do not have as a deserter."

Jules turned his face to the window, not answering.

"If not for yourself, then for the people I need you to protect," Eliot said softly. His hand was still extended, gripping the blades.

Jules glanced at them, world narrowing to that beautiful steel. He could almost taste their power. Eliot was not asking him to kill, but to *protect*.

"I only have to wear them?"

Eliot nodded.

Muscles heavy with reluctance, Jules reached out, grasping the leather straps that loosely held the blades crossed together. "Who do I need to protect, Eliot?"

The motion of the train made Selene's fountain pen roll gently across the closed dossier and Eliot stilled it with one hand. He set his jaw, saying nothing.

"If you can't tell me that, who am I protecting them *from*?"

Eliot ran a hand over his face. "Half my story isn't mine to tell. The other half risks you more than it helps you. But I'll tell you what I can of the pieces in between." His voice was muffled as he rubbed a hand over his mouth. "I was exiled because, for whatever reason, somebody high up saw me as a threat."

"But seven years ago you would've been—"

"Twelve, yes. A child. But I wasn't a threat because of my raw power or my training. I didn't have either of those back then. I was a threat for another reason, because power isn't just about that. In Rome, power is about influence and control."

"Influence and control?" Jules echoed.

Eliot nodded. "Our system is one of strict hierarchy, with exorcists at the top. We have nobles whose families populate the Academy—but that is no guarantee, because you must also have innate ability. From the age of seven, we are taught to do what we do. Those who cannot are weeded out."

Jules frowned. Eliot was barely scraping the surface of the truth.

"And sometimes they die," Eliot murmured, glancing away.

Jules spread his arms across the seat back. "Who teaches you?"

"Instructors. Older exorcists. It's a system that reinforces our power structure. Ability primarily runs through blood. Old Roman families, for some reason, have the best chance of thriving. The Alleva family, for instance. Selene's father was a powerful exorcist before he died. And her uncle is the Imperium Bellum."

Jules racked his brain for the Latin. "*Bellum* means war, yes?"

Eliot nodded. "Imperium Bellum. Lord of War. The Vatican's military leader. As long as the Holy Vatican Empire is at war, he'll be the most powerful man in the empire."

"Would that be raw power?" Jules asked.

Eliot's lips tipped slightly. "Now you're getting it. The answer is yes and no. Cesare Alleva does have raw power, but he has even more influence. His brother was the prodigy when it came to raw power. He would've become Imperium Politikos in time."

Jules nodded slowly. "You're telling me that Cesare's the most dangerous man in Rome."

"No." Eliot shook his head, his mouth curling into a strange smile. "I'm telling you he's the most dangerous man in the *empire* and that you need to keep your head down. He knew me. He *exiled* me. Selene is playing a dangerous game by bringing *me* back to Rome. She's gambling on the fact that it's less dangerous than telling them who you really are—and taking *you* into the lion's den."

Jules rubbed his thumb over his lower lip. "So whether he fully believes I'm you or if he figures out I'm me, either way I'm—"

"Fucked. Yes."

Jules glanced toward the door. "You didn't say this in front of the *Macellaia di Roma*, why? Shouldn't she know this about her uncle?"

Eliot spread his hands. "She knows but she doesn't care. He's not dangerous to Rome."

"And?"

"Selene will always put Rome first. She thinks Rome needs him, like she needs him."

"*Does* Rome need him?"

Eliot grimaced. "Maybe."

"How did you graduate if you were exiled?"

"I completed my training in Nice. The Academy is the pinnacle, but I had already completed six years there. For the last four I essentially did on-the-job training."

Jules ran his thumb over the raised pattern on the hilt of one of the swords. Wrought in dark metal in contrast to its pale sister. "Your family are exorcists as well, right? Like the Alleva family."

Eliot nodded, following the movement. "Yes. And these are our family blades. Each captures something of the sun and the moon because we will do what we must to fight, whether it be day or night."

The platinum filigree on the gunmetal moon blade was so intricate, there was more decoration than steel. So much it seemed to be lit from within.

"Then why don't you come back? We can think of another way to get me in. You know Rome. You know Cesare. And . . . I'm just a liability."

Eliot glanced up. "I don't believe that." His expression grew more serious and he drew a notebook from his pocket, but held it clamped between his palms as though to keep it sealed. He looked as though he were at war with himself.

Jules sighed. "Eliot, if you hold that any tighter, it'll combust. Tell me or don't."

Eliot's liquid dark eyes were rather lovely as he shot him a dirty look. But Jules's words had the intended effect and he opened the notebook. "This is everything I know from Nice and Saint-Jeannet. Study it. In Rome, Selene will take lead, but you must have the answers if they ask. They'll be interested in you because—"

"Because they think I'm you?"

"In a manner, but it isn't necessarily about me. Matteo, my mentor, was Selene's father." *Was*. Jules made a mental note to look into that later. "He was a good man. He saw something in me." Eliot smiled slightly, voice drifting into memory. "When I was at the Academy, he would check on my progress when he visited Selene and Niccolò." Seeing Jules's expression, he hesitated a moment before adding, "Selene's brother. We were all close. Grew up together. Matteo wasn't allowed to administer their tests, but he did mine."

"What kind of tests? Tests to see who can look prettiest in black and gold? Who can wear the biggest, fanciest buttons?"

Eliot leveled him with a look and dismissed the question with a wave of his hand.

Another secret. Of course.

Jules thought of the Tsarina's words on the battlefield. *The Holy Vatican Empire, and all those beneath their aegis, have forgotten much.* Was it any wonder? With so many secrets, the truth was bound to get lost somewhere along the way.

"All you need to know is that the most important test decides if we'll be an exorcist or an artificer. I'm sure Matteo would've administered that test for me too, but . . ." Eliot shook his head.

Because of his exile? Jules wondered. *Or because Matteo was already dead?*

Jules leafed through the pages, glancing over Eliot's notes. "The demon went to the church?" he asked, remembering the spark in

Selene's eyes. *Église Saint-Pierre?* she'd murmured. And, like a fool, he'd given her even more reason to think he was somehow connected to this . . . Baliel. This *Duke of Briars.*

The name sent a shiver down his spine.

Until his last day in Ostrava, Jules had seen demons as monstrous things. Twisted creatures, borrowed corpses. They rarely even resembled humans. But the weather demon had been something else entirely. And so had Baliel.

Their beauty. Their power. It was far more terrifying. No wonder the Vatican didn't want them to know.

Giving Eliot a lingering, dubious look, Jules smoothed open the pages and began to read in earnest.

When the train eased to a stop in Nice-Ville, Jules tossed the notebook back to Eliot, who snatched it from the air and tucked it into his pocket. He stood, nodding his thanks. As he passed through the cabin door, his coat flared out behind him and a folded piece of paper fluttered to the polished floorboards.

The train whistle sounded.

Jules glanced at the door to the corridor. Eliot was far too trusting, leaving him alone. No sooner had he considered the possibility of escape than he heard Selene on the platform. Standing, he looked out. Selene and Eliot stood close, their dark forms shrouded by billowing steam.

Bending, Jules picked up the fallen paper.

"If you change your mind, we can think of another way to get him in."

"How?"

"A body bag. Oh, don't give me that look, Eliot."

Eliot chuckled.

Jules glanced down at the fallen paper in his hand and stilled upon seeing the newspaper clipping. Eliot had folded the torn edges neatly as though to frame a black-and-white photograph of Selene that had made the news. Her hand was raised against a paparazzi flashbulb and, caught unawares, she was utterly compelling. There was a vulnerability in her eyes that he had not seen during their interactions.

A final whistle sounded, warning late travelers to hurry, and the thunk of steel on steel announced the train's departure.

Au revoir, Nice.

"I hope I can do this," he heard Selene say, her hair flashing past the window as she leaped onto the steps.

Eliot walked alongside the train. His eyes never once left Selene, so he didn't notice Jules watching. "I know you can. You're something special, Selene." A grin flashed across his face. "*Captain.*" He infused the word with deep affection.

Clipped footsteps announced Selene's return and Jules fumbled the photograph, tucking it into his inside breast pocket. He sat back when the door opened, donning his most innocent *of course I wasn't eavesdropping* smile.

She did not appear convinced.

CHAPTER FIFTEEN

Leaning his temple against the window, Jules stared into the midnight dark as the train eased out of Nice. He watched Selene's reflection in the glass and considered her words.

Who are you really, Jules Lacroix?

Selene had switched gears between breaths, manipulating him with ruthless skill until he told her more than he'd intended.

Now they were alone. At least Eliot, with his innate calm, had seemed to rub off on her.

They were spared any obligation to speak to each other by the arrival of what looked like an empress's high tea of tiny sandwiches. Jules ate everything himself, while Selene radiated her lack of interest across the compartment.

The movements of the train shifted and Jules leaned his forehead against the glass. "Strange."

"What is?"

"We're turning inland."

Selene moved to the window. "You're right."

"*Huh.*" Sarcasm wasn't beneath him.

She marched across the cabin and Jules followed, curious what she intended to do. Demand they reroute for her personal convenience? But before she reached the door, it snapped open.

She stepped back, bumping into his chest. Instinctively Jules caught her slim waist in his hands to steady her.

"Get *off*." Selene jabbed him in the ribs with a pointy elbow. Jules kneaded his ribs. *That* would leave a bruise.

"Forgive the intrusion, *mademoiselle, monsieur*—" The conductor nodded to each of them. "We've had a slight diversion. We'll be arriving in Rome via Milan." Selene's expression darkened, and he hurried on. "I'm afraid the order comes direct from Vatican City. We have no choice. *Je suis terriblement désolé*."

Through the window beyond the brass-appointed rack stacked high with expensive luggage, the coast dwindled away as they turned inland. Going via Milan would add hours to their journey. Irritably Selene waved the conductor away and collapsed back into her seat.

Jules watched her as she flipped through her portfolio, spreading a few loose pages across the seat beside her. She turned her face away, hiding a yawn.

He nodded to the pages. "What're you reading?"

"Nothing." *Of course.*

Bored, he took a huge bite of baguette sandwich.

Selene scrunched her nose. "Don't choke."

"That wasn't very sincere, exorcist," he said, spraying dry crumbs.

Her face twisted in distaste. "How could you tell?"

"I suppose you must be used to it by now."

"What?" she asked, voice dangerously soft.

The words came faster than his teeth could stop them. "People dropping dead around you."

Her gaze bored into him, each subtle shade of honey a fragment of loathing. Did he really want to taunt a girl who could kill him a dozen different ways before his next breath? But the way she stared him down, and her extreme self-possession, coaxed forth a self-destructive impulse he couldn't resist.

"You *are* used to that, aren't you, *Bouchère de Rome?*"

"I don't know. Maybe we should test the theory." Her fingers made a move toward her boot knife.

Jules grimaced. *Touché.*

When she turned back to her pages, it was his turn to smother a yawn. But he refused to be the first to sleep. Jules was unsure when their mutual exhaustion had turned into an unspoken competition to see who could stay awake the longest, but he was determined not to fold. He'd lived in the trenches, sleeping in stolen seconds between gunfire. He could outlast the Vatican princess.

He swallowed his last bite of France and brushed baguette crumbs from his hands. It did nothing to fill the hollow in his chest. Homesickness. Or maybe loneliness. He'd only been back in his motherland for a day. He didn't want to leave again so soon.

There were so many things he didn't want. He sank lower in his seat and put his boots on the one opposite, watching her reflection.

Selene pressed her fingertips against her temples.

He repressed a grin. "Sure is getting cold. Bed sounds real cozy right about now."

With saintly patience that didn't fool him for a moment she replied, "Well, don't let me keep you up, Lacroix. I need a cappuccino."

Lightweight. If she was already resorting to caffeine, he could win this. With sleep deprivation the prize.

Setting her sword on one shoulder, she stepped over his legs. "I'm going to the dining car," she said tightly, then under her breath, "where I can breathe."

Her barb landed like a roundhouse. No longer smirking, Jules waited until she was gone to sniff his shirt. Yeah, he needed a shower.

Jules stepped out of the adjoining shower room later to find Selene had returned. He rubbed the towel against his hair, watching her from the doorway.

She turned her face away, smothering a yawn. So stubborn.

Her contradictions and sharp edges were fascinating. The Butcher of Rome, right here. If only he could tell Farah or his regiment about this. They'd never believe it. Stories about Rome's exorcists sometimes reached them on the front. He'd always assumed most were fiction, but since he'd met this particular exorcist, he was no longer sure. Even on the front, they'd rarely seen exorcists in action. Only when things went *really* bad.

"You know, exorcist, if I'm going with you to the Vatican fortress—"

"We don't like that name," she interrupted, not looking up from her writing—filling page after page with that same intriguing hand.

"I don't really give a shit." He filed the information away for later. "On that note, thank you for perfectly illustrating my point—"

Her eyes narrowed. "What point?"

"*Patience.*"

"I have none."

He smirked and lingered on that for a moment. At least she was self-aware.

"I know nothing about what goes on in the Vatican. Not nearly enough to convince everyone I belong there." He grabbed the D'Alessandro blades and tossed them at her feet. They landed with a heavy thunk. "You think having these will be enough to fool anyone?"

She was silent. *Point.*

He sat opposite her, plastering on a charming smile. She looked faintly irritated. "You know I'm right."

"And?" she snapped.

"This Milan detour gives us some much-needed study time. I want you to teach me about the Vatican."

She sighed. "I suppose we could begin with the history of Rome—"

"Um, that's fine," he interrupted quickly. "I'll just ask questions."

"Well then, I get to ask you questions too," she retorted.

He blinked. "Why?"

She threw up her hands. "I don't have time to waste answering asinine questions."

"*That's* rude. You're just assuming my questions will be *asinine?*"

"Obviously."

"Huh."

She set aside her papers, interest finally lighting her eyes. "Go on, then. You can go first."

"Well, it's a lot of pressure *now.*"

She snorted delicately. "Just do it so I can gloat."

"Fine." He raised his hands in surrender. "Why did you want to become an exorcist?"

She smothered a frown, her eyes going a little distant. "My father was an exorcist. And my uncle, too."

"Was?"

Her expression sharpened. "No follow-ups."

"Wow, this is turning out so fun. Your turn, I guess."

"It's not *meant* to be fun." She tapped her chin as she plotted her question. "All right. What's the highest class of demon you've ever faced, and how did you dispatch it?"

He snorted. "Fuckin' exorcists."

"*Excuse* me?"

"Nothin'. Besides, you cheated. That was two questions."

"I used a conjunction."

He repeated his curse and this time she didn't pretend not to hear.

"If you don't want to answer my questions, we can always stop," she said archly. The threat was clear. *You wanted to do this, not me.*

Jules carded fingers through his hair. "I don't know anything about classes. Forgive me," he said, voice dripping with sarcasm. "I wasn't classically trained, like some."

She rolled her eyes and waved for him to hurry up.

"It was in Ostrava." He moved aside the D'Alessandro blades and sat cross-legged on the floor, lowering his voice as he got into the rhythm of the story. "The demon was seven feet tall, her skin pale as ice—"

"*Seven* feet?"

He scowled.

She gestured for him to continue. "Proceed."

"No interrupting."

"Fine!"

"She was a weather demon. Terribly beautiful. Too many teeth."

She looked intrigued now, and eased off the tufted leather seat to join him on the floor. "And you killed her?"

He smirked. "*Obviously.*"

"How?"

He echoed her again. "No follow-ups."

"Subsection One says I already asked how you dispatched her in the original question."

He groaned. Arguing would be futile. "Pike through the gut."

"A weather demon . . . ?" she echoed, sounding skeptical. "Sounds like a Level Five. A Viscount?" Her intense gaze didn't move from his.

He widened his eyes. *And?*

"Impressive." There was a shift in Selene's expression, as though she was reevaluating him, and he decided he didn't entirely dislike surprising this girl. It could become addictive.

"All right," he murmured, thinking for a moment. "Tell me about a time you made someone cry."

"Does today count?" She bit back a smile, but he saw it there at the corner of her mouth.

He chuckled. "Someone other than me."

She leaned her head back against the seat, staring at the ceiling. One leg stretched out beside his knee, close enough for him to touch the shiny leather boot hugging her shapely calf. "There are so many possibilities."

"I bet."

Finally she jerked upright. "Oh! This one's funny. So, one time Gabriel—he was a couple of years ahead at the Academy—told Eliot that sometimes exorcists go insane and sate their bloodlust by eating little children, right?"

Jules stared, wide-eyed. "Uh-huh?"

"Anyway! I told Gabriel that he was actually *right*. That it was this big secret, and that if they found out he knew, they'd eat him."

"And he cried?"

"Oh yeah. Loads of tears. I got in *heaps* of trouble. What a wuss."

"Was he right?"

"Not the eating children part, as far as I know. What was your biggest accomplishment before you went to war?"

Not the eating children part . . . Jules shook it off, deciding against chasing the scary rabbit down that particular rabbit hole. "Probably . . . not dying in the cruel institution where I was raised?" He played with the leather laces of her boot, tugging until they nearly came undone.

She pouted out her lower lip. "Grim."

He snorted. "And your thing wasn't? What's your biggest regret?"

The air seemed to chill. Jules looked up from the bow he'd almost completely untied.

All color had drained from her face.

He drew his hand back to his lap. "What?"

She shook her head. "Nothing. Just . . . That won't help you."

"Afraid to expose your soft underbelly, exorcist?" He smirked to cover up his discomfort and pulled on his gloves.

"*No*," she said icily.

"Fine, I'll ask a different one." At that, blotches of color appeared on her cheeks—she clearly hated him seeing her weakness nearly as much as she'd hated the question. "What was your childhood like?"

She looked away and he instantly regretted the question.

The air had grown noticeably colder inside the cabin and the gas lamps flickered low. The train was moving through the mountains now. Outside the window was an eerie vista of night-bright snow and nothingness. Jules didn't mind the cold. The concept had new meaning since Ostrava. But Selene was clearly feeling it. Her long, elegant fingers were bone white.

Jules drew off his gloves and extended them to her. A peace offering. One he hoped wouldn't bite his ass, this time. They were all he had left of his kit other than his boots, and the soft leather was only slightly charred.

Other than the tinkle of glass tassels on the lanterns, swaying with the movement of the train, the sounds of the steam engine were muffled. Even the steady thrum of the iron wheels charging toward Rome had faded away.

Her amber eyes held his for a long moment before Selene took them. "Thank you." She traced the cognac stitching with her thumb, then tugged them on, pulling them taut at the wrists. A soft sigh escaped her at the warmth. Her hands looked absurdly small in his large gloves.

Jules smothered his smile when Selene returned her attention to him and cast around for a safer question. "I didn't learn a lot of history." Perhaps he'd been too hasty when he dismissed the subject earlier—now it sounded good and safe. "Tell me something interesting about the Vatican. Make it good or I'll never give history another chance."

Selene leaned back to pull her coat off the seat and over her shoulders. "All right." Her eyes were distant. She tapped a finger against her cheek.

"Can't think of anything?"

"The opposite," she replied. "The list is too long." She crossed her legs and retied the bow he'd untied. "Do you know anything about the Academy?"

He knew what it was, of course. The elite school for training Vatican exorcists. But what happened within those walls was far above his pay grade.

"I really, genuinely, know nothing. I promise I'm not just being modest."

She snorted. "You, modest?"

"Exactly."

She nodded. "Interesting, you say. All right. Not many records remain from the early days of the Holy Vatican Empire. I suppose the previous system collapsed and *was* rebuilt in a time of war."

A smile tugged at his lips as he listened to her speak.

"But we do know that during the first years of the Academy they tried to train everyone as exorcists. The death rate was . . . terribly high. Now the Academy tests for aptitude before dividing the cohort. And that's when it's decided whether you'll become an exorcist or an artificer."

"Artificer?" he asked.

"They're more like you soldiers. Their weapons do the heavy lifting. Caterina and Lucia are artificers."

He snorted. He'd seen Caterina and Lucia in action. They were nothing like the soldiers he knew.

If Selene was trying not to look annoyed, she was failing. "Think what you want, deserter."

"I shall, exorcist."

"Why are you so irritating?"

He smirked. "Born that way."

She rolled her eyes, but then a reluctant smile stole onto her mouth. "Their magic is less potent and temporary." She continued as though he hadn't spoken. "Just enough to give them an edge in a fight."

"An edge? Caterina's made like a damn throwing star."

"You saw her grumpy side."

"She has another side?"

Selene considered that. "Not really, no." She thought for a moment. "Do you have a hidden talent?"

"Maybe . . . luck?"

"Try again, Lacroix." Her cheeks were blotching red from the chilled air.

Rubbing his thumb over the marks on his knuckles, Jules smothered a yawn. Could killing be considered a talent? He sure was good enough at it.

Selene went unnaturally still. "What are *those*?" she asked softly.

He turned his hand in the guttering light of the gas lamps. His marks were stark slashes in his skin in the odd light. He curled his fingers into fists as though to hide them, but that only made the silvery scars across the ridge of his knuckles stand out more.

Selene reached for him, her slim hands swallowed by his large leather gloves. Taking his hand, she turned it in her own, examining it like one might examine a relic. Impatiently, she tugged off her gloves and leaned closer, tracing her thumbnail over a scar.

Jules froze. Her fingers were so gentle—so different from the sharp little elbow between his ribs earlier. And with his mind fogged by exhaustion and heart bruised by grief, he *let* her touch him.

It was the first gentle physical contact he'd experienced in days—since before Kian died—and it felt so good. Even from her, this exorcist who'd said not a single kind word since they'd met.

"You did these to yourself?"

"Yes," he breathed.

Her eyelashes dipped low, casting crescent moons against her cheekbones.

Maybe they weren't so different after all. Selene, too, knew what it was to kill. She'd survived to walk away from fights where others had died. She'd lost friends.

"Why like this?"

He let himself really look at the marks. Countless now.

The words slipped from his tongue. "Because I wanted to carve my hatred into my skin. To remind myself *why* I kill. So that if I ever forget, all I have to do is look at my hands." He flexed his fingers. "If it's been a few days between attacks, they remind me not to become complacent or I'll become one of these." He traced one of the horizontal lines with his pinkie, flicking a glance up at her. Her expression was somber and he could see no recrimination there. "So instead, I make more of these." He traced a vertical line—the demon kill. "It started with my original crew. The five of us who survived our first battle together."

Without a word Selene held his wrist in one hand and turned his sleeve. Rolling the cuff again and again. And *again*. Finally she stopped, her eyes darkening with realization. "I see." Her fingers fell still against his skin and he felt her touch intensely. Like it might scorch him to his core.

Jules yanked away from her, rolling his sleeve down. He wasn't ready for this—this *intimacy*, if that's what it was. They breathed the same air, him and this strange girl who knew more about him than anyone should. Farah had been the last to see them. Selene acted like she understood, but she didn't—*couldn't*.

"Lacroix . . ." She drew a steadying breath. "I read the reports, of course, but it doesn't really . . . I had no idea."

Her eyes were large and earnest, and he knew he was seeing her for the first time. *Really* seeing her.

"Hard to describe wholesale slaughter, is it? Didn't whoever wrote your reports have a thesaurus on hand?" His voice had a bitter edge, but she didn't move away, so neither did he. He could practically count each one of her long dark eyelashes.

Selene knelt up and flipped the portfolio case open with a fingertip. "I don't know," she said so seriously he knew she was playing along. "Perhaps you should ask an officer by the name of—"

With a sudden jolt, the train's wheels squealed against the tracks.

CHAPTER SIXTEEN

Eliot's ancestral blades slid across the floor as the train tipped on two wheels in a partial derailment. Thrown completely off balance, Selene landed heavily—rump first—in Jules's lap.

Dio.

Large hands grasped her hips, attempting to steady her.

Thud-thud-thud. The squeal of brakes was accompanied by the rumble of falling luggage.

"What the hell was that?" she demanded.

They were too close. Far too close. Her cheeks flamed and she squirmed to climb out of his lap.

His scorching fingers tightened. "Stop moving. I'm *begging*—"

"Let go of me, Lacroix!" She twisted, shoving at him.

They pushed each other away. Jules sprawled on his back, whacking his head on the floorboards as she scrambled to put distance between him and her rear.

Casting him a dirty look, she slapped her hands against the door. It resisted, opening only an inch before slamming closed again, followed by the sound of more baggage falling.

Red liquid leaked beneath the door, spreading over the shiny floorboards. She backed away.

"A tragedy," Jules murmured. She looked at him, alarmed. He laughed. "Wine."

"Wine?"

"Bordeaux red, if I'm not mistaken."

She snatched a blanket from the ornate cupboard beside the foldout beds, using it to soak up the liquid and prevent further encroachment.

With a final lurch, the train came to a halt.

The windows unlatched easily, opening wide enough for Jules to lean halfway out. "We've stopped," he reported back.

Selene made a sound with her nose that she very much hoped he would understand to mean *no shit*.

"Looks like a small avalanche on the tracks," he said.

This was what she got for getting on the first train out of Saint-Jeannet, rather than going through the proper channels. They never would've been diverted via Milan if she'd requisitioned the entire train. *Too late now.* This way, she reminded herself, she'd be able to explain her unexpected arrival back in Rome to Cesare *personally*. Better to have that conversation face to face.

In the steady flurry of falling snow outside, a gaggle of conductors paced alongside the train, holding lanterns aloft as they inspected the damage. One stopped beside their window, the golden light illuminating his features. "We'll get moving in no time at all. Please make yourselves comfortable until then."

Selene squeezed in beside Jules at the window. "We're *trapped*," she told the conductor.

"Only for a little while," he assured her. He raised the lantern higher, and the pool of light widened. A few feet behind him the ground dropped away in a sheer cliff. Along the track, snow mounded around the train engine, half burying it. "The snow will be cleared very soon."

The merest hint of jagged mountains blocked out the stars along the horizon, their edges etched out of the darkness by snow. The altitude made the sky look terribly large, but it was beautiful in its vastness.

"No. *We're*—" Selene indicated between herself and Jules. "*Trapped*. In here. *Together*."

He looked confused. "Are you not one party?"

Selene narrowed her eyes and tried to slam the window shut in answer. She didn't engage the latch and it bounced open again so a large clump of wet snow dropped onto the open pane.

Jules smirked as she shoved it off with her bare hands.

She was shivering by the time it was closed. "Thanks for your help."

"You seemed to have it under control."

She yanked the curtains closed. The room was freezing now and Selene battled teeth that wanted to chatter. By the time she turned around, Jules had his head tipped back against the seat cushion, eyes almost shut.

"Fine." She tried not to sound as resigned—as utterly, inescapably *done*—as she felt.

"Hm?" He smothered a smile, but not well enough.

"I'm going to sleep."

His expression briefly flashed with something very like triumph. With more clattering and stomping than strictly necessary, she pulled down the bed on the far wall and shrugged off her coat. Designed to be converted from day to night journeys, it wasn't the height of comfort. But the mattress had a cushion top so it would do.

She shed her boots, climbed the ladder, and shuffled under the covers. The sound of silk ropes snapping was her only warning before the bunk collapsed, dumping her out.

Jules lunged, dropping the coat he'd been folding, and caught her before she could hit the floor. And for the second time in ten minutes she was pressed up against his large, warm body.

She shoved him, trying to get her feet on the ground. "Get off."

"Can you please stop throwing yourself at me?"

Heat rushed to her cheeks. "I can assure you, if it happens again, it'll be dagger first."

He grinned and set her back on her feet.

Stalking away from him, she shot a betrayed look at the bunk. Her breath puffed in the cold air and, depleted as she was by the magic that had coursed through her body, she felt the chill more keenly than she usually would.

Jules tested the integrity of the lower bunk with a hand, bouncing it a few times. "Here." He sounded softly amused. "Take this one."

"I couldn't possibly." Selene tried to ignore the tone in his voice. First she'd thrown herself at him—a train derailment didn't make *that* any less mortifying—and now this.

She shook herself. *Get it together.*

Jules carded his fingers through his hair. "Consider this me deferring to my superior officer." Eyes sparking with humor, he added, "Besides, I don't mind sharing. We can keep each other warm."

Why, that little—

She plopped down on the bed and fluffed up the pillow, determinedly ignoring the fact that she could still feel the heat of his large hands, the raised scars beneath her fingers.

"Good night, Lacroix."

When Selene woke—alone—the train was underway once more. A gentle tone signaled their final approach into Rome. Sitting, she muffled a groan in her hands. The punishment she'd put her body through over the last few days was catching up with her. Her muscles were kinked and her temples ached horribly.

Dio. She regretted *everything.* Most especially she regretted telling Jules Lacroix so very much. And touching him with her entire body.

Jules was sleeping peacefully on the opposite seat. He didn't appear to be actively suffering, so she nudged him with her boot. "We'll be in Rome in an hour."

"So?" he mumbled.

She looked down at him, again questioning the sanity of their plan. If looks were all, that would be one thing. Seven years was a long time and their classmates probably hadn't thought about Eliot since his sudden departure. But looks *weren't* the end of it. Eliot was noble-born. Jules was . . . something else.

Dangerous, her mind supplied unbidden. With the air of a man who might not always start the fight but who'd certainly finish it.

More importantly, how did he look so damn comfortable?

"So?" she echoed with a hiss. "You're not *dressed.*" Her head throbbed. *Goddamn it.* That pillow was a crime against humanity— worse, against her specifically. She ought to bring charges.

A soft snore was her only answer.

His hand curled over his pillow, Jules's fingers were scarred with dozens of kill marks. She took a small step back and drew his gloves from underneath her pillow, setting them beside his head. Despite herself, she felt like she understood him a little better now. Could she really hold desertion against him when he'd killed more in his short life than most would ever, *could* ever? Most would never survive that long.

Impressive. And a little disturbing.

Selene rubbed her shoulder, grimacing as a twinge went through her new skin and muscle. The ligaments and tendons and nerves that Lucia had rebuilt. She couldn't remember a thing after her arm was burned.

The final moments of her fight with Baliel were distant, as though they were taking place on the other side of a frosted window. Utterly frustrated, her gaze returned to his sleeping face.

"Who *are* you, Jules Lacroix?"

The rich aroma of coffee filled the café car. Selene breathed into her steaming cup, pressing her cold fingers to the porcelain. As the train crawled the last few miles into the city, she considered the wisdom of bringing Jules to Rome.

Jules and Baliel were on parallel paths: Nice, Saint-Jeannet, the Genealogical Library. Perhaps it was a risk, but leaving Baliel unchecked was a bigger one. And whoever Jules turned out to be, he was the only thread she had that connected to Baliel.

A chill infused her skin and bones, and even the heat of her coffee didn't warm her. Baliel, Duke of Briars. She never thought she'd live to see a demon duke in the flesh.

And even in her most ruthless and ambitious moment, she had never wanted to.

Selene set her cup down, leaving a small stack of notes on the table. But by the time she returned to the cabin—feeling only fractionally more human for the double-shot latte—Jules was gone. Battling panic, she reasoned it out. The train hadn't stopped anywhere. What was he going to do, fling himself from a window? Snatching up her bag, she ran down the hall, poking her head into unlocked compartments until the train let out a hiss. Selene navigated the suddenly packed corridor, past passengers carrying ornate travel trunks and embossed leather cases, and forced her way to the front. Skipping down the steps, she turned on the platform in case Jules slipped out another door. She was the first onto the platform and she couldn't see him anywhere.

But something else drew her eye. A Vatican delegation. Six in all. She recognized two golden heads among them. Florentina and her superior, Gabriel Notaro. Selene wound her way through passengers toward them. Florentina's eyelids were heavy with boredom and when she saw Selene she sighed. Ignoring her rival completely, Selene stopped in front of Gabriel. "Hello, Gabriel. To what do I owe the pleasure?"

"Selene. The Imperium Bellum requested we meet you."

How Cesare had learned of her early return, she wasn't sure, but this was a message. She reminded herself not to underestimate her uncle. They didn't call him the Shadow of God because he was *incompetent.*

"I don't need a babysitter."

"Escort only, I assure you."

"Quite unnecessary. I'm sure I can find my way to St. Peter's."

Besides the indignity of being marched back, she didn't want any of them to see Jules. She wasn't ready for that yet.

More importantly, neither was he.

Gabriel sighed. "We won't be going there, I'm afraid. We've a funeral to attend."

She raised a brow.

"Three killed in Ostrava. Their bodies arrived on your train." He nodded along the platform and Selene turned. Three coffins, draped with the tassel-edged flag of the Exorcist Primus, were being carefully unloaded.

"They came via Milan, I suppose?"

He smiled. "Quite. Good of you to escort them home." She nodded mutely, turning her back to the somber affair.

Gabriel reached to tip her chin up. "Don't be like that. Come, how about we ride together?" His eyes shifted from her face, settling on something over her shoulder.

Selene pulled away from Gabriel's touch, following his gaze. Her breath caught in her throat.

"Who's that?" asked Florentina.

Selene recalled Jules's cocky expression from yesterday. His irrepressible grin. The smirk that played on his lips before he shoved an entire baguette into his face. Even now, hours later, irritation still blossomed in her at the memory. But Jules had changed—no, *transformed*—and she could hardly believe her eyes.

Jules Lacroix stood at the top of the train's three steps, pushing his hands through his damp dark hair, slicking it back so that only a few stray strands fell across his forehead. Tied at his hip, he carried the twin blades of the D'Alessandro family with careless ease, as though he'd been born to them. The military-style Vatican uniform suited him. The jacket stretched taut across his broad shoulders, but she was the only one who'd notice. She'd have another tailored for him soon. Tall black boots stopped before his knee, accentuating his long, lean legs. Gold epaulettes engraved with the Deathless God's crucifix and spear were sculpted over his shoulders and even though she'd seen this uniform every day of her life, it looked remarkably different on him.

Jules rubbed his freshly shaved chin, sleeve brushing the engraved gold plate at his throat.

"Is that . . . *Eliot D'Alessandro?*" someone asked quietly.

"Eliot?" Florentina drifted forward. "Eliot D'Alessandro? Is it really you? It's been years, darling! Years."

Selene bit her lip. *Dio* . . . She hadn't anticipated seeing anyone from their class so soon. Their ridiculous study session from the night before hadn't taught him nearly enough to survive this encounter. Half the exorcists in this cohort had been at the Academy with Eliot.

Before Selene could interject, Jules plastered a smile on his face and flung open his arms.

Florentina squealed in delight and leaped at him. Jules spun her around as he hopped off the last step onto the platform, holding her in his embrace. "Tell me absolutely everything I've missed," he said conspiratorially in Italian, somehow crushing all but the slightest hint of his Niçois accent. Even before the Vatican Empire had mandated that Italian should be the administrative language of government in Provence, Nice had been a playing piece on the Italian chessboard.

And yet she couldn't help but notice Jules was *incorrigibly* French.

Florentina launched into a report of the last several years of dirty little secrets and scandals. Eyes shining as she gazed up at him, she added, "You look divine. France has been good to you."

"I think you mean puberty," Jules replied with a wink. Florentina laughed, hanging off his arm.

Selene tried to ignore the way she pressed her breasts against his bicep.

"I didn't know Eliot's banishment had ended," Gabriel murmured, surprise flickering across his face. The crease between his brows deepened. "Is your fiancé back for good?"

Selene felt more than saw Jules's full attention zero in on their conversation.

This had to be punishment for past sins.

She shot Jules a narrow-eyed glance, alarmed at the hint of amusement in his expression. *Fiancé?* said the smirk that played at the corner of his lips as he gently shook Florentina off.

"I am indeed." Circling her waist with one arm, Jules tugged Selene back against his chest. "Didn't you tell anyone I was coming?"

He looked down at Selene, holding her gaze. "Did you want to keep me all to yourself? How selfish of you, *mon petit lapinou.*"

My little love bunny.

He pressed a kiss to her temple.

Little other than an iron will forged in the Vatican's military academy prevented her from inflicting grievous bodily harm in that moment. Smiling a smile that felt like it showed too many teeth, she pinched his chin between her fingers. "Who can blame me for wanting to keep you all to myself? After last night, I thought your *conversation* skills could use a bit of practice."

"My conversation skills are just fine."

She raised one shoulder in a casual shrug. "Maybe for Nice. But in Rome we pride ourselves on being a city of great conversationalists. There's room for improvement, that's all I'm saying."

Jules bit back a smile. "That doesn't sound like me."

"I can assure you, it was." She yawned.

A flicker of amusement lit his eyes and he dropped his lashes, acknowledging defeat. He loosened his arm but kept his hand against the small of her back.

Something Gabriel said slithered back to her. "What do you know about Eliot's exile, Gabriel? I wasn't aware you had any insight."

While Gabriel gave no visible sign he'd even heard her question, Jules's expression shuttered.

Her lips twisted in annoyance. She hated being the last to know something.

"Didn't Eliot tell you? He was banished by Imperium's decree and I was there to ensure it was done. Your uncle . . ." Gabriel trailed off, seeing her face. "Your uncle asked me to see him to the train."

Jules squeezed her hip in warning.

"He personally approved Eliot's return," she lied tightly. "So obviously that's changed. I'll have to make sure word gets round so you don't get thrown in the Vatican dungeons."

Gabriel narrowed his eyes. "You seem different, Eliot."

"It's been seven years, Gabriel. Give him a chance to find his feet."

Gabriel ignored her. "What was the last thing you did in Rome? Just curious." He tried to stare Jules down but couldn't. Jules had inches on him, and it gave her a vicious surge of delight that Gabriel couldn't intimidate Jules in his usual boring way.

Sensing danger, her fingers bunched in the back of his jacket.

Jules ignored her death grip. "I visited the Trevi Fountain and tossed three coins over my shoulder."

How did Jules know about the Trevi Fountain legend? By ensnaring three promises with three coins, you ensured your ticket back to Rome, love, and a wedding day near at hand.

"Though I only really needed two." Looking down at Selene, Jules held her eyes. "Because one . . . one was already spoken for."

His breath was a low purr that stirred the loose hairs at her temple. *None* of it was Eliot. The delivery was all Jules, and it made her heart stumble. He lied so smoothly even she almost believed him.

"Of course," Gabriel said quietly. "I forgot."

Selene felt as though she'd been knocked over. Nothing made sense right now. "How did you know?" she asked Gabriel in a low voice.

He blanched. "I was there. I took him there as a last request before escorting him to Roma Centrale. I . . . I ensured his exile was complete." He wouldn't look at her and betrayal slid between her ribs like a knife.

Gabriel had been their upperclassman, and *he* had been the one to force Eliot to leave. He had been the knife at his back.

And he'd never told her.

As Florentina dragged Jules toward the idling town cars, Selene fell into step beside Gabriel.

How many times had Gabriel lied to avoid telling her the truth?

And how many times had Cesare?

CHAPTER SEVENTEEN

The funeral was a quiet affair. The Exorcist Primus of Rome did not attend, surprising nobody, which meant Cesare led the service. It was a solemn aspect of his role. Something of a residual limb from before demons attempted to kill God—but at least it kept her uncle occupied. Selene had no desire to speak with him here. Not under the scrutiny of so many watching eyes, all intent on seeing her fail.

When the service was done, everyone proceeded to one of the large garden courtyards. Jules leaned against the rough bark of a parasol pine. Pine needles dusted the paving stones and floated in the still water of a fountain.

When they had a moment alone, she said softly, dangerously, "*Mon petit lapinou?*"

Jules shifted on his feet, tugging at the button at his throat. "I had to sell it. I would've loved a heads-up that we're betrothed." He hesitated, then corrected himself. "That you and Eliot are betrothed."

"We're not."

He raised both brows.

It had been their parents' arrangement. A powerful alignment of exorcist families. Selene smothered a sigh, not particularly wanting to explain to Jules that she'd ended their engagement. Now the only man she was betrothed to was *him* in the guise of a rather suave Eliot D'Alessandro.

"I broke it off with Eliot." Selene enunciated the words. "I hadn't told anybody yet. Now it's *too late.*"

The contemporaries of the dead exorcists told stories, laughing about school-age shenanigans, but Selene hadn't known them well—they'd been years ahead of her at the Academy. Instead, she guided Jules through the clusters of somber people, introducing him. Or rather, reintroducing *Eliot*.

Nobody had questioned his identity. A dark-haired man wearing the priceless D'Alessandro swords could only be the banished scion of the family.

Jules hadn't shown a flicker of surprise when Gabriel told her it had been Cesare who banished Eliot. Of course. Eliot would have warned him. But why hadn't Eliot mentioned it to her?

She thought of Cesare's words before she left Rome. *I'll put in a call to the Nice office and have someone meet you.* He hadn't known that Eliot was working that office. Not then. And then it had been too late. She was already on the train and Eliot had been dispatched to meet her. Events had been set in motion that even the Imperium Bellum of Rome could not prevent.

Another thought occurred to her then, and her stomach soured. When she had telephoned Cesare from Nice-Ville, he had requested she greet her fiancé on his behalf. In doing so, had she unknowingly conveyed Cesare's subtle hint that he expected Eliot to keep the truth of his banishment secret? That it had not been their Academy masters who had sent Eliot away, as she'd believed, but an order from the Imperium Bellum himself?

Florentina waved excitedly, bouncing on her toes. With effort Selene resisted the temptation to roll her eyes.

Jules raised a hand in a lazy wave, then leaned into Selene. "You might have to stake your claim, *mon cœur*. No big deal, but she wants my—" He broke off as two mourners passed close by and lowered his voice. "Let me put it this way, she wants a personal session with *the* D'Alessandro sword."

"Charming." Selene slid her hand into his and linked their fingers. Resting her chin on his shoulder, she gazed up at him from beneath her lashes. "Is this better?"

Color bloomed on his cheekbones and he tousled a hand through his hair, thoroughly messing it up. "Much." He cleared his throat. "Even I'm convinced."

Florentina appeared somewhat crestfallen.

"Oh, you were *right*."

"What can I say? I know when I'm wanted."

"But not when you're not?"

"Oh, yes, very droll."

Selene laughed and mirrored Florentina's grip from earlier, sliding her hand around his bicep. But she knew what Florentina could not; the skin beneath her fingers told a story of slaughter.

Despite her earlier concerns, Jules was flawless in this role. Which was fortunate, because many of their contemporaries were curious to meet the new Eliot. There was only one classmate who might have picked Jules for an impostor, but he wasn't here. Her twin, Niccolò.

A booming voice broke the moment of stillness between them. "Wonderful to have you home, my boy. Wonderful. A sad day, but a happy one."

Smiling broadly, Jules met the outstretched hand of the man who had once been her father's mentor. "Likewise, sir—"

"Adriano de Sanctis, Imperium Politikos," Selene whispered against his shoulder.

Jules swallowed. "And thank you very much, Imperium. I'm honored."

Long before Cesare had stepped in to take his place, Adriano had been a staple in her life. He'd drifted away, no doubt disappointed in the part she played in her father's death, but he looked at her kindly now. "Selene, I see you found your fiancé in France?"

Selene curled her fingers slightly tighter around Jules's bicep. "It surprised me too, sir. I didn't know he was in Nice."

"Adriano, please, Selene. You *know* this." She smiled, and Adriano turned to Jules, fondness melting into what she imagined Jules might call his *war face*. "You look after her."

Jules nodded earnestly, his eyes lingering on her. "She's my sun and stars, sir."

Adriano made a sound Selene took as approval and sauntered off.

"The Imperium bloody Politikos of Rome, Selene? Really?" Jules sat somewhat heavily on the edge of a stone wall.

Shrugging, she tried to extract her hand from his. Even through the gloves he wore to cover the kill marks, she could feel he was beginning to sweat. "My godfather."

"I feel a little faint."

From the corner of her eye, she saw Florentina start toward them. Selene stepped between his knees, draping her arms over his shoulders so she could play with his hair. And for a moment Jules seemed not to breathe—probably dissociating.

Not wanting to be a third wheel in their little moment, Florentina veered away.

"Whose funeral was this anyway?" Jules asked.

She met his eyes, noting again the lovely green. "Lorena, Vissia, and Tobio. They were killed in Ostrava." She forgot for a clumsy moment why Ostrava rang a bell.

The color drained from his face and he glanced back toward the chapel. "Did . . . did Tobio fight with a pike?"

She nodded slowly.

He swallowed. "Remember how I said . . . ?"

The memory of their study session flashed back. "The weather demon."

"Yeah."

She looked him over, reassessing him. He'd put down a demon that had already killed three Academy-trained exorcists. *Incredible.*

"*You!*" someone shouted, barreling toward Jules.

Jules's hand moved to his sword before he stilled, shocked by his own instinct for violence. Even here, far from the front. Even now, at a genteel funeral.

"What are you doing here, maggot? Why didn't you die in the mud like you were supposed to?"

Selene intercepted the tall man staring daggers at Jules. "Enough." Her voice rang overloud in the garden and people turned their way. Despite their difference in age, she was his superior. "Explain yourself."

Jules straightened to his full height at her back, one hand resting on the hilt of a D'Alessandro blade.

With eyes that promised murder, Selene stared the man down. In the moment or two of silence that followed, Jules finally recognized the man, recalling the words he'd spoken when they met in Ostrava. *Very good, grunt.* This was not good at all.

Selene tipped her chin higher. "If you're accusing him of something, Tommaso, spit it out."

"This is none of your business, *Captain* Alleva." He spat to the side, showing what he really thought.

She laughed, stepping closer. "You're mistaken. This is my fiancé."

"Then why did I see him a week ago covered in mud and shit?"

Selene laughed. "I can't speak for Eliot's recreational activities—"

"In *Ostrava*."

She bit her lip, eyes narrowing. Despite the danger they were both in, she didn't waver. "You're mistaken."

"No."

Jules stepped around Selene, forcing Tommaso to back up. "You heard her. You're mistaken." His voice was soft. "And never spit in front of Selene again. Filthy dog."

The man's eyes widened, teeth flashing as his lip curled up. "How *dare*—"

"How dare *you*?" Jules channeled Eliot's posture, the noble blood that ran in Eliot's veins. He tipped his chin and looked down the length of his nose at him. "You come here and disturb this gathering for Vissia and Tobio? For Lorena? Conduct yourself like a filthy foot soldier in front of my fiancée? Have you been in Ostrava too long, Tommaso? Anyone can tell you I was in Nice." Jules spread his hands, looking around. "Should I ask the Imperium Bellum to come over here and confirm?"

Tommaso's eyes darted from Cesare Alleva to Selene.

"No," Tommaso muttered, and stalked off.

Something about these people made Jules uneasy—they had an iron scent reminiscent of blood. Metallic and dangerous. Compounded here where they gathered together. It brought to mind the French corruption of a well-known Roman saying about the

Vaticano Nero—the black they all wore. *L'avant-dernier noir que vous verrez jamais.* The second-last black you will ever see.

Jules let out a long breath, watching Tommaso go. "Who knew funerals could get even *more* fun?" he murmured.

Selene plastered on a smile and laughed, as though the altercation was nothing. Even Jules was almost convinced. She drew him back to the edge of the gathering. "Do you want to head back to my rooms? I need to stay a bit longer." She glanced toward Cesare Alleva, who was busy entertaining a crowd of sycophants.

"You trust me out of your sight?"

She let her eyes roam up and down his length. "You've proven yourself. Besides, we had an agreement. I can offer you access that nobody else can." She cast a meaningful look at the pale dome of St. Peter's Basilica looming over them, and beyond, the forbidding towers of the new Vatican complex stood starker for its light. A fortress indeed. There was no way he'd ever get in if he wasn't welcome.

"All this so I can get into your library."

Surprisingly, a smile flashed across her face. "Yeah. A tad academic for a soldier."

He pressed a hand to his heart. "Ouch. My Achilles heel."

She rolled her eyes. "*Go.* Before Tommaso comes back."

He pushed his hands into his pockets as he strolled away, taking in the lush gardens. Towering cedars edged the park, growing taller even than the dome of St. Peter's. The grass beneath his feet was smooth and spongy. Pencil pines lined walled gardens, creating pockets of privacy. It was unbelievable he was here at all.

A gold-lit fountain drew his eye and he skipped down a handful of steps into an enclosed garden, surrounded on three sides by trees and thick shrubbery with gravel paths disappearing in three directions. Approaching the fountain, he leaned his hands against the stone. Coins winked at him from underwater. Sparing a glance around, he dipped his hand in and pocketed a few. Waste not, want not and all that.

"That's *enough*, Selene."

It took a moment for Jules to place the deep velvet tones of Cesare Alleva. He could win hearts with that voice, the Imperium Bellum.

Their voices drifted closer, and almost too late Jules realized that they were coming down one of the paths. He leaped over the stone wall and disappeared beneath the trees. He wasn't ready to meet another Imperium.

Eliot's contemporaries had been surprisingly easy to fool, through a complex blend of disregard for the Eliot they'd once known and belief in the power of puberty. But Jules had the strong suspicion that the Imperium Bellum wasn't the kind of man to make such mistakes.

Cesare sighed. "Forget Baliel. It sounds as though you removed him from the equation. I'm more concerned about you over-extending yourself." He paced back and forth, then stopped suddenly, looking down at her. "I've *told* you. Other exorcists can train their bodies to withstand their own borrowed power. But yours flows through you from *God*. It is too much for you. You're burning yourself out until there is nothing left."

Jules didn't understand. Was this some religious hyperbole or did exorcists actually believe it? He wished he could see Selene's face. Was Cesare getting the stubborn frown? Or maybe the crumpled brows Jules got when he *really* irritated her.

"I understand, uncle." Selene's tone was flat. "But I want you to know I'll use it if I must. As I did in Nice. I *had* to banish that demon—imperfectly, granted, he'll be back—but there was too much at stake."

Jules cocked his head. Why was her uncle lambasting her for saving Nice, instead of lauding her success? She'd almost lost an *arm* in that fight. And even though Baliel had been consumed by his own flames and Selene had been unconscious long before the demon spoke his final words, she had fought fiercely. Cesare should be proud.

"Selene—"

"*Even* if it pushes me to the brink of death. Even then, I will do what I must. I respect your opinion, but I—"

"This is *God's* power you're playing with." Cesare's deep voice cut across hers. "Remember that. You're not strong enough, my darling girl. Your body, your *soul*, and your mind will wither and burn long before God's power dries up. I will not bury you too."

His words were layered with love and concern, but Jules sensed an undercurrent of something cold and calculating beneath. It took Jules a moment to realize what that was: Cesare was *afraid* of Selene.

Whether he believed what he was saying or not, Jules could tell Cesare wanted her small.

Before they parted ways on the train, Eliot had warned him about Cesare Alleva, the Imperium Bellum of all Rome. Cesare had condemned his own brother—Selene's father, Matteo—to death. He'd *crucified* him.

Ruthlessness was a baseline concept for the man.

Selene had fallen silent. Jules's hands were fists, his nails biting his palms. A strange sense of protectiveness filled him. He didn't need to hear more. The Imperium Bellum was a beautiful, terrible creature. So like Selene in many ways. It was clear to him now that she'd learned at Cesare's knee. Jules felt his instincts quicken. The man was a threat. Perhaps even an enemy.

Cesare sighed. A few beats of silence passed, then he spoke

again. "You're expected at the Carnival Masquerade at the Colosseum. Bring Eliot, since it appears he is here anyway. Your attendance is not up for discussion."

"Will you be there?"

Cesare snorted softly, and that was answer enough, even for Jules. He gently touched her cheek, thumb smoothing along the high bone. "I don't want to lose you." He kissed her brow and disappeared in the direction of the Vatican proper.

Selene seemed smaller somehow. Even among these men who took up so much space, she didn't *usually* look this small.

Jules wanted to undo what had been done. Wanted her to take up space again. *Light* it up.

He hopped silently down to the grass, bending below the draping needles of a weeping pine. His footsteps were soundless as he stepped up behind her, covering her eyes with a hand. She was a blur of movement as she twisted, slamming into his solar plexus as she threw him. Jules stumbled and they fell in a tangle of arms and legs and sweet-smelling dark hair. And the kind of curses that should rightly be reserved for a sailor, not the beautiful lush lips of Selene Alleva.

"*Vaffanculo, idiota!*"

She slammed him into the water, gun pressed to his forehead as she knelt over him, rear pressed against the one part of him that should not be showing interest right now. Not in response to this bloody monster.

His fingernails scraped algae from the shallow fountain as he shoved himself up, gasping for breath as water trickled down his face.

"*You—*" Selene snarled, grabbing his shirt to yank him an inch closer as though intending to bite. A fraction of his mind noted the way she lowered her gun to her side, but a more significant part was occupied by the tightening of his pants. He was a sick man.

And if Selene noticed, she'd make him no man at all.

Jules attempted a charming smile. "Surprise?"

Her lips curled over bared teeth, very much *not* smiling.

Selene holstered the gun at her thigh and palmed a knife. Its point tickled his chin.

"What on earth happened here?" Florentina asked, surprising them both.

Selene flipped the knife, concealing it against her wrist.

"How romantic," another voice added, dripping with sarcasm.

Gabriel too. Of course it had to be him, strolling unhurriedly down the steps with his hands tucked in his pockets. How would Selene explain threatening her fiancé at knifepoint? A beat passed where neither moved.

Jules took her wrist, further concealing the knife. "Please don't kill me for this," he breathed, and caught her lips in a kiss.

His fingers tightened, holding her wrist captive between them. Her bones felt absurdly fragile. She let out a little sound of surprise and he tangled his other hand in her hair. Her mouth softened beneath his and for the briefest of moments he tasted her.

Jules smoothed her hair back from her face with his palms. "It's good to see you too, *bellezza*, but next time there's no need to tackle me into a fountain."

"How dare you?" she breathed, eyes flashing like flat gold coins in her fury.

He smothered a smile.

Furious was an improvement on whatever emotion she'd felt before with Cesare. Ignoring the danger, he drew her closer and tucked strands of her hair behind her ear. Her eyes held his, and her lips parted but no words came.

Florentina scoffed, breaking Selene's stillness. Jules felt the loss of her full attention.

"Crazy in love, Selene?" Florentina asked. "I'd never pick you as the type."

Selene pressed the lightest kiss to the tip of Jules's nose, and only then spared Florentina a bored look. "Can you blame me?" She flicked her eyes down to where his wet shirt clung to his skin, translucent against the planes of his chest. Her thighs still brushed his hips. She plucked at his sleeve, tugging it away from his skin. *Hiding his scars.*

Florentina laughed, though it was devoid of any humor.

"Come now, if you stay in there you'll become waterlogged," Gabriel said, his voice rich with suppressed amusement.

As she stood, Selene uncurled her fingers from the knife. It fell toward the water and Jules caught it neatly as he reached for her proffered hand, sliding it into his sleeve.

As she pulled him up, Selene hissed viciously against his ear. "Don't think I didn't notice that you're hard."

CHAPTER EIGHTEEN

Back in her rooms, Selene let the uncomfortable silence stretch between them. *Let him sweat.* The only sound in the echoing silence was the *click, click, click* as she opened her gun's chamber to count and recount her bullets. Enough to kill him many times over. Jules adjusted the button at his collar, his eyes on her fingers.

Tearing his gaze away, he deliberately circled the rooms, peering into the small library before pushing open the double doors to her bedroom. His eyes widened at the sight of the bed.

It *was* rather large. Especially compared to the narrow bunks on the train. *No,* she corrected herself, *especially compared to the trenches.*

Sometime during the funeral, their luggage had been delivered. Selene checked on the portfolio containing Jules's file and found it untouched, still tucked inside her winter coat. Jules's smaller suitcase—borrowed from Eliot, detailed with his initials on a brass plaque—sat beside hers. She took the handles and carried both after Jules, making a point of not noticing him. Even though he *was* standing in the middle of her space. Seeming particularly tall and broad-shouldered. Which was a problem.

Eliot had no rooms at the Vatican.

He'd left when they were both at the Academy and sleeping in the dorms. She could requisition some, but Vatican administrative processes were notoriously slow when it came to non-demon-related paperwork.

A problem for tomorrow.

Cesare's earlier words came back to her. She had disappointed him again. And *he* had disappointed her by dismissing her concerns, as she knew he would. When she told him that she suspected Baliel was coming to Rome, he'd laughed. She felt it to her bones and he'd *laughed*. Worse, he had admonished her for using too much power. Against a *demon duke*.

And this was why he couldn't know about Jules. When she'd brought it up—hesitantly, feeling disloyal for even voicing the thought—Eliot had agreed. It was best not to *bother* Cesare with this. Eliot had chosen his words carefully, and she would too. Cesare was busy with his own role and picking up the slack from the Exorcist Primus's infirmity. She would continue her investigations until she had something meaningful to share. Something beyond her gut instinct. Something he couldn't laugh off.

Jules poked his head into the main bathroom, whistling between his teeth, before moving to relieve her of the luggage. He set Eliot's small case on one of the window seats. The stained glass at the top of the window colored the planes of his face as he snapped open the buckles. He drew out a fresh white shirt to replace the wet one. She tried to ignore the way every fold of saturated fabric emphasized a different muscle, from sculpted biceps to the hard lines of his chest and stomach.

"How did you know about the Trevi Fountain?" she asked.

He raised a brow in question.

"Earlier," she clarified. "You told Gabriel quite a story. I thought you were making it up as you went. But . . . his reaction."

"Eliot told me. He didn't tell me his wishes were about *you*." He picked up a photograph of her parents, his thumb smoothing over the glass.

She tried to assemble her features into something more *Selene* but failed. She could tell he'd caught her stricken look.

He set the picture down. "Why do you think he didn't tell me?"

"I don't know." She spread her hands. "We were children when it was all decided, and the last time I saw him he was my best friend and nothing more. I haven't thought about it for years. It's probably the same for him."

He smirked. "Sure it is. And Gabriel? What is he to you?"

She narrowed her eyes.

"Isn't this something I might need to know?"

He was right, damn him. "He was our upperclassman. We knew him growing up. And he was my superior when I first left the Academy."

"That's all?"

"Absolutely." She shrugged off her jacket and tossed it over the velvet chaise.

"Well, I think he likes you."

She chose not to dignify that with a response. Turning her full attention to the bar cart in the corner, she sifted through the bottles until she found what she was looking for. Jules continued to circle the space, fingertips trailing over the walls as he looked around with open wonder. He paused in the doorway to her bedroom, his broad shoulders briefly eclipsing the sunlight streaming through.

How dare he take up so much *room*?

She poured herself a Scotch.

Selene's rooms were much like her. Utterly beautiful. He smothered a grimace at the resurfaced memory. *Bellezza*, he'd called her. *Beauty*. Because she was. Terrifying, yes. But also beautiful. And then she'd promptly cut him down to size with that razor tongue of hers.

He slid a glance her way. Her gun was back at her thigh, its many bullets chambered once more and ready to kill a man. Probably him. She had taken the time to count each one with deadly patience—something he had never expected from her, and hoped never to see again.

He glanced around the lounge. Where the walls were lustrous and ornate, the doors and architraves were pure white. The large sitting room was wallpapered with painted midnight silk, details picked out in beadwork. It was as though the Vatican gardens had been captured and brought inside. Pressed into the walls. All their palms and flowers and birds. Fat pomegranates and raspberries fought for their place among large ruffled peonies, plum blossoms, white lilies, and fronded plants. Cranes in flight stood out against the deep blue background.

Jules brushed his fingers over the beading of a luminous bird. Tiny gold beads created the impression of a bright, alert eye. He stroked his fingers over the thousand more that defined its wing feathers in pretty waves, the tiny discs sewn directly to the fabric.

The bed was vast and postered, draped with gauzy curtains beaded with seed pearls. There were miles of plush bedding, and pillows piled high enough to swallow a man. Selene, by contrast, appeared severe in this heart of opulence. Her dark uniform, tights, and fine leather boots that ended above her knee; the delicate pauldron sculpted to her off-shoulder, its overlapping gold scales forged to look like feathers. And all of her still rather damp.

He tipped his head, reevaluating her.

Seeing her private space did nothing to lessen his regard. Quite the opposite. Selene had all the comfort she could ever want, and still he'd seen her throw herself into the fight with all the ferocity of a starving wolf.

Water dripped off the hem of her short black dress, puddling on the floor. He stepped up behind her, looking down at her delicate hands as she stirred a drink. Her shoulders stiffened, but that was her only reaction. Still furious.

But that only made winning a smile a challenge worth attempting.

Jules stepped up behind her, his presence warm at her back. His heat seemed to soak through the damp wool layers of her uniform and into her skin. She smoothed her mask, not showing any of her thoughts on her face.

He eyed the glass in her hand. "You know what I'm thinking?"

"No."

"I'm thinking—"

"I mean *no* to whatever you're thinking. Emphatically."

He reached over her, snagging the glass from her hand, and raised it to his lips. He watched her over the rim, taking a sip. She shifted, warmth coiling in her belly at the memory of those lips on hers.

Damn him.

"I'm thinking we play the question game again. But make it interesting."

"The question game? I thought it was a *study session?*"

He grinned. "It was."

"And now you want a drinking game? No."

"Well, that's not fair. How else am I supposed to figure out this place if I don't make it into a drinking game?"

She turned. There was no space between them. Barely a breath of air. "What do you want to know?"

"Everything."

She rolled her eyes.

"What I need to know to survive," he amended with a sigh, handing her back the glass.

She took a sip, not taking her eyes off him.

"Selene, please." Her name sounded different now, though she couldn't place how.

Returning the glass to Jules, Selene poured herself another. She raised her Scotch. "To surviving all of—" She angled her wrist, glancing at her watch. "Six hours in Rome without being discovered."

His lips curled into a slow smile as he touched their glasses. "It's gonna be a long week."

Jules looked good like this. Relaxed. Damp clothes hugging every line of his body. All but his shirt, which was only partially buttoned. She yanked her eyes back up. *No.*

Focus.

There was no way on earth she could let herself be distracted by the most irritating man she'd ever met just because he knew how to kiss—and *Dio*, he knew how to kiss.

Perhaps a little distraction wasn't all bad. But . . . not *this* man. Not with his kill marks and an unknowable connection to Baliel. *That* was a dangerous game. Not that she was unused to dangerous

games, but it was one thing in the streets, entirely another between the—

No.

She let out a long breath. "It would take all night to tell you
everything, but I'll tell you what I can."

"But no drinking game?"

"My liver wouldn't survive it."

He grinned, eyes bright. "But it *would* be fun."

And God help her, that smile would get him everywhere.

It had been a long time since she'd had more than a finger of
Scotch, and she suspected Jules had never had access to quality
hard liquor. The first half hour was spent reciting the names of her
classmates and their ranking. And then Jules had decided he was
no longer interested in learning. He was bored to death and losing
his patience.

And his clothes.

"No, Florentina ranked second, *Fiorentina* was seventh," Selene
corrected him. Her brain was foggy and the world spun pleasantly
around her.

"I don't even *know* her." Jules was trying and failing to untie
the D'Alessandro swords from his hip. "Where did Caterina rank?
Higher than you?"

"Nope." She knew she sounded smug. "I was top ranked. Besides, Caterina and Lucia were ahead of me by two years."

"Huh." He tipped his head back, staring at the ceiling. "But
you're their boss?"

"The empire runs on—"

"*Nepotism.*"

"Meritocratic principles—*what?*"

"Nothing." He stole her glass, downing it to avoid her eyes, and
brought her another.

"At least I can untie a knot," she muttered into her drink.

"Let's ask the question game again."

"Play the asking game?"

"That's what I said."

She rolled her eyes. "Fine. Umm."

Jules tossed his hands up, finally giving up on the sword tie. "*Fine*, I'll take the whole belt off." He began unbuttoning his shirt.

She laughed, pressing the crystal glass to her cheek to try to cool it down. "Oh, I know. If . . . if you could do *anything*, what would you do?"

"Fly," he said, falling hard. He sat on the floor, forgetting his shirt buttons and fighting with the swords once more.

"No—no, *no*. Like a job."

"Oh." He stilled, apparently thinking very hard, his eyes unfocused.

She stomped over. "Answer!"

He laughed. "Or what?"

She snorted, trying not to laugh. He was much funnier than usual tonight. "Maybe something. Maybe nothing."

"Well, okay then." He whistled through his teeth, once again thinking hard. "Maybe what you do?"

She scoffed. "Exorcist?"

"Yeah. Why?" He stood, grasping for her shoulders to keep his balance. "You think I couldn't do it?"

"An exorcist who doesn't even know how to un—unbluck—"

"Un-*bluckle*," he said confidently.

"Yes, that. You need to do that if you want to be a good exorcist. Good exorcists can't just wear their swords forever, you know."

He looked dejected. "Makes sense."

She reached for him, fiddling with his buckle with clumsy

fingers until the whole belt fell to the floor with a heavy clunk. "There. Fixed it."

He beamed. "All right, all right . . . a question." He strolled a few steps away, then turned. "If you could kill anyone without any consequences, who would it be?"

Her brows furrowed. "But I can already do that?"

"Oh." He thought about that for a moment. "Then I get another one."

"That's against the rules."

"Subsection Three says—"

"*Fine.*"

"Ha!" He grinned as he resumed his attempts to undo his shirt buttons. She watched his large, scarred hands struggle, his brows pulled together, as he scowled darkly. Finally he yanked the shirt up over his head and dropped it to the floor. His skin looked remarkably tanned and smooth in this light and she wondered if it felt as hot as he looked.

She took a step closer. "What are you doing?"

"Going to sleep." He slumped onto the bed, leaning against the headboard carved like palm fronds. "You always look so sad when your family comes up. Where are they?"

She bristled, the question something of a cold splash of water, though her edges still felt fuzzy. "I did not look sad."

"You did."

"Gone." Her back was to him. "Some dead. Some just gone." The crumpled white shirt looked a hell of a lot more comfortable than the still-damp clothes she was wearing. She picked it up. It was still warm. "If you won't wear it, I will."

"Be my guest," he slurred, somewhat muffled by the bedding.

Toeing off her boots, she pulled her shirt off and slipped Jules's on. Her fingers were clumsy as she tried to do up the top button. In the bathroom she kicked off her tights, finally shedding the last of her damp clothes. She returned with a glass of water and knelt on the bed beside him.

At her urging, Jules obediently wrapped his fingers over hers and guided the glass to his lips. "Have you ever stolen something?" he asked.

Selene bit her lip, trying not to smile. "*This,*" she said, tugging at the hem of the shirt.

"Mm-hmm." He smirked and seemed about to say something more. Heavy-lidded eyes trailed down her body. Then he flopped unconscious into her pile of feather pillows.

She shuffled back to the armchair. She shifted around, hanging her feet over the edge. Nothing she did made it more comfortable. Sighing, she wriggled her bottom to squish deeper into the seat.

The sound of Jules breathing barely reached her over here, just enough to remind her he was there . . . in *her* bed. In her Egyptian cotton sheets. He sounded deeply asleep. And very drunk.

She dragged her gaze away and shifted around, curling up like a cat. Nothing worked. She groaned loudly and flounced to her feet.

He didn't stir. Not a twitch.

Tiptoeing over to him on quiet feet, she hesitated by the bed, bare legs chilly. Her bed looked awfully inviting and it was the only thing that wasn't spinning.

Jules was a heavy sleeper. She'd witnessed that on the train. And *this* time he had more liquor than blood in his system. Surely he was too drunk to notice her slip under the covers and back out again before he woke up? She carefully shuffled in. The cold sheets felt sublime against her skin.

Jules rolled over, his hand perilously close to touching her. Still and silent, she waited until his breathing evened out again and then wriggled deeper under the covers.

She sighed. *Bliss.*

And Jules's soft snores didn't bother her at all.

CHAPTER NINETEEN

Selene woke tangled in sheets.

She groaned, pressing a hand to her throbbing temple. *Dio . . .* There was a soft breath. Her head whipped around and the world spun dangerously. Asleep beside her, Jules hugged one of her feather pillows to his naked chest.

Carefully sitting up, she glanced at the water she'd set beside his bed. It was drained. Maybe *he* wouldn't have a splitting headache to show for their evening together.

Then she froze like a startled rabbit. Had he woken up and *seen her*?

Selene rubbed her temples, and the laundered cotton rustled when she moved. She was still wearing his shirt and not much else. Searching her bleary mind, she remembered the order of events— drinking, questions, explaining things that would keep him alive, and him getting so distracted halfway through undressing that she had declared that if *he* wouldn't wear his shirt, *she* would. She dropped her forehead into her hand and peeked through her fingers at Jules.

Lines were blurring. And that was something she couldn't allow. The kiss had been a farce. She *knew* that. So why did it make it so much easier to picture him in her bed for different reasons than late-night drinking games? Today she'd figure out where he could stay. No sooner had she decided than she reconsidered; the thought of sending him alone into the Vatican left her cold. Looking at him now, soft and pliant in sleep, it was far easier to believe they were almost the same age.

All his sharp angles came from neglect and war, rather than training like hers. Beneath it all, he hid an incredible gentleness. She'd seen it when he'd risked his life for a child. She'd seen it again last night when he knew the right questions to ask to pry away her armor.

Tentatively she reached out to push a lock of hair off his brow, brushing the backs of her fingers against his forehead to feel the heat of his skin. He could be hard, even cruel. And sometimes he used his humor to wound. He enjoyed taunting her with cold one-liners and half-formed smirks. But now . . .

His lashes fluttered and he mumbled something against the pillow.

She yanked her hand back and his hair flopped against his brow once more. What was she doing? Jules Lacroix wasn't a lost puppy. He was a dangerous weapon. He'd proven as much when he'd shown her the kill marks swirling across his skin. It didn't matter how charming he could be; nobody survived a fight to the death with as many demons as he'd killed without their own dark side. And he was a weapon with invisible threads binding him to Baliel. An unparalleled threat to Rome. First and greatest of the demon dukes. Selene could not allow herself to feel anything for Jules. Not until she knew who he really was.

The only reason he was here at all was because for every one of his hard angles, she could show him one of *hers*. Each honed to a razor edge. She wanted him for her purposes, but if she didn't know she could control him, she would never have risked inviting him into the heart of Rome. But, despite everything, she *liked* him. *Dio.* When had her feelings become so inconvenient? Another thing was true too. Cesare was a threat she would protect Jules from so long as he was useful to her.

Crossing the room, she leaned her temple against the window-pane, hoping the chill would seep beneath her skin and calm the heat that still flushed her cheeks. Beyond the glass, Rome was quiet. Quiet as she ever was in those moments before dawn, basilicas and domes illuminated in autumnal hues that fought off the night. It was an *illusion*, this quiet, this . . . *safety*. Because, for the first time in a hundred years or more, Baliel, the first and greatest of the demon dukes, was making his slow, dreadful way toward Rome.

It was an illusion the Vatican lovingly cultivated, paying the price to subdue demons wherever they appeared. Humans were adaptable creatures. Despite the incursions into their world—despite the death—they had achieved a balance in Rome. A tithe paid in blood. It was a lie that was already cracking around the edges, but if anyone could finally shatter the illusion of safety in Rome, it would be Baliel.

There would not be blood enough in all Rome to pay Baliel off. Even if the wards kept him at bay, they weren't infallible. He would get in, and when he did he was powerful enough to wreak all kinds of chaos before they could stop him.

The sky opened and rain streaked the glass, taunting her with the echo of a moment she'd rather forget.

She was glad to be home. She *was*.

But Rome held within her cobbled streets so many painful memories—they weren't always so sharp and near to the surface, but they waited within touching distance. She remembered the freezing rain. It had run in rivulets across her skin as she mounted the steps to the Imperium Bellum's dais. The petrichor scent of cold rain on warm stones had been thick in the air.

She'd fallen to her knees in front of the Imperium.

He'd watched her, bemused.

Behind his shoulder, his bodyguards had stood poised. The woman, Ginevra, towering over six feet tall, was one of Selene's instructors at the Academy. Now she watched Selene with a look so cold, intent to kill. Selene knew she'd find no kindness there.

Only a year later, Ginevra had expired—lost to the dark magic in her blood. She had been cut down in a mercy killing by Mirco, the man who loomed at the Imperium's left hand.

Black as polished walnut wood, Mirco's bald head shone under the lantern light. He hadn't moved since her approach, observing her sagely from beneath lowered brows.

One wrong move and she'd be dead eleven different ways. Ginevra and Mirco were the pinnacle of what an exorcist could be, and despite the trauma of the night, she remembered thinking that she wanted nothing more than to be like them. Even if it damned her family. Even if it ruined her name.

She bent her head and shouted to be heard above the drumbeat of falling rain and the thunder of her own heart crashing against the cage of her ribs. She shouted of treason, shouted of betrayal. At barely eleven years old, Selene had sacrificed that which was irreplaceable—her *family*.

"Imperium, *ignosce me*. And forgive the sins of my father. May God have mercy on his soul."

"He will not."

Cesare Alleva stood. And if Ginevra was six feet, he was taller still, and feared for more than his title. Lord of War. Natural head of the Vatican Order and Prince of the Church. The marble steps seemed to tremble as he descended toward her.

She bowed her head further, hoping he wouldn't see the rogue tears streaking her cheeks. Even though she'd had every reason to reveal what her father had done, she couldn't smother the agony of knowing what her father's future held.

Her father was as good as dead. Her family might still be saved.

Selene was an exorcist in training; she believed in the justness of the Vatican's choices. If they said she was guilty by association, she would bare her neck for the executioner. If they took her family for her father's crimes, she would accept it. But she would not stand *idly* waiting. She'd fight until her last breath to save those she could. "Please, I beg you, forgive my mother and brother. They shouldn't be punished for my father's sins. Please, uncle."

He was silent and she dared glance at him.

He stroked his chin with a thumb. "Because of your loyalty and in . . . acknowledgment . . . of my brother's past endeavors for the empire, I'll spare his wife and son. They will live out the remainder of their lives exiled from Rome."

She held her breath. He sounded as though he'd say more. Maybe . . . ?

"But I can do nothing for Matteo." His words crashed over her. "He'll be crucified at dawn."

Death. And, for her, exile.

Selene closed her eyes against the words.

So ended her ambition. The Academy in Rome was all but the only path to the blood—becoming an exorcist was beyond her reach now. The Imperium gently lifted her chin. In the depths of his eyes she saw the same grief she felt. "You'll join my household. I've already heard great things about your talent, Selene. We need exorcists like the one you'll become."

And despite the chasm in her chest, his words had lit a flame of warmth inside her.

She squeezed her eyes shut, taking a deep, steadying breath. Now was not the time to lose her composure.

Nor could she afford to underestimate her enemy.

Jules shifted in the bed behind her. She turned to see the curve of a bicep, the tousled mop of sleep-mussed hair.

He is not a puppy, she reminded herself. Jules was a *soldier*. He'd seen things she could only imagine. And he'd lost people too.

Before her mind flinched away, she saw Benedetta's lightbulb smile. Then she saw her sightless eyes. The image was there and gone again before she could dismiss it. Sickness twisted her gut.

War was the same. Boys and girls thrust into battle against demons with little more than a flimsy spelled blade. They never stood a chance. She couldn't even remember if conscripts were trained before being dropped into the trenches.

She showered, letting the steam fill the bathroom until condensation trickled down the forest-green tiles.

By the time she finished, Jules still hadn't woken. He'd rolled himself into the middle of her enormous bed, burying himself in feather pillows.

Taking a steadying breath, she tiptoed over to him. Plush jewel-toned rugs covered the herringbone oak. The rich silken strands swallowed her footsteps.

He had one arm flung over his face.

She shook his shoulder, trying to ignore the heat of his skin. It seemed to scald her where it stretched hot and taut over defined muscles. She felt raised scar tissue against her palm and grazed her thumb over a long-healed bullet wound just below his collarbone. Absently she traced her thumb over it again. How many scars could one boy have?

He shifted, and when she looked, his eyes were open and un-readable. She drew back, rubbing the heel of her hand against her thigh.

"Morning."

He pushed himself languidly to one elbow, a dark brow edging up. She couldn't decipher the look.

"What?" she demanded. Heat rose in her cheeks.

But when Jules lightly touched her wrist, all thoughts flew from her mind. He drew her hand close, letting her fingers brush the bullet wound again. He was still heavy-lidded with sleep, one foot still firmly in his dreams.

She shifted closer, tracing the hard line of his shoulder blade to find the healed exit wound. With a delicate fingertip, she measured the difference between life and death. It had exited his left shoul-der, missing his heart.

"You were lucky," she commented softly, not really meaning him to hear.

He smiled, dropping his head so his hair fell around his face. "I was fast."

Selene scoffed and pushed him back an inch with her fingers spread against his chest. She narrowed her eyes as she looked into his. "Nonsense. Nobody's that fast."

Jules's smile tipped higher on one side, showing a flash of teeth before he yawned widely. She covered his mouth with her hand and he blinked, shaking himself awake as he pulled away from her. "Whatever you say, exorcist. You're the expert."

Jules smirked to himself, rolling so he could press his face tight into the pillow to yawn against the cotton. His biceps shifted with the languid motion and she moved off the bed, taking a few long steps back. On his bicep was yet another scar. Brambles like deli-cate calligraphy twisting and snagging across his skin.

She checked her watch to avoid looking at him. "Get up. We've things to do." She reached for the D'Alessandro blades strung from his belt over her bedpost and tossed them on the covers between them, a clear dividing line. *Do not cross.* "I'm taking you to the dark side of Rome tonight. You'll need those. From what I read, you're good with a blade."

Jules was fully awake now, his hand fisting in the sheets to pull them aside.

The swords thumped heavily to the ground. Line. Crossed.

She took an involuntary step back, putting more distance between them. "I read your war record and the desertion report they prepared. It said that even though you earned gun rights with your most recent promotion, Corporal Lacroix, you still preferred to fight with your exorcist-forged blade. Forty kills to a sword—impressive, most would be lucky to outlast their weapon—"

Jules's green eyes lost their warmth. "*Fifty.*"

"Pardon?"

"Fifty kills. One sigil per ten kills. Five sigils per blade. Fifty kills. Believe me, I'd remember. Miscalculate and you've got a broken blade and an angry demon who *just* watched you kill a buddy."

Her lashes lowered in admission. He stalked across the room, throwing open his case. The powerful muscles in his back flexed. He pulled out a shirt and reached inside for something she couldn't see.

"I know, you know." She was surprised by the gentleness of her own voice. He half turned to face her, a notebook in his hand. "You were a valiant soldier. Your superior, Sergeant Bachelet, spoke highly of you."

His face paled, his expression devoid of the usual spark that lit his eyes. She desperately wanted to take back whatever she'd said wrong. "Jules—" It was the first time she'd said his name instead of Lacroix. It felt different on her tongue, rounder than the sharp angles of his surname.

"*Don't.*" He dropped his face into one hand, staring blankly through his fingers.

Selene bit her lip and left without another word. Once the bedroom door shut behind her, she slid down the wall and dropped her forehead against her knees. There was near silence from inside the room and she tried to convince herself that was all she heard.

Silence. But that would be a lie.

Instead, she heard the muffled sound of Jules crying.

Later, a knock came at her door.

Finally. Only liquid espresso direct to her veins could set the day on track. She needed it as dearly as she needed her next breath.

But before she could move, the double doors swung open. The visitor was not, in fact, the catering staff. Her uncle raised one dark brow, observing her position on the herringbone floor. This was not Cesare Alleva, uncle, this was the Imperium Bellum at her door, dressed in his vestments of power, flanked by his latest bodyguards.

"Lovers' quarrel?"

Wordlessly she scrambled to her feet, spine stiffening at his unexpected presence. Before she could think of anything to say, the bedroom doors behind her opened, and Jules stepped through. He reached for her, one large hand spread over her hip. "Of course not." His voice carried a touch of insolence.

Selene swallowed.

Jules folded into a low, exaggerated bow. "Imperium Bellum."

His shirt was open, showing a stretch of smooth tanned chest while managing to hide the marks on his arms. Scars where Eliot would have none.

"Eliot," said her uncle finally.

Cesare's dark eyes slid to his exorcists, the look enough to have them backing up to position themselves outside the door. He stepped around Jules, pausing on his way to the armchair, his eyes following a trail of discarded clothing through the double doors to her bedroom.

The corner of Jules's lips tugged up in a crooked smirk.

Dio. That look boded very ill indeed.

CHAPTER TWENTY

Cesare Alleva circled the room. A predator.

"So kind of you to visit on my return," Jules said conversationally. "Or are you planning to send me away again, personally this time?"

Selene gave him a *look*. One that hinted at how brutally she'd murder him if he didn't shut up right now.

He shut up.

Cesare was tall—almost Jules's height—and broad at the shoulder. He had the same dark hair as Selene, but unlike her, he had eyes that were nearly black. Their unfathomable depths made it difficult to tell what he was thinking.

He flicked a bored glance at the messed-up bed.

Jules hooked his thumb in his pocket and waited to see what Cesare would do. The moment he'd heard him outside the door, his well-honed sense of danger had sparked to life. Cesare had personally exiled Eliot, which was no small thing.

"Eliot. What brings you back to Rome?"

Uncertain what answer to give, Jules remained silent. Eliot hadn't told him why he'd been expelled from Rome. It could make this meeting difficult to navigate.

He could play it safe—be *polite*. But that didn't suit him at all.

The Imperium Bellum was a handsome man, as forbidding as he was tall. Calloused hands attested to long hours spent training. This man had not let power make him soft. Rather the opposite. Power had tempered Cesare like a blade—and by impersonating Eliot, Jules had slipped into the shoes of his enemy.

With effortless dignity, Cesare folded his tall frame into the large armchair. Beside the Imperium Bellum's immaculately shined shoe sat a button from Jules's shirt that had rolled under the armchair the night before. Jules followed the trail of forgotten clothes with his eyes, and not for the first time, he wondered what was real and what had been a dream. He thought he remembered waking with the honeyed dawn to find Selene in his arms, but when he woke again, she'd been totally composed.

Cesare tapped the armrest with his index finger. It was the only outward sign of his impatience.

"I was under the impression you approved my return?" Jules said, curtailing the lengthening silence.

Cesare adjusted his attention, regarding Selene impassively. "Is that so?"

Jules had to figure out why Eliot had been exiled. To protect his own neck, because to survive he had to make sure he made no misstep, but also because he was *curious*. He wanted to know everything there was to know about Selene, and as much as she might deny it, Eliot was a crucial fragment of her past.

Selene crossed her arms loosely. "I don't know if you recall our telephone conversation, uncle. You told me to say hello to Eliot, remember?"

"When I said to say hello, I did not expect you would take that to mean bring him back to Rome." His voice was soft and low; if there was any recrimination, it was only in his eyes.

"He's my second on this case. This case is not done. Besides, *I* didn't know *you* sent Eliot away." Selene raised a shoulder, eyes narrowing. "Perhaps this is less my fault than yours, uncle." Heat blotched the high angles of her cheekbones, and Jules could almost hear the angry thunder of her heart as she stared Cesare down.

He couldn't look away. This countered so much he thought he knew about Selene; a consummate professional, and utterly respectful of her uncle and his position.

"How could you?"

Jules felt a stirring of jealousy. Was this Selene's defense of Eliot? The *real* Eliot?

After a moment's stand-off, Cesare sighed heavily and dropped his gaze. "You're right. I'm sorry. You were children. I didn't think your attachment was so strong. I . . . miscalculated."

Selene seemed mollified at that.

"You sure did." Jules indicated Selene with a nod. "Selene's incredible, sir. Seeing her in action . . . I'm more in love than ever." He glanced at her.

Selene had her full lower lip caught between her teeth, and when their eyes met, she looked quickly away.

He added quietly, "And if you'd seen her in Nice, you'd be so proud."

At least, he *should* be. But Jules wasn't so sure. Cesare hesitated, eyes flicking to Selene. "I am."

"Her power is a credit to your training."

Cesare's jaw tightened, a muscle flickering beneath smooth skin. When he finally smiled, it was the barest twitch of his lips. "I appreciate that. Eliot, Selene, I have a meeting. We will catch up again soon, no doubt." A promise and a threat.

Jules watched the Imperium leave with narrowed eyes. Returning to the bedroom, Jules threw open the suitcase—unconcerned by the buckles scraping against a beautifully beaded beetle sitting on a wallpaper fern—and stilled when his fingertips brushed the hard leather cover of the notebook he'd first glimpsed among his things last night.

He heard Selene's footsteps before her furious hiss. "What the fuck," Selene breathed, "was *that*?"

He flicked a glance at her. "Your turn."

She raised a brow in question.

"I want to see the library. *Now*. I've had enough of playing with the elites." He didn't even attempt to keep his voice steady. "Much as I enjoy rubbing shoulders with Imperiums, you have a deal to uphold."

He was still furious. He'd schooled his expression, not wanting her to see how effectively she'd hurt him. He wanted to slink away and lick his wounds in peace. But so long as he was here, in this place, he wouldn't be allowed the freedom to do so.

He also wanted a smoke. Preferably one of Farah's slender black cigarettes.

But they were gone, and so was she.

The casual way Selene had brought up Farah had been an unwelcome reminder. An intrusion even. He'd let Selene and her world swallow him whole. But . . . Kian was still dead. Farah, dead. And Jules was more alone than ever. No matter how brightly Rome glittered, no matter how beautiful Selene was when she smiled at him . . . *he* was more alone than ever. He no longer even had his name.

Selene observed him with a military eye, as though assessing risk. Lashes lowering to hide her light eyes, she said, "Fine."

He nodded but didn't immediately follow her, turning the

notebook over in his hand. It wasn't Eliot's notebook as he'd thought. This one had a marbled cover and a spine of stiff leather scrawled with the notation *vol. ii.*

"What's that?"

He gave her a sharp, irritated glance. She was as silent as a cat.

He opened it at random. His eyes settled on the page, widening as he tried not to drop the book. He knew that man. Recognized those eyes captured in dark Indian ink. In his memory, they burned so blue they veined the skin around them black.

The Duke of Briars.

Selene's breath caught in her throat and she stepped up behind him, trembling fingers reaching to touch the page. Her breath ghosted against his bicep, warming his shirtsleeve as she let out a shuddering sigh. "My father drew this."

He swallowed, taking in the expert lines. The looping, confident script.

Each line was delivered with the self-assurance of someone committing fundamental truths to the page. Only one who wrote like this could create such a daughter.

Jules turned, the book between them. Again they were too close. But he could tell she wasn't really there; her amber eyes were utterly distant.

He offered it to her.

She snatched her hand back as though burned, tapered fingers curling against her chest. "I— No." But her eyes were still drawn to the page.

He rubbed his thumb over the picture of Baliel, then turned the page. The next page was filled with tiny script. The one after that contained a sketch of the Pantheon, streaks of light captured in the spaces between dark pen strokes rendered in faded black ink.

"Wait," Selene said quietly.

When he looked up, her cheeks were bloodless. He wanted to reach out to her, but knew it would not be welcome. He spread a protective hand over the notebook, concealing it from her sight. "Is this too much?"

She dragged her eyes up to his. "My father's dead."

"I know."

Her eyes went half-lidded. "Seeing his handwriting, it's like seeing a ghost."

They stood like that another moment, and Selene drew a steadying breath. Finally she nodded. When he turned another page, a scrap of paper fluttered out.

Selene snatched it from the air, holding it as though the ink might burn. "It's from Eliot. He says that my father never allowed him to see the writing inside and he respected that, even after his death. He took it from his office before—" Her voice trembled.

Jules eased the paper from her hand, surprised by her lack of resistance.

Selene,
Matteo never allowed me to read these pages, and I still have not.

I retrieved the notebook from Matteo's office before his execution. Before they stripped it. Before my exile. Even as a child, I knew the words on these pages were dangerous. Matteo did not trust them with anyone else in life, nor would he in death. But now that Baliel has returned, I suspect you will need your father's guidance.

Eliot D'Alessandro

Jules flipped to near the beginning of the book and began to read.

> *I must untangle truth from dogma. I refuse to blindly accept the words of a demon.*
> *~~Even when my gut says he is telling the truth~~.*

Jules frowned, rubbing the aged paper with his thumb. The indigo-blue ink had faded noticeably, but other sections appeared to have been added later in black Indian ink. The final sentence, struck through, was one such example.

It suggested to Jules a man at war with himself.

Selene made no move to stop him. Glancing sideways at her, he saw her eyes trailing the words as she read over his shoulder.

> *On the day God stepped into our world, we teetered on the brink of death.*
> *Rome burned. Countless died. But God would not watch His people suffer. Accounts of that day tell of how God appeared in St. Peter's Square, prepared for battle. He was immensely tall and powerful and nothing like our scholars or priests had said. He was so much more. Beyond anything humanity could have imagined.*
> *He was God, for who else but God would appear to protect humanity from demons?*
> *Who else but God ever could?*
> *He gave His life for humanity that day, our Deathless God. Now He exists in perfect stasis within the Vatican. Neither fully living, nor fully dead. And we have learned our lesson well. We will be ruthless;*

we will be cruel. Demons must not be allowed a second chance to kill God.

Jules turned the notebook, reading a line of text written vertically in the margins.

We became the very thing Valeria and the Kairos feared we would become.
Demons cannot be given an opportunity to finish what they began two centuries ago.
Si vis bellum para pacem. If you want peace, prepare for war.

M. A. 15 September MMVII

And on the next page, in tiny writing around the edges of an earlier drawing of the Vatican obelisk:

In the beginning, ~~there were humans and demons~~.
There must be more.
In the beginning, there were two worlds. Ours and theirs.
Demons wielded unimaginable power, power that ran through their veins like blood. We were blind. Ever ignorant to all but ourselves, we were unaware of the visitors who oh so rarely walked among us. Unaware of the fissure between our worlds.
Once, demons were united.
The demon king wished to protect humanity from outside influence. Selected for his unparalleled power, he was considered a great leader, beloved by all. But he

had a secret. Sometimes he walked among humans. It was on one of these visits that he fell in love.

Valeria, Duchess of Razors, knew that given half a chance, we could destroy her people. She saw the greed and cruelty of humanity and believed that we did not deserve more from demons than we afforded each other. She visited the human world, each time hoping to witness something that would change her mind. Something redeeming. Each time she left disappointed.

She was the first Kairos. To the Kairos, our world was a vast resource to be utilized. Humanity a threat.

The Elysian faction formed in opposition, and ancient grievances festered in the name of a new rallying call. To the Elysian, we were a curiosity.

And still Valeria of the Kairos would visit Rome, where the boundary between the worlds was thinnest.

She saw nothing worth changing her way of thinking. Her loathing grew.

Until she fell in love.

But it was too little, too late. Their war spilled over into Rome. And still it burns.

Ad pacem. Toward peace.

M. A. 28 March MMXV

Our family motto rings truer for me now than ever. Animas nostras pro populo. Our lives souls for the people.

Selene's brows were drawn together as she stared down at the notebook, consternation pressing out her lower lip in a slight pout.

"Duchess of Razors?" Jules murmured. "A friend of the Duke of Briars, I assume?"

Selene shook her head slowly. "I have never heard of such a creature. There are only twelve demon dukes, but each of them is named. Each of them is known."

She reached for the book and then hesitated. Changing her mind, she leaned closer. Her hair smelled of orange blossom. "I am also confused by this." She hovered her smallest finger over the word *Kairos*. "I do not know of this. *Elysian* too. They aren't taught."

"But your father knew."

She shook her head, eyes clouding with pain. "He might have known, or maybe he was mad. We'll never know because he's dead." She straightened, forcibly sweeping away any hint of pain in favor of a cool mask. "Put it away. You wanted to visit the library, so let's go."

The marble halls of the Vatican rang with silence. Jules felt it like a physical thing pressed to his skin. Selene led them deeper into the complex, through antechambers and frescoed hallways, and the hairs on the back of his neck rose.

He flicked a glance at Selene's watch. Barely midday. Why was it so damn quiet? It reminded him of the orphanage at midnight. The stark hard beds had been arrayed in military rows. The breathing, snuffling, and snoring a constant litany until you stepped out into the chilly hall. Then it was cold and silent. But this was different. Where the orphanage was full of blossoming life, this place was opulent but putrid with the scent of death.

Jules raised a gloved hand, touching his nose. This wasn't the stench of other exorcists, redolent with their own blood even in their crisp military uniforms. Even Selene smelled faintly of her own blood where she'd fought and bled, but it didn't bother him as much. Selene's heels clicked as she strode ahead of him.

Halting, she glanced back with an arched brow. *What is it?* the impatient look said. *Idiot.*

He had no answer. It was like nothing else. "Where are we?" he asked hoarsely.

Her brows crumpled in irritation. "St. Peter's Basilica?"

Selene was the only person he'd ever met who could say something so patiently it circled right back around to impatience again.

"I know *that*," he snapped.

"We're about halfway to the library. It's on the other side of St. Peter's."

Conversation over, she continued walking.

He lowered his hand cautiously, taking a breath of rancid air. Perhaps it wasn't a scent at all . . . maybe it was the atmosphere of this place?

Selene pivoted on her heel the second he stopped moving. "What is it now?" she snapped.

"Death," he said, his voice low and gravelly. He cleared his throat. "Don't you smell it?"

She looked around, as though she might find a corpse hanging from a chandelier. "No?"

"How much farther?"

"Not far." Her expression cycled through annoyance to concern.

He swallowed. "Good."

"Are you all right?" she asked. Reaching for his hand, she added his name in a whisper. "Jules?"

He grasped it, holding it tightly in his own as he pulled her down the hall. If they were almost there, well and good, but the smell was stronger around the next bend and he reared back from it, fingers tightening on Selene's.

Her cheeks paled from his hard grip, but she didn't make a sound.

Jules pressed a hand to his nose, clamping his teeth over a leather-clad finger in hope of stopping his guts from coming up his throat. His heart thundered and he pulled her back, turning in place, trapped by the reek of desolation, of death, of all those things and worse.

"What are you doing here?" The harsh voice crashed over him like a wave.

Some of the panic receded as he straightened his shoulders.

You're Eliot D'Alessandro, he reminded himself.

Selene turned. "Excuse me?"

"Oh, Captain Alleva. I'm sorry, I didn't recognize you."

The liveried guard stepped closer, circling them, eyes on their joined hands. On Selene's bleached knuckles. Jules tried to loosen his grip, but his fingers felt stiff. His heart still thundered as though he'd run a fast mile.

"I suppose I can turn a blind eye to your mistake." Selene moved in front of Jules, their fingers still loosely linked behind her back. "*This time*," she added haughtily.

"Thank you, Captain. Unfortunately he is not allowed here." The guard nodded to Jules. "Authorized personnel only this close to the *Cor Cordium*."

"The *Cor Cordium*?" Jules echoed faintly.

The guard gave him a strange look, hand tightening on his wicked black-hafted spear.

Selene straightened. "I think you're very much mistaken; *however* . . . we'll go the long way." She forced Jules into motion. Coaxing him to take one step, then another. She wrapped her hands around his arm so she could pull him along with all her strength.

She kept her expression haughty. "Come on, Eliot. The nice guard wants a demotion."

The words broke through his daze and he gave a soft gasp of

a laugh. The resulting quick pull of rancid air almost made him vomit, but it was worth it. The strain on her face eased and she met his eyes, a small smile stealing across her mouth. "What?"

"Nothing."

Her smile melted away. "What *was* that?"

"I don't know," he breathed. "I really, truly don't know."

Selene pulled Jules along, worry coiling in her gut at his slow pace. It was as though he'd lost his strength. Usually she strode through here quickly as though she had somewhere else to be. But in truth, she hated these hallways. She tried not to look too closely at the columns, the shadows they cast. Shadows long and deep enough to conceal a small girl.

No . . .

Selene tried not to remember, she really did, but even as she hardened her mask and lengthened her stride, the memories came for her throat.

Memories of soft bare feet on marble, in a hallway where she had no business being.

Memories of long ago.

If her teachers caught her on this side of the Vatican, Selene knew they'd be *furious*. Morning was meant for reading, they said. For writing, symbology, first aid, sometimes even—dreaded—geography. Being discovered near the training rooms meant punishment. But she was small enough to easily melt into the shadows.

A crisp tap of boots made her press her back to a column. Footsteps passed her as she owned the dark corners. Edging around the column, Selene risked a glance at the retreating figure, realizing with a jolt it was her father.

It was unusual for him to be here. His offices were on the other side of the Vatican entirely.

Curious, Selene quietly ran after him.

He only looked back once, and even that was almost one time too many. She was slow to react, only ducking behind a draped velvet curtain at the last possible second. Her heart skittered with excitement and maybe some nerves. Then she dashed to catch him again.

St. Peter's Basilica had grown terribly quiet. As ominous shadows deepened, Selene noticed it. Usually the vast marble halls echoed with every tiny sound. An unpleasant chill started in her bare toes and tickled up her neck, and she resolved to shout out to her father soon.

When she spotted a familiar painting, large enough to fill an entire stretch of wall, her heart climbed her throat. She knew this particular hallway. Her father was going to the heart of the Vatican.

Toward *the Deathless God.*

Selene fought a shiver at the thought of one place within the Vatican she'd never been, and would be glad never to go. The thought filled her with terror. Most of the time Selene could make herself forget that she shared a roof with a real god. That His divine presence filled this place. She had heard stories of what happened to people who looked upon Him, that all but the Vatican's anointed would burn at the sight.

When she stepped around the corner, Selene drew breath to yell for her dad. Instead, she clamped both hands over her mouth. Two guards lay flat and a pair of huge double doors yawned open. Only blackness beyond.

"Papa?" she whispered, but her voice sounded thready in the vast space. She tiptoed carefully past the nearest guard and peeked in the door. She pretended she couldn't see the spreading puddle of blood.

They were only *sleeping* . . .

"*Selene!*" Florentina stood in the courtyard ahead of them, a longbow in one hand.

Selene jolted out of her reminiscences. "What?"

"Are you all right?" Jules breathed softly.

She nodded, her smile bitter at the edges.

Kindness wasn't something she deserved. Not from anybody really, but especially him. Not after earlier. The pain on his face when she'd mentioned his dead superior was still vivid in her memory. She made a mental note not to stumble into his grief like that again.

Florentina grinned toothily, eyes sparking. Selene's guard immediately flew up as they stepped into the cool air and she saw the others in Gabriel's team similarly armed. Then she realized they were in training gear, not the official Vatican black.

"Perfect timing." Florentina smiled. "We should make sure you're back in form after gallivanting around France."

The second they got outside, Jules's color improved. The pale cast washed from his features. He smiled easily at Florentina, though Selene could feel his muscles tense beneath her hand. But he needn't have worried; Florentina wasn't speaking to him.

"I was *working*," Selene replied dryly, "not on a wine tour."

Florentina grinned, looking around at the others. "Oh yes, *working*." She gave an exaggerated wink. "Curses and demons that don't even qualify for a number don't count, Selene."

Selene stepped away from Jules, closing the distance between herself and Florentina. She smiled as she looked into her eyes.

"It's Captain Alleva to you, Florentina. We're not at the Academy anymore."

"I noticed."

Selene stiffened. What did *that* mean?

Florentina didn't make her wait. "We don't see you training anymore, do we? We don't even know if you're keeping your skills sharp. You only train alone, we hear. Which would be fine. If your subordinates didn't keep ending up dead."

"Or maimed," added Chiara, an artificer.

Florentina nodded affably. "Quite."

Pressing her lips into a tight smile, Selene stepped around Florentina. "I don't owe you anything."

Florentina moved quickly and Selene shifted, tensing for an attack. Instead, Florentina blocked Jules's path. "What about you, D'Alessandro? Don't you want to join us for a bout or two?"

Jules smiled easily. "I kind of do actually. Given I really *was* in France for years—" The color drained from Florentina's face at his quiet tone. "Fighting, what did you say? *Curses and demons that don't even qualify for a number?* Yes, I'm *definitely* tempted."

"*Eliot,*" Selene said warningly.

A beat passed before Jules tore his eyes from Florentina, catching her gaze. "Fine."

Selene pivoted on her heel. This was no time to be drawn into a training bout. Jules had already said he wouldn't touch a weapon; what was he going to do in the ring against Academy-trained exorcists? Much as she hated admitting it, Florentina was good. Not so good as Selene, of course, but still a strong opponent.

"Scared?" Florentina taunted.

Selene stopped, boots skidding on the slick cobbles.

Jules touched her shoulders. "Selene . . ."

But Florentina wasn't done. "Are you afraid I'll kick your ass?" she asked sweetly. Selene could picture her smile, though she resisted the urge to turn.

"No," Selene bit out.

Jules chafed her biceps, thumbs making small circles.

"Or maybe . . . *maybe* you're worried Eliot's improved? He's a foot taller than you now. With *that* reach—"

"I was the *best* in our class." Selene turned, shoving Jules aside so she could see Florentina.

"I don't deny it. But I want to know if you're *still* the best."

Florentina nocked an arrow, drawing it to look along the shaft at Selene.

Jules's muscles tensed, but Selene didn't move, only narrowing her eyes. *Oh well.* Maybe this was good. Burning muscles would force her mind away from dark memories and distract her from her guilt.

And maybe she'd get her ass kicked—no less than she deserved— although she doubted it. The only one capable of hurting her was her dead father and his words from beyond the grave. She hadn't even been able to *touch* the notebook. Jules had it tucked into his inside pocket against his skin.

Why had her father gone to the *Cor Cordium* that day? Why had he removed the spear from God's body and broken every rule they'd ever been taught? Every rule he'd ever taught her?

Before Florentina could form another jagged taunt, Selene spread her hands. "All right, let's find out."

Florentina's eyes sparked with challenge and she let the bow-string loosen. "You'll let me pick your opponent?" She looked around, gesturing broadly at their classmates training around them.

Selene didn't follow Florentina's eyes. "You won't fight me yourself?"

"Where's the fun in that?" Florentina asked, teeth flashing in a grin. "I want to see you beat Eliot."

Around the courtyard attention sharpened on their conversation. The clang and grunt of combat training died as the others stopped pretending not to care.

Selene looked around. They were dying to see her beaten.

Jules drew a breath, following her eyes. "I don't mind." He smiled slowly. "My love, it can't be any more strenuous than last nigh—"

"Fine!" she shouted over him. Someone wolf-whistled.

Jules grinned. He seemed to be enjoying this a little too much.

CHAPTER TWENTY-ONE

Jules had let himself forget that the Vatican was the beating heart of the empire's military power. A mistake he wouldn't make again. Around the training yard pairs of exorcists sparred with quick, decisive movements and an array of deadly weapons—not a practice sword to be seen.

A covered walkway wrapped the entire courtyard, edged by an impressive colonnade. And in one corner a great skeletal tree stretched toward the open sky. Dormant, not dead. Waiting for spring.

Selene stepped onto the sand covering the flagstones, glancing at him. Jules tried to ignore the promise in her eyes—she'd make him pay for that. "Weapon of choice?"

At his hip were the D'Alessandro blades. Deadly and tempting. "Hand to hand."

She scoffed. "You want us to pummel each other to pulp, *cuore mio*?"

Oh, so it would be like that. He rubbed his jaw, glancing at the weapons arrayed along the walls. Pausing before a racked great sword, Jules was briefly tempted by its sheer size. Neither slim like the D'Alessandro blades nor stocky like the swords he'd fought with on the front, it was a different beast entirely. But wielding that five-foot abomination would make his inevitable loss to Selene and her sleek black blade even more devastating. Next, he ghosted his fingertips over a pair of vicious-looking poniards.

"You'd forgo your reach?" Selene asked innocently, leaning around him to look at the display.

He grinned. "I don't need my reach to beat you, *vita mia.*"

A light dusting of pink graced her high cheekbones and Jules smothered a smile. *Point.*

She spread her hands, walking backward into the middle of the courtyard. "Oh, don't get me wrong, it wouldn't *help* you. Only make this fight more interesting."

Her confidence was magnetic. Unable to take his eyes off her, he followed, spotting an exorcist who held a quarterstaff across his shoulders. Jules raised a hand.

The exorcist tossed it over and someone whispered, *He's not using the D'Alessandro blades?*

Jules tested the balance of the staff. At seven feet long, it had a heft to it that he liked. The hard oak had been worn smooth by many hands. From the notches beneath his fingers, Jules knew this staff had faced a sword before. His fingers flexed. He had no experience fighting with a staff. They weren't suited to war. Much better for single combat. Still, it was nothing more than studded wood, and the last thing on earth that would hurt the Butcher of Rome.

"I'll use this." He raised one brow at Selene.

She nodded, a smile playing at the corner of her mouth. "A quarterstaff. How quaint."

Jules chuckled. "I thought you were concerned about my reach." He gave the staff an experimental spin.

"Now you're all reach and no bite," she said, amused.

Maybe, he mentally conceded.

As they met in the middle, she drew her sword from her back.

Before he let anyone see him bleed, Jules would show her what he could do. He wanted Selene to *see* him. And he'd do it with a humble quarterstaff.

She circled, sword leveled against her metal armguard.

He winked and blew her a kiss.

Selene tilted her head, battling a smile. "Don't be cocky, *amore mio.*" She laughed, a soft sound that made the people gathered around them fall quiet. He spared them a quick glance. Even more had come to watch.

The moment he looked away, she struck. *Fast.*

He moved before conscious thought, bending away from her blade. If he hadn't shaved that morning, she would've had some of his stubble. As it was, the blade whistled past his chin with nothing to spare.

"Oops." Selene twirled the blade, shifting onto her back foot.

Jules pressed his thumb to his chin, checking for blood. He wasn't bleeding. No thanks to her. He laughed darkly, subtly shifting his stance. He wouldn't wait a second time.

But Selene didn't give him a moment to take ownership of the bout. She met him halfway and they were dancing.

Jules felt her blade graze his skin. He spun the quarterstaff to divert her sword and stepped inside her guard. She twirled away, her hair catching and glinting in the dilute winter light. He followed, powerless to resist even when it brought his throat right to her blade.

"Check."

"Different game, *tesoro mio.*"

"Not so different," she whispered.

He pushed her hair out of the way and leaned in, letting her blade slide along the staff until he was close enough to brush a kiss against her neck. Her pale skin barely hid the delicate blue veins and he could feel the hurried steps of her pulse. "We really need to sell this thing," he breathed. Then before she could finish him, he fell back.

When she followed his feint, sensing an opening, he came up within her guard from beneath.

She met him with a dagger. He hadn't seen her draw it, but that didn't matter because suddenly it was there, catching his quarter-staff at her throat between her crossed blades. Their noses almost touched. His muscles, taut with strain, trembled against her incredible strength. This close she was more dangerous than beautiful. More deadly than alluring. And yet he was nowhere near strong enough to resist. With the eyes of everyone on them and the game afoot, he leaned forward and captured her lips in a searing kiss.

Her mouth softened beneath his, and for the briefest moment she kissed him back.

Then her boot met his chest and his back met the stone.

Worth it. The winter-gray sky turned overhead.

Selene smiled as she leaned over him and her hair brushed his cheeks. "Do you forfeit, *luce dei miei occhi?*"

Selene three, Jules two. Not satisfied with merely kicking his ass, she'd wielded the endearment like a knife.

Light of my eyes, she called him. He filed that one away.

Jules groaned. "Yeah. But only because I already got the prize."

"Oh?"

"A kiss from the *principessa.*"

She laughed. "You're concussed."

He grimaced, rubbing the back of his head. "Maybe."

Heavy silence filled the courtyard. Dragging his eyes from

Selene, Jules glanced around at the shocked expressions, noting the way these trained exorcists now held their weapons in a white-knuckle grip.

Florentina's skin was alabaster pale.

Selene stepped closer, her fingers gliding up his neck to rest against his jaw before she brushed the softest, sweetest kiss to his mouth. A kiss no more substantial than the touch of butterfly wings. All that ruined the moment was that everyone watching thought Selene was kissing Eliot, when it was most undeniably Jules Lacroix.

Still holding his jaw, Selene flicked a bored glance Florentina's way. "Are we done here?"

The Vatican library was everything a library should be. A thousand gilt-edged books across three levels. A thousand more bound in stiff leather. And even some covered in enough jewels to feed everyone in Nice for a year. Selene walked ahead of him through the stacks, tipping her head back to look at the frescoed ceiling.

Jules pushed his hands into his pockets, not hurrying. "You said we're going somewhere tonight?" *The dark side of Rome.*

"I have a compact to witness," she said as she marched across the inlaid marble, following the reference number clutched in her hand. She made no effort to explain what that *meant*. "And maybe there'll be answers to be had, if we're lucky and play our cards right."

They passed a series of enormous portraits. Imperiums past, Jules supposed. Each appeared serious and intimidating, but he paused to read the plaque below one that looked a little different to the rest.

Selene turned, looking at the portrait he was interested in. "He was the last Imperium Politikos who was not also an exorcist."

Jules nodded slowly. *That's* what it was.

He found the portrait of a slightly younger Adriano de Sanctis, who seemed to have become less austere as he aged. Jules was glad not to have met the man when he was younger. "Does he still . . . you know . . . kill demons?"

"His role is political. He can still do it, but he will never be deployed by the Imperium Bellum."

"Why?"

"They're technically on the same level. Cesare has no power over him and vice versa."

Shallow winter light slanted in through a tall window, landing on a more ornately framed portrait of a shrunken old man whose bushy brows obscured eyes that had sunk into the dark hollows of his skull.

"But this guy does, right? The Exorcist Primus." Jules leaned closer to read the brass plaque, whistling below his breath. The painting was over fifty years old—no way he was still around. "If he was alive, that is."

"He *is* alive," Selene said simply. "And yes, commanding the Imperium Politikos is his only external means of power. The rest lies within the Vatican walls. In the hierarchy itself."

Jules whistled again. "I hate to guess how he looks now."

Selene crinkled her nose. "Much like . . . *that*. But even older."

Grimacing, Jules turned back to her. "So, your uncle's one of the most powerful men alive. And, even better, he still looks it."

She raised her eyes to the heavens, but Jules felt sure he could see a dimple in her cheek as she bit back a smile. Leaning around a stack to make sure they were alone, she said, "Yes and no. Yes, particularly given he's become the mouthpiece for the Exorcist Primus, who hasn't been seen outside his apartments for years."

Selene pulled out a book and flipped through the pages, but it was clear she wasn't really seeing it. Across the vast room, a librarian who looked almost as old as the Exorcist Primus was shuffling back and forth from a library cart, shelving books one at a time.

"And, no?"

Selene pressed her lips together, and for a long moment he thought she wouldn't tell him. Then: "When they're recalled, the college are more powerful still." Even bathed in pale winter light, Selene seemed to shiver. "Individually the Extremum Filum fall below the Imperiums, but collectively they have more power than anyone."

"Even the Exorcist Primus?"

Half turning away from him, Selene pushed her hair behind her ear. "Their power begins and ends with the Exorcist Primus. The college is only called to appoint a new one when the old one dies. Otherwise they stay . . . elsewhere." The look in her eyes changed and he could see her shutting down.

Secrecy was a way of life here, Jules was beginning to learn.

Shoving the book back onto its shelf—still upside down—Selene walked away, gliding her finger along the reference numbers.

"What are the Extremum Filum? Have I met one?"

"No. And pray you never do." She looked ashen.

Jules wondered what could frighten the Butcher of Rome.

"You see . . ." Selene continued in a measured tone. "There is a threshold we exorcists must not pass. When an exorcist exceeds their own limits, one of three things can happen. In the best case, they're killed swiftly *before* they lose themselves. Or they can become less than human and little more than a monster. They must then be killed by their fellow exorcists. Sometimes this mercy killing happens too late and lives have already been lost."

"Obviously that's the worst case."

Her expression twisted. "No."

But her willingness to speak about the secrets of her world seemed to be drying up. Before she could retreat farther down the row of bookshelves he pulled her around by the hand. "Selene, you can't leave it there." He smiled to hide his frustration, stepping closer. "You said there were three things. Where do the Extremum Filum come in?"

She hesitated, then continued. "The worst case is you use too much power, but it happens slowly and there is time for the Vatican to act. In this instance, an exorcist can be arrested at the precise tipping point before becoming something completely other. But it is no life at all. I would rather die."

Her eyes looked haunted.

Jules felt as though a vast hand pressed against his chest.

"Here," she breathed, scrunching the paper in her palm.

The line of shelves was full to the brim with great, bound books. Their spines were stamped with dozens of French cities. Jules walked along the row, tracing city names with his fingertip: Cannes, Lyon, Marseilles, Paris, Toulouse.

He retraced his steps. "Nice isn't here," he breathed.

Selene came closer, head bent to read the spines. "What do you mean?"

"Nice is *missing*." Jules set his hands flat on the empty shelf. Folding almost double, he swallowed a yell. "The records are already gone."

CHAPTER TWENTY-TWO

O n returning from the library, they took a different route back to the rooms. Jules paused at the skyway between Selene's building and the one next door, where a trio of arched windows decorated each side of the covered stone footbridge. To his right, the Basilica's great dome dominated the skyline.

When he caught up to Selene, she was patting her pockets in search of the key—an ornate monstrosity tasseled with pale blue silk. Each leaf of the double door was decorated with a coat of arms. *Her* coat of arms, he realized, reading the motto from Matteo Alleva's journal. *Animas nostras pro populo.* Our lives for the people.

His eyes trailed over the spread wing of the lion rampant. Rearing on its hind legs, it dominated the left-hand side of the shield. And above its noble head, a crown. On the right-hand side was a serpent wrapped around a sheaf of keys.

Inside Selene's rooms, they parted ways and Jules strolled into the sunroom. He withdrew Matteo's notebook and thumbed through the pages. Noticing a tear, he ran his index finger along the gutter where the pages were sewn into the binding, and felt a ragged edge.

A page had been removed. He tossed the book aside.

Sighing, Jules slouched into a chair. So much for Rome and her libraries. *Another* severed thread.

Selene walked in, carrying an envelope and wearing a frown.

He watched as she read the card, her expression unchanging, and tried to see beyond the mask. Figure out what she was thinking. Annoyed? Bored? When she ran her fingernails so firmly across the paper's crease that it threatened to fatigue and tear, he rubbed his hand over his mouth, smothering a smile. *Definitely* annoyed.

She caught him watching her. "It seems as though we have no choice but to attend the stupid Carnival ball."

Jules raised a brow in question and she tossed the card to him. Snatching it out of the air, he flipped it open.

The Lord Chamberlain is commanded by Her Imperial Majesty, Ofelia Augustus, Empress of the Holy Vatican Empire, to invite Captain Selene Alleva, Heir of House Alleva, to the Empress's Carnival Masquerade held on Saturday in honor of His Holiness Alexander II, Exorcist Primus of Rome.

"I don't see why I have to go. They only commanded the heir of House Alleva."

Selene ignored his smirk. "*Cesare* said. It wasn't a request." She sighed, rubbing a finger between her brows.

"He said I had to come?"

"Look underneath."

Jules flipped it. On the back was a personalization in sloped handwriting reminiscent of Selene's that had to belong to Cesare.

Eliot & Selene

The Imperium Bellum had pressed so hard on the *t* that the ink bled. "Oh."

When Jules handed the invitation back to her, his knuckles brushed against her chilly fingertips. Ever since their training match, he'd felt the electricity of awareness any time Selene was near. He smiled to himself as the fight played behind his eyes. Unlike every teasing word, every *amore mio*, the kiss had been real.

He *wanted* her.

It had been a long time since he'd wanted anyone like that.

The telephone's shrill ring split the quiet. Ruefully, he watched her go. Later, he followed the sound of her voice and found Selene curled in her armchair with her feet tucked up under her. Seeing him, she extended the phone his way. "It's Jules Lacroix on the line." She flashed a smile.

"What?" He scowled, leaning into the receiver. "Hello?"

"Hello," Eliot replied, voice crackling across the connection. "I couldn't exactly call as myself."

"But you used my name? Are you a complete idiot?" Selene pulled the handset away, but he snatched it back, ignoring her *look*. "Don't get yourself killed using my name, D'Alessandro."

Eliot snorted. "Likewise."

A stretch of uncomfortable silence made him feel almost as bad as Selene's death glare. Jules cleared his throat. "What news?"

The line was scratchy with distance and Jules could imagine Nice in the background. The sun, the white pebble beach. If he closed his eyes, he could almost taste it.

"I think it's safe to say Baliel was hunting someone," Eliot said, "but I'm not sure it was you. At least, not at first."

"What do you mean?"

Eliot added more softly, "He could have been hunting your mother."

Jules's skin prickled. "Why do you think that?"

"Because he made another stop in Saint-Jeannet. *Before* the church. And he made inquiries."

"Inquiries?"

"We found a survivor. Apparently he asked about a woman. Whatever he learned took him to the church. *À l'église Saint-Pierre.*"

"Does Selene know?" Jules met her eye across the room. She nodded, but her mask was in place and he couldn't tell what she was thinking.

"Yes," Eliot said at the same time. "One more thing. Further results have come back from the fire at the orphanage and I can confirm we've found no evidence of human remains. None at all."

Jules drew in a sharp breath. "Destroyed?"

"Not hot enough. The demon fire burned itself out and the rest of the orphanage was destroyed by ordinary flames."

He frowned. It had seemed hot enough to him. But he held his tongue. After the dead end at the library, perhaps a little hope wasn't the worst thing in the world.

Selene tapped her watch. He nodded, only half listening to Eliot as he watched her leave the room.

"Eliot, I need to know why you were exiled," he interrupted.

The hollow sound of the phone line crackled between them. "I'm not sure I was ever told. I was in no position to fight the banishment. My mentor was newly dead and power in Rome was shifting. Those who knew about it assumed my exile was linked to Matteo's crimes. Nobody wanted to say the words out loud. Better to quietly accept it. My family thought Cesare was doing me a kindness, merely sending me away instead of killing me." Eliot took a shaking breath. "But in hindsight I think it was because of Selene. Her mother and brother were newly exiled. Without me she had no one but Cesare."

After that, nothing could salvage the day. Jules poured himself a drink.

It was impossible not to like Eliot, but a sullen feeling gnawed at his gut. *Jealousy*, he realized, remembering the way Selene had curled in her armchair, her chin propped on her knee. It had felt intimate.

Patting his inside breast pocket, Jules found the newspaper clipping that Eliot had dropped on the train and brushed his thumb over Selene's photograph. The Imperium Bellum had sent Eliot away because, even as children, Cesare knew he cared for her.

Maybe even loved her.

Jules pressed a small, bitter smile to the crystal rim of his glass. He *wanted* her. And he was impossibly jealous of Eliot for their shared history. Not even Selene's smoothest Scotch could take the edge off this new realization.

Slouching into a chair in the corner of the sunroom, Jules propped his feet on a marble chessboard. Knowing what he did about Selene, he imagined it was probably the most use the chessboard had ever had. He let his eyes roam over the star-painted ceiling, and lazily swirled his drink in one trailing hand.

Jules absently flipped through the notebook, thinking about the man who had written it. It was dense with information, full to the edges with skillful drawings and architectural studies. He turned again to the missing page, running his thumb over the ragged edge.

"What are you doing?"

Jules glanced up. "There's a page missing. It was ripped out."

Selene snatched the notebook from his hands, frowning as though she might intimidate the truth out of it. She angled the page into the light. "There's an impression on the next page."

He dropped his boots to the herringbone floor, knocking over the white king as he stood. "Really?" He set down the glass.

She nodded, moving to the grand writing desk and pushing open the rolltop. In a flurry, she opened drawers, tossing aside scraps of paper and empty ink pots. Each drawer seemed to require a complicated series of twists and tugs, but she unveiled each hidden compartment with ease.

With a pleased sound she whipped out a lead pencil with a flourish.

He snatched it from her, turning the pencil to rub the flat lead against the page.

A string of numbers.

He frowned. "Well, that's disappointing."

Selene fished in her pocket, pulling out the crumpled scrap of paper on which she'd written the library reference number, and smoothed it out.

Together they looked between the tracing and Selene's looping hand.

"Your father went in search of the Nice records too," Jules said quietly. "I wonder if he found them?"

Selene's voice was pensive when she finally said, "Well, isn't that the question?"

After learning about the missing records, Jules had been certain nothing could improve his mood. How wrong he was. Midnight was closing in when Selene stepped out of her dressing room, thumbing the final button on her left hip. "Ready."

Oh, *how* wrong. His fingers spasmed on his glass. *Holy shit.*

She glanced up, then returned to what she was doing. "What?"

She wore a crisp, close-fitting white button-down, but her shirt wasn't what gave him pause. Her legs were clad in skintight leather—if that's what it was, he couldn't say for sure—with four large gold buttons up one hip, four up the other. And, by God, if he didn't finally appreciate Vatican-stamped buttons.

"Nothing," he said, voice hoarse.

Now she was annoyed. "No, seriously, what?"

Jules swallowed. "Is that leather or, um—"

"Lambskin."

"—paint?"

"What?"

"Nothing."

Selene's eyes narrowed, her long lashes only exaggerating the menace of the expression. *Oh, no.*

"*Paint?* You think my hunting leathers look *painted on?*"

He wasn't an idiot; he knew a trap when he'd already stumbled into it. "No?"

"I heard a question mark."

"No, you didn't."

"I'm going to change," she said grumpily. Dark hair slid over her face, obscuring her expression, but he thought he saw flushed cheeks in the mirror's reflection as she turned.

"Wait." Before his mind caught up, Jules crossed the room, hands curving around her hips to stop her. Her body heat had suffused the soft leather. Her shoulders stiffened, and—God protect him—so did he. Touching that warm leather felt just like touching *her*. The illusion was all but perfect, if not for the chill of the damned Vatican-stamped buttons beneath his palms—his opinion of them had changed again—and it was as though an electric current bound them together. He couldn't have moved even if he'd wanted to.

He didn't want to.

With her back against his chest, Selene tipped her head so she could meet his eyes. The position only emphasized the difference in their heights. From this close, even the kohl around her eyes looked sharp enough to cut.

"Hello." His throat was suddenly dry.

She tried to turn but he held her in place. She would notice his predicament the moment she faced him. Then he'd die.

Dieu, she was beautiful. He wanted to tell her so, to wipe away any lingering doubt his words had triggered. Carefully he angled her hips with a hand, and drew her hair over her shoulder with the other.

"Just look." He nodded to the mirror in its ornate gilt frame. "You look . . ." He searched for a word to sum up what she did to him without getting himself in worse trouble. "Incredible. Don't change. I'm . . . I'm just—"

"An idiot?"

He grinned sheepishly. "Yeah."

She wasn't looking at herself; instead, she watched him.

He raised his brows.

Finally, reluctantly, she shifted her gaze. "Jules. They're just *hunting leathers.*"

Unable to fathom the vast difference between what he could see and what she did, he shook his head wordlessly. She was so *beautiful,* but he couldn't say that. Chafing his hand lightly against her hip, he was unprepared for the spark of awareness when his thumb met soft skin.

"Don't change. They suit you."

She pressed her lips together.

Skeptic, he thought, amused.

He consciously shifted his thumb back to the relative safety of her waistband. Touching her skin wasn't helping his predicament at all. *Think bad thoughts,* Jules coached himself. *Not those thoughts. The other kind of bad.*

"And I bet your maneuverability's excellent," he added.

She nodded at that.

"So, um, tell me all about the gross, disgusting demon you slaughtered last time you wore them."

"Are you mocking me?"

"Not at all. I just love war stories. *Brutal* ones."

She seemed unconvinced but finally relented. "It *was* rather brutal."

Selene thought her heart might beat out of her rib cage.

Breathing, a thing of the past. What she could manage had become soft little gasps—like the fluttering of moth wings.

Jules touched the naked skin of her hip, smoothing with a slightly roughened thumb. *Dio*, he didn't know he'd met skin. And she certainly wasn't going to tell him.

"Good," he said, his voice strangely intense. "Tell me more."

"I-it was a midlevel demon possessing the body of a small boy. Maybe four years old. Very creepy. Too many mouths." She drew a line on her cheek. "Big long tongue."

"Great, excellent." He sounded oddly relieved.

Finally he moved so she could see him properly. His proximity was distracting, and the casual lean against the mirror's gilt frame, with his arms loosely folded over his chest, only emphasized his biceps. But at least those large marked hands were no longer touching the sensitive skin over her hip bones. Why, then, did she feel disappointed?

"Really, you look great."

She rolled her eyes, not deigning to reply.

"Like a total professional," he continued, raising his hands as though framing his next words. "The consummate Vatican exorcist."

"Charmer." She used the excuse of reaching for her watch on the dresser to turn away.

Why was he always like this? Did he take nothing seriously? She wasn't always sure where the mocking ended with him. She didn't have her footing around him, and she hated that. She *always* had her footing.

Now was not the time to lose her edge. At least, no more than she already had. She considered the earlier call with Eliot. He and Caterina had turned up a survivor in Saint-Jeannet. The woman's testimony all but confirmed that Baliel had been tracking someone, that it was no coincidence that he went first to the church where Jules had been abandoned in Saint-Jeannet, then to the orphanage where he was raised in Nice. Both now destroyed. She had known it in her gut, but now she had *evidence* to support her theory.

It was almost enough to take to Cesare.

She glanced at Jules again. Dark hair flopped over his forehead, and his high cheekbones were dusted with color. His eyes found hers and a half smile tugged at his mouth. She found herself beginning to smile back and crushed it.

Almost, but not yet. First she would learn the nature of Baliel's interest in Jules on her own. She buckled her watch single-handed. Cesare had been distracted lately. Now was not the time.

Besides . . . She didn't want to throw Jules to the wolves.

"*Enough*," she snapped, cutting off whatever Jules had been rambling about. "Let's go, shall we?"

He smirked, flicking his eyes down meaningfully at her trailing laces.

Of course her boots were untied. She knelt to thread the laces up her calf, tweaking them until they were taut to her liking.

Reaching for the coat draped at the end of the bed, Jules swirled it over his shoulders. He decided against putting his arms through the sleeves, instead crossing them over his chest as he leaned against her bedpost. She was *far* too distracted to notice, looping her laces around the hooked eyelet before tying a tight knot. With no more excuses, she looked up.

Dio. It was almost frustrating how good the Vatican uniform looked on him. Some people let the uniform wear them, with its close tailoring and gold details, but Jules had the build to pull it off. A body refined by fighting for survival. All lean legs and narrow hips and—

She dragged her eyes away. *Enough.*

"*Deus, desiderium meum,*" she muttered in Latin, "*in Jules Lacroix averte.*"

"Hey."

"What?" she asked flatly, shooting him a look.

"Did you just curse me out to *God*?"

"No," she said airily.

"We're only, like, a thousand feet away."

"Three hundred."

"Even worse. What if he comes for me?"

"Stop getting on my nerves and move. *Dio.*"

"You did it again."

"Get your ass out that door or not even God could save you from me."

Raising his hands, Jules backed out of the room. Then he lazily tucked those scarred hands into his coat pockets.

And again Selene prayed. *May God protect me from lustful thoughts about Jules Lacroix.*

CHAPTER TWENTY-THREE

The frigid air was sharp and sweet, promising snow. Jules adjusted the collar of his black wool coat. The slim-fit Vatican uniform was an excellent cover, disguising that he was perhaps a little too hungry for a Roman noble. When they'd swept through St. Peter's Square, people had ducked their heads, afraid to look him in the eye.

Selene led the way across the Tiber via the Aelian Bridge only minutes after midnight. The Castel Santo Immortale rose up behind them, imposing in its rotund solidity. The carved demons along its length made his neck prickle. They passed a demon whose hair looked soft enough to touch. Jules pivoted, half expecting to catch it watching him, but it gazed into the distant horizon. The demon held a column upraised, and its billowing cloak almost gave the impression of wings.

But that would be silly, Jules thought. *Demons don't have wings.*

Dressed as though for war, Selene strode ahead. Her black coat flared in the night breeze, revealing the shoulder holster for her gun. Matte-black guards were sculpted to her shoulders, detailed with delicate gold chains that glinted with her every movement.

Jules trailed a few steps behind, not only for the view of her blessed legs but because he couldn't help but linger. Rome was a glittering jewel. Gas lamps burning in ornate iron braziers lined the street, and for every balcony draped with a constellation of fairy lights, there were dozens more stained-glass lanterns flickering with real flame. Like on the front, Romans couldn't depend on electric lights or telephones.

He noticed graffiti on the walls and cracks in the stucco. Plants tumbled from balconies. A few small restaurants and trattorias were still open for the late crowd, soft voices and clinking cutlery tumbling onto the street whenever someone opened a door. Outdoor tables had been folded away for the night, and only a few people sat on the steps, watching them without a word.

His shoulders unknotted as they passed from pristine cobbled streets to the grittier parts of town. It felt real to Jules. No pretty mask to hide a dirty truth.

Adjusting her holster, Selene ensured her usual white-handled gun was snug beneath her breast. A twin to the one strapped to her thigh, this one was white with black filigree and gold detailing—the Alleva family crest stamped into the grip.

She brushed her fingertip over the emblem of the Holy Vatican Empire and the Deathless God stamped on the grip of the black gun. This one was no less beautiful, matte black with delicate filigree in gunmetal gray, with subtle gold detail you could only see when the light hit just right.

"You're nervous," he said, eyes following the movement of her fingers.

Her eyes snapped up. "No."

A smirk played across his lips. "Yes, you are."

She strode down the street as though she owned it. Rome was *her* city. Its people hers to loathe and protect. Its streets hers to bleed and shed blood on, and only hers.

Damn anyone else who tried to kill someone on *her* streets.

If he hadn't noticed Selene caress the emblem like some kind of touchstone, he would never have guessed. She was *nervous*. Which made *him* nervous. He glanced over his shoulder, checking for tails, but they were alone.

When Jules faced the front again, he was suddenly nose to nose with Selene. He skidded to a halt and gripped her waist. Arms crossed over her chest, she angled her chin up. He had no choice but to meet her steady gaze.

"I am *not* nervous," she enunciated.

To disagree would be to take his life into his own hands. Her eyes glittered like the carapace of a nasty beetle. *Go on,* she challenged him, without ever saying a word. Her flash of irritation lit an answering spark in him, and, God help him, he *wanted* to provoke her. And not for the first time he questioned the wisdom of taunting a girl with carte blanche to kill him, and the rare skill to follow through.

"We're stepping into Rome's filthy, disgusting underbelly." Her nose wrinkled. "Crawling down there with the dogs and the rats." Jules wanted to smile at her vehemence, but his will to live won out. "Even I have no place there," she finished softly.

He didn't remember when they'd switched to French—probably around the time he started taunting her—but he enjoyed her accent in his language. *Rome's filthy, disgusting underbelly* rang beautifully in his mother tongue.

He indicated her uniform, the distinctive sword crossing her back. "You don't have to step out as the Butcher of Rome. So why?"

She smiled slightly, showing teeth. "I may have no place there, but I can still intimidate them."

Jules nodded. Yep, he could see it.

She let out a puff of breath, blowing unbound hair off her

cheek, and the tension eased palpably between them. She watched him expectantly.

He raised a questioning brow.

"*So . . . ?*" she prompted.

He was still touching her. Carefully, he lifted one hand off her waist at a time. Looking at them as though they should be someone else's problem.

Her brows crumpled in confusion. *Not it.*

Visibly losing patience, she said, "So, as you see, I'm not . . . ?" She waited expectantly for him to finish her sentence.

"Oh! Nervous," he guessed. Her expression darkened. "You're *not* nervous. Right. Sorry, I was wrong."

She seemed mollified.

As her footsteps retreated, Jules tipped his head back. He let his eyes unfocus and stared between the stars into the darkest void he could find. So that was what it felt like to have your life flash before your eyes? By the time he caught up to Selene at the next intersection, she'd smothered her nervous tic—crushing it beneath her will.

"I got you these." She drew a pair of black gloves from her pocket.

His lips curled slowly and he took them, smoothing his thumb over the supple leather. Gloves made of the same impossibly soft leather she wore. The snug fit made his fingers look long and strong, concealing the telling scars without hindering his movement.

He flexed his fingers, adjusting them at the wrist. "Thank you."

She tore her gaze from his hands and met his eyes. "You're welcome. Before we arrive . . . You already know there are secrets. Compromises we've made for peace." She glanced at him from beneath her lashes. "Ones that . . . that I'm not exactly *proud* of."

She had the hollow-eyed look of someone deeply ashamed of her doubts. Perhaps she felt it was a failure of her faith—but he disagreed. Jules was quietly impressed that after a lifetime under the Vatican's thumb she thought to question what had been handed to her so easily.

Her next words made him draw a sharp breath.

"Where we're going you'll meet half-demons, part-demons, and others with barely a drop of demon blood in their veins—"

He gripped the brick wall, holding himself steady. "So it's true? They . . . *breed* with us?"

There were always rumors. Sometimes tabloids that turned up at the front speculated in licentious detail about the Caspian Tsarina's demonic features, and her pointed teeth that she filed down daily to look smooth and pretty. None of it true. He had witnessed her power with his own eyes. She'd looked entirely human until she *hadn't*.

Because you're like me, Stigmajka.

He thought about the wide eyes around the training courtyard earlier. Pride had flooded him, but now he wondered how he'd kept up with Selene. She was Vatican-trained. Everyone knew exorcists were *more* than human. Their magic made them superior to others. Faster, stronger. And from what Selene had said in the library, he knew they were martyrs. They sacrificed their own bodies for the ability to fight demons.

Selene nodded, a flicker in her eyes. "Yes. And they can be powerful."

Jules rubbed his hand over his jaw, crushing down his panic as best he could. "What kind of power?" he asked, his voice surprisingly steady. Meanwhile, his traitor heart dashed itself against his ribs. Surely she'd hear it.

"Similar to high-level demons. Fire. Or weather. Or ice." She paced away, then returned. "Sometimes they control creatures. Or plants. The corpses of ravens."

He had no such abilities. Only an aptitude for knowing just when to strike. And perhaps strength and speed that outstripped his fellow soldiers. And maybe healing.

Selene shifted, again touching her gun. "They're dangerous."

Jules looked up sharply. "You kill them?"

"No, but . . ."

Her expression was strange, but the limpid quality of her eyes in the lamplight made him think it was not about him. This was all her—and some inner conflict she didn't want to own.

Heart thundering, he waited for her to continue.

"When we allow them to live, we must ensure they're no threat. Do you understand?" Jules nodded, but he wasn't certain it was true. His mind crowded with thoughts, making it difficult to focus. "I—" She bit her lower lip. "Oh, never mind." She pivoted and strode on.

The world felt as though it had been ripped out from under him. He had to pull himself together before Selene looked back, and so he battled hopelessly to get his recalcitrant heart under control.

But then she was there, drawing off her glove to press cool fingers to his forehead. He closed his eyes and leaned into her touch.

"You're hot," she murmured.

"So are you." He could picture her rolling her eyes. "I'm fine. Honestly."

"All right." She sounded doubtful but lowered her hand.

They walked in silence through the quiet nighttime streets. Up a cobbled incline, down an unexpected flight of ivy-strangled steps, and the world seemed to right itself. As they passed through a puddle of buttery light, a symbol stamped into the cast-iron lamp-post caught his eye. He traced the shape. An upright key.

Keys were everywhere in Rome. Selene's own coat of arms had a set of three keys wrapped in the coils of a serpent. But this one looked different. The teeth of the key resembled an intertwined *E* and *K*. Why did those letters spark meaning to him? Then he remembered Matteo Alleva's notebook. *Elysian. Kairos.*

"Selene—" He lengthened his stride and caught up with her, guiding her by the elbow to the next lamppost. He indicated the symbol. "What's this?"

"It symbolizes that the compact between the Vatican and part-demons holds sway here. These streets are not entirely our own." She began to turn away, but he stopped her.

He traced the letters for her to see. "*Elysian. Kairos.*"

She stilled. "*Dio Immortale.* I think you might be right."

He straightened, his jaw tight. "If they're here—in Rome, I mean—does that mean we can live in harmony with demons? If . . . if we create offspring together, doesn't that mean we're not so different?"

That was a whole new horror he refused to consider. The scars on his arms seemed to throb with his stumbling heartbeat.

"What?" Her brows drew together. "No. It doesn't mean that at all . . ." She selected her words carefully. "Don't mistake my . . . regret . . . for hesitation. Demon offspring are an abomination before God." There was no waver in her voice. "I know it's distasteful. It's a complication. But their existence doesn't change why I was created. I was born to kill demons."

He knew Selene didn't like shades of gray. But part-demon children . . . ? That made it messy.

"And the children?" he asked quietly.

"I cannot personally kill each and every one of them."

"But you would if you could?"

She didn't speak for a long moment, still walking half a step ahead of him. Eventually she said softly, "I might try." He could see the side of her face and the shift in her expression. "Thankfully . . . I have never been asked to do so. I hunt the demons who've broken through, and nothing will stop me from doing that."

Stopping abruptly, she pounded her fist against a studded wooden door flanked by potted palms.

His stomach knotted as the echo of her knock sounded. They were going to meet demons.

A judas window slid open in the door, framing a set of dark eyes.

Selene didn't say a word, and for a moment neither did the woman beyond the door. Jules had the impression she was deciding whether to pretend Selene wasn't there at all. Finally, the door swung open.

"*Ciao, Giulietta. Dov'è Sparrow?*" Selene seamlessly switched back to Italian.

Giulietta was a slender woman, her slinky black dress draping low between her breasts so that he could see the slight dip of her ribs beneath smooth brown skin. Aside from the dress, she wore the ugliest expression Jules had ever seen on a beautiful woman. And every inch of it aimed at Selene.

Selene, for her part, wore her dead-eyed look. The one Jules associated most with her mask—pretending she was only a Vatican exorcist and nothing more. Which raised the question: mask or shield?

"*Cosa vuoi, troia?*" Giulietta spat at Selene.

"Oh, shit," Jules whispered in his mother tongue, backing up to get out of the danger zone.

Selene shot him a bored look.

Giulietta seemed to notice him for the first time. Her expression shifted to something sultry and heavy-lidded. "And who are *you*, cute boy?" she asked in heavily accented French.

"I'm alive. And I'd like to stay that way," Jules replied in Italian.

"You trained the fun right out of him," Giulietta sneered at Selene. "Sparrow's on the roof. He'll be *so* pleased to see you."

Selene was already gone, and her voice drifted back. "About as pleased as I am to see him."

After a last glance at the woman, Jules caught Selene at the top of a flight of spiral stairs. She didn't appear to notice—or care—but when they reached the top landing, she gave him a measured look. "Stay on guard, *cute boy*." Her hand hovered near the gun at her thigh.

She waved him onto a busy rooftop terrace ahead of her. Rome was spread out beneath them, glimmering in the dark. Flowering plants had been brought outside, their leaves lit in yellows and golds from dozens of brass lanterns. And all around the edges, banisters were wrapped with tiny lights. But none of it really registered as his focus narrowed on the screaming youth being branded with an iron across his back. The boy's voice broke from the agony, and Jules realized what Selene hadn't said. *This* was how the Vatican bound the power of part-demons.

Jules was knocked back on his heels by the wrongness of it.

Half turning from the horror of the scene, Jules noticed a man with a presence unlike any he'd felt before. He stood to the side with one arm draped over the banister, watching the branding with a taut expression, and held a cigarette pinched between two fingers. Blue smoke trailed into the night. He looked up sharply when Selene stepped onto the terrace.

With a broken yell, the young woman wielding the branding iron dragged it away from the boy's skin and plunged it back into a burning brazier. The assembled people cheered, surging around the boy to embrace him and ruffle his hair. More than one jostled to pour drinks down his throat.

But Jules's attention was focused on the man with the cigarette. He was beautiful.

That was the only way to describe him, with his knife-edge jaw and column of throat that dipped into an open-necked shirt. Light from a brazier illuminated pale scars that sliced through his brow and one eye. Jules could feel his attention as he watched them approach with an eye that burned like blue fire in stark contrast to the milk-white of his ruined eye. And yet it took nothing from his looks.

If anything, it made him more handsome.

And the impression that he saw *everything* even more unnerving.

CHAPTER TWENTY-FOUR

I t was busier than usual. Three dozen people were crammed into the space, with Rome spread out beneath them. She had felt Jules flinch at the first yell and tried not to react in kind.

It was awful.

It was *unavoidable*.

"These . . . are demons?" he breathed.

She glanced his way. "It would make it easier if they all looked like monsters, wouldn't it?"

Monsters they were not. More often than not, they were born lovely. And dangerous.

"Why do this?"

"We have a compact. As part of this compact with the Vatican, they brand their part-demons. Once their power is bound and they are no great threat, we mostly turn a blind eye to their existence."

Sparrow stood to the side. If not for his incredible presence, he might fade into the shadowed edges of the tableau. But he wasn't the kind of man who could avoid attention. He looked at them, expression unchanging, then tossed his cigarette over the balcony and cut his way toward them.

"Selene. To what do I owe this pleasure?" He indicated the

branded boy. "You're here as witness? That's unexpected. Isn't this below your pay grade?"

She watched the boy drink, holding the bottle with shaking hands. "I should arrest you," she said mildly.

"Go ahead."

"Don't tempt me. I could find *something* and make it stick."

"Promises, promises."

The boy pulled a tank top on, its low back baring his raw flesh. Adrenaline would keep him warm.

"I need information."

Sparrow gave her a long look. "It must be important to bring you all the way here, *Macellaia*. Last time we spoke you weren't interested in what I had to say."

"If I recall, last time we spoke you said nothing of use. Things have changed. I should have listened then, but I'm here now."

He straightened, clearly surprised by that, and whatever else he saw in her face decided him. "All right. You should speak to Kalindra."

She nodded toward a young girl shrugging her jacket down, baring the curve of her spine. "Another one?"

"Vatican-approved."

"I didn't ask."

He huffed a sound that was not quite agreement.

They watched in silence, both of them witnessing the branding. Nicely done. Like the first.

When metal and flesh had stopped sizzling, Sparrow led them down an open-air staircase to a smaller terrace that wrapped around what had once been a clock tower. Green shutters stood open, and beyond were French doors.

Holding open the door, Sparrow watched Jules with intense

appraisal as he entered the room. It was the first time he'd shown any sign of noticing him at all.

Inside, Selene leaned against Sparrow's desk and continued their earlier conversation. "As long as you follow the compact, I have no problem with what you do here. No matter how many baby demons you find."

His blue eye flicked up and pinned her. Sparrow didn't respond immediately, but when he did his tone was ice-cold. "Liar. You sound smooth to everyone else, *Macellaia di Roma*, but you can't fool me. You would prefer to see them in the ground."

She barely smothered a sneer. "Believe what you like. Honestly, I don't give a—"

There was a loud knock. Giulietta leaned in, pointedly not looking at Selene. "Boss, there are people here. People like *her*." She jutted her chin at Selene.

"*Ex-or-cists*," Selene enunciated. "It must be difficult having all your major developmental milestones between your collarbones and navel."

Giulietta flounced off and Selene followed.

Pausing beside Jules, Selene lowered her voice. "Stay here. You two can talk about how cruel I am among yourselves. I'm sure it will keep you busy. Maybe Sparrow knows something I don't. Doubtful but possible. And, Jules, do try to stay out of trouble."

On the street below, Giulietta started left but Selene turned right, calling over her shoulder, "Tell them to wait on the street. I'll be there shortly." Then she slipped down the alley to the right, knocked twice on the glass door, and let herself in.

Kalindra's shop was always dark and close, even during the day when it opened. But night was when her real wares were on sale. Information and black-market items. It was filled to the rafters with dried plants and growing ivy. A large macaw sat overhead, watching Selene with beady eyes.

The information broker stood in the corner, smoking a long pipe. Her eyes were filmy with age. Selene strongly suspected Kalindra was almost as old as the new Vatican itself, born in the tumultuous years after demons tried to kill the Deathless God. But Kalindra's mind remained sharp, and despite her demon nature, she'd proven useful to Selene and the Vatican.

Kalindra raised a hand. "I have nothing to say to you, girl. Not now."

So it was going to be like that.

Selene pressed her teeth together, forcing a smile as she slid a sheaf of papers from her pocket. "I figured that might be the case. Which is why I brought five clean approvals. Already stamped with the Primus Seal. *Five*, Kalindra. You know how valuable they are."

Kalindra scowled darkly, popping a sweet into her mouth and sucking on it as she stared Selene down. "Not enough. Not with the change in the air. Not even for five lives."

Selene narrowed her eyes. Five certificates would mean Sparrow could take in and brand five part-demon youths. Kalindra would never turn down such an offer. "What are you scared of, old woman?"

Kalindra scoffed. "I'm not afraid."

"You seem it. Not even ballsy enough to save five kids."

"Says *you*—you're the one who'll cut them down if I don't."

"Probably," Selene acknowledged, leafing through the pages to count the writs. She paused meaningfully. "Oh. I miscounted. I seem onto have seven."

Kalindra twitched, reaching out a bony hand. "Give."

"Not until you tell me what's happening on the streets of Rome.

I don't need you to tell me something's afoot, I can work that out for myself. I want *details*."

Selene didn't want to direct Kalindra with leading questions or tell the information broker anything she didn't already know. That Baliel had returned to their world. That he was on his way. That he was *hunting* someone . . . and she suspected that someone was upstairs.

"The underground is in chaos. Sparrow can barely shelter those under his protection. Old alliances are tearing this city apart. Anyone with demon blood in their veins is being forced to choose a side. And each and every one of us would kill to know why the Duke of Briars is here again—"

"In Rome?" Selene interrupted. "Already?"

Kalindra laughed. "Yes, in Rome. After so long away. Long, even for me."

Selene thought of Baliel's likeness captured in her father's hand. His face sketched in incredible detail. So even Kalindra didn't know he'd been back some ten years ago. Just a few short years before her father's death. "If that's free, what *aren't* you telling me?"

The murky corners of the shop seemed to edge closer.

Kalindra curled her gnarled fingers. "Give me the five, and I'll tell you. Then you give me the two."

Selene hesitated. It'd be something of a bad deal if Kalindra reneged, but she wanted the information more. Smirking, she dropped the papers onto the table.

Kalindra snatched them, burying them somewhere in the layers of her clothes. When her hand reappeared, she held glinting hexagonal coins. "These are breaking," she said, dropping them into Selene's palm.

The metal was freezing. Turning them between her fingers, she shivered. A greater cold seeped into her bones as she realized what these were. Vatican seals—the ward coins protecting Rome.

"Who did this?" she asked softly. Dangerously.

Though only a fragment of the immense network, they were vital to defend the Deathless God. Without them, the Vatican fortress would fall. Given their importance to exorcists, they could be unpopular with Rome's demon-blooded population.

Lower lip jutting, Kalindra thrust out a hand, waiting for the final two approvals.

She'd get nothing more from her tonight. Nodding, Selene gently set the certificates into Kalindra's soft, wrinkled hand and held it between her own. Leaning closer, she whispered, "You tell me when you know more, Kalindra. Or I'll forget the compact and kill every branded child in this city. Understand?"

Kalindra yanked her hand away, spitting wordlessly after her as she left.

Selene slowed at the door, where a little half-demon girl peeked around the doorframe. "Hello." She reached into her coat pocket and pulled out a brightly colored caramel.

After a moment of stillness, the girl snatched it from her hand.

Very seriously, Selene asked, "Would you like one more?" There was much eager nodding and Selene set another in the girl's outstretched palm. In thanks, the girl hissed like a cat and scampered off, shoving the colorful sweets into her ratty coat pocket.

Smothering a smile, Selene watched her go.

Ambrose was waiting for her on the street.

The hexagonal discs clinked as she transferred them discreetly to her inside pocket.

His jacket was open from his shoulder, revealing the shiny metallurgic monstrosity of his new arm. She forced away a twinge of guilt at the sight. Why should she feel guilty for not saving his arm when he stuck it between razor teeth of his own volition?

She raised a faux-curious brow in response to Ambrose's sneer. "Should've known."

"What?" she asked, bored.

Ambrose trailed his eyes up and down her, then leered up at Sparrow's tower. Selene didn't dignify his filth with a reply, though she dearly wanted to.

He cupped his groin with the metal hand. "How about you give me a go? Better than a demon, I'll bet. Or maybe you like it taboo—?"

Her boot knife found its way into her hand and the blade against his tongue urged him to be silent.

"I really wouldn't go on," she breathed close to his ear.

His tongue worked against the flat of her blade.

Selene eased closer, turning the dagger so she could hold it between his teeth and still boop his nose with a finger. "Ambrose, I know you're mad about the whole *arm thing*. But that's on you. Why would you choose to get that close to a demon's filthy mouth? And I really do mean that. They're filthy. If you make such a vile suggestion again, well . . ." She trailed off, letting the steel shoved between his teeth speak for her.

Abandoning her favorite boot knife, she turned on her heel.

Be smart, Ambrose, she thought. *Don't do it . . .*

But the moment her back was turned, she sensed him move with intent. She twisted and slammed her fist into his face. A searing line of agony burst across her knuckles where her own blade sliced her to the bone, and the world briefly dimmed at the edges.

Worth it.

It was worse for Ambrose.

A gruesome smile split his cheeks and he dropped to his knees. Her knife clattered to the ground. She grabbed his hair and tipped his head back to force him to look into her eyes.

Blood dripped from her other hand onto the cobbles. "You ever try to hit me, or any other Vatican officer again, and I swear to the Deathless God that you will be crucified by the coming dawn, understand?" She tugged his hair, puppeteering a nod.

Blood soaked into the neck of his Vatican jacket.

"Get yourself healed up. Lucia's still in Nice, so good luck finding someone skilled enough to keep the scarring to a minimum." She had no energy to sound convincing. "Oh, also, I acted as witness for the branding. It's done. Write the report, then you're off this assignment."

He spat, pushing himself to his feet. "*Captain.*"

Scooping up her knife, she returned it to her boot. "Go," she sighed.

The cut was no longer bleeding freely, but it hurt. Injuries were part of this life she'd chosen, but where adrenaline faded, pain lingered. She grazed a thumb over her knuckles, wincing. She could get it fixed in moments, even if she had to find someone other than Lucia to do it. But she thought not.

No, this was a scar she should keep. A reminder.

She wasn't certain she'd dealt with that as well as she could have.

CHAPTER TWENTY-FIVE

S parrow drew a silver lighter from his pocket as Selene's foot-steps faded. "She hates the brandings," he murmured. "I think she sees it as demons escaping natural justice."

Jules shook his head. "That's not true." He remembered the internal conflict underlying her words, the faint flutter of expression behind her inscrutable mask. "She doesn't like the brutality of the solution."

Even as he said it, he knew he was right. She hated what the Vatican did to part-demons. It was cruel where Selene was not. Un-compromising at times, and hell-bent on success, but never will-fully cruel.

Demon offspring are an abomination before God. Her cutting words echoed in his ears, but more memorable was her quiet relief when she told him she had never been asked to kill the children.

Instead of responding to that, Sparrow said, "You're a long way from the front."

Jules tried to keep the tension from his shoulders, but Sparrow's knowing gaze was hot on his neck. When he'd schooled his expression, he turned.

Sparrow tapped out a cigarette and set it at the corner of his mouth, flicking the flame but not lighting it. He watched Jules with an openly curious eye. Sparrow was twenty-five at most, but something about him spoke of experience in life and all things.

Jules felt out of his depth. "What gave me away?"

Sparrow huffed out a low laugh, extending the lighter to Jules, who took it curiously. He turned it over in his hand, as though expecting to see what Sparrow wanted him to. It was unadorned, without sigil or design. Flawless silver. He raised his eyes. Sparrow took the cigarette from his mouth, setting it on the window ledge. "Keep looking."

Jules glanced back at it, and as his eyes relaxed, instead of the shiny silver he saw himself reflected back. And he saw what Sparrow saw. *The soldier.* He flicked his gaze away to the window, to the door, to Sparrow, never settling as he sought danger. Even now, he was waiting for the next attack.

He lit the flame, letting a bitter smile curl his lips.

"Yeah . . . Yeah, I see." Jules protected the flame with his hand and extended it to Sparrow.

Retrieving the cigarette he'd set aside, Sparrow put it between his lips and leaned in without taking his eyes off Jules. Its golden light lit the planes of his face and dark hair. Those high cheekbones. His scarred brow and sightless eye.

Dieu, he's beautiful, Jules thought again.

He was also tall. Almost inhumanly so. And Jules had to remind himself that there was no *almost* about it. Selene had said, *It would make it easier if they all looked like monsters, wouldn't it?* That Sparrow was so striking was the point.

Seeing the direction of Jules's gaze, Sparrow pointed to his own ruined eye. "Rome," he explained, making the entire city culpable for the damage. He still stood close, tipping his head to breathe smoke toward the ceiling.

There was something about Sparrow that made Jules's muscles unwind. He struck Jules as capable. If Jules only watched him, he could allow Sparrow to watch the windows and the doors, no?

Yes, that felt right.

So he watched Sparrow as the man shifted closer, corralling him back toward the wall. Jules pressed a hand against Sparrow's chest, halting his approach.

Sparrow laughed softly but didn't push it.

And even though Sparrow stilled, he did not move away.

Jules could feel the heat of his smooth skin and the heavy thud of his heart beneath his fingers. He glanced down, seeing the ridge of collarbone disappear into the neck of his shirt.

Sparrow let him look, then: "Have you slept with her?" He cocked his head toward the door. Jules didn't reply and Sparrow took his own meaning from that, laughing in a dark rumble that sounded like far-distant thunder. "That's a no, then. Have you ever slept with another man?" The question sounded darkly taunting.

Jules narrowed his eyes slightly as the tall man backed him up toward the wall. Selene was nowhere in sight. He was silent a moment, evaluating him. "I have. In the past." He cleared his throat. "But my tastes are rather specific these days." He thought of Selene, and the kiss he'd stolen. It had cost him a few bruised ribs. Still worth it. "But I wanted to try it and I don't think there's anything wrong with it, so if you think you're getting to me with this, then—"

Sparrow's hand settled on his hip, pressing him back against the wall in a reversal of Jules and Selene earlier.

He broke off. Then, "*Oh.*"

Sparrow's lips curled just slightly at the corners as realization dawned. "*Oh,*" Sparrow echoed, his deep voice full of amusement. "Yes. I was hitting on you. *Not* teasing you. Well, maybe a little."

"I see that now." Jules felt his neck heat up, but laughed before he let embarrassment take hold. It felt easier to hold Sparrow's intense gaze now—the pale eye and the ruined one. "Thanks."

"You know where to find me, if—"

"Yeah. I do." He couldn't ignore a jolt of lust.

If he'd been here alone, maybe he'd take him up on the offer. Just for fun. But he wasn't. He was here with Selene, and when he thought of her he pictured the light gilding her cheekbones and the full curve of her lower lip. The way the lantern light had limned her hair. She was bright and vital and dangerous. And so he was glad not to be alone, because that would mean being without her. Aware of the play of emotions across Jules's face, Sparrow took a step back, sitting on the window ledge. "It's something of a miracle," Sparrow mused. "That you've survived Rome this long."

"Is Rome really so bad?" Moving to the standing globe beside Sparrow's desk, Jules traced the route the train had taken from Nice to Rome. It already felt so long ago. Then he found Ostrava, which felt like a different life entirely.

"Well, surviving Rome is one thing. Surviving *her* is quite another."

"Now you sound like Giulietta," Jules replied, an edge of reproach in his words.

Sparrow's chuckle was low and did things to Jules's stomach. "Selene. Exorcists. *The Vatican.* That's all I mean."

Jules circled the room. It was clear this was not Sparrow's bedroom, but it felt more intimate than an office. He could see a conservatory through a pair of French doors and what appeared to be a small jungle growing beneath the glass.

Sparrow stepped into his path, nodding toward his bicep. "Can I see?"

"See what?" Jules asked.

"Your brand."

"My *what*?"

"You have a brand." He drew a circle around his own bicep, just where Jules's thorns were on him. "Here."

Jules shook his head, a fresh wave of uncertainty rising in a tide that threatened to drown him. He had no brand. Only demons had brands. "No, I have a *scar*."

Sparrow looked confused for a moment, his ruined eye beautifully pale as he watched Jules sharply with the good one. He was more handsome for his flaws. The scar through his brow made the hard lines of his face and the soft fullness of his lips look like something out of a painting. "Show me?" Sparrow asked quietly.

Jules swallowed, forcing down the hollow cry that wanted to claw its way out. Without taking his eyes off him, Jules dropped his jacket over the back of a chair and undid his shirt buttons, shrugging the white shirt off his shoulders so that his bicep was exposed. For a moment he hesitated, not wanting Sparrow to see the number of marks on his arms, but it was his shame to bear. There was no use hiding what he'd done. So, averting his eyes from Sparrow and staring into the darkness beyond the window, Jules removed his shirt completely.

The hushed hiss of air between Sparrow's teeth revealed the moment Sparrow saw the marks. Jules resolutely raised his chin an inch, not looking at him.

But then Sparrow took half a step closer, and Jules couldn't *not* look to see. Anger darkened Sparrow's brow, and his good eye had sharpened to something dangerous. "Who made these marks?"

"I did."

"You did them to yourself?"

Jules nodded. "They mark the dead."

"The dead," Sparrow echoed.

"The ones I killed." *The demons I killed.*

Sparrow's expression opened with realization, then he turned his attention on Jules's thorns and said nothing more about it. "These—" He traced one of the lines lightly with his index finger. "How long have you had them?"

"As long as I've been alive, just about." Sparrow gave him a look, doubt clouding his expression. "I was abandoned when I was a baby. The doctors think I was only a day old. These were already carved into my flesh." He glanced at the scar, his brows pulling together.

Sparrow saw the question in his eyes and his own softened. "Your mother did it, most likely in the minutes after you were born."

Jules raised both hands in a warding gesture and stepped back, knocking over a Murano glass lamp that smashed with a dramatic rain of sparks. He righted it and backed away toward the door, still holding one hand up between them. Sparrow's mouth opened as if to speak, but Jules cut him off. "Don't."

"Jules—" Sparrow followed him, grasping his wrist and pushing his hand down.

Jules was tempted to deliver an elbow to his cheekbone, but he did have such lovely cheekbones. The thought was feverish, there and gone again like tattered cloud whisking across the sky.

"Not another word."

His chest expanded with gasping, ragged breaths. It felt too hard to breathe.

He had pushed this feeling away since that day on the battlefield. Now Sparrow stood in front of him, the blue of his eye burning like Baliel's flames, and Jules knew he wouldn't be able to run anymore.

Sparrow's hand was gentle as he settled it against the back of Jules's neck, but his fingers were unyielding.

Jules couldn't move. His eyes burned, the edges of the world blurring slightly. He shook his head. *No.*

He wanted to run. But he was held in place by Sparrow, whose eyes were gentle and solemn as he confirmed his nightmare. The voices of soldiers echoed through his mind. *Lacroix. How many kills?* He traced his own fingertips down his forearm, feeling the faintest ridges.

In four years? Not hundreds. *Thousands.*

"Just—" Sparrow began.

"*No.*"

Sparrow sighed, tipping his head back as frustration tightened his jaw. Reaching for Jules's shirt, Sparrow dropped it over his shoulders, concealing the damning scar once more. Jules clutched it to himself as though the starched cotton could cover up unfortunate truths.

"Does Selene know?"

Numbly he shook his head.

"Good. At least there's that." Sparrow's expression was dark. "She's their creature through and through. You *cannot* trust her. You should stay here with—"

"With people like me?" Jules snarled, his lips curling back from his teeth. He held his forearm an inch from Sparrow's nose, forcing him back a step. "You think I'd be welcomed here with a thousand demon deaths written across my skin?"

Sparrow's expression twisted and he looked away. Jules had found his mark. He always did. No matter what strange affinity he and Sparrow shared, there would be no home for him here. He had locked the door on that possibility before he knew it existed and thrown away the key. Had sacrificed *all that* to be the Holy Vatican Empire's loyal soldier, giving them his every waking hour for four years. And more than once he'd tried to give them his blood.

But he'd never managed to die, unlike everyone else he had come to love. Farah killed by demons, Kian killed by Baliel.

His heart fluttered like a caged bird against the bars of his ribs. Half-human, half-demon. And not enough of either to count for anything.

"*What?*" Sparrow said, his voice rough. His blue eye darkened with some emotion Jules couldn't quite name. Anger, perhaps? Fury, even—and Jules realized he'd spoken the last part out loud. Sparrow stepped closer, his hand rising to catch Jules's jaw and tip his face. "Never say that. You are not *half-human.* You are not *half* anything. You are a demon. Every drop of your—"

He broke off. The bloodless expression on Jules's face had silenced him faster than a knife to the throat.

Jules sat heavily on the edge of Sparrow's desk. He had assumed he was like the people on the roof. Human, with tainted blood in his veins. But Sparrow had dashed that hope.

You are a demon.

Perhaps deep down he'd suspected it since Nice. Why else had he forsworn his sword? On the battlefield outside Ostrava, the Tsarina had handed him a nightmare with a smile. He hadn't accepted it then. Now he had no choice. Born and raised a human, with demon blood in his veins.

"You could tell?" Jules heard his own voice as if from far away.

Sparrow shook his head. "Not right away. Your scar binds you. I thought you had a brand, because I could only feel the faintest flicker of your demonic essence when . . ." He cleared his throat. "When I was very close."

"I remember that," Jules murmured, a smile tugging at his mouth. "Tell me more." It hurt, but it was not in his nature to rail against reality.

Sparrow spoke with the cadence of a storyteller, guessing at

Jules's torrent of emotions and gentling his voice to match. "If this was done when you were a babe, then it was your mother. Most likely in the minutes after you were born. At first I didn't recognize it, because this is something I've only ever seen once before."

A feeling unfurled in Jules's chest. Relief, warm and golden. "You've seen this before?" Perhaps he was not entirely alone.

Sparrow smiled faintly as he pulled back the eyelid of his ruined white eye to reveal a small black mark pressed into his sclera. It looked like a teardrop. Or a fang.

"A tear?"

He touched Sparrow's arm lightly to let him know he could release his eyelid. Sparrow blinked dark lashes and rubbed his eye with a sheepish grimace. "It is the symbol representing the Duke of Teeth. It bound me before I destroyed it."

A sacrifice to reclaim his birthright.

"So that's how you knew. You have one too." Jules frowned, rubbing his thumb over his own bicep. "I thought you said it was Rome that ruined your eye?"

"In a way it was. Without the Vatican we would be safe."

The French doors blew open and a flurry of snow came in, falling wet and heavy before Sparrow caught the windows and latched them shut. The papers on his desk rustled, then went still—as still as Jules felt, heart leaden in his chest.

He shook his head. "Without demons we—*they*—would be safe."

Sparrow brushed that off, unacknowledged. "Your scar tells me much. I think your mother must be related to the Prince of Thorns somehow. One of your parents certainly."

His parents. His *demon* parents.

"The Prince of Thorns?"

"Perhaps you know him by another name, the Duke of Briars?"

His knees weakened. If he hadn't been leaning on the edge of Sparrow's desk already, Jules would've sat heavily on the floor. The Duke of Briars—*Baliel*—he knew.

His knuckles whitened where he gripped the desk.

Kian's killer was his blood. His lungs constricted, burning as though he breathed hot embers, and Jules crushed the thought cruelly down—unable to deal with it right then. It threatened to split him open, baring his insides to the world.

Even though he trusted Sparrow—trusted him more than he'd trusted anyone since arriving in Rome—he didn't want him to see so deep. Nor so clearly. His guilt. His *crimes*. Those he was happy to share, but his weaknesses were his alone.

"The night Selene and I met, she fought him. He arrived at the orphanage where I was raised and—" He faltered, cleared his throat. "Baliel killed Kian, my childhood friend. My closest friend."

"What else?"

"What do you mean, *what else*?" Jules's hand was a fist against his knee, then he recalled the words Baliel had spoken as his body burned. "And he told me the Vatican was my enemy."

"He told you that? Then you must believe him—" Sparrow broke off and Jules heard it too. The crisp tap of Selene's boots. Jules slid his arms into his shirtsleeves and buttoned up. He wanted to dig his fingernails into the scar on his arm and shred his flesh to get it off. If she found out he was a demon, Selene would kill him. He could run, but she knew this city. These were her streets and she'd hunt him down.

If he asked, Sparrow would let him stay in spite of the marks on his arms—no matter how much trouble Jules brought to his door—because Jules knew how to use his smile.

But he didn't want to stay.

When Selene stepped into the room, her hair glinted in the

lamplight as she turned to find him, and he knew he would be leaving with her. His eyes trailed over her, the curve of her hip, those long legs clad in tight leather, and he crushed down his rioting emotions so she wouldn't immediately know something was wrong. No matter how cold she pretended to be, she saw more than she let on.

Farah would have told him to run from this, but he had always barreled headfirst into danger.

"Ready to go?" he asked, running fingers through his hair, mussing it so it stood on end.

Sparrow closed his eyes.

Selene nodded, pressing a cloth to her knuckles. "Quite."

There was a crisp click as Sparrow flicked open the silver lighter. The flame played over his eyes so he was a different creature entirely from the man he'd been with Jules. Reaching for another cigarette, Sparrow lit it between his lips.

Selene wrinkled her nose. "Sparrow, that's a vile habit, I'll have you know."

He breathed out a coil of blue smoke. "Noted. I'll take your personal preference into account from here on out." Somewhat inevitably, Sparrow seemed to take it as encouragement. "So?" he asked, voice almost back to its usual timbre. "What did Kalindra tell you?"

Selene raised one shoulder in an easy shrug. "Did I say I'd share the information I was given with you, *L'occhio della Malavita*? Ask her yourself."

"An open book, as ever. Can't you try to be a little fucking mysterious for once?"

Selene smirked. "Don't pretend you can *read*."

CHAPTER TWENTY-SIX

Selene looked at the coins in her hand. Hexagonal. Gold or gold-plated. Each with the crest of the Vatican and the Deathless God worked into them. Like the one she'd taken off Ambrose, each one was fundamental to protecting their city, but these were shiny as a new-minted coin. So how had they come to be rattling around in her pockets instead of where they should be—at significant points around Rome, working together like knots in a net to keep high-level demons out.

It meant parts of Rome were vulnerable.

The thought of the broken wards squirmed up her throat until she wanted to gag.

And . . . the Duke of Briars was already here.

They walked out onto the street, with Sparrow acting as escort, which was certainly not a courtesy he'd ever extended to Selene alone.

Whenever Jules looked her way, she glanced the other way or angled her wrist to check the time. *Dio, how pathetic.* In spite of the valuable information she'd gleaned from Kalindra, her mind kept returning to their soft voices. On her return, the tone of their conversation had struck her and she'd paused down the hallway to listen.

There was an intimacy to the way they spoke, confiding in one another with words she couldn't hear. Jules had immediately relaxed with the demon. Relaxed in that particular way you did when you sank into a hot bath and your muscles uncoiled. A way she wasn't sure he'd ever relaxed with her.

Of course, she wasn't surprised Sparrow was interested. Jules was impossibly gorgeous and Sparrow liked beautiful things. Not that it mattered. Jules could like whoever he wanted . . . Except he was *her* prisoner and that kind of made it *her* problem. Other than that, she didn't care. *At all.*

She shook herself. She was never this distracted.

Jules was work. Sparrow was a filthy demon. And *Rome*—Rome was in *danger.*

She tightened her bandaged hand around the coins and slipped them into her pocket.

Feeling Sparrow's eyes on her, she said, "You have to see us off your street, Sparrow? I promise we're leaving." She flicked her eyes around. "I wouldn't stay here a moment longer than necessary."

"Easy, exorcist. I have places to be. The other one's for you." Sparrow nodded over her shoulder and she turned, realizing he'd been looking past her as two cars pulled up. They were sleek black beasts that didn't particularly suit him, except that they were expensive and Sparrow liked nice things. Biting her lip, she glanced at Jules. Nice and beautiful things.

Jules met her gaze, his eyes crinkled at the corners. She couldn't help but smile.

"Shall we?"

She nodded, a wave of relief almost knocking her back on her heels. "Yes."

When the car slowed to pass through the checkpoint into St. Peter's Square, she moved the discs into her inner breast pocket before pulling on her gloves. It would be unusual for them to search an exorcist, but if the wards were breaking, anything was possible.

Jules leaned closer to her, breath stirring her hair. "What are those?"

She jumped. "What are what?"

She'd been so careful not to let Sparrow see them and refused to believe for one second that Jules had noticed what Sparrow had not. She tucked her hand into her pocket, fingering the hexagonal discs. One was missing.

"What is *this*?"

She turned, finding Jules rolling one between his gloved fingers. She slapped her hands over his, clamping down on it, and gave him a death glare. He'd definitely noticed. While Sparrow had been distracted by Jules's ass, Jules had been watching *her*. She suddenly became aware of his warmth and yanked her hand away again quickly.

"You *pickpocketed* me."

She lunged for him.

He laughed as she came away with only his glove, the coin glinting in his other hand.

A rap on the window made her jump as a Vatican guard waved the car through and Jules disappeared the ward coin into an inner pocket, as though it had never existed at all.

The moment the door to her rooms shut behind them, Jules flicked the coin into the air with a taunting grin. It turned, winking in the low light. In her pocket, Selene's fingers tightened on the supple leather of his glove. As the coin fell between them, he lazily reached for it with his naked hand.

Her body moved on its own. She snatched the ward coin from

the air a moment before his fist closed over it and crashed into his chest, her shoulder colliding with his solar plexus. He caught her hips as his back hit the wall so she didn't slam into it too.

"What's your problem?" he demanded, confused and a little angry.

She tightened her hand around the disc, unsure why she'd reacted the way she did. Ward coins were harmful to demons, not to orphan soldiers.

Jules scowled, kneading his chest. "What *are* they?"

"I don't know."

Lie. She knew what they were, but she didn't want *him* to know. "Selene—"

"They're not *toys.*"

He grabbed her wrist, holding up the hand with the coin in it. "So, if it's not a toy, what is it?" Hadn't he seen another one like it around here somewhere? Releasing her, he crossed the room and reached into his coat pocket, shaking out the coins he'd liberated from the fountain.

"What are you doing?"

He ignored her, searching until he found the hexagonal coin. It was different from the others. The symbol on the back was a face, the mouth slightly agape. "What *are* these?"

Her eyes were wide as she watched him, chest rising and falling with quick breaths.

Fear? Surely not.

He frowned, spinning the coin between his fingers to look at the other side. "What does this writing say?"

SOPHIE CLARK

"What writing?"

Frustration bit at him and he dropped his hand. She was still watching him with that strange look on her face. "Do you have to look at me like that? Like a fucking idiot?"

Her expression clouded over. "Do you mean *you're* the idiot or am I?"

A fair question. He scrubbed his fingers through his hair, dropping his gaze as his ears grew hot. "Me."

"Liar."

Jules looked away, shifting back to lean against the bureau. Its marble top felt cold under his naked fingers.

Selene held out her hand, trembling slightly. "Give me the coin."

He scoffed quietly, but her eyes had an intensity he couldn't ignore.

When Jules held out the coin, she snatched it and wrapped her fingers around it tightly. "Not that you deserve an explanation, but there is nothing there. Nothing I can see anyway." She stalked away from him and put the coins into her desk, closing and locking the lid.

He turned away, eyes settling on the bar cart. Shedding his remaining glove as he went, Jules crossed the room and plucked out the stopper of a crystal decanter. He dropped it with a dull thunk onto the bar top and poured himself two generous dashes.

"Selene?"

"Hm?" Her eyes were distant, a pinch of concern between her brows.

He wanted to ask her more questions, but he remembered how she'd tucked the gold coin into her fist and away from his eyes. Remembered her shaking hands, and the words she said she couldn't see. She sequestered information away like a squirrel before winter, but at least that part had not seemed like a lie.

"Why didn't you want me to touch them?"

Silence.

Unbuttoning his shirt, Jules leaned back in the armchair, pressing the crystal tumbler to his temple. The fingers of his other hand traced the lines of his scar, the raised thorns and leaves. *No*, he thought bitterly. *Briars.*

Who would do such a thing to a newborn babe?

"What are you thinking?" she asked, searching his face.

If you knew what I'm thinking, Bouchère de Rome, *you'd kill me. Just like that.* He shook his head wordlessly, a bitter smile on his mouth as she came closer. And *Dieu*, if she wasn't the most beautiful killer he'd ever seen. Turning the crystal glass in his hand like a kaleidoscope, he watched her through it.

She pushed aside the tumbler so she could see his face. "The wards are old," she began, taking his silence for anger. Her words were a gesture of good faith. "We are only taught a little about them at the Academy. I always understood that they were older than our records."

"How can that be?"

"It was chaotic in the days after the Deathless God saved Rome. Until then, humanity had only faith to comfort them. God was a *concept*. Then He stepped into our world with fire in His eyes as a warrior god. It overturned everything we knew to be true."

Her lilting voice was soothing, so Jules listened.

"Every understanding had to be rewritten to account for a corporeal God who was very much present in our world. And for those of us in Rome, present in our lives. Right here."

"You're teaching me things I already know, exorcist."

A smile touched her lips. "I know. But can you *picture* it? The Vatican had to scramble to catch up with the new world order and at some point the wards were erected to protect God, so demons might not finish what they started. No one alive now knows how they were made or how they're being destroyed. The knowledge is lost. If Baliel is behind it, I can only imagine that his goal is . . ."

"*Dieu Immortel*," Jules murmured, still tracing his scars.

"And so I must kill him."

Such a cruel imperial agent when she had to be.

Selene shifted closer to sit on his knee as she pushed his shirt aside, shadowing his earlier movements as she trailed fingertips along the lines of the kill marks on his arms, tracing each one in turn until he lost count and his muscles unwound.

"I would not choose anyone else to stand beside me when I face down a demon duke." Her voice was so soft, he barely heard her.

The cloth bandage around her fist was beginning to soak through with splotches of crimson. He set down his glass and reached for her hand. Turning it over in his palm, he frowned. "This won't do. You'll get gangrene."

She rolled her eyes at him, unwilling to accept the same comfort she had given.

He leveled her with a look, jaw ticking. "You should bind this properly."

"It's fine. I'll heal."

He lifted her out of his lap, growling with irritation as he left the room. In the bathroom cabinet, Jules found an untouched first-aid kit. With care, he selected a brown bottle of liquid. Sniffing it, he confirmed it was iodine. Oh, this would sting.

Carrying a bundle of supplies to the bed, he patted the covers. "Sit."

She moved closer, perching on the edge as though she might take flight.

With careful fingers he unbound the makeshift bandage,

grimacing as the wound was revealed. "*Dieu Immortel*, is that bone?" he murmured.

She was determinedly looking anywhere else. "Probably."

He soaked a cotton pad with iodine, being generous because he still felt cross. She was being stubbornly stoic. His eyes returned to the cut bisecting her knuckles. "On three."

"Honestly, just do it."

"One . . ."

"I'm quite capable of—"

On two, he pressed the iodine against her knuckles, pinching the cotton to soak the wound. She hissed, spitting at him like a feral cat as she tried to pull away. He dodged her hand as she slapped for his head, fingernails nearly gouging out an eye. He didn't relinquish her wrist.

"You son of a—*shit*! Shit!"

Jules wrestled her back onto the bed, holding her down. "*Just do it*, she says. *Quite capable*, she says."

Selene snarled at him, lips curled over her teeth. "You did this on purpose."

"I sure did. I purposefully saved you from losing those lovely fingers. You're welcome." He pinned her down, holding her eyes as she stopped writhing. "*You* . . . you have no idea how much you test me, do you? When you yell, when you get hurt . . . everything you bloody do."

She arched her spine, shoving against his weight. "*Good.*"

He shook his head, his fingers releasing slowly as he began to laugh, and he shifted to the side, pressing the heels of his hands to his eyes. "You really mean that, don't you?"

She rolled away from him, curling on her side. "Yes."

"You live to torment me."

"You, personally," she said waspishly.

He laughed more, tears springing to his eyes. "Well, fuck my life, I guess."

The sun was barely above the horizon when something woke Selene. Morning light streamed in, painting the gauzy curtains a delicate gold. Jules was asleep beside her on top of the covers with one arm thrown over his eyes. Her knuckles throbbed, but not enough to have woken her.

Then came another knock.

Damn. She pulled on her jacket and boots and strode to the outer suite, softly closing the door behind her so she wouldn't wake Jules. When she answered the outer door it was to find one of her uncle's aides.

She'd been summoned.

When she arrived in Cesare's office, it was clear he had just returned from training. His discipline was one of iron. His wet hair was slicked back, highlighting the silver at his temples, and his face was solemn. He was the Imperium today, through and through.

"Good morning, Selene. I missed you at training." He snapped out a starched white shirt, his corded forearms dark with tattoos. Where Florentina had twenty, he had at least fifty. Selene's eyes trailed over the symbols. Each a word of power. There were many that she also had. He had been her teacher, after all. Though hers were carved into her bones.

But he had unique words too. *Wisdom. Stratagem. Fortitude.*

The words were as old as the walls they'd built around the Deathless God in the two centuries since he was almost slain. Where they had come from, she wasn't sure anyone living knew.

He pulled on the shirt, concealing them. "I heard what you did to Ambrose."

She grimaced. That snitch.

Cesare went on, ignoring the face she pulled. "Maiming him like that is beneath you, Selene. But I can't have you losing privileges now, not when you're my spear." He frowned. *Disappointed.* This was even worse than she'd thought it would be. Cesare sighed, running fingers through his hair. "So, I'm promoting you to Exorcist First Class, effective immediately."

Her stomach clenched. He tossed her a velvet box. Opening the lid, she found her new insignia gleaming within. *Not like this.*

"Say thank you," Cesare growled, his patience running out.

She could barely get the words out, her jaw was so tight. "Uncle, I've worked so long for this. Don't give it to me now. Not like this. I want to *earn* it, not—"

"You *are* earning it. You're earning it through your foolishness. I'm promoting you to get you out of trouble, and to show everyone watching on that I still have faith in you." After a beat of quiet, he added in a consoling tone, "Besides, your work in Nice was admirable."

This was salt to her wound. Cesare hadn't thought her work in Nice good enough for promotion on her return.

"I understand," Selene said dully.

"Congratulations."

"Yes, uncle."

She paused at the door, looking back. "You've diverted more exorcists out of the city—can I ask why?"

He didn't look up, his eyes already flicking over a report. He turned the page, reading another paragraph before he replied. "I diverted them to search for Baliel."

"Sir—"

"I know." He looked up.

His soothing tone only made her more irritated. "Then, why? If you heard me when I said he was coming *here*."

Cesare sighed, finally setting aside the blasted report. "Selene, you told me about your gut instinct. You can hardly expect me to allocate personnel based on that alone? Of course I sent teams to see if they can find a trace of him."

The words devastated her, and for a second she thought she couldn't quite breathe. Her hand curled around the ward coin she'd slipped into her pocket before leaving the rooms. Palming it, she slammed it onto her uncle's desk between them. "And what of this? Wards are breaking. Is it a coincidence?"

He stilled. "A single ward coin—"

"Not a *single* ward coin. There are more."

He took it, turning it over in his fingers. "I do not see Baliel's name written on this coin, Selene. Why do you think the Duke of Briars is involved? Do you have other evidence to suggest he's in Rome?"

Cesare wouldn't be impressed by her answer. "Kalindra."

"The information broker?" he said softly, the cutting edge to his words making it clear he meant, *The demon?*

"Her information's good—"

"Enough. When the Primus dies, the first thing I do will be to *reconsider* the value of the compact." She drew a sharp breath. His words were tantamount to treason. Cesare opened a wooden box on his desk and tossed the coin in before snapping closed the lid. "Instinct is one thing, Selene. I always encouraged you to follow your intuition. But conjecture based on loosely connected events is not enough for me to act. I hold lives in my hands. I have a war to manage. You need to do better. Do I make myself clear?"

"*Yes.*"

He raised a hand. "But you will not. Because I have handed this task along. You are here in Rome. Baliel is not." His dark eyes were steady, warning her against arguing. "And if you don't want Eliot sent back to Nice on the next train, you will not pursue this. Do you understand?"

All this time, she'd believed he trusted her. "I understand."

He nodded, turning back to the paperwork on his desk. The phone rang and with a sigh he scooped it up, glancing at Selene as he listened. "Oh, Selene." His soft voice stopped her in her tracks. "You're representing the Alleva family tonight. Remember that."

CHAPTER TWENTY-SEVEN

Jules woke alone. Morning sun slanted through the windows, painting the parquet floor in gold stripes. He reached for Selene beside him, but the sheets were cool. He sat up and pressed the heels of his hands to his eyes, grimacing against a dawning pain. Sleep had kept it just out of reach, but now it drew closer. *You are a demon.*

He screamed into a pillow without making a sound, the hollowness inside him rupturing. Somehow he'd held himself together in front of Selene, but the reality was ripping him apart. What did it mean that he was all demon without a single drop of human blood in his veins? And how many demons had he killed? He shrugged off his crumpled shirt and flexed his bicep, making the pale scars stand out against tanned skin. To know for sure, he'd have to count the marks. But not yet. He dreaded the knowledge.

After a shower, Selene still wasn't back. He couldn't wait here for her to return—he'd go mad—so he reached for the twin swords and strapped them to his hip. He needed to walk, then maybe he could outpace his racing thoughts. Retracing their steps from the night before, he soon found himself climbing the stairs at the

Castel Santo Immortale. The castle near the statue-lined bridge was the exorcists' deployment point and armory, connected via a tunnel to the rest of the Vatican. No sooner had he cleared the doors than he spotted a familiar golden head. His expression soured and he pushed his hands into his pockets, hoping Gabriel wouldn't see him.

And as Gabriel crossed the bridge toward him, walking ahead of a column of other exorcists, he almost didn't. At the last possible moment, he looked up, spotting him. "Eliot." He looked around, seeming disappointed not to find Selene. "I need you to take an important message to Selene. We were just called out for a demon at Palatine Hill, but instead we found a broken ward." His jaw tightened beneath his skin. "I'm going to report it to the Imperium Bellum, but tell her to keep her guard up."

Jules nodded. "Will do." He wanted to ask about the wards, but he couldn't without risk of exposing himself. Clearly Eliot was supposed to know. Selene had avoided his every question last night. She was impossible.

He crossed the Aelian Bridge and wandered into Rome, threading through narrow stone streets that branched into even smaller alleys, with doors so low he needed to duck head and shoulders to pass. He smiled when he saw the first lamppost decorated with the *E* and *K* key, and turned to go deeper into Sparrow's territory.

Beneath an ivy-covered bridge that spanned a wide alley was an old church decorated with skulls and carved dancing skeletons. One fleshless head appeared to be screaming. "You and me both, mate."

"Talking to yourself?"

He smiled, unsurprised by the rich, deep voice. "Sparrow. I was hoping we'd speak again."

The demon's eyes were warm. "Jules." Strolling closer, Sparrow looked him up and down. He wore a long wool coat, his slacks belted at his narrow waist and tightening again before the ankle.

"I'm talking to *him*," Jules said by way of explanation, nodding at the howling skull. "I call him Benoît."

"Benoît? For how long have you been doing that?"

"I named him just now. But I think it suits him."

"Certainly, *blessed* seems like the perfect name for a screaming skeleton."

They walked on together, and Jules told Sparrow what Gabriel had said.

His good humor died. "It was not the first."

"No," Jules agreed. "Kalindra gave Selene a handful of ward coins last night."

"So *that's* what the old woman told her."

"You know, I don't really believe in coincidences," Jules murmured, "which means the failing wards must be connected to Baliel, no?"

They passed through a wide piazza full of market stalls. The air smelled of sugary sweets and roasting nuts.

Sparrow nodded, expression taut. "I think that's a good guess. Why he's back, or what he wants, I have no more answers for you, I'm afraid. I just know it bodes ill." He glanced at Jules. "I don't know enough about his bloodline to tell how you might be related. Even if you share blood, he could be a threat to you."

"Tell me what you wanted to say last night. About the scar. About my—"

Mother. The word caught in his throat.

Sparrow's gaze settled on Jules's bicep, as though he could see the scar through his Vatican black. "I believe your mother was powerful. She carried you to term here in this world with the exorcist threat hanging over her head, then she did this to protect you."

Jules hung his head.

Sparrow's good eye searched his face. "Why do you look like that? It's true."

Jules shook his head bitterly. "I don't know if I can admire her. She bound my . . . *power* . . . before I ever knew I had it. How would you feel if your mother clipped your wings before you ever left the nest, Sparrow?"

Maybe it was lucky she had. Even with her mark, he was a monster. How much worse would he have been without it?

"But she didn't," Sparrow murmured, expression gentle. "This is much more sophisticated magic than the crude Vatican brands. Comparable to using a sledgehammer to amputate a finger." He flicked his eyes up, holding Jules's gaze. "This magic is sublime. And from a woman who had just given birth."

Jules ran his palm over the raised scar on his bicep. "I understand the concept of *half*-demons. They have a human parent. It makes some kind of twisted sense." In truth, the thought repulsed him, and he couldn't entirely keep it from his voice. "But I've *seen* demons. They're rarely—" Jules looked at Sparrow. "*Beautiful.* Perfect."

Sparrow's gorgeous mouth was tempted to a smile. "A good question. The answer is that you and I were made in this world. Long ago it was much easier for demons to come here."

"Why?"

He shrugged. "I'm not sure anyone knows. Maybe Baliel. Or someone who was alive back then." Sparrow leaned closer, his voice conspiratorial. "And back then demons were not monstrous."

Jules thought about Baliel and about the weather demon he

had crossed blades with on the battlefield. Perhaps *they* were what demons used to be. He withdrew Matteo Alleva's notebook from his pocket. "This belonged to Selene's father." He opened the book to Matteo's sketch of Baliel.

Brows crumpling, Sparrow turned the notebook between his hands. "You're sure this belonged to Matteo Alleva?"

Jules nodded, puzzled. "Why?"

"Demon dukes aren't your typical demon. They're immensely powerful. Their presence here is like a stone dropped in a pond. Demons usually know when one is here." Sparrow frowned. "I suppose we missed something." They stopped in the middle of one of the many bridges spanning the Tiber. He handed the notebook back to Jules.

"Don't you think it's strange? An exorcist knowing a demon duke? Knowing him well enough to commit his face to paper so clearly?" Jules ran his thumb over the sketch, wondering how this man was related to him. It still seemed unlikely.

"It would be," Sparrow began slowly, deep voice considered. "Except that Matteo Alleva was crucified."

"By Cesare." Jules's fingers tightened on the notebook, knuckles turning ghostly white as he dug his nails into the leather. "His own brother, no less."

Sparrow's face was grim.

"Do you know what he was executed for?" Jules asked.

Sparrow's eyes drifted to the notebook. "Would that I did. All I know is that the Vatican declared him an apostate."

Jules thumbed the notebook pages, wondering what Matteo knew that had made him reject the Vatican so completely that his own brother killed him for it.

He frowned. "I need to read this."

Upon Selene's return to her rooms, she found a scrap of paper with a scrawl of messy writing on the sideboard in place of Jules.

Back soon. J

  Surely that couldn't be all? She turned it over, searching for more, then scrunched it in her hand. *Damn him.*

She stormed out of her rooms and down the hall.

Useless. Why bother leaving a note if that was all he was going to write?

Striding around the corner ahead, Jules grinned when he saw her, eyes flicking down to the crumpled note in her fist. "You found my message, I see."

"Is *that* what you call this?"

"Of course," he said simply, rocking on his heels with his hands in his pockets. He looked too damn pleased with himself, a teasing smirk curling the corners of his mouth.

"What if I'd needed to find you?"

He shrugged. "You didn't, did you?"

Throwing her hands up, she stalked past him. He was being deliberately obtuse.

Falling into step with her, he lowered his voice. "I bumped into Gabriel coming back from Palatine Hill. They found another broken ward."

The blood drained from her face, uncertain which part of that alarmed her more.

His large hand landed lightly on her shoulder. "I didn't mention anything," he reassured her softly, his eyes skipping over her face. And sure enough, her heartbeat gradually slowed. "Told him I'd tell you. That's it."

The clipped sound of boots on slate announced a whole swath of Academy grads from her year. She turned, watching them go.

"Coming to train, Selene?" called Chiara, one of Gabriel's artificers.

Jules stepped up behind her. "Do you think you can defeat me?" His breath made her hair tickle her neck, and heat flooded her cheeks.

"I already did. Yesterday."

He shrugged, smirking. "I don't remember it like that."

By the time they arrived at the training yard, Selene had her mask securely back in place. She pictured her expression as marble, like the demons that flanked the Aelian Bridge. No flush stained her cheeks, betraying what she hid inside her ribs. But what exactly was she hiding? Fingertips smoothing over the bandage Jules had tied around her hand, lingering over his careful butterfly knot, she realized she couldn't put a name to this feeling.

A strange disquiet made her feel as though events were slipping out of her control. The unpleasant sensation redoubled when Florentina lit up upon seeing Jules.

Short memory, Selene thought caustically.

Flipping her long golden ponytail over one shoulder, Florentina bounded up to Jules, molding herself to his side. "You're not cross with me, are you?" Florentina pouted out her lower lip, as though he might be so easily swayed.

"How could I be cross with you?" Jules smiled easily.

Men.

Florentina shot her a triumphant look over Jules's shoulder.

Selene forced a smile. With teeth.

Watching them talk, it was as though something large and

particularly toothy was gnawing at her intestines. Perhaps this was what it felt like to be possessed. Unpleasant, certainly. Regrettably, she wasn't possessed. More like *obsessed*. The ward coins jangled in her pocket and her new insignia weighed heavily on her lapel, yet all she could think about was the way Florentina put on her most gregarious act for Jules, forcing a surprised laugh out of him.

It was similar to how she'd felt last night, whenever Sparrow had looked at Jules like he was a delicious morsel. And damn it, he was, but Sparrow had no business noticing. Nor did Florentina. Then again, neither did *she*.

Selene pressed a hand to her forehead. She was probably sick. The stress of this past week. That had to be it . . .

After training—and a long, hot shower—Selene joined Jules in the sunroom. He was poring over her father's notebook again.

She thought Eliot had been remarkably optimistic to imagine her father might have anything useful to add seven years after his death, but when she'd voiced the thought aloud, Jules had waved the sketch at her again. "Matteo's the only exorcist who met Baliel. Everyone else is under the misapprehension he hasn't been seen for a hundred years."

Dio Immortale, she was sick of seeing that face.

Despite herself, she drifted closer and plucked the book from his hands. "How do you know that?" she said absently, running her fingers along the green leather spine. Even if it was useless, it was a beautiful object. An intricate Alleva *A* decorated the spine above the *vol. ii.*

"When I showed Sparrow the picture of Baliel, he mentioned it."

Sparrow. She tried not to react to his name, but felt the bitter twist to her mouth. She bit her lower lip and returned to the pages. Near the end, her father's handwriting became so tiny it took on an incomprehensible slant. She turned it sideways and tipped her head, hoping the change of angle would illuminate the situation.

No, not incomprehensible. *Latin.*

"I think he's written in code. Or the best he could manage in the time that he had."

"I thought you knew Latin?"

Grimacing, she shook her head. "Not enough."

She flipped through the book, scanning the pages. Words jumped out at her and she paused.

Jules looked over her shoulder. "*Initia: Deus et Daemones.* Well, that one sounds intriguing."

Selene nodded. "That much I know. *The Beginning: God and the Demons,*" she said, running her fingertip over the pictures around the edge. Her father had drawn an intricate labyrinthine border with symbols she recognized. *Divorare. Protezione. Ritorno. Fortuna.* They were symbols for triggering magic. *Devour. Protection. Return. Fortune.*

Jules frowned, pointing at four symbols she barely recognized decorating each corner of the next page. "These were on the hexagonal discs."

"What discs?" she said absently.

Jules snorted. "The ones that made you lose your—"

She shot him a warning look.

"The ward coins."

He still sounded sullen and she struggled not to roll her eyes. Then his words sank in. *Legamento. Sigillo. Proteggere. Guardia.*

"*Bind. Seal. Protect. Guard,*" she murmured. She grabbed his hand, pulling him out of the room and into the corridor. "Come on. We're going to the language library."

This library was inside one of the smaller domes. The floor was a vast marble mosaic of aigikampos, winged hippocampi, and other sea monsters. The walls were unknowable, covered as they were by tall shelves. Selene took Jules up the hidden staircase and found the books on translation on the top walkway, just below the dome.

She piled thick leather tomes into Jules's arms and drew him to a desk by one of the ceiling windows. The dome was dark, what little light there was came from two chandeliers that hung halfway to the floor below.

At last, the books she needed were spread out before her and she held her fountain pen poised. "*Oh.* I don't have paper."

Jules flipped to the back of a book and ripped out a blank page. She gasped.

He rolled his eyes. "Oh, come on. Nobody else needed it."

Her silence was condemnation enough. Still, she accepted the page. Holding the notebook open with a finger, she juggled one of the Latin dictionaries and held the fountain pen between her teeth.

With a laugh Jules claimed the pen and slid the torn page in front of himself. "I'll transcribe." Limned in pale winter light, he looked otherworldly.

Finally, she dragged her eyes away and began to translate.

The Vatican does not often speak of its origins. We forget because we do not wish to remember.

And by any accounting, two centuries is time enough to forget much. Even as I watch, Rome, who survived empires, crumbles around me. As we fight for our city and our people, I can't help but think it's not reason enough to forget that demons were the ones who gave us the means to fight and protect.

Selene paused at that, frowning. It was *known* in the Vatican, among those who graduated from the Academy, how they got their borrowed power. They all went through it. So what did her father mean, exactly? She skimmed the page again, then flipped through to the first entry they had read. It reassembled itself before her eyes. The dashed-out sections. The corrections. The way he had written the known dogma and replaced it with . . . *discoveries?*

She read on, eyes skimming the Latin as she grew more comfortable, but she didn't speak the next part aloud for Jules.

*Demons gave us the symbols we use to kill them.
And they gave us the wards.*

Jules looked up. "Selene?"

She stared at the page. "Sorry . . . I don't know how to translate the next bit, hang on." She flicked through the pages and then closed the book. "Let's take this with us. We'll do more later." Or she'd find a way to lose the notebook, because her father was mad, wasn't he? There was no way demons had given them the wards. Even as she thought it, she felt her confidence waver. Could the reason her father died be written in these pages?

She jumped when Jules closed the large book, releasing a puff of dust. "It's interesting. I heard something similar recently."

"Hm?" Selene glanced at her watch, only half listening. *Damn.* It was long since time they started getting ready for the masquerade.

Jules drew doodles around the edge of the page, staring out the window with unfocused eyes. "On my last day in Ostrava, I met someone on the battlefield who said something like, *The Holy Vatican Empire, and all those beneath their aegis, have forgotten much.* Or words to that effect."

She frowned, searching his face. His easy smile was gone, replaced by an expression taut with pain. Not for the first time she wondered what had happened that day. What had driven him from war when he'd been so deadly proficient at it?

"Who—and I mean this in the *strongest* sense—the absolute fuck said something like that on a battlefield?"

His eyes snapped up to hers. They were bottomless and a self-preservation instinct made her want to lean away. She ignored it. Even if he seemed far away and unknowable, he was still *Jules*.

"The Caspian Tsarina," he said in a voice not quite his own. "After she wiped out my entire battalion."

CHAPTER TWENTY-EIGHT

Just as they arrived back in her rooms, the telephone gave a shrill ring and Selene scrambled to snatch up the handset. "Captain Alleva speaking."

"Vatican switch . . . transferring . . ."

Selene waited, impatient and curious. Only outside calls went through the switch. Eliot or Caterina, then. Or, if she was really unlucky, it'd be Lucia.

"*Little French shit!*"

Selene pulled the phone away from her ear, wincing. "Caterina?"

"I'm going to kill him."

Selene's heart leaped to her throat. Was she talking about Jules?

"Goddamn . . . slippery . . ." In between swears, the line crackled loudly.

Selene gritted her teeth. "Caterina, for the love of God, speak into the receiver. And *slow down.*"

"Captain! There you are!" Caterina's voice was only a little clearer. "We're—" What sounded like a train whistle drowned her out and her next words were shouted even louder to be heard. "Gotta go, boss. We're coming back to Rome. The train's—"

Another protracted whistle.

"There he is!" shouted Lucia excitedly from the background.

Click. The line went dead.

Selene stared at the phone, feeling as though she'd experienced a very confusing week in double time.

"What was that?" Jules sounded amused.

She turned, finding him in the doorway watching her with a strange expression. *Damn.* He also looked gorgeous, lazily leaning against the doorframe, adjusting his cuff links. Formal white tie looked good on him. Unbidden, a treacherous little voice added, *Everything looks good on him.*

If only he could wear the medals he'd earned on the front. Of course, that was silly. Eliot had no medals of honor to wear.

The trailing ends of his white tie caught her eye and she stepped closer. Voice failing her, she swallowed. "Do you even know how to tie that?"

"I'm not an idiot," he said, eyes sparkling.

Selene smothered a smile as he turned to the mirror, crossing one end over the other, proceeding to look very much like an idiot. She pressed two fingers to her lips so she wouldn't laugh.

"Come here."

Her heart seemed to sit too high and beat too fast, tripping over itself by the time Jules stopped in front of her. She untied the clumsy knot and smoothed down his collar. Even her fingers were trembling.

"It's quite simple."

He nodded, his eyes roaming over her features. She swore she could feel the heat of his gaze on her skin.

Carefully she did up the white tie, taking longer than necessary.

Her fingers brushed his throat and she felt the flutter of his pulse.

Jules broke the silence. "What was the call?"

"Caterina," she explained. "It sounded . . . chaotic. I have no idea what's happening. They're coming back to Rome apparently."

"From Nice?"

"I suppose so."

Selene finished and ran the backs of her fingers lightly against his jaw. Stubble pricked her fingers and a coil of heat burned in her belly. *Dio*, she had it bad. "Did you forget to shave?"

"Damn. I *knew* I forgot something." He yanked at the tie, preparing to rip it all off so he could shave.

Her hands covered his. "Wait."

"Selene, I don't want to be late."

She drew his hands down from his throat and pulled him into the bathroom. "Come with me."

He fell silent as she guided him to the edge of the bathtub. When she found the shaving kit, she handed him the brush and soap and draped a towel around his shoulders. Jules soaped up, still watching her intently. Trailing her fingers along the selection of ivory-handled razors, she made her choice.

He swallowed.

"I'm very good with knives." Selene tested the edge with her thumb. Wicked sharp. She smiled.

He made a choked sound that wasn't quite a laugh. "Believe me, I know."

"So you have nothing to worry about." She rolled her eyes, stepping between his knees. "Head back."

With the same dedication she gave to her work, she started to shave him with long, smooth strokes. Wiping the blade on the towel, she smoothed a thumb over the clean skin and made a soft sound of satisfaction.

Jules gripped the bathtub with one hand. His other hovered, as though he wasn't sure what to do with it. Then, taking a breath, he settled it lightly on her waist.

His touch was like fire. Hotter than Baliel's flames. An impression that only worsened when he began to trace patterns against her side with his thumb. She shivered, tightening her grip on the ivory handle.

At her urging, he angled his head, exposing the column of his throat. But she could still feel his undivided attention, and it made warmth coil in her stomach. "What?" she murmured, not looking up. She couldn't risk their eyes meeting or he'd see the truth there.

Would that be so bad? asked a traitorous little voice. *Yes.* Jules couldn't know how much she wanted him. Neither of them could afford the complication. Or the distraction.

"Nothing." He sounded somewhat strained.

She paused to clean the blade. "No, seriously, what?" Daring a glance, she was arrested by the intensity of his gaze.

A smile played at the corner of his mouth. "You're beautiful."

Heat rose to her cheeks. It was frankly quite rude of Jules to have such lovely eyelashes.

"I'm serious—"

She hushed him, pressing the edge of the blade to the last remaining patch of lathered skin. "Hold still, unless you want me to slit your throat."

He fell silent, but his hand on her waist shifted, thumb drawing slow circles against her ribs as he tipped his head further back to let her work. And *oh*, that distracting thumb. He was lucky she truly was the best in the Vatican with a knife.

There was a loud rap at the entrance to her rooms, and from beyond the closed bathroom door came a flurry of activity. "Oh. That's for me." She was loath to leave, taking her time with the final stroke. Setting aside the razor, she patted a towel against his skin.

"Done?" he asked in a husky voice.

She touched his perfectly smooth cheeks with her fingertips, and with no more excuses left, she met his eyes. "Done."

He grasped her waist between his palms and seemed about to say something more when a knock sounded from the other side of the bathroom door.

"A minute," Selene called, not breaking their gaze. The knocking increased in enthusiasm. She dragged her eyes from his to glare at the closed door. "I said, a minute!"

"Rome wasn't built in a day, *mia signora*, and you won't be made fit for the empress in one hour!"

Jules grinned, sliding his hands higher. "*Mia signora*," he murmured, teasing.

His fingers were too strong against her ribs, his touch far too warm. "Shut up."

Jules waited in one of the smaller chambers between the wing of St. Peter's where Selene's rooms were located and the center of the dome, exiled as he was from the apartment. None of the ladies who arrived to help Selene get ready seemed eager to countenance his presence until their task was done.

As he looked out the vast window at the empty piazza below, he heard Selene before he saw her, and turning, he forgot to breathe. Whatever those bossy women did was nothing if not some unspoken Vatican magic, because she had been transformed.

He'd always found Selene frighteningly attractive—literally, frightening—but now there was more to it than the way his body reacted to hers. The dress she wore was the kind of black that swallowed the light, like only the most complete shadows. She was still dangerous, but there was a softer edge to her beauty. And maybe it wasn't all about the dress. It was something in her eyes . . . an unspoken spark of possibility.

His traitorous heart grabbed on to it.

Yes, it beat in reply. *I want you too.*

The fabric moved like liquid as she descended the stairs. He wondered if it felt as good as it looked where it dipped against her slender waist and over her hips. He wanted to touch it. But maybe that was only because he wanted to touch *her*.

She held her scabbarded sword loosely in one hand. Even if she'd been descending these steps at his execution, he doubted he would have noticed anything but her legs. A long slit opened up the side of her gown, baring a stretch of smooth thigh to right below her hip. Where some panels were daringly sheer, others were opaque and had been sewn with gold embellishments, stars and constellations, as though she'd captured the starry night in her skirt.

He swallowed, adjusting his cuff links to stop himself adjusting his pants. A dress like this one should be illegal. Praise the Deathless God that it wasn't—but it *should* be.

He let his eyes roam over her, from the beaded straps on her shoulders to the sheer skirts.

She paused halfway down the stairs and raised a brow.

He jerked his chin up. Now he knew how the field mouse felt under the eye of a hawk.

"Where are you looking?" she asked, expression unreadable.

"Just admiring the tailoring. It looks, um, proficient."

Her lips tipped into a small smile. "*Really.*"

He leaped up the steps to meet her, taking her hand. "Not at all, no."

As she led them through the halls of the Vatican at a quick clip,

Jules was a man on fire. He could still feel her touch. The blush dusting her cheeks was a sight he'd never forget. But most surprising of all was how patient she'd been as she shaved him.

Of course, he knew by now she could be gentle with those slender fingers of hers. He knew they got chilly fast and touched softly, but the electricity of the contact had felt different today. He wanted to believe there was a chance.

Dieu. Every moment she'd pressed the blade against his skin, he'd fallen more in love with her. Infatuated by the way she bit her lip. The pressure she applied at the edge of his jaw.

It didn't even matter that for a moment he thought she might slit his throat.

And that was the crux of it. If Selene learned what he was, she would kill him, not love him.

Maybe tonight he could hold her. But then he'd have to run. One more night. Even just a moment. Couldn't he have that?

The thought broke him.

He walked half a step behind her, careful not to step on her gauzy dress. The plunging back showed off her shoulder blades and a series of minuscule tattoos along her spine. He raised his hand to graze his knuckles against them. They held a remarkable similarity to the elegant elongated symbols from Matteo's journals. He felt sure he recognized one.

Proteggere. Jules mouthed the word.

His footsteps faltered. He could smell blood. It crept up on him, choking him. Filling his nostrils.

Selene glanced over her shoulder and her brows tugged together at whatever she saw on his face.

The scent of blood was overwhelming. He turned his hands, looking them over. Were they covered with blood? Was that where it came from? Sometimes, when the Vatican sword shattered, all that remained was the blood dripping between his fingers. As though he'd ripped the demons apart with nothing but his hands.

St. Peter's was quiet. Distant footsteps sounded through the halls but he couldn't see who they belonged to. What was it about this place that triggered his fear response? And his battle instinct, too? He thought he could kill someone. Right now.

"Jules?" Selene whispered his name.

Turning sharply, he angled his head and inhaled. The hairs on his neck stood on end—if he were a wolf, his hackles might rise. He strode past her, grabbing her hand. "Hurry."

"What is it?"

Her heels clicked on stone as she ran to keep up with him, holding her dress in one hand.

"God, do you smell that?" he muttered.

Selene frowned, responding in French. "I don't smell anything, Jules."

He was confused a moment. He'd reverted to his mother tongue. Unease climbed his throat, and he felt penned in by the reek—he was an animal, and all he wanted was to run.

So he did.

They ran past paintings and sculptures worth more than the orphanage he was raised in. More than Nice itself. Selene kept saying his name, softly at first, then louder. Nothing broke through and he only stumbled to a stop at a dead end.

His pulse and the howling in his ears was louder.

Selene pulled him back, grasping his jacket. Then she tried to grab his hands, her fingers digging into him. They stumbled together as she became increasingly frantic in her efforts. "Jules, please—" But the rest of her words faded away as they slammed into a pair of double doors, sprawling to the marble floor.

The scent was less overwhelming here, but it still lingered in the air, acrid as burned citrus.

Jules pressed his palms to his temples, tempted to crush his skull between his fingers. What was this agony? This . . . this yearning? This desperate wail into the abyss to please—*please* . . .

Jules didn't know if the thoughts were his own. He couldn't separate what came from him and what came from elsewhere, and that frightened him. His mind pressed back against the pain and it felt as though only a shimmering membrane held his mind apart from oblivion.

Tipping his chin back slowly, Jules looked upon the face of the Deathless God, and tears ran through his lashes and streaked down his cheeks.

Towering over them, crucified on the great burned oak beam of an ancient cathedral, was a beautiful god. A great spear pierced him through.

His lean, languid limbs were shrouded in deep shadow, as though the darkness loved him. But then so did the light. His bent neck curved in such a way that a rogue bar of pale light picked out the delicate bumps of vertebrae beneath pale skin. A silken fall of dark curls shadowed his features.

Jules devoured the sight. If not for the steady drip of lustrous golden blood along the length of the spear, he could be sleeping.

"*Dieu Immortel.*"

His words weren't a prayer but a curse. For the thing in front of him was no god. He was a *demon*.

Jules's hands slid on the warm marble. No, that wasn't right. When he tore his eyes off God, he saw a luminous pool like liquid gold spreading from beneath his feet.

Blood. *So much* blood.

It filled the chamber, making the space echo with a constant hollow dripping that he'd first thought was water.

His hands were soaked in it.

The Deathless God's voice resonated through Jules's veins. *Let me—please* . . . When Jules angled his wrists up, they sang with it. Aureate and breakable as a crescent moon. He ran a finger over one of the glowing veins, not quite understanding.

Somewhere he could hear Selene screaming, her voice breaking as she ordered someone to *Get out or I'll kill you myself.* Or maybe she was speaking to him.

But . . . that didn't matter.

Everything beyond the high, sweet thrum in his veins felt smudged.

A primal plea seemed to pass through his blood and bones, echoing in his skull as though a tuning fork had been struck. *Please, let me die.*

Selene pulled him away, gasping as she hauled him up and stumbled with him against the wall, tearing down a tapestry as they fell together. She pressed her hands to his wrists, covering the spiderwebbing gold veins from sight as she hurried him through the depthless halls. When they passed a gilded mirror, he caught a glimpse of himself and he wasn't crying tears but *blood.*

Somewhere else, somewhere where the stench was less and the song was quiet, she slid with him to the marble floor, her hands cupping his face.

"Jules . . . *Jules!*"

His unfocused eyes finally found her.

"*Dio*," she breathed, relief stealing her remaining strength. "I thought . . ." She trailed off, dropping her forehead to his chest.

He tangled his hand in her hair. It was so dark and fine it felt like silk. His fingers felt rough and clumsy in comparison. "You thought what?"

His voice was hoarse. Perhaps some of the screams he'd heard had been his own? He couldn't quite remember.

"I thought you were going to die. Like anyone else." Selene blinked away tears. "His blood burns." She smoothed her palm over his fingers, using her silk shawl to wipe away gold liquid. Blood. All over his hands.

"*You* aren't dying."

"No, but I'm an exorcist. We're immune to the divine touch." She pulled his sleeve aside to see his wrist, her fingers gentle as she turned his hand. His veins had returned to normal—faint blue lines beneath pale skin. Tentatively she trailed a fingertip along one as though he might disintegrate beneath her touch.

"I've never seen anything like this. What was it?" She pressed her thumb against his pulse point and his heart stuttered. He wanted to pull away from her, to shift from her touch—so different from earlier—but he couldn't. Her long, tapered fingers were unyielding.

He shook his head. "I don't know."

One of the Vatican's great bells began to ring, echoing through the empty halls.

Jules's hands trembled like leaves and he started to turn away. "I can't go to the masquerade."

Selene took his shirt collar in one hand, forcing him to face her. "Eliot would never disobey an order. The Imperium Bellum *ordered* you to be there tonight. He's already watching us, Jules. Don't give him a reason to suspect anything is amiss. This is both our lives now."

She helped him to his feet.

Jules trailed behind her, touching the skin of his wrists. Despite how it had looked, when his blood ignited, it hadn't burned. And he had a valuable new piece of information. Selene's *God* was a demon like him.

She couldn't know. She would never question her god, and she wouldn't be able to fake her faith.

Which raised the question, did the demons know? Was this why the Tsarina had sacrificed waves of her men assaulting Rome's borders? And why demons attacked Rome more than anywhere else in the empire?

All the questions made a deeper throbbing begin at his temples, and he leaned against the wall to catch his breath. He needed to speak with Sparrow about what he'd learned, and soon. Before he made a mistake in front of Selene and she decided to finish him off herself.

"Come on," she urged.

Jules scratched at his arm. His skin felt tight and hot.

Selene glanced back and came to a sudden stop. Following her gaze, he saw crimson blotches like flowering poppies on his white sleeves. Heart stammering in his chest like a moth trapped inside his ribs, Jules tore at his shirt cuffs. Every one of his kill marks bled, even ones that had been healed for years. His blood ran thick and dark in the guttering light of the Vatican halls.

His thoughts were panicked. This was punishment from the Deathless God. A false *god* but a *real* demon. Jules had killed hundreds of them during the war. His throat tightened. He was a killer, and the only rationalization he'd ever needed was that they were demons and he was not.

He scratched his arms, as though trying to pull away his skin and see what was beneath. *He* was a demon too. What twisted, corrupted being hid beneath his flesh? He clawed at the dozens of bleeding crucifixes on his arms, splattering dark blood on the black and white tiles beneath his feet.

Selene made a wordless sound of horror, grabbing for his hand. Her fingers slid between his own—strong and warm. She pulled him along, taking him somewhere. He was unaware of all but the sound of her footsteps.

"Jules, *stop*." Her voice cut like glass, and he stopped.

His back was against something cold and hard. When he shifted, he felt ironwork. A distant dripping echoed. The swirl of panic receded as he tried to match his breathing to hers. She was panting too, muscles trembling at the effort she'd gone through to fight him and prevent him from mutilating himself. After a few more deep breaths, her muscles relaxed, fingers loosening on his but not letting go.

"Where are we?"

He could see the delicate blue veins on her eyelids from here, and the way his breath stirred her hair. Beyond her, dark stairs curved upward.

"The Vatican necropolis."

His hand tightened reflexively on hers. "Not the most popular place in the building?"

"Kind of avoided actually."

The chill in the air was deterrent enough. Beyond the ironwork gate, stone coffins had been arrayed in the necropolis and disappeared into the darkness. He finally dared a look at his sleeves. The white fabric was stained scarlet. Shaking, he tried to unbutton his shirt, pulling at the tie around his throat. She pushed his hands aside and made quick work of his buttons. Her pulse was still up— he could see it in the flutter of her throat.

Reaching for her, he pressed his thumb against her wrist, counting the beats of her heart until his own seemed to settle. "I'm sorry . . ." His words sounded papery. "Sorry for scaring you."

Her lashes trembled. "I wasn't scared."

Resuming her task, she pushed the shirt off his shoulders. Her eyes lowered and she stilled. "This scar—" She dropped the shirt and it fluttered toward the ground. Jules snatched it out of the air before it could land on the cold stone, but his whole attention was on her fingertips tracing the briar thorns carved into his skin.

He shrugged, walling off his feelings.

Her expression clouded over. "Tell me."

"I've had it as long as I can remember. Since before I was found. Since I was a day old, I suppose."

She scanned his face and he couldn't quite recognize the intense look in her eyes.

"Do you know what it is?"

"Nothing. Just a scar. Or a birthmark." He brushed her off, putting a foot on the first stair.

She twisted his bloody shirt between her fists. "I'll get you another shirt."

She swept past him and Jules dropped his face into shaking hands, grinding the heels of his hands into his eye sockets as her footsteps faded away.

CHAPTER TWENTY-NINE

At some point between the Vatican necropolis and her rooms, Selene kicked off her heels. In truth, it was muscle memory that got her there at all, her bare feet slapping against the floor just as they had when she was a child. She felt no more capable now—more helpless than ever for the sword clutched in her hand and nobody to use it on.

Pain resonated from inside her ribs, making her lungs constrict so every breath felt like an impossibility. By the time she arrived at her rooms, she was gasping, dragging at the bodice of her dress as she tried to get enough air.

There'd been so much blood. Gold blood and red blood and the beautiful, terrible face of God impassive above it all. And Jules . . . Fear spiked through her and her fingers curled, wanting to grasp his shirt or touch his face. He was really all right, wasn't he? Why hadn't she checked his pulse one more time before she left?

She ripped the room apart, searching for something for him to wear before finally spotting another white shirt and vest hanging on the doorknob. She reached for it and saw her bloody hands. Stained with Jules's blood. Stained with God's blood.

"No . . ." she whimpered, sliding to the floor in a puddle of midnight silk. "Not again."

Stories about the Deathless God were as common as the rats in Rome's gutters. But Selene had known from the first moment she laid eyes on Him when she was a little girl, when she had followed her father into that sacred chamber, that none of them did the awful truth any justice at all.

The truth was simple: their once-absent God had stepped forward as Rome's shield and sword against the demons who wanted only destruction.

After a battle of many days and nights—nights lit bright as dawn from demon fire—God had defeated the most powerful of the demons as Rome burned around them. But not before He was impaled on her great spear. The colossal battle had crushed part of the Vatican, and God's body had been pinned to an immense beam at the heart of the ancient building, neither dead nor fully alive. So they had rebuilt around Him.

As a child of eleven, she had been unprepared for the reality. The memory played through her mind with perfect clarity, even seven years on.

She had edged around the sleeping guards. No longer tempted to call for her father, she bit her lip. Buried deep in the confines of her rib cage thrummed a dreadful realization: her father was doing something terrible. She shoved down her pain until it smoldered inside her.

There was a pale glimmer at the far end of the shadowed *Cor Cordium*.

As her eyes landed on His face, a gasp had been torn out of her as she flung up a hand in front of her eyes. *Too slow.* She saw Him before her hand blocked the sight. Tears streamed down her cheeks as she blinked the afterimage away. The *Cor Cordium* was dark, with only a few guttering candles lighting the corners, yet the curve of His neck, the gilded softness of His hair and the jut of His cheekbones amid the shadows were enough to burn her eyes.

When she touched her cheeks, her tears were running red.

Careful not to look directly at God again, she used the shadows to steal closer.

The chamber was so large it almost made God look small, but when she saw her father standing at his feet, she could see that the Deathless God must be eight feet tall from the crown of His head to the tips of His toes. Metallic gold pooled beneath His feet, dripping down the dais steps.

Her father gave this pool a wide berth, gazing up at the God with no hesitation in his eyes. They burned with a feverish light that Selene had never before seen. After circling the shallow pool once, Matteo Alleva splashed through it, grasping the haft of the spear with one large hand. He stilled, candlelight painting his face in stark relief.

For a moment the scene looked as though he had just plunged the spear deep into an enemy's chest. Her breath caught and she was unable to make a sound. It was magnificent. Even her heart seemed to slow its hurried beat to a steady thrum. Fresh tears dampened her lashes at the sight.

Her father drew the spear from the Deathless God's chest, splattering the wall opposite with the aureate gore. *Blood*. The pool was fresh blood. Selene cried out wordlessly.

Her father turned and his expression twisted with horror. "Selene, you can't be here. *Run!*"

Behind him, the Deathless God twitched. His great head lolled an inch to the side, and as blood ran down her cheeks, she met His terrible gaze as one eye opened, peering at her through the fall of His hair.

Green eyes, she remembered now.

A wave of energy so intense it might have stripped the skin from her bones slammed her back against the wall, but her father's body sheltered her as he held her against himself. His leg snapped like a twig against one of the columns that circled the chamber.

Selene was tossed away, limp as a rag doll.

Something clattered across the floor toward her, stopping shy of the pool of blood.

Whimpering in pain, Selene dragged herself toward it. She took the heavy wooden spear haft in both hands; her fingers were barely able to grasp it. The sharp obsidian point dragged on the ground as she approached the stirring god.

His long, elegant fingers twitched.

Selene knew what she had to do. He was the *Deathless* God, neither living nor dead, and her father had committed a sin. She had to fix it.

Her entire life was an exercise in patience as she waited. Waiting to be big enough to hold a blade in one hand. Waiting to be strong enough to swing it.

Waiting to be old enough to take the vow.

But now her father had ruined everything. If she couldn't fix this, her waiting would never end. She'd *never* be an exorcist. She'd just be dead with the rest of her family.

She thought of her twin and their mother.

If she fixed this, maybe she could beg the Vatican to overlook her father's crime. She hadn't even finished the thought before her mind shut it down. Even as a child, she was not that naive. Her father was *dead*. All she could do now was beg for her family.

With a primal scream of rage and agony, Selene swung the spear with both hands.

The muscles in her arms strained as she used momentum to swing it around and up and slammed it back into the Deathless God. Her vision wavered as agony like none she had ever known tore through her. It burned up her legs from her bare feet, puddled in God's blood. It was as though something hotter and whiter than fire ignited in her middle. She was *dying*.

A wash of hot liquid soaked her hands as she sagged against the spear. It was all that held her up, anchored between God's ribs. She hoped He'd be the last thing she'd see, not her father with blood haloing his head. The Deathless God's blood burned her hands and feet, and down the column of her throat. She could feel it scouring her out of existence. On her lips, on her *tongue*.

Selene pushed herself up and washed her hands, turning them under the gushing water until they were spotless. She carefully collected the fresh shirt and vest and walked to the door. Catching her reflection, she ripped out the dozens of diamond-tipped pins from her hair and let it fall around her face.

Yanking the door open, Selene bit back a gasp of surprise. Cesare Alleva looked down at her, bemused. "You're still here?"

"We're just on our way out." Selene tried to relax her grip on the shirt. "Of course he forgot his shirt."

"*Of course . . .*"

"And of course he had to train, right before the masquerade." She forced a wry smile, rolling her eyes. "Men."

"We're a curse," he replied, watching her closely. "Are you all right, Selene?"

"Quite. You know I hate being late. And I don't suffer fools."

Cesare smirked slightly at that. "I noticed. Eliot will be on the couch tonight, I presume?"

Selene pressed her lips into a tight smile. "I have to go."

"Yes, you do." He glanced at his watch, raising one brow. "Don't be late. If you are, I'll be convinced Eliot is a bad influence on you. I cannot afford for you to lose your edge."

She nodded, almost running away from him. Turning the corner, she glanced back.

Cesare's gaze was directed at her bare feet, his dark brows pulled together in thought.

Jules lifted his head when he heard footsteps. He'd lost track of how long he had been inside the Vatican necropolis, though it was long enough for the chill to have slid into his bones.

Selene crouched beside him, smoothing his hair from his brow. He leaned into her hand. "It's funny . . ."

"What is?" she asked, concern in her eyes.

"In Ostrava the cold didn't bother me. But now I feel like I might die of it."

She moved closer, rubbing his shoulder with her hand. "It's the shock. We need to get you moving." She swallowed. "And we need to go."

He met her gaze. "The masquerade?"

She nodded, still rubbing his shoulder. Her hair fluttered in a draft from within the necropolis.

A hint of foul blood.

Jules covered his nose. "What's that smell?"

He could practically see her patience fray at his repeated mention of something she couldn't sense.

"I don't *know*."

But he did, he realized. It was the carrion scent of their captive god. The scent of His torment.

"You don't *know*? Is it just me who has to put up with this stench?"

Selene almost looked afraid. Concern warred with confusion in her expression. It made him angrier. He closed the distance between them so he could take the shirt roughly from her hands. As he pulled it on, he caught her looking at the scar around his bicep again, her expression drawn.

"You're staring."

"Did you do that?"

"No."

"Tell me what it is," she demanded, her voice tightly controlled.

"I told you, it's just a birthmark—"

"*Liar.*"

Jules tried to ignore the barb, but it hooked itself right into the fabric of his raw emotions.

"Who are you to say that? You lie as easily as breathe." He spread his hands, looking around. "Not that I can blame you, raised in this twisted place. It's *rotten*, Selene." He leaned close to breathe against her neck. "This place reeks of corruption."

She barked a laugh, although her cheeks had gone blotchy with anger. Her reaction reminded him of the first night on the train from Nice when she was all razor edges. He'd hit a nerve.

He already regretted the words, turning to pace away.

"Oh, I'm sorry. Do you miss the glory of the trenches?"

The trenches. Everything darkened. He prowled closer, getting into her space. "*Don't.*"

Selene snarled wordlessly against his face, teeth bared.

He laughed, trying to cover a sliver of genuine fear. "You look half feral."

"At least it's only half. *Dio*, I pity your poor Sergeant Bachelet. I couldn't stand to have you on my team for longer than five minutes. Insubordinate. You skated by on raw talent alone, and not an ounce of discipline."

A fist closed around his heart and he took a quick pull of air, jerking back from her.

Selene's eyes were glassy with anger. "You must've been a nightmare. Always sure you knew best. Always blaming yourself for every death. It was a *war*. You didn't have to take personal responsibility for every casualty. But you *did*."

Jules shook his head.

These were things Selene couldn't know, and it broke his heart that she was paraphrasing things Farah had said. "Did she say that?"

Selene must have heard something hollow in his voice, because for the first time she faltered in her tirade.

Her eyes flicked up to his and held. "Say *what*?"

"Farah . . ." he said listlessly. "Did *she* say I was a nightmare?"

"No, I—"

"Just you, then?"

"Jules . . ."

His expression twisted and he held up a hand. When she ignored him, he pushed her back a step, his hand nestled above her collarbone.

He needed space. When her lovely lips parted to say more, he pressed a finger against them, perhaps pressing harder than he should.

He couldn't *think*. All he could do was lean closer until they were separated by an inch that felt like a mile. A thousand miles.

More distance than he could fathom as he stood once more on the battlefield in Ostrava and she stood here, now, in the Vatican.

"Farah died. She's *dead*. Don't ever quote her words again, Selene, or I swear to that thing you call God, I'll deliver you to hell myself."

Her lashes trembled and he saw a flicker in the tight line of her jaw where she ground her teeth when she was cross, but Jules still couldn't feel a thing. A distant part of him screamed that none of this was right, but he could barely hear it. Everything that had coursed through him from *Dieu Immortel* had left him feeling frayed and not quite himself. It was as though the magnitude of that being, and His mind, had displaced something of Jules when it broke through.

And Selene *saw* that.

Jules tried to bite back his rage, but it snarled to be released like a dog from its chains.

"I don't know what's wrong with me, Selene. I acknowledge there's something. But you—*all of you*—are twisted too." He glanced at the pale skin of his inner arms. "With your captive god and your tainted magic. You reek of corruption."

Pain lanced through him at the cruel words because they weren't exactly true. He remembered the morning in Rome when he'd woken to her hair in his face. She had smelled of sun-warmed sheets and star jasmine, something citrusy and, yes . . . *demon blood*, but mostly she smelled sweet to him.

Her eyes widened. After the moment of surprise, they darkened with anger and hurt.

But it was nothing compared to his rage, which was just hitting its stride. "I can't help what I am. But you . . . you chose to *become* this." Contempt dripped from his words.

He dropped his hand, then dreamily lifted it again to brush his thumb over her lips. They were red, as though kissed, and he feared for a moment that he'd bruised her with his roughness. Stumbling away from her, he collided with the ironwork gate and gripped the freezing metal in his fingers. "Everyone here chose to become what they are. Tell me, Selene, who within your Vatican knows how to summon demons?"

Her eyes shuttered.

He couldn't fight a small, bitter smile. "You aren't only the protectors you claim to be. And your blood doesn't smell like it should. It burns my nose, acrid and—"

"You're *boring me*. If you don't move—*now*—Cesare will send you away." Her words were razor sharp, and if a tone could cut, he'd be bleeding. "No more access. No more chances to figure you out. It'll all be over."

She cocked her head. "So are you coming with me or not?"

A dark veil crossed her heart as Jules handed her into a waiting town car. Her teeth ached, and she consciously tried to relax the muscles in her jaw. Leaning her scabbarded blade against the door, Selene wished she was going anywhere else. Somewhere she could actually use it, perhaps. Anything to burn away this *feeling*. This dawning dread as she realized she had entirely lost her objectivity. Jules was neither merely an asset nor even a dangerous unknown; somewhere along the way she'd grown complacent. Not something an exorcist could afford.

Worse, in her carelessness, she'd started to care what he thought of her.

Rome whispering her name wasn't enough to disturb her sleep . . . but the thought of Jules learning what she'd done to her family terrified her. Jules, who had never had a family, wouldn't understand the decision to destroy her own.

He'd never look at her the same way again.

She propped her cheek on her hand, gazing out the window. The atmosphere in the car was thick and she could feel Jules's eyes on her. He fidgeted in her peripheral vision.

A part of her wanted to reach out and still his hands.

The fight had affected him worse than it had her. That was no surprise. After all, he hid an incredible softness somewhere beneath the rest. She'd witnessed it the night they'd met, when he'd tried to save a child with no reasonable expectation of surviving himself. She'd seen it again when he'd cried for the Deathless God.

The words that had spilled out of them both in the necropolis haunted her. Guilt twisted in her gut like a knife. She regretted saying what she'd said. *To a point.*

There had been a moment when he'd looked at her with such anguish, as though afraid he'd hurt her. But he hadn't. Scowling, she wiped smudged lipstick off her mouth. Even at the height of the argument, those powerful hands had been so gentle against her lips. Even with the blood of a thousand scars drying on his skin and the trauma of battle fighting for space inside his head, he'd touched her like she was breakable.

That man *would* blame himself for every life lost in a war he didn't start.

Silk swirled around her legs as she pulled one knee onto the seat so she could face him. The taut tug of her brows loosened as she took in his expression. He was shaken. She could see that so clearly now. Even though his long limbs were loose where he draped himself in the seat, his knuckles were white where he gripped the door handle. And his high cheekbones were pale beneath the gold lights of passing Rome.

She remained utterly still, only moving to adjust her dress strap when it slipped down her bicep. In the window's reflection, his eyes followed her fingers as though captivated. Even furious as she was, she realized with a terrible urgency that she wanted to protect him.

Selene bit her lip to hide her pain.

In the *Cor Cordium*, he had burned as though his veins were on fire. The memory of terror seemed to bubble in her chest, refusing to make room for oxygen or pumping blood. Did he burn because he was a disgrace before God?

She pushed the thought away, unable to wholly consider it.

Instead, she thought about her father. He had tried to pull the spear from God's body—betraying the Vatican in the process. But why? Her father was an exorcist and had faith—had *taught her* his faith.

"Tell me what really happened just now," she said.

"Do you mean . . . the fight? Or before that?"

Her sense prevailed and she flicked a glance toward the driver and shook her head minutely. They couldn't talk here. But when they were alone, she wouldn't lie to him. She'd furnish him with every gruesome detail of how he'd gone limp and insensible in her arms, and how she'd had to drag him like a corpse through the elegant halls of St. Peter's Basilica before he . . . before he returned to himself.

The truth she'd tried to ignore was burying its teeth so deep she could no longer fool herself.

She'd seen Jules's veins burning with holy light, as though God Himself was rejecting him. And she'd seen the briar scar, binding Jules tight since birth.

Dio . . . She raised a shaking hand to her temple.

Jules had cut through all her defensive layers as though they never existed. When she thought he was going to die, it was worse than any fear she'd ever known.

Greater even than the fear of death.

If he walked away now, it would break her. The beaded strap slipped down her arm again and Jules slid it back into place, thumb stroking her collarbone gently.

She'd been raised in the Vatican, where shades of gray existed between the pillars of light. There were immoral men and women here, and she was one of them. Raised to serve humanity. To *kill* in order to save.

She had one enemy.

The thought settled heavy, like a stone in her mind, an uncomfortable weight that hadn't been there before.

One thing she knew for sure—*Jules* was no shade of gray. He was a light so bright it could blind.

And he was a demon.

CHAPTER THIRTY

Masked strangers swirled around them in a frenzy. Beside him, Selene stood impossibly still, as though carved from marble. Her demeanor more akin to when she was on duty than attending a glitzy masquerade. Rather than joining the festivities, they lingered on the outer edge, which suited Jules.

Their angry words still echoed in his ears. And when he wasn't being consumed by thoughts about the argument, his mind drifted back to the *Cor Cordium*. Even now, he couldn't shake the sensation of vast power trapped inside that chamber at the heart of the Vatican. Even now, he could still feel the blood that had covered his hands and streaked his arms.

He had felt with the sleeping god the same affinity he felt with Sparrow. Echoed, too, in his memory of the battlefield, and the ozone scent of storms as the weather demon drew closer. *Demon.* The truth had resonated through Jules's bones in the same way the Deathless God's voice resonated through his veins.

Let me die.

Jules hadn't guessed how magnificent the restored Colosseum would be, with arches lit by shifting lights. On every tier, people mingled, champagne flutes clutched in their hands. Crumbling statues to Roman greats littered the space and wisteria coiled around stone columns and balustrades, dripping with amethyst flowers even though it was Rome in the middle of winter.

The Imperium Politikos circulated amid select guests. Jules had seen him from a distance, and once, when Selene had drawn him to a standstill and forced him to bow low, Jules had seen a hint of the shadowy throne where the empress sat.

It was undeniable that the Colosseum was bursting at its glamorous seams with Rome's elite—her noble families—and all of them watched Selene.

Even in her mask, she was recognizable. Selene Alleva, *Macellaia di Roma.*

Perhaps for the first time Jules understood the allure she held for the people of Rome. Was she a monster? A guardian? Fear and respect and caution warred for primacy when they glanced her way and hurried to make room for her wherever she went.

But wherever Jules looked, fear won.

No matter what Selene had done for them, it would never be enough. They'd never appreciate her as they should. Instead, they treated her like a tamed wolf, knowing the wild in her could not be suppressed forever.

Jules shifted closer, touching her wrist with his little finger.

She pulled away from him. "Don't touch me."

Her mask carved around the edges of her face, accentuating her honey-colored eyes and her knife-edge cheekbones. The rich blue and brilliant gold stars adorning the mask only managed to fade when compared to her. She looked ethereal.

"You know—" he started, but the skin around her eyes tightened and Jules cut himself off.

"Selene!" Adriano de Sanctis strode toward them.

Selene plastered on a smile. "Imperium."

Before she could bow, he captured her hands. "No need for that." He pressed a kiss to each hand. "Matteo would be so proud of you." Clearing his throat, he nodded at Jules. "Eliot."

"Imperium."

"You should be dancing."

"Oh, you know . . . I got a little rusty in Nice." Jules snatched a champagne flute, chuckling until he drowned the laugh with alcohol.

"My goddaughter is far too young and lovely to be relegated to the edge of the dance floor, Eliot. If you don't dance with her, I will." Adriano laughed, but there was an edge of warning to the words. Jules knew an order when he heard one.

Squaring his shoulders, he barely stopped himself saluting with the champagne flute. "Sir." Setting down his glass on the next passing tray, Jules swept into a low bow of his own for Selene, holding out his hand as he lowered his eyes. "Dance with me."

She laughed a brittle laugh.

Adriano wore a beatific smile. "Go," he urged her. "You'll make me so happy."

Jules almost thought she'd refuse, but finally he felt her hand land in his as light as a breath. He smoothed his thumb over her knuckles and she stiffened.

He'd ruined everything.

Her fingers felt brittle in his hands, bone, muscle, and tendon all denying his touch. So different from when she'd smoothed careful fingertips over his jaw to check the closeness of his shave. They were different people now. Maybe they'd had a future then. It had certainly felt as though there was a spark of possibility. Now they had ashes and angry words. His stomach churned with regret.

Unlike Selene, Jules had never learned to waltz, but he followed the couple dancing beside them, matching their movements a fraction of a second delayed. But Selene was a natural lead.

Every time she twirled away, he felt a spike of panic. As though he'd lost her forever. Only once did he pull her back too soon, unable to quell his rising pulse. Her expression was stormy, but she didn't comment on his mistake.

With his hand on her waist, Jules could feel the slightest dip of her ribs beneath his thumb as he ghosted it beneath the sheer silk of her dress. Her expression was taut, but she dipped with the grace of a dancer. He spread his hand against her spine, holding her as her unbound hair trailed across the floor.

"Selene—"

"Hold your breath."

"What?"

"I stink of corruption, so hold your breath." He pulled her up, stepping between her knees as his hand smoothed down her spine to hold her close. She smiled with teeth as she hissed against his ear, "And don't stop."

His jaw worked. He couldn't fake a smile like hers, it hurt too much.

Tugging her closer, he made her miss a step. She slid a furious look his way.

"You can't deny there's something wrong there."

"Wrong?"

"Corrupt."

She scoffed, holding his shoulder as she leaned back in a half dip.

In retaliation, Jules released her waist, letting her fall for a fraction of a second before he caught her. "Oops."

"You bastard." She pressed up against him, forcing him back a few steps with her body, and he felt something sharp against his groin. He didn't dare look but she pretended to brush a kiss to his neck, her soft lips trailing the fast-beating pulse at his throat. "Drop me and it'll be the last thing you do as a man."

He swallowed, hands loosening a little on her waist, and he drew his fingertips featherlight up her sides. Her breath came faster and after a beat she yanked the knife away from his crotch. "Don't touch me."

"You don't touch me."

"I'm not touching you." But she was; one hand was bunched in his hair as she pressed their foreheads together. "I hate you."

"I—" *Love you.* He almost said it. But the words wouldn't come.

"Captain Alleva?"

Selene pulled away from him, breaking all contact as she turned, brow arched in question.

An imperial valet had his hands linked behind his back, trying studiously to look unobtrusive. "I see you're carrying your familial blade. You'll have to disarm. Please come with me."

Selene's lip curled. "Took you long enough. The empress is *right there.*"

The valet's expression didn't change.

A tall woman appeared from behind the valet, her dark eyes crinkled with a smile. "An indication of the crown's trust in you, Captain Alleva. Exorcist First Class now. Congratulations."

Her flawless complexion belied her age; the woman had to be in her late forties, though she could have passed for younger. A companion of the empress, Jules assumed. And even here in the heart of Rome she wore a stunning royal-blue-and-gold qipao.

Selene nodded. "Thank you, Lady Yajin."

"Please, come." The woman indicated with an elegant hand.

Selene shot Jules a look that could wither fruit on the vine. *Stay*, it said, or maybe, *Die*. Possibly both.

A faster waltz struck up and Jules watched the feathered, silken Carnival masks and their people circulate on the floor. Then he saw a maskless face. A young man cutting through the crowds.

Jules elbowed through the dancers, hopping on one foot to dodge behind a swirling skirt. He saw the pale flash of the man's face before he placed his mask on with spread fingers. Then he passed behind one of the pencil pines edging the Colosseum's main floor, disappearing from sight. But Jules still felt him, the same resonance of familiarity as he felt with Sparrow.

He pushed past a man, his gold hair glinting. "D'Alessandro!"

Jules barely even registered Gabriel as he turned in place, looking this way and that until the faces around him blurred. He plunged into the dancers again, leaning back to avoid the tickle of ostrich feathers as ladies were dipped by their partners, before he was ejected out the other side.

His quarry had completely disappeared.

"I see you're wearing the mask of the Duke of Briars. How very curious." The young man leaned against a crumbling column nearby, hands loosely tucked into his trouser pockets in a relaxed posture. Jules couldn't say exactly what it was—nothing outright triggered his honed instinct for danger—but something stirred his unease.

"Who are you?"

Overhead, snow had started to fall. Whether it was real or manufactured Jules couldn't say, because it never reached the dancers, dissipating as it passed between strings of lights. The man stepped closer. His gold half mask had laurel leaves at the brow, lending him a regal bearing. Then Jules saw the truth beyond the obvious.

He staggered back. "*You—*"

The young man touched Jules's mask right between the eyes. "*Me.*"

An enigmatic smile on his face, his touch heralded a subtle twist of magic as blue flames ghosted across his skin.

Only feet away, entertainers dressed in jewel-toned silks for Carnival performed in their harlequin masks. But he might as well have been alone, because *Baliel* stood only inches away. The demon's blue eyes burned in the depths of the mask that hid his face. His glossy dark hair fell over the laurels carelessly. He was tall and long-limbed, though perhaps not quite so tall as he had been when they'd met at the orphanage in Nice.

Jules's fingers itched for a blade. He wanted to pay Baliel back for Kian. But he was unarmed and the demon just about stank of raw power barely contained. Jules clenched his hand into a fist. Nausea was like a moth fluttering in his stomach as he looked around at the helpless guests, dressed in their insubstantial finery. Baliel was a wolf among sheep.

Jules raised a hand to rip off his own mask.

"*Stop.*" A command, Baliel his general.

Jules almost laughed but his muscles seized.

On the upper balconies of the Colosseum, contortionists twisted themselves into shapes upon request, and magicians delighted and dismayed, disappearing champagne flutes and priceless jewelry in exchange for laughs. Even more and varied acts threaded among the throng on the main floor: a feathered youth; a snake-eyed waif of indeterminate gender and unspeakable beauty; dancers who spun in a complex ballet that had them leaping and twirling overhead.

All that faded into the background, leached of all color, until it was only him and Baliel.

The demon's glittering blue eyes watched him through the

mask—staring through Jules and into his soul. Jules fought to twitch even a finger but could not. Fear prickled his skin.

"Why are there only twelve masks?" Baliel continued rhetorically, his voice thrumming rich as overturned soil. "One for each of the twelve demon dukes, yes, but they are not the greatest of us. There should be thirteen." He said it with finality, as though that explained everything.

Jules watched his mouth and jaw, observing the parts of him he could see. Even though it was clearly a new body—not the same wrecked and twisted thing he'd worn last time—he *recognized* Baliel. Both from then, and from the drawing in Matteo Alleva's notebook. It was as though Baliel had sculpted this body to be a shadow of his real one.

"Why do you look different from before?" Jules asked.

"This new body is more suited to me. Though it is rather young. My essence isn't ripping it apart to get out."

"Why not?"

"Demon blood." Baliel touched his chest lightly with long fingers. "This one has a demon in his family line somewhere. Long ago. If I am careful, I can leave his body whole when I'm done with it. He will be—well, if not *none* the wiser, at least alive."

Jules grimaced. "Generous."

"If I do not borrow this body, I cannot walk in this world. I wasn't born here. I do not have my own body." He waved a hand. "I have very little say in the matter, Jules."

The sound of his name on the demon's lips made a shudder crawl down Jules's spine and he shuffled back an inch, putting some distance between them.

Baliel looked around, his lips twisting with distaste. "Look at them, dancing on the Deathless God's living grave." Contempt dripped from Baliel's every word. "Do they question nothing?"

"You know him," Jules guessed. "And you know he's not God."

"Of course he's not God." Baliel laughed, though the sound was humorless. "They once had another god, you know. They unthinkingly stitched a demon into their religion, warping the stories to fit."

"Who is he? The man they call God."

"He is our king. Yours and mine. The Elysian king."

Jules felt a muted spike of surprise. It made a kind of twisted sense that *Dieu Immortel* was important to the demons. Jules pressed a hand to his chest, heart beating in panicked little skips. Baliel knew what he was, too. The wrongness he'd felt earlier returned to him. The scent of death. His realization that their god was a demon and that he was *suffering*. The realization that exorcists had trapped him inside their walls for power.

Did they know? Did *Selene*? No, he thought not. Even if she feared the Deathless God more than loved him, her faith was real. The realization soothed his frayed thoughts.

Jules leaned heavily against the marble column at his back. The Deathless God had been nailed and chained to the great burned crossbeam where he'd fallen all those centuries ago. And the Vatican as it stood now rose up around his body. The cult of the Deathless God seamlessly making a home for itself in the carcass of the old religion. And the carrion crows of this world still lived with that, even at the cost of their god.

Jules withdrew Matteo's notebook from his pocket, finding the page he'd looked at more than once: Baliel's face, sculpted from graphite and shaded so he looked pensive. He held it up. "Good likeness."

Baliel tipped his head. "Indeed. But can you read the words?"

Jules shook his head. "I know a little Latin, as much as anybody, I suppose. Well, not as much as them." He nodded toward the shadowy throne, using the Roman empress to encapsulate the spectre of the Vatican and all the exorcists within it. "Can you?"

"Of course."

Baliel took the book and flipped through the pages, then handed it back, looking slightly bored. Jules blinked, the residual imprint of blue flames momentarily trapped in his retinas after Baliel used his magic. When Jules glanced at the page, he froze. The script was legible for him to read, and so he did, *hungrily*.

Baliel, Duke of Briars

Even Baliel looked faintly amused as Jules scanned the short-form observations around the sketch. Many were things he knew from having met Baliel before—things he could know now by glancing up at the man opposite him, as those distinctive blue eyes beyond the mask watched him back.

Still, he read.

Baliel's power was vast, manifesting as blue flame. He had the ability to possess living human bodies and adapt them to his needs. He was very old, though he did not look it.

Then he read a passage that gave him pause.

Baliel is the one who gave us the wards, and he'll be the one to break them.

"You made the wards?" Jules asked, looking at Baliel with surprise.

"Not all of them. I made the first, then they made more, imitating me as best they could with their lesser magic."

"Why?"

Baliel responded with the resonance of an answer to a question, though it was not the one Jules had asked. "Do you ever wonder why they left him like that? Neither dead nor alive—" Baliel choked off, as though someone had grabbed his throat in their fist.

Jules shook his head. "Of course I wonder. But why tell me about their god? Why tell me he's a demon?"

Baliel watched him, interest sparking in his eyes. "You sound unsurprised." A small smile tipped the corner of his lips. "Have you been into the very bloody heart of the Vatican, Jules? Have you seen him?"

Unable to put the experience into words, Jules just nodded.

The demon did not seem to mind his silence. "Remarkable."

Jules shrugged that off so he wouldn't have to think about the way Baliel's admiration made him feel. "Why did you destroy the records? *All* of them. Because of you, I don't even know who I am."

Baliel smiled. "I have *tried* to destroy them all, but not to thwart you. It's always been about protecting you."

"*Protecting* me?" he asked, voice caustic with doubt. "And what do you mean, you tried?"

"The Vatican records were already gone when I looked. Destroyed, I hope."

"Who by?"

Baliel was thoughtful for a moment. "A man I knew a few short years ago, I believe. *Matteo.*"

The word was like an electric current through Jules, though he had already suspected they'd come into contact. "Matteo *Alleva?*"

Baliel's gaze sharpened and *that* was answer enough.

Jules slouched against a pillar, watching the demon. "What do the wards have to do with the Deathless God?"

"Everything." After a beat of silence, Baliel began speaking in earnest, his voice filled with the timbre of a storyteller. "It was hastily worked magic, the wards I created. I had little time and much to protect. In the same working, I bound a truth into this city, into the wards that protected it from my kind—that would eventually protect it, even from me. It expended a great deal of power. I was weakened. I am weakened still."

"What *truth*?"

"Only a demon can kill him. Only a human can free him."

"Why would you do that?"

"Why? Because I cannot *change* the laws of nature. I can only bend them. So I restricted who could strike the killing blow, and that is all. And then I ensured no demon could get close enough to do it."

"Except me."

"You, I did not anticipate." Baliel watched Jules a long moment, his eyes deep with some emotion Jules couldn't name. "I had hoped that a human would free him, but in two hundred years I have only been disappointed." His eyes darkened. "I miscalculated. I forgot how fleeting a human life could be. The humans who had been alive to witness their god were in his thrall. But that faded with time. And then they learned the power in his blood and he was too valuable to them sleeping."

Sleeping. A tender way to put the torment Jules had felt in echo.

Jules looked away, wondering what Selene would do if she knew the truth. He couldn't say for sure that she'd yank the spear free. "He doesn't *look* like a demon. I don't think they know what he really is. I only knew because I . . . felt it." He bit off his words. He could still feel the smothering desperation, the pain, and couldn't continue without his voice breaking. "He's . . . beautiful. Nothing like the demons I've seen."

Baliel was silent a moment. "The demons you've seen are not their true selves. With their essence compressed into a shell so unsuitable it is akin to torture. It stretches, trying to fit around you, twisting and breaking and cracking, *pop-pop-pop* along the bones and up the spine—"

Jules repressed a shudder. The description was far too visceral, as though he could feel it.

"Eventually it becomes some approximation of what you've left behind, something that can, for a time, hold your spirit captive in the flesh—" Baliel broke off, barking out a laugh and pushing his hands through his hair to smooth it back again from where it had fallen over his forehead. "Forgive me . . . He—the one they call their god—is what we really look like, Jules. He is a true demon. The only true demon in this realm. His body uncorrupted, though his spirit is still trapped."

"Why is it like that?"

Baliel frowned. "He forced the door shut in a last bid to protect humanity. It takes a vast amount of power to cross, and it trapped many of our kind here to wither and die. All to protect the ones who ultimately held him captive for centuries."

Jules thought back to the voice that had begged for death inside his mind. "He wants to die," he murmured.

Baliel looked up sharply.

"He asked me to kill him. He was speaking to me. It was—it was awful."

Jules wanted nothing more than to forget it.

Baliel reached up, catching his chin in strong fingers. "Quiet."

Obediently Jules fell silent.

"He *will not* die. I won't let him." The words sounded raw with conviction and Jules realized that Baliel cared. *Really* cared. The demon had a personal stake in this. Baliel glanced around the gathered people, but no one paid them any mind. They were too distracted by the tumult of entertainment thrown at their feet.

"What is he to you?" Jules asked.

His voice was steady even though he had not stopped processing the wretchedness he felt at standing eye to eye with Kian's killer and having a cordial conversation. It felt almost as strange as speaking to the Tsarina among the bodies of slain friends. Although Baliel felt a thousand times more dangerous—and more unknowable.

A ghost of a smile touched Baliel's lips.

His voice was low. "The better question would be, what is he to *you?*"

Jules frowned in confusion. He was God.

Baliel waited, silent, and once more Jules felt as though he was being read. It was an uncomfortable feeling, but not because he was afraid of Baliel. Despite all he'd been told, he found himself unable to fear him.

At last Baliel sighed. "He is my son. And he has been trapped here long enough."

Impossible . . .

Jules wanted to denounce the words, but the truth of them sang through his bones. Baliel meant every word. His unceasing air of rage and grief suddenly made sense. Unable to hold his eyes, Jules looked away.

This demon was the father of God.

Jules had been raised believing in the Deathless God. This was sacrilegious. He felt almost ashamed to believe him—but believe him he did.

He is my son. The echo of Baliel's words taunted him. *The better question would be, what is he to* you?

Fighting a sense of dread, Jules dampened his lips. "And who am I?"

Baliel huffed a laugh. "You are *his* son."

CHAPTER THIRTY-ONE

S elene had one color and that was military black.

Among a painter's palette of bright dresses, she stood out like a shadow on a bright day. The bodice hung from her shoulders on slender beaded straps. Silk flowed like water around her legs, and a gold chain wrapped around her waist, adorned with small jeweled replicas of the Alleva sword and the great spear that impaled the Deathless God.

And across her back was the actual Alleva sword, resplendent in its ceremonial scabbard.

The mask she'd been given did little enough to disguise her anyway, but it was useless, armed as she was. Who but the Butcher of Rome would dare wear a blade before the empress? But right now, Selene didn't give a damn for the rules. In fact, a good fight might work off some excess aggression.

Lady Yajin led the way down a flight of stone steps flanked by six-foot lions.

"Why did you sneak in the back, Selene? Her Imperial Majesty wanted to speak to you and Eliot when you arrived."

They'd arrived fashionably late, and Selene had ordered the

driver to take them to the back—hoping to avoid the ceremonial entrance entirely. "I dislike a fuss."

The woman smiled but said nothing more.

Selene paused, feeling a familiar presence. A tall figure stood in the shadows beyond one of the lion statues. The tip of his cigarette burned ember bright before fading away.

Of course. Sparrow *would* be here.

He casually matched his pace to theirs, finally joining her at the edge of a stone balustrade that had been set up as a weapons check. The demon cut a handsome figure. Too tall, almost inhumanly tall—nearly enough to make him stand out for the wrong reasons—broad in all the right places and narrow at the hips. His face was cut glass in the low light and his ruined eye only made his other features more startlingly perfect by comparison.

Behind the balustrade, an elderly valet glanced between them with a blandly polite expression. "She's with you, sir?"

Sparrow leaned a casual hip against the stone, angled to watch her reaction. His eyes danced with amusement. "I wouldn't say that."

Selene set her sword on the weatherworn balustrade between them, leaving her hand on top.

The man's expression sharpened when he saw the blade. He bowed at the waist.

Sparrow slid a gun across the balustrade and the man took it carefully, lifting it into a bank of heavy weapons lockers against the wall.

Sparrow leaned close, breathing against her ear. "I've always wanted to see you without your sword on."

"Shut up." Despite her mood, the words held no heat.

As the valet locked away Sparrow's gun, Selene drew her sword an inch, taking a second to inspect the blade before slicing a tiny cut in her thumb. She pressed it against the Alleva family crest on the scabbard, leaving a smudged crimson thumbprint. A blood lock only she could release. And stealthy enough that neither man noticed.

"Is your handsome friend here?" Sparrow asked.

"My fiancé?"

Sparrow smiled around his cigarette. "We both know he's not *that*."

She flicked her gaze to him, eyes narrowing in warning. Lady Yajin watched from a polite distance. Far enough not to be privy to their conversation, but it was still dangerous. When the valet returned, Selene shoved her sword at him.

"Bye, Sparrow. This was fun."

The valet cleared his throat.

Lady Yajin stepped forward. "Aren't we done, Gilbert?"

"Not quite, Lady Yajin."

Selene scoffed.

Gilbert extended his hand again and after a beat Selene grudgingly set a dagger into it, followed by a slender holster with a pair of matte-black throwing knives.

"That's all."

Sparrow shifted, crossing his arms over his chest, and raised a brow, letting his eyes slide down her body. "Nobody believes that."

She plastered a false smile on her face. "Well, you're wrong. *Shocking*."

Gilbert didn't move, that same painfully bland expression on his face as he waited. Apparently he and Sparrow were of one mind. Selene reached through the slit in her dress and undid her thigh holster, slapping it down on the balustrade. Turning her back on them, she drew a spoke-like stiletto from the inseam of her bodice and set that on top of the holster.

"Now I'm done."

Gilbert finally appeared satisfied.

Chuckling, Sparrow moved closer, fingering a line of gold embellishments along the edge of her plunge back, tugging until he withdrew a slender gold knife no larger than a letter opener. It swung between his fingers on a beaded thread that seamlessly matched the detailing on her dress. Then he let it drop and the point embedded itself a quarter-inch into the stone.

Selene shrugged. "Oops. *Careful*—" she warned Gilbert before he could touch it. "I'd handle it with gloves."

Sparrow extended his arm in a grand sweeping motion—*lead on*—and fell into step beside her.

"You need to protect Jules," he said softly. "It's important."

Skin prickling with heat that could be jealousy, her lip curled as she answered. "Important for you, you mean? Oh, Sparrow, we're not friends. The things you want are things I want to prevent. Kind of by definition."

"You care about him." He spoke past the cigarette held between his lips.

Her teeth creaked as she tightened her jaw. "*Don't.*"

She pressed her hand against her heart, trying to coax it to slow. Her ribs ached. Even hearing Jules's name hurt. Seeing him—*seeing* him was exquisite torment. Each time she looked at him she had to remind herself that Jules was, in fact, a dangerous enemy. Behind that beautiful face, he was a monster. Whatever human blood ran in his veins bound him to this world so it was his just as much as it was hers, but in many ways he was more dangerous than a full-blooded demon. And being Jules, he was certainly more of a threat to her.

Sparrow stepped in front of her, blocking her way. "Did you see the mask they selected for him?"

She could barely breathe the reply. "Of course I saw."

"Something of a coincidence."

"One of the Twelve. It's considered an honor."

Sparrow laughed at that. "Ironic, isn't it? In this society built on loathing demons, your most sophisticated Carnival Masquerade has one special feature: twelve masks in honor of the demon dukes."

"I always thought it was in bad taste. But . . . *tradition*."

"Ah, yes. See, that's what I don't get. Who started this tradition? When? How many years after we killed your god?"

"Enough."

Sparrow laughed bitterly.

She pressed circles against her temple with a fingertip. "They gave him the mask of briars. I saw. What of it, Sparrow? What are you getting at?"

"I just think it's a coincidence given Baliel's in the city. And that Jules is . . ." He trailed off. "Well, I'm sure you know."

She tried not to react, but Sparrow saw through her anyway.

Selene carved her way through well-dressed guests, searching for Jules. When she spotted his familiar broad shoulders, she moved with renewed purpose, every nerve in her body attuned to him.

"And who am I?" The pain in his voice was so jagged it hurt to hear.

"You are *his* son."

In her single-minded focus on Jules, she made the mistake of getting too close. She felt the telltale tug on her senses and realization crept over her. *Baliel. Dio*, he was powerful. He kept himself so tightly bound inside his human shell that his power was indistinguishable from barely seven feet away.

She pressed her back to a column, heart clamoring somewhere in the vicinity of her throat. Did Jules know who he was speaking to? Betrayal was the iron tang of blood on her tongue. Pressing a shaking hand to her mouth, she drew back. If she'd had a single weapon on her, Baliel would already be bleeding . . . but unarmed, her magic locked beneath her skin, inside her blood and bones, she was helpless.

More now than ever.

She needed her sword. Had to alert the empress's guard. *Kill Baliel.* Preferably with a minimum of collateral damage.

She forged through the crowd, heading for the stairs to the weapons lockers.

"Selene!"

A hand caught her wrist, pulling her around as Jules tangled their fingers together. His touch burned and her ribs gave that terrible constricting ache.

She rounded on him, teeth bared, then the breath left her lungs in a gasp. She'd been expecting the mask of the Duke of Briars, like some cruel joke. But instead, it was a different face. Crueler still. A mask she'd never seen before.

A mask for the *Deathless God.*

"I need to—" Jules began breathlessly.

"What—what's that mask?" she interrupted, feeling the heat drain from her cheeks. The world seemed to waver around her. "Jules, what are you wearing?"

His hand rose, touching it. "I don't know."

"You look like . . . like the Deathless God."

Jules tore the mask from his face and looked down at it. But Selene didn't look away, searching his features. It really had looked like a stylized Deathless God. But . . . this mask was in the style of the twelve demon dukes. It was the face of a demon—a second pair of eyes angled beneath the first.

Heart thundering, Selene observed his dismay.

"It . . . suited you. But it wasn't much of a disguise." She stepped closer, taking the mask from his hand. "The moment I saw you it was like I was looking straight through the mask to *you*." She smoothed her fingers over the lines of the mask, a fleeting pain sliding between her ribs. What she said was true. And it made no sense. "Will I never escape?" she said softly, addressing the mask.

"Who?" Jules asked as though he already knew.

"*Dio Immortale.*"

"Why do you need to escape a captive god, Selene?" His voice was so quiet it might have been her imagination.

Wanting to run, she took a half-step back and collided with someone. A flashbulb popped, making her vision dance with spots. Stepping between them, Jules protectively blocked the offending camera with his hand.

"If it isn't Rome's most talked-about couple! Aurelio Sabatino, reporter. Smile for the birdie! You look beautiful, Miss Alleva."

"*Captain,*" they said together, and shared a look.

When a reluctant smile tipped her lips, it was impossible to ignore the flare of hope in his eyes.

Or, she thought cynically, *I have residual shadows in my vision.*

"Whatever, stand together, please." The reporter circled them, holding a press camera to his eye. "Our readers aren't interested in . . . well, *this*—they want romance! Can't you get a little closer?"

"I'll tell you what—" Selene began, taking a threatening step toward the reporter, but Jules grabbed her around the waist and hauled her back.

"Very good, Lieutenant D'Alessandro. Put your hand on her hip. Or kiss her?"

Selene scowled. "Oh, you'd like that, wouldn't you?"

The photographer shoved a champagne flute into her hand, ignoring her completely.

"A toast for the happy couple! Do you have a ring?"

Jules blinked, totally lost. "I, er, yes?"

"Hold her closer, pull her in a bit. Don't tell me you're scared of the Butcher of Rome, D'Alessandro? Have you been in Nice too long?" The photographer lowered the camera, grinning. This upstart reporter couldn't be older than she was. "That's it, hold her tighter. You better do it or I will." He winked.

Selene could feel Jules's irritation mount as he obediently tightened his arm around her waist, his other hand lightly holding her hip.

"Great!"

The camera flashed sparks and Aurelio Sabatino disappeared—no doubt off to harass someone else—leaving them both a little stunned.

Selene swallowed, not turning to look at Jules. His breath stirred her hair, and her anger dissipated. Maybe like this, without looking at him, she could tell him the truth.

"You asked—" *Dio*, why was he so warm? His hands branded her waist, burning through her silk dress. His breath ghosted the back of her neck, lips grazing the point where her neck met her shoulder, so softly she might have imagined it. She refused to turn, drawing a fortifying breath that shuddered in her chest. "I'm afraid to tell you why I need to *escape a captive god*."

"Why?" He murmured it against her ear.

"What will you think of me? Once you know everything."

Jules's hand tightened on her waist, like he might turn her. She resisted and his hand grazed her ribs, his thumb sliding until he found skin instead of silk.

"Not less." He swore, his voice gravelly. "Never less."

He didn't know what he was promising.

CHAPTER THIRTY-TWO

A figure sidled up to Jules, holding a tray of champagne. He cleared his throat.

"We're good," Jules said, annoyed, without looking away from Selene.

"Wait." Selene reached for a fresh flute. "Thank you."

Out of the corner of his eye, Jules saw a flash of bright red hair and his heart leaped. *Kian . . .*

Then it fell.

Not Kian. Never Kian again.

"Hey! You there!" A figure hared across the dance floor. She skidded, barely avoiding a waiter with a tray of empty glasses—unfortunately she stumbled right into the path of a second waiter carrying glasses full to the brim.

Lucia Scavo. As bubbly liquid splashed to the floor with a crash, the sister of medicine seemed to point directly at Jules. *Shit.*

No, *past* Jules.

The waiter lingering nearby whipped off his mask. "Hello, Jules!" Kian grinned, his copper hair caught the light of a dozen lanterns and Jules could only stare. "Oh yeah, *not* dead. Surprise!" He handed off the tray of flutes he'd been holding.

Jules blinked, sure he was losing it.

"Kian . . ." he whispered, a tear carving its way down his cheek.

The floor seemed to tip, but it wasn't the champagne.

"How?"

"I'll explain later!"

"Wait, Kian . . ." Jules said, the words barely audible as he reached out an unsteady hand.

Selene's hand tightened on his bicep. "Uh . . . Jules . . ."

"*Fermatevi!*" He recognized that voice. Caterina. He predicted her words before they came. "I'll make you red mist!"

"Gotta go!" Kian tugged his forelock, nodding to Selene. "You look beautiful. If you want a real man instead—"

"STOP! Vatican."

"—come find me. I'll probably be in the Vatican cells. Or dead."

The tinkling of two dozen glasses hitting marble heralded Caterina and Lucia's approach.

Kian ran.

Jules took half a step after him, but Caterina blocked his path.

"Do you know that redheaded corpse, kitten?"

"Uh . . . no?" Jules tried to dodge around her.

Dieu. Kian was alive. But for how long? *That* was the question.

"Altamura, you're making a scene," Selene said, her voice dangerous.

Lucia sashayed up, clutching two glasses of champagne—both very much for her.

"Hello! Oh my, don't you look dashing, *D'Alessandro*?" She gave an exaggerated wink.

Selene waved after Kian. "I forbid you from killing anyone at the masquerade."

Jules's pulse seemed to thunder in his ears. "What do you mean, *corpse*?"

"He's *meant* to be dead. All the records say so. And Caterina basically promised to kill him the first time he ran, so either way it's true. Fun!"

"*First* time?" Selene echoed faintly.

Caterina scanned the crowd. "This has happened before."

Lucia leaned closer. "More than once," she confided in a stage whisper. She missed Caterina's narrow-eyed look as she knocked back a flute, her little bone-saw earrings dangling merrily.

Jules wasn't totally surprised to hear it. Absconding from trouble was his and Kian's shared legacy. However, Caterina and Lucia were formidable. He gazed after Kian. If he left to find Kian himself, Caterina and Lucia would tail him for sure. Jules circled Selene's waist with an arm, hissing by her ear. "Hey, sweet cheeks, tell them if they kill my *best friend*, I'll—"

"I'm on it, *amore mio*," she said through her teeth.

Many eyes were on them now.

He slid his hands to her hips. "I'm serious." He emphasized the words by pulling her so tightly to him that her champagne sloshed.

"So. Am. I." Selene punctuated the final word by stomping on his toe with her stiletto.

Pain—like nothing he'd ever known—assured him she'd won this round.

"Altamura." Selene smiled, extricated herself from Jules, and went nose to nose with her subordinate. "*Caterina*. If you kill his friend, I kill you. Then everyone you've ever loved—"

Caterina snorted, unimpressed. But Selene wasn't finished.

"—and all the ones you don't, too. I'll kill anyone you've ever *tolerated*."

The nun pressed a hand to her throat. "You wouldn't."

"Watch me."

Lucia popped an olive in her mouth. "So you'd kill me?"

Selene didn't look her way, holding Caterina's gaze. "I'd be forced to, Lucia. It would be a shame. You're an adequate subordinate."

The blond shrugged an easy shoulder. "*C'est la vie.*"

There was a flash of red on one of the upper balconies.

"There he is!" someone cried.

Caterina and Lucia took off running. People watched on, ratting Kian out every time he made a move. Romans still liked their games in this Colosseum. Eyes settled on Jules and Selene. There were cries from the empress's personal guard.

Selene's hand was pale in his grip.

A table with a pyramid of champagne coupes caught his eye. He could make a love declaration—bratty Roman elite style—as a distraction. Even before he'd formed his plan, he knew Selene was going to kill him.

"You'd do it for me, boyo," he muttered under his breath.

"What?" Selene murmured distractedly.

Jules climbed atop the table and kicked crystal glasses out of his way. A waterfall of champagne splashed to the floor, fizzing at the feet of the Roman elite. "Attention, everyone!"

Selene stared as though he'd grown horns.

Hundreds of eyes pinned him. His heart stuttered. It was working . . . maybe a little too well. Every second, more people decided Jules was better entertainment than an escaped fugitive. He snagged the last intact coupe from where it teetered at the edge of the table, angling it at Selene. "My lovely fiancée. The most beautiful girl in the room. Any room—sorry, ladies." He forced a grin. A titter of laughter. For her part, Selene only looked about half as murderous as he expected. Some of the guests cast sidelong glances toward the shadowy throne. *Damn.* Jules hadn't anticipated insulting an empress today.

"So much wasted champagne tonight," someone whispered.

He was losing his audience.

"I, er, I want to raise a toast to Selene, my fiancée, did I say that part already? To Selene. Beautiful in the way only the deadliest things are. Marry me, won't you?"

A flash went off, momentarily blinding him.

"When can we expect a wedding?" Aurelio Sabatino's voice contained all the verve of a journalist chasing a hot lead.

Jules blinked against the spots in his vision as he searched for Selene in the crowd and found her. Still unimpressed.

"Er, tonight? Or tomorrow? Very soon, in any case."

Sabatino looked thrilled at this. "Now that's what I call *romance!*" he said, pivoting in place to get a photo of Selene, who stood with one hand beneath her chin and the other propping up her elbow, watching Jules inscrutably.

The crowd in the room seemed to agree, warming up to the show.

Jules leaped off the table to applause and approached Selene, tossing back his champagne for strength and handing the coupe to someone in the crowd before extending his hand. Softly he said, "Selene, can't I have just one more dance tonight?"

Eyes guarded, Selene hesitated, then she set her hand in his.

He pulled her close, hand sliding around her waist.

Selene was silent, her cheek on his shoulder.

"Are they still watching?" he asked.

She looked over his shoulder. "Oh yeah."

"So I guess it'd look bad if I went running after two nuns and a redhead?" He leaned back enough to see her face.

Her lips tipped into a reluctant smile. "Might ruin the romance of you declaring your intention to marry me tonight."

"Or tomorrow."

"How could I forget?"

Jules's smile faded. Unsuprisingly, she hadn't yet forgiven him. And even though he was loath to make things worse, he had to tell her: "Baliel was here."

Baliel, Duke of Briars. *His grandfather.* The Prince of Thorns. And who knew how many other names he had been given over the centuries?

Her eyes seemed to clear. "I know. I saw him."

"Why are you so relaxed about this?"

"If I could do anything about it, I would . . . but he's in a new body. He's got his magic bound so tight, even I can't feel him. The only way I find him now is if he wants me to."

Jules nodded slowly, remembering how Baliel had simply melted into the crowd of glittering dresses and handsome evening suits so effectively he couldn't feel even a hint of stray power. "You're telling me I should have kept him talking?"

"Maybe." She shrugged. "But if he planned to do something at the ball, I imagine he would've done it by now."

He should really know not to underestimate her sharp intelligence.

I am a demon. And so is your god.

Jules twirled her away, holding her tighter on the return.

The final strains of music faded, leaving them pressed together, chests heaving as they stared into each other's eyes. Selene pulled back an inch, as though suddenly desperate to escape the clinging crowd and watching eyes.

She pushed past masked guests and waiters whisking heaped trays of candied figs, Sicilian olives, wrapped prosciutto, and Roman artichokes. He could barely keep up and the distance between them widened. Selene was hurting, and he could only make it worse the way he was. The grandson of her sworn enemy, and one of the demons that monstered her world. Who knew when their accord would crumble and they'd be thrust onto opposing sides of this by whatever Baliel was planning? She was nearly out of reach.

He lunged after her, catching her hand, his knuckles white in his desperation. Selene whirled on him, her beautiful lips curled over her teeth in a slight snarl.

"Please . . ." he whispered, consciously gentling his grip.

Around them guests gorged themselves, wheeling in frenetic dance and screaming with laughter at the performers who twirled overhead. But here, between them, it was utterly still.

She raised a hand and tucked dark hair behind her ear. A ruby droplet of blood slid down her thumb and he caught her wrist, pressing a handkerchief to it before it could drip onto her dress and be swallowed in the black. Again he caught the faint scent of iron and twisted magic.

Softly, he said, "You have the blood of demons in your veins, don't you?"

Her eyes widened in surprise.

A secret, then. One nobody should know.

They weren't so different. They *both* had demon blood in their veins. What he would never say was that his was natural, hers an abomination. An *aberration*. Something loathed by nature.

Even though a distant part of him was pleased at surprising her, he instantly regretted his question. He shouldn't know this— *humans* couldn't smell blood. The fragments of the last hours still felt jagged-edged and didn't fit comfortably together, but it was too late now; the words had been spoken aloud.

"Answer me," he urged more quietly still.

She nodded.

"Maybe," she said finally, tugging at his glove to expose his inner wrist. She lightly touched his skin, as though to test it wasn't hot or cold to the touch. All his visible scars were silvery again, the veins their normal blue. The luminous gold was so impossible to imagine, it might've been a dream. "But this isn't about me. This is about you. And about Baliel. What did he want?"

With his free hand, Jules rubbed the crumpled line between his brows. If only it wasn't so complicated. He needed his head clear so he could think. If his world had already been turned upside down in the Vatican's *Cor Cordium*, then the conversation with Baliel had tipped it even further off its axis.

An unfamiliar expression twisted her lips.

Selene took his hand. "Fine, tell me later. But rest assured, Lacroix, you will tell me."

The world drew in around him. All he could see was her slender back, all he could feel were her warm pianist's fingers drawing him in her wake to a brass-appointed lift. She pressed a button and the pointer flicked past four levels.

When they stepped out, it was into blessed solitude at the top of the Colosseum.

The bitter night breeze whipped Selene's hair against his cheeks, and through the dark strands he could see Rome spread out beneath them. Jules pushed a strand of windswept dark hair behind her ear. "I'm sorry for the things I said." She shivered and he chafed the backs of his fingers against her bicep. "For hurting you with my words and—"

"Jules, stop."

He quieted.

"I was hurt, but I also know it wasn't really you. In the necropolis, you were like a cornered fox. You were bleeding. You witnessed our god in all His terrible beauty. You looked upon His face. You were . . . tormented. I still don't know by what. By war? By . . . by *God*? And I hurt you, too." She drew his hand to her lips, pressing a kiss to his thumb. He caressed her lower lip, tugging it slightly to reveal a flash of white teeth. Her eyes were impossibly dark as she looked up at him from beneath her lashes. "And even though you are strong enough, you were never once rough with me. I saw it written all over your face, the fear that you'd damaged me. But I'm stronger than I look and you're much, *much* gentler."

"You promise?" he breathed.

"I promise."

Jules searched her face, but he couldn't read her beyond the filigree mask. Her usual mask was gone and here she was wearing a literal one instead.

Selene reached up to touch his cheek. He hadn't been able to bear the thought of putting his mask back on. Not once he knew who he looked like when he wore it.

Untying Selene's mask, Jules let it fall in a flurry of ribbons to the stone and touched the side of her face, thumb smoothing beneath her eye. Rome at night was more beautiful than the sky, but both paled to insignificance when her mask was removed. "I missed your face."

"Liar," she breathed.

"Yes." She tipped an unimpressed brow and he grinned. "But not about this. *Never* about this."

He couldn't leave her, but he had to. Baliel's blood was a curse. Pain ached through his ribs, as though he'd finally met the wrong end of a knife. Her eyes were the amber gold of Rome's lit domes and so intense it hurt. Unable to hold them, he looked away. He wanted her and he was tired of pretending he didn't. But telling her would be a watershed moment, and he wasn't sure how she'd react.

Across Rome, bells began to chime ten o'clock. When the final bell faded to nothing, he shook himself. "Selene, I can't pretend—"

She silenced him with a kiss so searing he thought he might die.

Holding her waist, he forced her onto the tips of her toes and deepened the kiss. When she pulled back, gasping, he whispered her name against her mouth. On their second kiss, he drowned in her, coaxing her lips apart so he could get a taste. To die drunk on Selene would be to die a blessed death.

When she carded her fingers through his hair, pulling his mouth more firmly against hers, he gave a soft growl that came right from his belly. *Dieu*, the way she lit a flame inside him. No longer a smoldering spark but a wildfire.

He smoothed a thumb along her jaw and tipped her face to his, granting himself greater access. Then Selene broke the kiss, one hand firm against his chest. Her hair fell over her face, shadowing her expression.

His breathing ragged, Jules leaned back to give her space even though he ached to touch her. For a delicious moment Selene had pressed her body against him, curving lithely against his chest and abdomen. He *knew* she'd felt the same fervent want he did.

But now she was pulling away.

And even though he'd removed her gilded mask, her expression was unreadable. She wore her armor and no honesty at all. His heart thundered, crashing painfully against his ribs. At least he'd tried, though it didn't make the agony of failure any easier.

Selene released a shaky breath. Gazing out over Rome, her brows tugged together as she took half a step toward the dark drop.

Wind whipped her hair against her cheeks and indecision crossed her face.

Always so hard to read, Selene.

But she wasn't alone. They stood together on the precipice.

When she smiled, he breathed again.

"Let's go somewhere. This party's the worst."

CHAPTER THIRTY-THREE

The Vatican's familiar hallways were theirs alone. Everyone else was at Carnival. Selene led Jules by their linked fingers. Though not to her rooms. Instead, she drew him up the angular spiral stairs of a clock tower, turning to face him now and then and coax him on.

She tried not to let him burn her through her clothes. Through her skin. Through the air itself. But it was impossible. He was light and heat, and she'd be lucky to burn alive throwing herself against him like a moth.

A familiar door with a familiar lock barred the way.

"Where are we going?" he asked, his hands sliding to her waist as he pressed against her back.

She laughed, swatting away his hand as he dipped his fingers beneath the silk bodice to feel her skin, delicately brushing the sensitive skin beneath her breast. "Wait and see."

If he didn't stop, she'd drop the key, then they'd never get in.

"You'd hate if I said that to you," Jules murmured, drawing her hair over one shoulder to press light kisses to her skin. "*Wait? Who do you think I am, peasant? I wait for no one.*"

"I do *not* sound like that," she protested half-heartedly, distracted by his lips. "And don't judge—patience is overrated."

Selene felt the curve of Jules's smile against her throat.

"You're telling me," he murmured, then trailed liquid fire across her skin as he kissed down her neck, pausing only long enough to move aside her beaded strap to nip her shoulder.

The scrape of his teeth was like lightning down her spine, igniting low in her stomach. A soft moan escaped her lips. In reaction to the sound, he surged against her, pressing his hips against her rear. She tipped her head back against his shoulder, as her whole world narrowed to the heat of him.

Jules slid his hand along her arm, his long fingers tangling between hers to guide the key to the door. Together they unlocked the room and stumbled in. The door hadn't had time to close behind them before Jules was turning her with his hands on her waist.

"Beautiful Selene." His voice lit fires in her.

One night. She would burn him out of her system until there was nothing left of how much she wanted him but ashes. Pressing him back against the door, she took his face in her hands and kissed him deeply.

Jules made a soft sound against her mouth and one of his hands drifted to her hip to pull her flush against his angular body, while the other dipped into the low-cut back of her dress, making sparks shoot up her spine.

The frosted glass of the clock face bathed the space in faint golden light. Then the ghostly shadows of the clock hands came together and the bells chimed, rumbling midnight through the space.

Jules pulled back, peering toward the oaken roof beams. "Selene . . . where are we?"

She tipped her head back, looking up at the raw beams overhead. "Clock tower. I used to come here as a kid."

Jules's fingers trailed absently up and down her sides as he looked around, the golden lights of Rome softly illuminating the tower room. "That's so weird . . ."

She was silent, sensing he had more to say.

He looked at her. "At the orphanage, there was a clock tower. It was nothing like this, though." He stepped away from her, and the empty places where his hands had been felt ice cold. Jules leaned on the sill, looking down over Rome. "It was kind of squat and—"

"Ugly," she supplied, stepping up behind him so she could lean her chin on his shoulder. "I recall."

He grinned. "Excuse you."

"You said it was squat!"

"And I would have said it was ugly too. But *I'm* allowed."

She rolled her eyes. "Ah, I see. Far be it from me to insult your squat little tower."

He laughed, pulling her in front of himself so he could lift her up onto the window ledge, pressing her wrists back against the glass. "Don't make me make you stop talking."

Her breaths were coming shorter and the silk of her dress felt thinner by the moment as his body heated up. She arched against him. "You'd be surprised what I'd do to get your attention."

Jules groaned softly, pushing her knees apart and ruching the dress up her thighs so he could step between them. "Mission accomplished, Captain Alleva. You have my attention."

She bit her lip and slid her hands to his pants, thumbing his button. "And? What else do I have?"

His body pulled taut at her proximity and she could feel the bulge in his pants. She palmed it, not taking her eyes off his face as his lashes fluttered. After a beat, he said hoarsely, "Anything. Everything."

She swallowed. The cold window at her back sent a tremor down her spine. His heat was all she wanted.

Everything, he said.

Everything was all she wanted.

Even though he was a demon. Even though he was her enemy. Even though tomorrow she'd have to say goodbye.

"Please . . ."

He groaned softly, sliding his hands to her hips beneath the dress. "You do not need to say please, *mon amour*."

Ignoring him, she pushed the jacket off his shoulders. "Jules, please . . ."

The words broke him.

She could feel the moment his control snapped and his strong hands tightened on her thighs, dimpling the skin as he lifted her and slammed her back against the stone an inch to the side of the window, crushing his lips to hers and pressing his hardness between her legs.

Jules's kisses were greedy and hungry and they stole her breath, so she fought back with enthusiasm, stealing nips from his full lower lip and battling his tongue with hers until he groaned and pinned her wrists over her head with one hand.

"What do I have to do to make you behave?" he murmured, voice husky.

She laughed. "Do you really want that?"

The following kiss was answer enough. He slid the straps from her shoulders, pulling her dress down so he could palm one breast, his lips dropping from hers to trail down her collarbone. Then she felt teeth, gasping at the starburst of sensation.

She wasn't certain how but she got his clothes off, shedding his shirt, troublesome button by troublesome button, only swearing when she couldn't get his pants undone.

He leaned back, looking down with hazy eyes. "Here, let me."

"I've got it!" she argued.

He groaned, pressing his forehead to the stone beside her shoulder. "This . . . all of this is very hard on me, you know."

She smirked, glancing at him. "It certainly is *very*—"

"Oh, ha, ha. Amusing."

Finally she growled and yanked his pants open, the button pinging against the windowpane. He kicked them off and stumbled back between her thighs.

There was a beat of stillness as he held her eyes. A moment between their frantic need and the answering of it. At last he pressed a slow kiss to her mouth as he entered her.

She cried out, hand bunching in his hair as she wrapped her legs around his waist, every inch of her clamoring to be part of every inch of him. Stars danced behind her eyes, or maybe they were in the sky as Jules lowered her onto his jacket below the window and captured her lips again. None of it was enough; she wanted more of him. More hands, more kisses. Until it all became too much.

She gasped, heart fluttering. She had to tell Jules that something was terribly wrong with her, but her fingers wouldn't obey her commands and only buried themselves deeper in his hair, and her own voice begged him for more.

And, God, she became the fire and it was glorious.

Jules bundled her against his chest and covered her with his jacket, pressing kisses to her hair.

He chuckled. It was infectious. Soon she was laughing too, trying to smother the sound against his collarbone. Her eyelids were heavy. She sighed, overwhelmed by the dueling urges to kiss every inch of skin she could find and to close her eyes. Jules burned like a furnace against her, lulling her into the warm embrace of slumber.

Jules drew Selene's smooth thigh over his waist, tracing lines against her skin with his thumb.

She was battling sleep with all the stubborn discipline she'd honed in her training. But tonight she was only a girl, and he brushed soft kisses to her ear, whispering, "Sleep, beautiful Selene."

She smiled, lashes trembling against her cheeks. "I don't want to sleep."

"Why?"

"Because then this will be over."

He shifted to lean over her, eyes trailing the length of her body to memorize every inch.

"Sleep, beautiful." He would never be able to use the word again—she'd ruined it for all other things. He lay back down beside her and traced up her ribs to her collarbone, gently thumbing a kiss mark he'd made, like an inexperienced boy. "Not everything should last forever."

Her brows tugged together, but sleep had her in its grip. She murmured in denial, but the words were lost. Jules frowned against her skin, unsure if he could have refused her if she had argued that no, some things should last.

But—heartbreakingly—she did not. There was nothing left for him within the Vatican. No answers he didn't know. Only the all-consuming pull of the Deathless God.

Not even Selene could protect him if they learned what he

was. He continued to draw patterns on her body with his thumb, mapping her. And if *she* ever discovered the truth, she'd hate him for this.

The thought was an iron spike through his heart.

She could never know. He never wanted her to regret tonight.

Carefully he eased up to a crouch, reaching for his clothes. The jacket slipped from her shoulders and ever so gently he moved it back over her. A rustle of paper drew him to the pocket, where he found a folded note.

Angling it to the dim light from the clock face, Jules read indigo words inked in a looping hand with aggressive horizontal slashes. Even before he read his name, he knew it had to be from Sparrow.

Kian is with me. Safe.
When you come, come alone – Sparrow

CHAPTER THIRTY-FOUR

Chill tendrils brushed Selene's naked limbs as she woke. The clock tower had a thousand cracks for drafts to slip through, and cold air twined among the gears overhead with a low whistle. She pulled Jules's jacket tighter to herself and sought him out with a hand. His place beside her was empty. A loose thread of worry tugged free. She sat up, reaching for her dress, and a glint of light on steel caught her eye. The twin D'Alessandro blades were propped by the door with her own.

No. Her heart plummeted. *He's gone.*

In a fugue state, she pulled on her dress, then stumbled down the spiral stairs with the D'Alessandro blades clutched in a hand.

He was *gone.*

She'd told herself that this would be goodbye, but . . . that was meant to be *her* choice. Now that Jules had made the choice for her, she wasn't okay with it. The stairs were achingly cold beneath her bare feet and her sword pressed painfully against the ridges of her spine.

She could catch him. She had to tell him not to go. *Please*—not a word she usually used, but she'd say it a thousand times if it made him stay. He was a demon and still she chose to sleep with him. *Just once to say goodbye.* The gossamer lie she'd told herself.

And now it was clearer than ever one night wasn't enough. She wanted him every day, forever. Demon or not.

Unshed tears burned in her eyes as she ran through the cold halls, feet frozen as she checked one corridor. Then the next.

They were dark. They were empty.

And Selene was alone again.

How had she been so *stupid*? She should have told him how she felt.

Far ahead of her strode a tall, familiar form.

"Jules . . . !" Her voice caught in her throat. The heat prickling behind her eyes broke free, sliding down her face. She broke into a run, picking up her pace as he turned a corner out of her sight.

Then another figure stepped into the corridor from a different hall.

Selene slipped behind a pillar, choking on her breath as she held a hand to her mouth to muffle her gasps—or her sobs? Was she crying?—so that Cesare wouldn't hear her. As she pressed her shoulders to the chill marble, part of her wondered why she'd hidden. Why was that her first reaction upon seeing him? But as her mind caught up to her body, she didn't move.

His footsteps brought him closer.

Cesare glanced both ways, then silently descended into the Vatican necropolis.

Jules hammered his fist against Sparrow's door, his heart thundering. He'd jogged here—cold sleet slashing against his face as he put as much distance as he could between himself and St. Peter's—so he wouldn't lose his resolve and go back.

Selene might be awake now. He took one step toward the Vatican. If he ran, he could lie down beside her and pretend he'd never left . . .

"You're here—" *Sparrow.*

"*Jules!*" Kian crashed against him, half climbing his body to smack kisses against his hair, hugging his head.

Jules squeezed him numbly. "Thank you," he told Sparrow, throat tight around the words.

Sparrow smirked. "I do what I can for our own."

Jules's shoulders tensed. "What?"

Kian slid down, backing up a step as he straightened his shirt cuffs. Beneath that mop of red hair, he looked shamefaced.

"He's like us. But . . . different," Sparrow explained.

Kian looked away. "I promise I didn't know, Jules. I was just meant to protect you."

Jules leaned his back against the wall and slid to sit on the slick cobbles, not caring that he was soaked through.

Sparrow crouched before him, placing a hand on his knee. "Come inside," he urged. "Get dry."

Jules ignored him, looking past him to Kian. "How are you—"

Sparrow cut him off, pulling him to his feet and giving him little choice but to move. "Come inside."

This time, Sparrow led them straight past the spiral stairs and took them deeper into the establishment. They passed smoke-filled rooms lit by low-burning gas lanterns. Felted card tables were occupied by hunched figures, not a face to be seen below drawn hoods. Jules raised an incredulous brow when he saw a stack of notes in the center of a table, a set of keys, and what looked like a Vatican-stamped blade. What a pot.

They went up a short flight of stairs to a bar. Only one barman remained, polishing glasses with fastidious care, but a single look from Sparrow had him wiping his hands and disappearing out the back.

"How?" Jules asked Kian again. "I thought you were dead. I could've sworn . . ."

Kian bunched his own shirt and shook it. "This is a stolen body. I wasn't born into it like you."

Jules stared at Kian, emotions raw on his face. They'd grown up together. They were basically brothers. How was such a thing even possible?

Jules dragged both hands through his hair and turned his back on Kian.

Returning from the bar, Sparrow set down a trifecta of drinks.

"Start from the beginning," he commanded Kian.

Eyes widening with something like alarm, Kian snapped his jaw shut.

Sparrow nodded seriously. "The beginning. If you don't, I will."

Kian sat heavily and suddenly he looked a lot older than his eighteen years. It was something in his eyes . . .

Jules swallowed, reaching for his drink. "Go on. I'm listening."

"All right . . ." Kian gripped his glass between his palms. "Jules, I knew your father years ago. Long before you were born. *More* than knew him—we were friends. Like you and I are friends."

"Basically brothers," Jules said quietly.

There was a foreign solemnity to Kian, who smiled slightly at that. "Brothers in every way that counts."

When Jules took a sip of his drink, his hand was trembling. "So you're a demon?"

Kian glanced through lowered lashes at Jules. "Yes. Elysian, like your father."

Expression carefully neutral, Jules turned his glass beneath his fingers. "So . . ."

Even though tension tightened Kian's jaw, his eyes softened as he waited for Jules's question—serious in a way Jules had rarely seen from his childhood friend.

Jules released a breath. "If you're some old demon, why were you such a dumbass our whole lives?" His face split into a grin.

Kian groaned, scraping fingers through his hair. "Oh, I should've fuckin' known . . ."

Sparrow's rich laughter washed over them and the tension fled the room. Jules grinned as he took a sip of his drink.

"If you must know," Kian said, tone measured, "I didn't know. I began to lose myself sometime during childhood. By the time we were ten, I was *your* Kian through and through." He rubbed fingers against his heart, smothering a fleeting expression of intense pain. "I still don't remember everything. Most things."

"You said you were Elysian, like my father. What does that mean?"

As though sensing his cascade of emotions, Sparrow smoothed a thumb over Jules's cheek. "I can explain that." Sparrow held his eyes as he explained in that low, reassuring way of his. "Kairos and Elysian have been fighting a long while, but we're the same people. Ultimately we're the same." He smiled. "And despite all the things driving us apart, you are a child of both. Remarkable really."

A child of *both*? "But how?"

Sparrow and Kian shared a look. "You mean, how did you come to be?" Sparrow asked.

Jules nodded. "Given my father has been trapped inside the Vatican for . . . for I don't even *know* how long."

"Your mother was pregnant with you before he was crucified. She didn't know about you—neither of them did." Kian chose his words carefully. "When she was cast out of this world, her essence was ripped out of her human body. And so it remained in perfect equilibrium. Neither dead nor alive."

"Like the Deathless God," Jules murmured, sensing it was only a fraction of the story.

Kian nodded. "As were you. Not yet born. Like an unspoken promise. Only once she clawed her way back here to her body, after living in it for a while, did she become aware of your existence at all. Until then, you were unknown to her. To your father. To any of us." Kian's eyes were fathomless and Jules could only see a stranger.

He rubbed his chest as if to ease a stab of pain.

Sparrow's eyes were on his collar. "Your buttons are all mismatched. Don't tell me we interrupted something?"

Following Sparrow's gaze, Kian was unable to hide a smirk. "You crawled out of that exorcist's bed to come here and see me? I'm flattered." And there was Kian, again. *His* Kian. His silence must've been confirmation enough, because Kian tried, and failed, not to laugh. "Are you fucking stupid? I always knew you were an idiot, but this, *this* is irrefutable proof."

Whistling low, Kian flicked up Jules's collar, showing Sparrow a lipstick stain.

Jules slapped his hand away.

Undeterred, Kian said grandly, "I hereby declare Jules Lacroix the dumbest bloody—"

"Shut up."

Jules trailed his eyes over Kian's familiar features as he howled with laughter. He was still the same, even if he was a demon. Clamping a hand over his mouth, Jules pulled him in, planting a kiss on the crown of his head. "I'm glad you're alive, boyo."

Kian had a teasing grin on his face. "Charm won't work. I still think you're goddamn stupid."

He pushed the dripping hair back from his face. The decision to leave Selene was a chasm in his chest and he couldn't joke about it. Not even with Kian. "It's better this way. She can never know what I am . . . She'd hate me."

Sparrow tipped his head back, sighing heavily. "She already knows."

"What?"

"She knows." Sparrow straightened Jules's collar for him and then gave him a shake. "I spoke to her at the ball and *she knows.*" He looked Jules up and down, his good eye taking in his mussed hair, the lipstick stain, and the mismatched buttons. "And apparently she doesn't care."

"*Dieu,*" Jules swore.

"Yep." Kian still sounded amused.

"She's going to kill me."

Sparrow nodded. "Probably."

Jules stood. "I have to go . . ." The part of him that had wanted to know his story forever screamed at him to stay. Kian knew his father. Kian could tell him everything. And yet he silenced that voice. "I have to go back." He spun on his heel and ran, leaping down the stairs.

As he burst out onto the street, the shutters on a window flung open and Sparrow and Kian leaned out. Jules skidded on the slippery stones but righted himself. Jogging backward, he cupped a hand around his mouth to yell up at Sparrow. "Look after Kian."

Sparrow raised a hand in silent acknowledgment, wincing as Jules cracked his skull against a lamppost. Rubbing the back of his head, Jules pivoted and sprinted for the Vatican, a stupid grin on his face.

Selene *knew* and she wanted him anyway.

And he'd left her naked on the floor of a dusty old clock tower.

Kian was right—he really was fucking stupid.

The ironwork gate at the bottom of the stairs was unlocked and Selene silently made her way through, walking down a handful more steps until her bare foot landed in an inch of freezing water. She moved more carefully after that, not wanting to alert Cesare to her presence.

She inhabited the shadows, tailing her uncle deeper into the Vatican necropolis. As she did, she lambasted herself for her suspicious nature. What had happened to her? Taking a demon to her bed and now, what? Investigating the Imperium Bellum himself? He was a Prince of the Church . . . But why was he down here, when the rest of the Vatican were at Carnival?

The soft sound of voices reached her, though she couldn't make out the words. Her uncle, she knew. But when she recognized the other speaker, her heart slowed as though frozen over.

She moved painstakingly closer. It couldn't be.

"I didn't expect your progress with the wards to be so slow."

"Humans, always in such a hurry." His voice resonated through her bones, playing along her ribs like a xylophone.

Baliel.

The Duke of Briars spoke in a softly amused tone that sang of years *and years* of waiting to get what he wanted. Patience such as this was chilling.

"And you wonder why we have so little respect for your lives." Baliel walked around the statue of a winged lion in the center of the space, water rippling around his every footstep, though it made no sound. "No sooner do you slip, squalling, into life than you rush back out again, as though you can't even pause to breathe—" He inhaled deeply, mocking her uncle. "Unfortunately your arrangement with our watered-down offspring has caused some difficulty."

Watered-down offspring. Could he mean Sparrow and the half-demons? "Even so, I'm almost done with the wards."

So it *was* Baliel destroying the wards. And even though she had warned her uncle that Baliel would be coming here, Cesare had diverted dozens of exorcists out of Rome—ostensibly to hunt for him.

She'd only been wrong about one thing: Baliel was *already here.*

Here, at the very heart of St. Peter's Basilica.

And Cesare had known.

Her uncle's voice broke into her thoughts. "When you came to me with this proposal, you sold it as mutually beneficial. So far all I have is a headache. I want this done. Fast."

"Fast?" Baliel drew out the word, making it sound especially languorous. "You are in no position to be making demands. I'm not as disposed to help you as I might otherwise be."

"Why?" Her uncle's voice was tight, his patience barely intact.

"After you sent your little lapdog after me in Nice."

"Perhaps if you had come when I called, I wouldn't have had to—"

Baliel laughed. The sound chilled her blood. "When you called? Such a genteel way of putting it, Cesare." He almost purred the name, no more cowed by Cesare's position than a panther might be. "When you hooked your magic into my essence and dragged me here, you mean?"

Cesare's jaw ticked.

Baliel was suddenly standing nose to nose with him. His blue eyes burned brighter than any other light in the necropolis. "Such statecraft. I do admire how effectively you talk around the sordid truth, but for once I would like your candor."

Cesare raised his chin slightly, his lips curling. "Very well. When I used my vast ability to drag you, the greatest of the dukes, into this world against your will. When I imposed my power on you and *won*. Is that what you want to hear?"

Baliel's expression didn't flicker, but Selene felt as though the room chilled by degrees. The dripping of water seemed to slow, as though it were becoming ice. Then he smiled. A beautiful smile that belied his profane nature.

"Exactly so. I am actually rather grateful to your niece. Without her intervention, I wouldn't have been able to break your hold. She's quite something. Her power . . ." He hesitated meaningfully, reaching for Cesare to slide a hand over his cheek, and where he touched, a cut appeared on his skin, seeping blood.

Baliel caught it and brought it to his lips, licking his thumb. "Her power tastes quite different from your own."

Cesare didn't move to wipe the blood, merely tipped a brow. "If you're done, I have work to do."

Without waiting for Baliel's response, Selene started her quiet retreat. Her movements felt mechanical, as though she'd been wound up like a pocket watch, her mind still turning over what she'd overheard.

Even as she moved out of earshot, she could hear her uncle's deep timbre. Could picture the touch of affectionate amusement that infused his voice—but only with her.

A stone sat heavy in her chest, crushing her lungs, replacing her heart.

Cesare Alleva was the Imperium Bellum. A Prince of the Church. And a traitor.

CHAPTER THIRTY-FIVE

Each step became a lesson in patience as Selene backed away, mindful not to disturb the water. Her every movement created a domino effect of ripples that disappeared into the dark, but she hoped there was enough disturbance from the steady dripping to disguise it. When her toe scraped against something that moved beneath the water, she froze.

A gleam of gold pierced the dark. She plunged her hand into the water, already knowing what she'd find. A ward coin. And ahead, the pale glimmer of an alabaster lion. What had once been a Vatican lion was ghostly in the dark. It was split down the middle and the coin that had been at its heart sat snug in her hand—already warming to her touch. A wave of terrible grief rolled over her. This was a reminder she needed about as much as a knife through the ribs that the one doing this was an enemy. And an enemy to all Rome.

Resting her hand on the lion's mane, she listened. She heard no movement. Only the perpetual dripping that filled the necropolis.

Her footsteps were careful in the depthless black water. She had to find Jules. Baliel had hunted him in Nice, and Cesare was pulling Baliel's strings. What did it mean? A dull ache throbbed through her temples as she tried to force the pieces together, but they didn't want to fit.

Once past the ironwork gate, she took the steps two at a time, favoring speed over stealth. The hall ahead was empty. She glanced over her shoulder, toward the necropolis's yawning dark.

Hands caught her waist and adrenaline shot through her. But she knew those hands. They were familiar. Large and warm.

"Jules!" she gasped, burying her face against his neck. He smelled of warm skin, of chilled Roman rain.

Stepping back, she let her eyes roam over him. He was soaked through.

He pulled her tighter to him, his lips roaming over her cheek to press to her temple. Then he moved to her mouth and caught her lips in a hard kiss. A kiss that took more than it gave. It was divine.

"I shouldn't have left—" he began.

"No, and you certainly shouldn't have come back."

Gripping his shirt in her hands, she pushed him, stumbling, back the other way.

Taking refuge in the language library, Selene moved Jules's hair back from his face. Then she slid her hands down his neck and shoulders, feeling him. His shirt was translucent from the rain and plastered to his skin. Where they were pressed together under a stone arch, beneath a stained-glass window that lit his face in hues of blue, the briars and thorns of his scar were clearly visible. How had she not realized he was a demon earlier?

In the necropolis it had seemed so obvious, and not just because of what had happened in the *Cor Cordium*, but also because Jules was remarkable. She tugged at his shirt, tearing it a bit as she pulled it down his bicep, her fingertips sliding over the scar's pale ridges. "This . . . *this* is why."

It was like a brand. Sealing the demon in him off from her magic and senses, as though it wasn't there at all.

His eyes were liquid as he watched her. "I think so. Sparrow told me he didn't know at first either."

She felt the blood drain from her cheeks.

Jules searched her face, brows drawing together with confusion. "I thought you knew."

And she thought he *hadn't.*

Walking away, she pointed. "Don't come closer." She ran her hands through her tangled hair and tipped her head back. Sparrow, *of course.* If he had told Jules he was a demon, it meant Jules had been lying to her since that night.

With obvious effort Jules obeyed, muscles shifting beneath his skin as he held himself in check.

"God, you must think I'm so stupid," she breathed.

"Selene—" He moved toward her and she snatched her favorite boot knife from inside the boning of her dress, angling it so it touched his solar plexus.

"Do not touch me, Jules Lacroix."

Anger flickered in his eyes, then he shuttered it behind faux curiosity. "What now, exorcist?"

Selene felt like crying but the tears wouldn't come, and she burned with humiliation. "Enough games. Sparrow isn't the only one with answers."

The scar on his bicep was a cipher, and suddenly she could decode the mystery of him.

"This mark belongs to one of the noble houses. The Duke of Briars. The demon you spoke to tonight. The demon I've been hunting."

His expression didn't waver. So he knew that too. It felt as though he'd wrenched her ribs wide—so much easier to crush her heart that way. But she was hell-bent on telling him something Sparrow hadn't. Even if it hurt.

Pacing, she continued, her words spilling out moments after she realized the truth for herself. "You were taken to the orphanage in Nice as a newborn, already scarred. Which tells me you were grown inside a demon's womb. Your mother wasn't some innocent girl seduced by a demon." She watched his eyes, but there was no surprise there. He knew that too. She nodded to his bicep. "Your mother did that." Her words were venom, but she couldn't stop them. "She carved her newborn's flesh."

Pain—but not surprise—flared in his eyes at her words. That a mother Jules had never known would hurt him? Or that *she* had?

He drew an unsteady breath. "I should have told you."

Selene shook her head, laughing bitterly. "No." The anger drained out of her as suddenly as it had come. "The irony is, I know you made the right choice." She turned away, disappearing the knife into her dress once more. Her hands trembled. "The only choice really. I could not have been trusted."

The warmth of his chest radiated into her back as Jules stepped up behind her. She wanted to lean into him but held herself rigid. A gentle touch—tentative—then he turned her with a hand on her waist. "I'm still sorry I didn't. But I'm not sorry for anything else. Not a *single* moment." He brushed her cheek with his thumb, frowning as he rubbed salt between his fingers.

Selene ignored the evidence.

Grasping her jaw in a hand, he tipped her head back so he could kiss her, softer than a flake of snow landing. She arched onto her toes, chasing the kiss when he leaned away. Laughing against her mouth, he wrapped his arms around her to hold her close.

Footsteps passed by and she pulled away, listening intently.

"I need to get you out of here. It's no longer safe."

She led him swiftly to the nearest garden courtyard, heart pounding double time as they kept to the shadows beneath a line of bending palms. Silhouetted against the night sky, the thick fronds were populated with large round nests. During the day, they were occupied by noisy green parakeets, but now the birds made only a few sleepy chirps as Selene and Jules disrupted the stillness.

Her bare shoulders prickled in the cold. The rain had stopped, leaving the night slightly overcast. She paused in the deep dark beneath an ancient cypress. "The Vatican ward was broken tonight." She reached into her dress, drawing out the hexagonal disc from the broken ward in the necropolis. "I don't know what the hell's going on or how it's all connected."

He reached for it, but she snatched her hand away.

"Are you stupid?" she asked, and she was pleased her voice came out steady if a little cold. "This was one of the most powerful wards in the city, Jules. It operated like a battery, charging the Vatican ward. They work against demons like you—" She broke off. How long had she suspected his true nature without acknowledging it to herself? A day at least. "It isn't because I don't trust you. I'm afraid for you."

His expression opened with realization.

She rolled her eyes and slipped it back into her clothes. "These discs were created specifically to guard against powerful demons and . . ." The enormity of the fact that he was somehow a full-blooded demon hung between them, overripe like the fat moon peeking through a tattered veil of low cloud.

"It broke tonight?"

"During the Carnival Masquerade. When I wasn't here."

When Cesare had *specifically ordered* her not to be here. But she didn't say it aloud. The pain was too raw.

At the far side of the garden she saw movement. A group of exorcists were knifing through the dark with an urgency that didn't fit the hour. She pulled Jules back and they ran low through the shadows until they could cut through to St. Peter's Basilica.

"Are there other wards?" he asked softly.

The early hour painted the Vatican in silver and gray. Shadows teemed in the corners, sinister in the way they had always been—but now she knew enough to admit it. She had never trusted her instincts when it came to the way this place made her feel.

Around the corner from the guardhouse, they stopped and she counted the moving silhouettes inside. Two. And one more outside. That was normal. If something was afoot, as she suspected, that could change. They had to move.

"Some. Wards like this take massive amounts of power to uphold. It's why we can't protect Rome as easily as the Vatican. Or Italy as well as Rome. Or Europe. Even protecting the entirety of Rome would be impossible. Some always get through."

"But never into the Vatican."

"Never. But now that the main Vatican ward has fallen, I don't know how long it will hold. There should be three, but, who knows, the other two could already be compromised. Meaning, theoretically, the demon dukes could descend on Rome."

Jules only frowned.

Selene slipped over the wall, keeping it between her and the checkpoint, and slunk low toward the guardhouse. The ember of a lit cigarette glowed in the dark as the checkpoint guard took a drag, illuminating his face. Tommaso, the exorcist who'd challenged Jules at the funeral. Just perfect.

Only a hundred feet separated them from the relative safety of St. Peter's Square where they could disappear among the citizens of Rome. She pressed her back against the wall of the Academy building, keeping the jutting corner between them and the guard-house. They'd be fine, so long as Tommaso didn't choose to stroll this way.

Jules took his place beside her and threaded their fingers. He glanced around the corner, then flattened her back with his arm. He shook his head in disgust. "Why does it have to be him?"

"One of the few who knows your face," Selene agreed in a whisper.

"Is it bad if the demon dukes get into the Vatican?"

"It's worse than bad. If they get through, they'll come for the Deathless God."

"Baliel won't. He doesn't want to hurt him."

"And he told you this?" she scoffed.

He nodded, watching her with trusting green eyes.

"Oh, well then, we don't have to worry about anything."

"That's not what I'm saying." His eyes were distant. "Baliel may not be a threat, but there are others."

"Be quiet for a minute." She pressed the flat of her palm to her forehead. "I have to figure this out."

Jules drew her hand down, rubbing his thumb against her palm. "Which part?"

A silver scar across her knuckles was all that remained of her wound.

"All of it." The distant sound of a door slamming made them both still. "We need to get out of here. It's not safe for you." Selene dared another look around the corner in time to see Tommaso kick away from the wall and toss his spent cigarette.

"Checking the perimeter," Tommaso grunted. "Watch the gate." There was no movement from inside the guardhouse.

Jules raised a brow in question. *Now?*

She held him back, hand pressed flat to his chest where she

could feel the powerful thump of his heart, waiting for Tommaso to turn the corner around the base of the ten-foot Janiculum wall.

Then, together, they slipped through the shadows, crossing inches from the rectangle of light that splashed onto the cobbles from the open checkpoint door. Inside, two men played cards and nursed steaming cups. No wonder they didn't want to step outside.

Complacency. Her lip curled.

Jules paused, looking curiously in, and she grabbed him, propelling him ahead of herself.

He whispered a protest. "The skinny guy's cheating."

"Do you want to go back?" she snapped.

He smothered a chuckle.

Outside the Vatican fortress signs of life were everywhere. A drunken group staggered down the middle of the quiet street, their laughter ringing loudly. A pair of old men played chess by the light of a lamp, breath misting in the chill.

"What I can't figure out is how Baliel knew my father. I learned Baliel hadn't been here for years."

"He came in secret," Jules said softly. "And he told me your father took the records."

She stopped. "But that means . . ." Her brows drew together. "My father destroyed records relating to you before he died. Years ago."

"Exactly."

"Who are you, Jules Lacroix?"

He smiled slightly. "The eternal question."

She sensed he wasn't saying something, but brushed it off, knowing where they needed to go. "Let's find out what else my father was hiding."

* * *

Even before she stepped inside her family palazzo, Selene knew it was a horrible idea. Musty air rolled out when she forced open the door, its hinges stiff with disuse. The dust motes glinting in the faint light of streetlamps could have spelled it out: *Wrong way. Go back.*

But Jules's warmth soaked through her like sunshine on stone, and his broad-shouldered frame filled the doorway behind her, locking her in. She couldn't back out now. No matter how dearly she wanted to.

Selene touched the wallpaper, gliding her finger along its ridges, and paused in front of a gilded mirror that had a film of dust over the glass. She looked like a ghost. Well, if that wasn't poetic irony. The girl in the mirror hadn't stepped through this door since before her father died. When her family was still whole. Now the ghost haunting these halls was the one who'd destroyed it all.

Jules gaped at the cobwebbed double-tiered chandelier. Selene noticed other things: a spilled travel chest of clothing at the foot of the stairs, papers and passports abandoned on the sideboard. Her family had been exiled—a dignified exit had never been on the cards for them.

As if in a dream, Selene walked farther into the foyer, tipping her head back to look at the coffered ceiling. Above it, her old bedroom, right next door to Niccolò's. Numbly she led Jules toward the library and her father's adjoining study at the back of the house.

Beautiful once, now draped sheets protected the books from fading and the library ladder had an air of being stationary for too long. The presence of her father was so palpably missing and she felt like a visitor in someone else's memory.

"What makes you think your father was hiding more than the records?" Jules blew on the dust-covered mantel, revealing forgotten trinkets. A rare fossil. An old sextant. A polished jade egg.

Selene averted her eyes. "Because he died for pulling the spear from the Deathless God's body. The more I learn, the surer I am that pieces are missing from this horrible puzzle."

"Apt description," he murmured.

An expression crossed his face like clouds over the sun. She knew enough to guess he was holding something back again. Maybe if they laid out what they knew . . . but that meant her being honest too, and the thought of cracking open her ribs and revealing her fragile insides made her flinch from the thought as though burned.

There'd be time enough later.

Wordlessly Selene entered the study, searching the desk and drawers before moving to the ornate boxes on the shelves. All locked. Her knife didn't care.

She tipped her head. Something didn't seem right.

Jules had ripped the sheets off the furniture in the other room, sending eddies of dust into the air, and without the lumpy sheets her suspicions were confirmed.

Against all logic, the shelves were set farther back in the library. Even though they both backed on to the same hallway, her father's study was six inches narrower. Selene slid her hands along the bookshelves, searching for a switch or a divot. Anything really.

Jules poked his head in. "What're you doing?"

She ignored him.

He waved his hand in front of her face. "Have you found something?"

"Not sure."

Jules caught her waist in one hand and kissed her bare shoulder, playing with the beaded strap of her evening gown. "I'm not moving until you tell me."

She set a hand on his chest, smiled sweetly, and shoved him out of the way.

He steadied himself on the shelf and it rocked forward, threatening to tip books all over them. Then, with a mechanical click, it swung open, revealing a second glass-fronted bookshelf beyond.

"*Dio . . .*" she breathed.

Jules brushed himself off. "You're welcome."

Again, she ignored him, her eyes roving over the hundreds of beautiful books.

"Death by twelve-foot bookshelves? Check."

"You can't check it off," she murmured. "You're not dead."

"I was checking it off my 'ways not to die' list."

She glanced at him, one brow arched. "You have a 'ways *to* die' list?"

A slow smirk swept across his face. "In the throes of—"

She pressed a hand to his face to smother his talking. "I've heard enough."

Surrounded by piles of books from the secret bookshelf, Selene sat on the floor of her father's study. She shook them out and tossed them aside, ignoring the clouds of dust that billowed around them.

Jules had a very different approach. He sat with a small pile of interesting books—books with gold foil and sprayed edges and decorative metal corners, and the ones overflowing with bright illustrations and diagrams of Rome's famous architecture—and he slowly worked his way through them without missing a page.

She sighed loudly. He ignored her now, too invested in his painstaking investigation. Selene threw another book over her shoulder and stood to sweep the contents of another shelf into a box, not caring that some spilled messily to the floor.

Jules clicked his tongue and scooped up one of the books that had fallen open, crumpling its delicate pages. But when he picked it up, he froze. "I think I've found something."

Jules held up the notebook, a twin to the one they already had. Scrawled across the pages were copious notes in her father's hand. Most of it Latin, again. Selene flipped through the pages and almost dropped the notebook when she came to a sketch of the Deathless God that covered two pages. The spear embedded in his torso had been meticulously re-created on paper—down to the swirls and carvings in the flared spear point and every stud along the line of the shaft.

Selene no longer felt her nails biting into her palms. Instead, she felt the smooth wood and the metal studs beneath her hands, the hot rush of blood that covered her and burned her until she thought she was nothing but bones, with sheer will holding her up.

"Oh," she said faintly, overwhelmed by the memory. "You might be right."

Jules caught her before she hit the floor. "Whoa." He cradled her to his chest.

Unsure what had happened—what continued to happen— she struggled to breathe. Her hands bunched in his shirt and she shuddered. Why couldn't she breathe? Jules was a pillar of warmth, but it was the ghost of a sensation compared to the encompassing memory of pain.

Her father lay crumpled just out of sight, and she was so small, with only a spear to quell the divine giant.

"Selene." Jules's voice was soft but firm. "Breathe."

He smoothed her hair back from her face, repeating her name. Then he captured a gleaming teardrop on his thumb and looked at it with an expression of deliberate wonder. "I didn't know you could *cry*."

The words finally broke through the fog in her brain. She laughed and Jules's eyes flooded with relief.

Darting in, she stole a kiss. *Dio*, she was stupid around Jules. Why did he make her feel like half a girl and only a quarter of the exorcist she was supposed to be? She could picture her gravestone all too clearly now: *Here lies Selene Alleva, Exorcist First Class, and one whole entire idiot.*

"I'm all right," she assured him, pressing their foreheads together. "Only—"

Her father's notebooks sat on the edge of his desk.

Volume i. She could feel its twin in Jules's breast pocket. She felt sick at the thought of more secrets uncovered. What had her father learned that took him to the *Cor Cordium* that day, intent on dragging the spear free from God? He'd started unraveling the Vatican's secrets ten years ago and it led to his death.

And Cesare . . . Her heart spasmed at the thought of her uncle. The pain of his betrayal was too intense. Her mind darted away from it. *Later*, she told herself. It had been such a long day already.

She nudged the book to Jules. "Can you look?"

He carefully leafed through her father's notebook. She saw diagrams of the Vatican, the buildings mapped out and labeled. The capillaries of the necropolis, the five-pointed corridor, and the solid lines of the walls. He turned the page, fingers flinching off the paper.

It was the drawing of the Deathless God. Her father had captured the light in the room perfectly, how it slanted across God's cheekbones at a certain time of day, illuminating a glint of pale skin and little more.

Jules cleared his throat. "*Devastatingly, what Baliel told me is true. The demon king was wounded to the brink of death during the*

Battle for Rome. Moving him would be a death sentence, and so a deal was struck—"

"Stop," Selene said. "No, this isn't right. Who is he writing about?"

Jules paused. When he spoke, the words were terribly soft. "*Dieu Immortel.*"

Selene strode forward to snatch the book from his hands. Unlike much of the rest, this page was written in slanted Italian as if her father was committing his thoughts to paper in a mad dash.

She continued reading aloud: "*The Vatican would shelter him until the spear could be safely pulled free. Baliel told me this, as all but the most tangential records of it have long been destroyed. I'm not sure even the current Exorcist Primus is aware of the truth. At some point the Vatican decided to let the truth die. I know the Imperiums are as blinded as the rest of us. I spoke to Cesare. He was horrified. And furious at my sacrilegious words.*

"*He will come to understand.*"

Selene shook her head. But it was undeniable. Her father's writing crowded in around the sketch of the Deathless God. It was quite clear that the notes and the drawing were connected.

She looked at Jules in confusion. "I don't understand."

Jules looked trapped, worry creasing his brow.

"Please, just say it." She wasn't ready, but she was sick of dancing around the fact that Jules knew something. "What did Baliel tell you?"

He groaned, pressing his face against her collarbone.

She carded her fingers through his hair and then tugged his head back. "Tell me."

He sighed, looking anywhere but at her. "The Deathless God is not what you think he is."

What, not who.

She narrowed her eyes. "Continue."

He turned his hand over and bared his wrist, as if to say, *Remember?* She touched his skin lightly, her fingertips trailing the blue of his veins.

"The Deathless God is a demon. Baliel confirmed it."

She coughed a laugh. "And we believe Baliel? A demon duke? Why?"

"He's telling the truth. Even before he told me, I knew it without a shadow of a doubt."

Selene felt as though the world had been yanked from beneath her feet. Jules must have sensed it too, because he gripped her elbow with one strong hand and held her steady. She feared she might fall off the edge of the world if he let go. "No, it's impossible," she breathed. "How could nobody know?"

Jules's face was too calm when he said, "How could they? Demons aren't allowed in the Vatican." He looked at his wrists, expression twisting into something complex. "And maybe that wouldn't prove anything anyway. Maybe it was just my blood." He swallowed. "Baliel told me . . ." He faltered.

Her lips parted. "What?"

His haunted expression played out the thoughts behind his eyes. He knew it wouldn't take much more to kill her faith. Finally, brutally.

"What is it? Tell me."

"He told me," Jules began, closing his eyes for strength. "The Deathless God is my father."

Selene took an unwilling step back. Then she remembered the way his veins had burned with gold fire. Gold like God's blood. Jules was a demon and *Dio Immortale*'s presence should have destroyed him. But Jules hadn't burned, he'd shone.

Her faith said it couldn't be, but the Deathless God's blood had triggered her magic the same way demon blood affected other exorcists. Even though it felt impossible, it made a bizarre sort of sense. Selene circled the desk, away from his warm, distracting hands.

She needed to think.

"Please, Selene," he said, sounding wounded, "I swear—"

"*Enough.*"

He stopped, eyes sharpening. She could see the killer he'd been. The one mentioned in Bachelet's reports, the one the Caspians called *Stigmajka*. She glanced at his arms. He'd rolled his sleeves up to his elbows, and coiling line after line of scars told of his brutality. His willingness to kill. Worse, his utter proficiency at it.

"I trust you," she murmured.

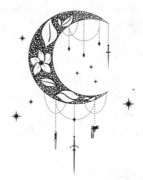

CHAPTER THIRTY-SIX

When Selene drew Jules up the stairs to her childhood bedroom, she didn't look around. Not at the dust coating
the banister or the cobweb-draped chandelier. His warm hand
grounded her and she stared straight ahead.

Canvas covered the windows, making the bedroom dark. Eyes
straining, she turned in place as Jules waited for her in the doorway.
The room was much as she'd left it. Her bed was undisturbed, the
artifacts of her childhood covered in dust on her dresser.

Once constellations had spilled across the high ceiling. Canis.
Aquila. Andromeda. Draco—her favorite. She could no longer see
them now.

She took three long steps and yanked the first of the canvas
window covers down. Nails broke and dust burst into the room as
the canvas billowed to the floor. She dragged at the next, and then
the last, turning to search the ceiling with hungry eyes.

The moon had nearly disappeared below the rooftops, but it
picked out the glimmering gold and tears pricked her eyes.

In the alcove of her window, Jules wrapped his arms around her
from behind and buried his face against her neck. Pain laced his
voice as he breathed against her skin, "I'm sorry I didn't tell you."

Reluctantly he let her turn to face him. She could see the last of the stars reflected in his eyes as he tipped his head back as though to gather himself. "I was afraid to tell you because you're an exorcist first. You protect Rome above all."

"You're not a threat to Rome." She said it like a warning. Or perhaps a furious plea.

He shook his head, *No.*

The taut muscles in her jaw loosened and she ran her fingers over his collarbone and down his bicep to find the raised kill marks. "I *have* told you once before, Lacroix, I don't want to kill you. That remains true so long as you're no threat to Rome." She delicately traced his scar, as if memorizing its intricacies.

He slid hands up her spine, curving her body against him. "I'll hold you to that, exorcist. My life is in your hands now."

How momentous his leap of faith had been, returning to her at all.

She leaned up on her toes, hands wrapped in his collar as she pulled his lips to hers with all the fury she had. It was angry and vicious, her teeth crashing into his lip before she nipped it and deepened the kiss so she could taste him.

Jules circled her waist, lifting her as he kissed her back with near-total enthusiasm, after a wince at the split lip.

"I'm still furious with you, demon." She pushed her hands into his hair, tasting his tongue until the need for air dragged her away from his lips. "Never leave me like that again."

"I swear."

Then he lifted her, beaded silk trailing across the dusty floor as he carried her to the bed.

Selene lingered in her mother's dressing room. She'd taken off the evening gown and dressed in some of her mother's clothes. Tall buttoned boots, fawn suede that hugged her legs, and a leather jacket with the Alleva family crest stitched in silk on the back. This place made her parents feel so close. She tried not to think of Cesare when she pictured her father's face, but it was impossible.

She plaited her hair loosely and tied it off with a velvet ribbon the color of Jules's eyes. He stepped up beside her just then, leaning to press the lightest kiss against her neck. Looking her up and down, he rubbed a hand over his mouth to hide his smirk.

She arched what she hoped was an unamused brow.

He raised both hands in surrender. "It's just a very Vatican-uniform kind of outfit. That's all." He ran his fingers over the lines of stitching, making her shiver beneath the leather. She was still so glad to have him back, too glad to be cross with him for leaving her.

And he was the son of God.

Reaching past her, he snatched up something that glittered like a star. Her grandmother's engagement ring. Looking at it for a long moment, he bit back a smile and slid it onto her finger.

She grasped his chin so he couldn't look away. "Do you know what this is?"

He smiled slightly. "Maybe. Maybe not. That depends."

"*On?*"

He pulled their tangled fingers to his lips, kissing her knuckles as his thumb played with the ring. "On whether or not you'll tell Aurelio Sabatino, that paparazzi photographer, that I finally got you a ring. He kinda hurt my feelings."

She shoved his face, but he laughed, pulling her with him as he stumbled.

"Idiot. Get dressed or dawn will beat us to the punch."

Only a few minutes later, Jules returned to find her standing at the window. Her face was a faint reflection in the rain-streaked glass. Beyond, the sky had opened, saturating the city, and a delicate lemon hue on the horizon threatened dawn.

She was a ghost of a girl, only the vaguest impression of an exorcist.

It was better this way. He had things to say, and if she turned, he feared the words would all dry up. Needing to occupy his hands, Jules tied the twin swords at his hip. His belt was the same dashing cognac leather as his boots. "I have to tell you something."

She didn't react at all and he thought perhaps she hadn't heard.

"Do you remember what we talked about last night? What we fought about? About the Vatican and where you get your magic?"

At first Selene only bent her head, then her quiet voice broke the silence.

"It's the Vatican's greatest secret. That we don't learn this power. We're not born with it. It isn't innate, or a gift from God. It's *stolen*." She spoke the words so softly he had to stand and move closer. Even though he'd already figured much of it out, Jules let her say the words, sensing she needed to speak them aloud. "We wield demon power. It . . . it *disgusts* me."

Her vitriol surprised him.

She touched her throat, swallowing as though she could taste it.

"And *your* power?" he asked softly. "Does it disgust you?"

"I didn't get my power the same way. I was on track to graduate when I turned sixteen. But . . . it didn't work out that way."

Jules could tell she was holding something back.

"How *did* you get your power?" He smoothed her cheeks with

his thumbs, turning her face to him. "Is the blood in your veins different, Selene?"

She hesitated before whispering, "It's God's blood in my veins."

His brows drew together, keenly feeling her pain. He'd suspected she was different from the other exorcists, and perhaps he'd even suspected this, but to hear her say it was different.

Earlier, when he'd told her about his connection to the Deathless God and watched the color bleach from her cheeks, that same instinctive part of him that knew how to find a killing blow in battle had warned him it wouldn't take much to kill her faith. Yet even now she *still* called him God.

A demon.

His father.

He ran a thumb over one pale cheek. She had weathered so many years of guilt for stealing God's blood.

Selene grazed her nails lightly against the delicate skin of her inner forearm. "When I use my magic, it's like liquid fire. I'm afraid of what I'll become when the power finally burns me out completely."

Cesare had embedded the thorns of that fear deep. Jules balled his fists and thrust them into his pockets as he paced. "I saw you use your power—*you have control.*" He emphasized each word.

Her lashes cast crescents on her cheeks. "Perhaps. But I mightn't always."

A knife of real pain eased between his ribs at the tears that caught on her lashes. He closed the distance between them. "Have you ever pushed the limits of your control? Used too much?" He took her face, his touch slightly rough as he forced her to look at him.

She turned her face away and her breath warmed his wrist.

Not looking at him, she murmured, "When your blood burned like His—*like mine*—I felt a little less alone. Ridiculous, isn't it?"

He stroked her cheek. "I don't think it is."

He remembered her words at the Masquerade when he was wearing the Deathless mask. *It wasn't much of a disguise.* How long had she suspected the truth?

When they were in the study, Jules had filled Selene in on everything Baliel said. The truth he had bound into the wards around the city—*Only a demon can kill him. Only a human can free him*—and how, when the final ward fell, Baliel planned to release God himself.

Selene had paled. "But then *Dio Immortale* will be be completely vulnerable."

Jules sat on the bottom step in Selene's family's huge house and looked at the notebooks. Volumes I and II together at last. The new one was indigo blue and utterly indecipherable. Only the one Baliel had handled was in a language he could read; the other was still in Latin. Jules sighed, pressing them between his hands, and felt a frisson of energy.

Barely willing to believe it, he opened the new book, finding Matteo's words. But instead of the Latin from earlier, his familiar sloped handwriting was now in Italian.

"Why couldn't it be French?" Jules muttered, looking the gift horse square in the mouth.

He turned to the page they'd started translating and continued reading.

> Demons gave us the symbols we use to kill them.
> And they gave us the wards.
> I shall sit down and write this long-form later, but I have learned something that must be remembered. Not

remembered like the first exorcists remembered, because they chose to forget. This must be <u>remembered</u>.

Disentangling the truth from dogma first written in the chaotic days after God was pinioned to that great crossbeam in the Cor Cordium has been difficult. In a real sense and an idealogical one. I do not like what I've learned about my people. And I'm afraid that we've gone too far. I'm afraid for my children.

I was able to reconcile myself with using demon blood. I believed that it was right. That the means were justified by the ends. I was foolish and blind, and I'm ashamed it took me so long to question everything.

I have learned that not only the means comes from the demons but also the method. Our symbols are also theirs. We twisted their magic against them and created the wards to keep them out, and, I'm horrified to admit, to keep the Death-less God trapped and immobile. It makes me sick to commit these words to paper.

Humans have ever been a devastatingly clever and devious race, but this . . . it makes me question everything.

Using the magic symbols they taught us, we bound God tighter and tighter.

Why? Because this living corpse of a captive God meant power.

His presence. His blood. It became the most valuable sub-stance on earth, used to make the most powerful weapons. Weapons we could use to fend off the demons who'd mistak-enly trusted us.

Is it any wonder we could not give Him up? Not even when he began to stir.

No, not even then.

Before they left, Jules hid the notebook Eliot had given him in the secret bookshelf, placing it inside a slender wooden box. He'd come back for it later, but he didn't want to carry it to Sparrow's door. It was too dangerous. If information like this had gotten Matteo killed, imagine what it could do to demons.

Dawn was no longer an empty threat as they passed through Trastevere in the rain. It crept over Rome, brightening the sky behind dark clouds and not much more than that.

Something shifted on the edges of Jules's perception. He halted. Everything was still.

"What is it?" Selene asked, hair curling around her face as water dripped from the ends.

"Nothing."

But it wasn't nothing.

The door to Sparrow's joint was visible at the end of the street.

Selene strode ahead, sword across her back, and hammered the flat of her fist on the door.

He felt it again. Like a torch flaring at the edges of his awareness. "Selene!"

"Time to shut up," Ambrose said, slamming his elbow into Jules's temple.

The world flickered, and by the time Jules hit the ground, darkness had swallowed him.

Selene turned in time to see Jules collapse, his face bloody from Ambrose's metal arm. When she reached for her sword hilt, a hand clamped over hers, twisting it up behind her back. She pivoted and lashed out with her boot knife.

Tommaso. He ducked beneath the wild swing.

Several more exorcists melted out of the shadows. Their skin glinted with magic that they'd used against *her*—sneaking up on them in the rain and the dark. Or, more likely, lying in wait.

In the moment of her distraction, as she swung to face them, Tommaso locked his arms around her.

Ambrose laid a boot into Jules's side, kicking him so he rolled over the cobbles. He was unconscious and unable to protect himself.

Fury ignited in her veins. "*Stop!*"

Selene had never been sick at the sight of blood, but Jules's split brow and the streak of blood across wet cobbles made her gag. A scream bubbled up from her chest as she kicked and squirmed against Tommaso's viselike grip. She couldn't reach Jules or Ambrose, or a dagger to trigger her magic.

She wanted to fight them—*kill* them—but they had their magic and she did not.

She should have risked tapping her own before they left the house. *Foolish mistake.*

Tommaso's bare forearms shimmered with loosed magic. It bolstered his unnatural strength, and without hers, breaking his hold would be nigh on impossible. Instead, she slammed her head back against his nose with a satisfying crunch.

Swearing bloody murder, Tommaso swung her around and slammed her face into a crumbling wall. Pressing his whole body weight against her, he crushed the breath from her lungs. Like the bottom feeder he was, Ambrose was drawn by the violence.

Leaning in, Ambrose breathed against her cheek while Tommaso held her pinned. "I knew you'd come here, *traitor.*"

The hairs on her neck prickled. Had Cesare been using Ambrose to spy on her . . . ?

She gritted her teeth, making her jaw ache.

Ambrose snapped at Tommaso. "Let up. There'll be time later."

She refused to look at Jules. She had one play—to be *Selene Alleva*, the Butcher of Rome—and that required her voice not to tremble. The moment Tommaso lightened his grip she shoved back against him so that she could stand tall. "How dare you? I'll be speaking to my uncle about you *today*." She shot a glare over her shoulder at Tommaso, who was binding her wrists. "And you."

Ambrose clicked his tongue. "Selene—"

"Captain Alleva," she corrected him immediately, even now loath to ignore his disrespect.

His fake smile died and an ugly expression twisted the scars on his face. "Not for much longer, demon fu—"

"*Ambrose.*"

Cesare.

Her uncle forced Ambrose back until his spine hit stone, then Cesare grasped his throat and slid him up the wall. "*Never* speak to her like that in front of me." His voice was so soft they all leaned forward. Ambrose choked, clawing at Cesare's hand. "Understand?"

A door flew open.

"What's the meaning of this?" Sparrow stepped out, walking into the middle of the exorcists as though he had nothing to fear. "This is neutral ground."

Sparrow grasped Jules beneath the arm and pulled him up. Groaning, Jules stumbled to his feet and spat blood on the cobbles. Holding him steady with one arm, Sparrow looked around the exorcists. More than one glanced away to avoid his steely gaze. "You have no jurisdiction here."

Selene had never thought she could love Sparrow—or like him—but right now she wanted to kiss his smug face.

Clearing his throat, Cesare dropped Ambrose. "Actually, Sparrow, I think you'll find we're just outside neutral ground." He touched the lamppost, smoothing his thumb over the Vatican seal stamped into the ironwork. "A shame. But we'll be taking lead here. I'll have one of my people send a report your way when we're done."

"I can't allow—"

Jules leaned heavily on Sparrow, and shook his head—*don't*—lips forming the words, *Protect Selene.* Sparrow quieted but remained in place.

Ambrose grasped for the sword hilt jutting over her shoulder and tried to draw it. But her magic bound it tight and she was flung to her knees as the leather strap snapped.

Too stupid to notice it was still scabbarded, Ambrose prepared to swing it like an axe.

A feverish light lit Jules's eyes at seeing Selene on her knees. He snarled, surging out of Sparrow's grip to meet Ambrose halfway, the D'Alessandro moon blade already in his hand, and with impossible speed thrust it through Ambrose's gut.

Blood trickled from the corner of Ambrose's mouth as he collapsed to his knees.

Jules rubbed his thumb against his lower lip. Behind the gesture hid a satisfied smirk. Then Cesare's exorcists closed in. Jules dropped the blade and backed away with his hands up.

They descended on him like crows on a carcass.

Sparrow watched, his expression raw with grief as they beat Jules bloody. Jules let out a hoarse scream as one bent his arm back, dislocating his shoulder. He only stopped screaming when Tommaso punched him so hard he couldn't breathe.

Selene hissed and spat and swore. The sounds of her own words never reached her, swallowed by the horrific cracking of bones as her traitor uncle snatched her off her feet and tossed her over his shoulder. His strength was undeniable.

Meanwhile, unobserved by anyone but Selene, Sparrow retrieved her familial blade and held it in a white-knuckle grip. Catching her gaze, he gave her a very slight nod before retreating inside.

CHAPTER THIRTY-SEVEN

Jules sat across from Cesare Alleva in a Vatican interrogation room. The high stone walls had been daubed with symbols in black paint. Though he couldn't read most, he could feel their power. More of the language stolen from demons. The vaulted ceiling disappeared into gloom, but he could sense the symbols hemming him in.

The flash of anger in Sparrow's eyes was fresh in his memory. Acrid guilt churned in his gut. When he'd asked Sparrow to protect Selene, he had chosen to ignore that Sparrow was most desperate to protect *him*. Jules rubbed at his chest, kneading his knuckles against his breastbone. But he knew something Sparrow didn't— Selene was more fragile than anyone realized. And if he couldn't watch her back, he needed someone he trusted implicitly to do it for him.

Opposite him, Cesare steepled his fingers. The silence stretched, until finally his expression twisted from its usual calm to something much more dangerous. "What are you?"

Jules spat on the table between them, tonguing a cracked tooth. Fragmented by the haze of agony, he remembered Cesare dragging Selene away, the sclera of his eyes black with tainted magic. Selene was a quarter his size and he was *still* afraid of her.

"I think you mean *who*, sir," Jules managed to drawl, though it was difficult to summon his usual laissez-faire attitude with blood streaming down his face and blinding one eye. "Eliot D'Alessandro. You know, I'm engaged to your niece? I guess your memory really does go to hell as you age. We spoke the other day, remember? You were staring at me like, *You're not good enough for her*. And I was like, *Yeah, well, sucks she gets to choose*. But only internally, because manners."

Jules stretched his arms over his head, smothering a pained wince. A nun medic he didn't recognize had belatedly shoved his dislocated shoulder back into the socket—which hurt worse than it had coming out—but Jules would die before he allowed Cesare *fucking* Alleva to see his pain.

Cesare checked his watch and grimaced. "Ambrose claims he has proof you're a demon."

Jules tipped one brow in mild curiosity. He knew from the train that anyone with the surname *Alleva* hated casual disrespect, so he lounged in his seat, ignoring the way the handcuffs limited his movement. "Make him prove it."

One corner of Cesare's mouth kicked up in a smirk. "You know I could." He scratched his chin, as though considering. "But I don't care. You see, I've read the file Selene had compiled. Orphan. Conscript. Soldier. Deserter. Demon or not, I have cause enough to have you executed."

Jules leaned forward with his hands spread on the table. "I'm a *what now?*"

Cesare ignored him. "I don't like you, Jules Lacroix. I don't like you as Eliot. I don't like you for Selene. And I don't like you breathing." He adjusted his shirt cuff. "Ambrose doesn't need to convince me of anything, because in my heart of hearts I hope it's true."

Jules's stomach dropped and he slouched down in his chair.

Cesare wasn't questioning him. He was creating plausible deniability. As though to prove him right, Cesare stood. "It's been long enough. You sang like a bird."

Jules watched Cesare leave through lowered lashes, tipping his head back. "Good. This overbearing-uncle thing is getting old. I get it, you don't like me. Kind of creepy, the way you want to be the only man in her life. But . . . whatever."

His expression impassive, Cesare almost had Jules fooled. But as he turned for the door, a muscle in his jaw feathered—just like Selene's did when she was irritated—and Jules knew his words had found their mark.

Gathering his composure around him like a tattered coat, Cesare suppressed the tell, and said, "As ever, you test my patience. A skill. No matter . . . You won't survive the day."

Jules forced a slow smile. "You know, you didn't send Eliot far enough. He still protected her." Eliot had been there to put Jules in Selene's orbit and make him stay. Eliot had watched out for her from Nice and ensured she wouldn't have to face this man alone. Jules sat up straighter, speaking through his teeth as he smiled wider. "Next time you want to isolate her, you'll have to look farther than Nice."

"Oh, I concur." Cesare didn't even turn back. "I plan to send you straight to hell, Lacroix."

With that parting shot, he slammed his fist against the door and stormed out when it was opened from the other side.

A pair of exorcists entered as he left. The hairs on Jules's arms prickled and he moved as far back from them as he could. They wore identical hard leather masks that had no visible eyes. The brow led to a smooth expanse where the eyes should be, a nose and soft cherubic lips. He didn't know the insignia on their military jackets, but he *did* recognize his executioners.

Fear was a torrent through his veins. They were armed to the teeth. And they were ready for him if he tried to resist. One came for him while the second, a woman, waited near the door, arm exposed. The tattoos covering her flesh looked like the runes tattooed down Selene's spine. Together they were ready for anything.

He went with them, unresisting.

Neither spoke as they led him through the cold and silent halls beneath St. Peter's Basilica, and they didn't lower their guard.

At a scuffle of movement, one exorcist jerked him to a stop.

The other drew a dagger, pressing his palm against the flat of the blade as he faced the direction of the sound.

Ambrose stumbled around the corner, using a bundled-up jacket to stanch the flow of blood that dripped down his front, teeth and chin stained red.

Jules sneered. Fucking Vatican and their damned healers. If not for them, he'd be dead.

When Ambrose met his gaze, his eyes flared with hatred distilled.

At least the executioners were utterly cold. They might be taking him to be crucified, but they harbored no specific resentment toward him.

Ambrose stumbled forward, leaning against the wall, and his hand left a bloody streak on the smooth stone.

"Halt." The female executioner tightened her grip on Jules's arm.

The male executioner reacted to his partner's change in stance, his weapon at the ready.

Ambrose's eyes narrowed. "Are you two *bloody* idiots? I speak for Cesare Alleva when he's not around. Didn't anybody tell you?"

He slapped his hand against his chest, leaving dark blood on his elegant stamped buttons. From experience Jules knew dried blood in the fiddly bits would be a nightmare to clean. "Nobody tells *me* to halt."

The executioners turned their masked faces toward each other, sharing some unspoken thought.

Even knowing the little he did of Vatican hierarchy, Jules was surprised. He sensed the difference in power between the executioners and Ambrose—they should be his superiors. Ambrose was just a thug. Any talent he had was squandered when he let his rage control him. The woman's head cocked only a fraction, but Jules caught it. He could almost smell the blood she was about to shed.

A tall figure stepped between the two groups. "You've lost a lot of blood, little Ambrose. I don't think you know what you're doing."

Caterina Altamura.

She leveled her gun at Ambrose's chest, shoulders squared in her familiar unyielding posture.

Ambrose's face twisted. "What are *you* doing back?"

"Saving the day apparently." Lucia poked her tongue out at Ambrose. "What were you even planning? The Imperium Bellum explicitly asked us to bring the prisoner to him." She stepped up beside Jules, tucking her knife under his chin. Jules slid his eyes toward Lucia. When no one was looking, she flashed him a cheeky wink, then set her face to neutral.

"He's preparing a public execution," Ambrose snarled. "Give the prisoner to me. I'll take him."

The executioners appraised the warring parties. Jules sensed their hesitation, though they didn't say a word. They had reason enough not to trust Ambrose, and Lucia was holding a knife to his throat. Rather too convincingly, Jules thought.

Caterina slung the gun over her shoulder. "Old news. Now he's doing it nice and private. Bloodier that way. More pain. He likes that, you know."

"You're with *us*?" Ambrose asked. "Last time I heard, you were loyal to Selene."

Jules didn't think he imagined Caterina's tension—the way her bicep shifted as she adjusted her rifle—and he strongly suspected she'd barely resisted saying, *Captain Alleva*. She smiled instead. It tugged at the scarred skin of her beautiful face. "Of course we're with you. With Cesare. Who would side with the *lesser* Alleva?"

Ambrose nodded slowly, his thumb picking absently at the opposite thumbnail. "True."

"So . . ." Lucia said, stretching her arms over her head, yawning widely before finishing her thought. "We'll be taking him now."

Ambrose took a stumbling step forward. "No! Give him to me."

Without further hesitation, the female executioner relinquished her hold on Jules's arm to Caterina, and the two of them walked away, passing either side of Ambrose without a word.

Caterina roughly gripped his bicep and shoved Jules in the opposite direction.

Down here, in the depths of the Vatican, the walls were smooth damp stone and thick black cables ran along the roof to ancient caged lamps. It was a testament to how little faith they had in the electrics that yellow gas lamps lined the walls.

"Where are you going?" Ambrose asked quietly.

Lucia wiggled her fingers. "To Cesare. The greater Alleva."

Ambrose frowned in confusion. "But he's in the *Cor Cordium*."

Caterina stiffened, her fingers tightening on Jules's bicep. It took Jules a moment to recall the Latin. Heart of hearts, where they kept the Deathless God.

"Don't let them go!" Gabriel walked down the hall.

The lights overhead flickered with an electronic hum.

Ambrose lunged forward, but Lucia spun on him, fingering her throwing knives.

"You're not here on behalf of the greater Alleva at all, are you?"

Lucia flicked her tongue against the sharp edge of a throwing knife. "Of course we are . . . *Selene* Alleva, the *greater* Alleva."

"You want to die with the demon?" Ambrose snarled.

Lucia laughed. "I don't think that's necessary."

"Traitors." Gabriel's eyes were heavy-lidded as he stared at Jules, looking bored.

Caterina stepped between them and they stared each other down.

Jules's muscles tightened as Ambrose grabbed his arm. Lucia gave him a dirty look, tugging Jules's other arm as though to pull him out of Ambrose's metal grip. With him still in chains they were evenly matched. Except that Gabriel was an exorcist and his sleeve was rolled up enough to show a line of tattoos on the pale skin of his wrist, a butterfly knife in one hand.

He'd have to go first.

With his magic at the ready, he was an immense threat. Jules had seen what Selene could do with a sword, but she was a thousand times deadlier when she tapped her God's stolen power. Gabriel was an unacceptable risk.

Jules surreptitiously shifted his weight to his back heel.

Lucia looked between Ambrose and Gabriel, expression darkening with suicidal intent. She was not one for rational thought, even at the best of times, and her finger tapped a rhythm against her throwing knife as the tension ratcheted up.

"Don't make me show you why I was top of our class, Gabriel," Caterina breathed. "Not today."

Gabriel's lips crooked lazily. "Scared of a little rematch, Caterina?" His sword hung on his opposite hip, just outside Jules's reach.

Tired of being ignored, Ambrose thumped his fist against his chest. "*I'm* in charge here."

Jules dropped to his knees, using his own weight to yank out of Ambrose's grip, and lunged for the hilt of Gabriel's sword with his bound hands behind his back. It was a split-second maneuver but his hands found only air as Gabriel whirled toward him.

Jules flung himself away, rolling across the floor to avoid Gabriel's butterfly knife.

Everything happened lightning fast. Caterina pulled a shotgun from her hip and Ambrose kicked it from her hand. Snarling, Caterina then swung the weapon from her back and bullets ate up the wall. The enormous gun was deafening in the confined space.

Lucia crouched with her hands over her ears, wailing, "Not the *big* one, not inside!"

But a manic grin was writ large on her face.

Jules's ears rang—deaf, but for the echoes of gunfire—and now that he couldn't hear Gabriel coming, he was completely vulnerable. Pivoting, he found the exorcist not a second too soon as Gabriel came for his throat with the butterfly knife.

Jules reacted. Muscles accustomed to fighting to survive tugged ligaments and joints, guiding bone and tendon, all before his brain could catch up. He caught the blade against the meat of his arm, sacrificing his bicep to protect his neck. The blade bit deep and his blood hit the floor. The pain, while terrible, was only just beginning. He screamed through his teeth as physical agony was displaced by a greater torment.

Heat kindled inside him.

It burned like coals as though his very bones had caught fire. And as his body ignited, the manacles on his wrists loosened. Melted. Sloughed, molten, to the floor.

Gabriel threw up a defensive barrier as he and Ambrose stumbled back. Snarling in pain, Gabriel flung away the knife that had flared cherry red in his hand.

As the pain running through his nerves faded, anemic blue flames danced across Jules's skin, devouring his flesh. Turning his hands over, Jules marveled at the tongues of flame licking harmlessly at his skin. He fingered his bicep but didn't find the wound he expected. Ignoring the blood, he found his old scar. The line of briar thorns encircling his arm had been bisected. With one slice of an exorcist's knife, whatever potent magic his mother wrought to bind his power had been undone.

Then Gabriel's magic slammed him down, like a giant palm crushing him into the travertine stone. Ambrose wore studded knuckle-dusters on one fist and he brought the points to rest against Jules's temple.

"Give me a reason, demon," he rasped. "I beg you."

Clink. Clink. Clink. Lucia's expression had gone slack with shock and her throwing knives fell to the floor.

Jules did not give Ambrose a reason. His body went numb as the flames died on his skin, and his senses faded. His ears and eyes might be better than a normal human's, better even than Selene's, when she wasn't hopped up on demon magic, but now his normal was dulled, as though the world were painted in shades of dullest gray where once there was color. The footfalls on marble, the hushed voices and shouts from the training yards, all faded to the suffocating silence of the hallway.

"It's true. You're a demon," Lucia breathed.

Ambrose crowed and punched the air. "That bitch really has

been fucking a demon. I can't wait to *ruin* her. Have you ever seen her cry? I can't *wait*—"

Jules lunged, his lips curled over his teeth in a feral snarl.

Gabriel tackled Jules, kicking his legs out from under him. His knees hit stone.

"Not so calm now, huh? She's trained you well," Ambrose goaded, as though he hadn't just fallen over himself to put distance between them.

"Don't talk about her." Jules looked at the scars of his Glasgow grin. "You really can't see how outclassed you are, can you?"

"This?" Ambrose asked, indicating his wounds. "She's in far worse shape than I am, demon. And far less pretty too."

Alarm coiled in his gut. He had faith in Selene, but he didn't trust Ambrose. If it was true . . . Jules's strength left him.

Gabriel adjusted his grip and held him up, keeping the dagger pressed to his throat.

Sensing victory, Ambrose strode forward and grabbed Jules's chin. "You can picture it as I brand you."

"I thought I was going to be killed?"

Ambrose showed even more teeth as he said, "You'll be executed. After."

"Then why brand me?"

Ambrose licked his teeth, thinking about that for a moment. "Because I *want* to."

Jules should've felt angry, but all he felt was pity. Ambrose's perverse joy in watching others suffer would rot him from the inside.

Please . . . Jules's eyes fluttered closed. The Deathless God spoke only to him. *Let me die.*

Ambrose made a furious sound and slapped his face.

Jules felt a sharp cut across his cheek and his eyes snapped open. He saw the golden blood before Ambrose did. It dripped from his cheek to the floor. Veins spiderwebbed his wrists, coruscating gold as though he'd swallowed a drop of the sun.

His kill marks bled and gold crucifixes soaked through his shirt, turning him from sinner to saint where he knelt on the floor. Angling his face blindly toward the Deathless God—trapped, tortured—he felt Ambrose's fear before he saw it.

Jules couldn't move. All he could do was bleed and whisper a thought to the massive consciousness pressing down against his own that he was sorry—because *he* would be the one to die first.

No, the Deathless God thought back. *You will not.*

Jules felt more alive than he ever had. The blood running through his veins flared brighter, escaping through the marks carved into his flesh, before they healed and faded beneath smooth skin.

Ambrose stumbled back and his fear made him angry, something he already had so much of. "Kill him. Kill him now!" he babbled.

Caterina's eyes were wide with shock.

She gripped her gun in a double-handed stance, but even if she *wanted* to help, the immense weapon was useless in such close quarters as long as Ambrose and Gabriel stood over him. And Jules was no longer sure she did, now that she knew what he was.

The voice in his mind grew clearer as though the Deathless God's attention had sharpened to focus in on him, aware of him in the same way Jules couldn't help but be aware in turn. He could almost perceive the personality, and perhaps even the ideals, of the one they called *God*. But still Jules couldn't move. It was as though his knees had fused with the stone, trapping him in a penitent pose. Gold blood dripped down his fingers.

With a flick of the butterfly knife, Gabriel scored the symbols tattooed across his knuckles with the barest hint of a laceration. The scent of terrible magic surrounded them, sparking in Jules's senses like a wildfire. He wanted to take flight. He wanted to *fight*. But he couldn't even move.

"*Non semper excitare.*" Gabriel spoke the words with the weight of a promise. You won't ever wake up.

Then everything went black.

CHAPTER THIRTY-EIGHT

The interrogation room was colder by degrees than the outside. Selene was dragged in by Tommaso and an artificer from Gabriel's team. Florentina Altieri was notable by her absence and Selene hoped she wasn't part of this. When she was thrown into the chair behind the steel table, she laughed—it echoed longer than the shriek of metal chair legs scraping against stone.

Warily taking a seat, Ambrose dropped the key around his neck.

She let a small smile linger around her mouth. It hid her rage and made him nervous. She only cared about the latter. And for perhaps the first time ever Selene was pleased that the chairs on both sides of the interrogation table were equally uncomfortable.

"Why did you pretend he was Eliot D'Alessandro?"

She gasped. "He's *not*?"

Ambrose slammed his fist against the table.

Rather than flinch away, Selene leaned closer. His gaze flicked to her cuffed wrists, as though checking she was still bound. Good. He still feared her.

"He's a soldier. And a demon."

Selene blinked in exaggerated surprise. "Who am I even *marrying?*"

All she could see when she looked at Ambrose now was his attempt on Jules's life with her stolen sword. His face made her sick with fury. She would never forgive the brother of medicine who had saved Ambrose, dragging him back from the brink of death. "I'm an Exorcist First Class. You can't keep me in here. Even my uncle has limits to his power."

"You don't know, do you?" Ambrose smirked, pleased to know something she didn't. "The Exorcist Primus is dead. Whatever limits there were are being dismantled as we speak."

A chill slipped down her spine. She slapped her palms flat on the table and pushed herself to standing.

Ambrose scrambled to stand too, puffing up his chest to look tough. It didn't work.

"You know, you made one mistake bigger than the rest," she whispered, so quietly he was forced to lean in.

She could practically see the gears in his mind moving. Since being wounded he'd been jittery. Erratic. Afraid of more pain. It made him weak. She flicked her eyes to look over his shoulder, as though someone stood behind him.

His attention wavered and she grabbed his head, smashing his nose into the metal table. Then, wrapping her knee around his neck, she encircled his throat with the chains on her wrists and held on.

Ambrose flailed like a Spanish bull, slamming her against the wall with his back.

She gritted her teeth against the pain, knowing she had to wait it out. He was tiring. Tightening the chain to give herself some slack, she slid her hand into his shirt and found the key.

His metal fist swung and missed, but his other connected, cracking ribs. The breath whooshed out of her. Devoid of oxygen, her lungs smoldered. Before he could take a third swing, she kneed him in the back. Then, with a turn of the stolen key, her handcuffs clattered to the floor.

Flashing a vicious smile, she drew a hidden stiletto from her boot—*not* her favorite boot knife, which Tommaso had relieved her of, but wicked sharp, and that was all she needed. Fear flickered behind the rage on Ambrose's damaged face as she carved the back of her hand, finding the marks on her ring, middle, and index fingers.

"You *never* use your magic—"

He was blasted against the wall.

Selene stepped over him and paused in the doorway. "You underestimate me. I use my magic when it matters."

It was achingly cold in the bowels of the Vatican complex. Selene cradled her ribs with a hand as she panted for air. What she wouldn't do to have Lucia with her now. She only had herself—her body and magic. Tearing a strip off her shirt, she wrapped it around her knuckles. She had to find Jules and get him out.

Soft voices came from the corner ahead. Leaning against the damp stone, Selene sidled closer to eavesdrop.

"Prepare St. Peter's Square for an execution at two o'clock."

"An execution? Whose?"

"*Eliot D'Alessandro.*" The name was spoken in a hushed tone, but it echoed in the serpentine hall. The second man choked on a breathless curse before he was sharply cut off. "I assure you, it comes from the top. Now get going."

One set of footsteps hurried away.

Selene rounded the corner and took out the remaining guard with ease. It should have been more difficult, but the exorcists her uncle had recruited had grown soft. Without the constant threat of death, they were nothing. Selene kicked him in the ribs once more for good measure, then shouldered open the heavy studded door, dragging him inside to cover her tracks.

If Cesare suspected Jules was a demon, there was only one place they'd hold him. Dropping the guard, she straightened and pain lanced through her ribs. Every breath hurt. She had no patience for a punctured lung.

What she was about to do was treason. And possibly impossible. *No going back.*

Selene dashed around the corner and slammed into a wall of muscle. Her broken ribs ground together, knees weakening at the agony.

Cesare held her biceps, supporting her until she found her feet. Then gently he released her.

Clutching her side, Selene shot him a reproachful glare.

His expression didn't soften. No hint of a smile around his eyes. None of the usual mannerisms that told her she was special.

"Where—"

"Think *very* carefully before you finish that sentence." Cesare's deep voice was taut with barely contained anger.

She knew better than to test him, but she did it anyway. "Where's Jules?"

"I told you not to ask." He sounded softly pained.

It was nearly two o'clock. Each breath burned as Selene watched the crucifix being erected in the square. Each minute that passed killed her slowly. Cesare was her uncle and the only father figure she had known since the age of eleven. As she watched him now, though, he was almost a stranger. But she held on to a sliver of hope.

"Imperium . . . *please*. Please don't do this. He hasn't done anything wrong."

"Nothing wrong? He infiltrated the Vatican fortress."

"I *made* him."

He ignored the words. "Worse, he went into our most sacred place."

She remained utterly expressionless. *How can he know that?* But Cesare could read her every nuance, and where others would fail to see the flutter of emotion cross her face, her uncle saw.

A tight smile, there and gone again. "It's true, then? He has been inside the *Cor Cordium*? How could you, Selene?"

"I've been with him every moment. He's done nothing wrong."

"He attempted to murder an exorcist. A capital crime."

"He was *defending* me." Cesare had an answer for every argument. Tears of frustration filled her eyes. But it was grief that made them carve down her cheeks and drip off her chin.

"I was there," Cesare said quietly. "So he didn't have to do that."

There were so many words unsaid between them. What she had heard in the necropolis. The truth about the Deathless God. Her belief that Cesare had betrayed the Vatican—and her. But she was trapped in a moment she had barely survived once before. "Please, Cesare . . . I can't see someone I love die here again. I watched when you killed my father. I didn't cry. You saw me. I made you proud."

He nodded, affection smoothing the hard lines of his face.

"You praised me for that, remember?"

His eyes softened. "I do."

"I'm *begging* you, please don't hurt him. I can't do that again. I won't survive."

Beyond the crucifix, people moved from the shadows of the building into the bright afternoon light. Jules had to be one of them. Caterina was dragged out first. Then Lucia.

As though sensing her gaze, Caterina looked up. Her lip was split and blood dripped down her habit.

Caterina's beautiful ruined face crumpled. She shook her head. *No good.* Or perhaps, *I'm sorry.*

Selene held her eyes, muscles trembling as she fought not to break. Her second always made her proud. The world roared in her ears as Gabriel and Ambrose stepped out of the shadows, dragging Jules. He wasn't moving. He might even be dead.

They'd crucify him anyway. Like their god.

Her own words echoed in her ears. *It's kind of symbolic.*

She became aware of Cesare watching her, his eyes on the side of her face. "You're right," he said quietly.

She bit her lip. He'd heard her.

"You're right," he repeated, taking her chin. "I can't make you watch."

The true meaning of his words resolved as he placed his hand on the back of her neck and propelled her along.

"No," she whispered, numb. She fought him, writhing and spitting, but Cesare tightened his fingers painfully on her neck. Flashes popped in her vision. "No . . . *Jules!*" She made herself go limp, a dead weight hanging like a kitten in his grip.

He tossed her down, clicking his tongue. Then, with a flick of his fingers, he summoned his bodyguards. "Bring her."

They overwhelmed her. She kicked and lashed out to slow them down, trying to catch a last glimpse of Jules. But it was too late. The sound of nails through wood split the air.

Crack.

She had argued her case too well. She wouldn't have to see Jules die.

Crack.

The bells tolled two.

Crack.

Now she would never see him again.

CHAPTER THIRTY-NINE

As strange as it sounded, the Vatican was not cruel.
Death by crucifixion had been refined over the centuries.
Now each crucifixion was choreographed to perfection. A ballet of death. Each spike exorcist-forged—artificed like their blades—with energy enough to kill a demon outright. They used these on their human victims, too.

Her father had died with the same nails through his wrists and feet. Jules too.

As they passed beneath one of the smaller domes in St. Peter's Basilica, a sudden burst of rain battered against the glass of the high windows. Just like the day her father was executed, when rain had carved down her cheeks like tears. But she had refused to cry where Rome could see her, and she had not cried since—not until today.

In her mind's eye she could see the Deathless God, beautifully motionless in his terrible prison. Her heart ached.

No, the Vatican was not cruel. Her father's pain had been brief. Death, quick.

It would be the same for Jules. So dreadfully quick.

Death would land with the final blow of the hammer, just a few seconds after the first.

She was an empty vessel. Ambition. Drive. Fury. None of them survived grief. Not even *vengeance.*

Grief subsumed everything else. It was the absolute hollowness left behind.

Cesare strode ahead, his tall form casting its shadow over her. She timed her steps with his, keeping pace with him like she used to do. Trapped between two of his men, Selene withdrew into herself, no longer entirely *there.* She watched the almond toes of her boots on the checkerboard halls, heard their smart click. But all of it was distant.

St. Peter's Basilica was a stranger to her now.

Even when her father died, she hadn't blamed this place. Now the seam in her heart was unraveling and she hated these columns, these corridors, these friezes, as though their cold remoteness had killed Jules and not the man to whom she'd dedicated her life.

But this pain, revisited, was so much worse.

Worse than her broken ribs.

Worse than the symbols she'd carved into bone.

Worse than her faithlessness, and worse than the realization the Vatican was utterly corrupt.

Dio, Jules . . . She loved him. It was too late to realize how much. An hour too late to kiss him again, and long, terrible minutes too late to save him.

Her muscles were tired and her body had been pushed to its limit. With Jules gone she had nothing left to fight for.

She'd spent her life worshipping false idols. Now came the reckoning.

Cesare turned his wrist, checking his watch. She despised this familiar tic. She did it herself. The gesture lit a fuse inside her. What did time matter *now*?

Worse, she knew it boded ill. Numbly she wondered what he was waiting for.

They stopped at the doors to the *Cor Cordium*.

"Why are we here?"

The usual guards were gone. A sense of foreboding settled heavy in her chest.

She backed away as her bodyguards moved to ease open the doors. Cesare grasped the back of her neck and propelled her forward. "We're here to finish what your father started. If not the way he wanted."

"What are you talking about?"

"Matteo came here to free him. He wanted to strip us of our god."

Selene frowned. "He isn't God. And you *know* that. My father told you, didn't he? He came to you and told you what he'd found. And you killed him for it."

Cesare's expression darkened. "He was my *brother*. He forced my hand when he did what he did. The Primus wanted blood."

Selene avoided looking through the double doors.

She didn't have to; the entire scene was vivid in her mind. That beautiful face and the tumble of dark hair so achingly familiar now that she could appreciate the similarities.

It was too late for Jules. The thought stabbed deep in her ribs.

"Are you telling me you want to free him?"

"Oh, no. That won't do at all. When Baliel takes down the last of the wards, I will kill him." He looked up, lips curling into a faint smirk as he touched his brow. "Our *Dio Immortale*." She could hear the note of mocking. Shattered faith had diminished him. She watched her uncle with an expression of cold curiosity.

Her religion was broken. The entire Vatican too. For the second time in two hundred years they had slaughtered a demon who had not deserved it. If this was their *god*, everything they'd ever taught her had been a lie.

She'd been the one to drive the great spear into God the second time. She'd condemned him to years more suffering. The Deathless God wouldn't die. Not by Cesare's hand.

No, he would be freed by *hers*. Even if it killed her.

Thinking back to her last moments with her father, Selene knew to the marrow of her bones that there was no *if* in this scenario. This was a suicide mission. A pact with death itself. She smiled, just the barest hint at the corner of her lips. *So be it.*

Head high, Selene strode through the carved double doors ahead of Cesare.

The *Cor Cordium* was not silent; the echoing quiet thrummed with nearly imperceptible sounds—the steady drip of blood, God's eternal heartbeat, thumping with the aching magnitude of a continental drift.

And for the first time in years, as she simply let herself *be* in this place, Selene dared look at God's face. His face was angled just so, and she could see the cut-glass line of his jaw, the hollows beneath his cheekbones. She drank him in. *Dio.* If she had just looked at him sooner—with eyes not shuttered by guilt—she would have seen the resemblance.

Jules was undeniably the Deathless God's blood.

Tears slipped down her cheeks unbidden. But this time she didn't rush to look away.

Exquisite pain thundered through her. Towering eight feet tall, the Deathless God's feet were pointed so the tips of his toes brushed the floor, his arms bound in chains, and cruel spikes had been driven through his body.

Jules had suffered the same.

This was how they treated their *god*? What did it say about her that she'd turned a blind eye for so long? Selene squared her shoulders.

She dropped to her knees, reaching to dip two fingers into the blood, and drew a rune on her forehead. But it was not veneration that drove her. And no expression touched her face as she moved with the practised motions of something deeply learned—all body, no mind. *This* was for Cesare's benefit.

Trick him, she told herself. Selene had to make him believe he could win her back to his side. All so that when she removed the spear impaling God and condemned herself—and destroyed the Church—it would hurt Cesare as much as he'd hurt her.

Arranging her face into a cool mask, she turned to her uncle. "Why are you doing this?"

Cesare unhurriedly circled the chamber.

Her lip curled in disgust. How could he be so composed when her world was breaking?

"Why do you *think*, Selene? We're under attack. For many years my predecessor—"

Selene scoffed. "He's barely cold, uncle. Be more careful. It's treason to speak as though you're already Exorcist Primus."

His eyes flashed with cold fury.

She compressed the hint of a smile. Make him angry. Then make him believe she could still be won over.

"My predecessor wasted our *primacy*. He wasted every opportunity to crush the demons once and for all. He didn't care that they're a threat—will *always* be a threat. He preached moderation." Cesare's expression relaxed as he warmed to his topic. "He wasted the years of division, when demons seemed to hate each other as much as they hated us. But that is *changing*. If they join together, we won't only be attacked from the borders, we'll be attacked from within Rome itself."

"You're the one weakening Rome. You helped Baliel destroy the wards."

Cesare flicked a bored finger, as though brushing off an invisible speck of dust. "Trivialities, Selene. The wards were weak. They would've collapsed eventually. You know, when they were first erected, no demons could enter Rome for decades? Wasn't it only this month that you cleared out an infestation in—"

"Trastevere," she said softly.

The thirteenth *rione* of Rome. Southeast of the Vatican, not too far from where Sparrow lived.

"Indeed."

She didn't respond. Let him grow desperate to convince her. Let him tell her more than he ever intended.

He continued. "In the last few decades, our power has been eroded from all quarters. Noble families hiring their own pet exorcists to ward their palazzos against demons. Can you imagine it? This is the corruption of the Church under our Exorcist Primus."

The silence hung heavy between them.

She let out a breath. "What are we meant to do about it? Demons are drawn to this place. To the Deathless God's power, most likely."

Even with his back turned, Selene could picture his expression. His charisma and sharp intelligence working to win her over. But what did Cesare really *want*? He already had the Exorcist Primus's power if he wanted it—and clearly he did—so what had driven him to bring her *here*?

"Why do you want to finish what my father started? And *how*?"

"As long as even a single ward stands: *Only a demon can kill him. Only a human can free him.*" The words were a remarkable break from his faith—faith he had once killed his own brother for. Cesare continued softly. "Baliel is taking the final wards apart as we speak; the last may have fallen already." He spread his hands, indicating the deadening silence around them.

She angled her chin so she could look up at the Deathless God's beautiful face. Unwilling tears traced paths down her cheeks. The natural physiological response to God—or whoever this being really was.

"Did Baliel tell you that . . . that without Him here, at the heart of the Vatican, the demon incursion might end?" She turned to face Cesare, quieting her voice as though in hope. It wasn't entirely an act. His answer wouldn't change anything. But part of her wanted him to be worthy of her loyalty. Her love. She'd never *forgive* him for this, but if he thought he was saving humanity, then it might blunt the cutting edge of her hatred.

Cesare looked up at God. "If we had a leader who was powerful enough to fight them as equals, we might have a chance. Power like that has never existed in over a hundred years, until . . ." He rubbed his hand over his mouth, brows drawing together in pain.

The words froze her. "Until me, you mean. Until I stole God's power."

Cesare's lack of answer was confirmation enough.

"But you're already the most powerful man in the world."

Frowning, he turned a new ring on his finger. The Primus's seal. "That may be true in one way. But not when it comes to *raw power.*"

"Even if I agreed with what you're doing, you still won't—" *Oh.* With cruel clarity she realized he didn't need to win her to his side. If she refused him . . . well, she was probably more useful to him dead.

Selene gripped her clothes over her heart, head tipping back to look up at the stone vault, the low, flickering lights of the chandeliers blurring in her vision. She hadn't thought there was still more he could do to hurt her.

"A warning, then, uncle. If you steal his power, it means harnessing magic that'll strip you down to your bones. You have *no idea* what it's like. You never did."

She paced away from him—toward God.

Closer . . .

Closer.

Golden ichor gilded the length of the great spear buried in his rib cage and dripped to the pool beneath their feet. Selene could easily reach it and plunge it home—but if what Cesare said was true, even that wouldn't give him the freedom of death. Not unless the last ward had fallen. *Only a demon can kill him.*

Good. Because the thought of killing this last beautiful piece of Jules hollowed her out.

She stabbed a finger toward God. "His power balances on the knife edge of agony. Sometimes . . ." Selene faltered. "*Sometimes* I'm tempted to let it rage. Sometimes I *want* to let it burn me out until there's no Selene left. I thought you understood?"

Cesare sighed heavily. "There's a reason an exorcist's first kill is what makes or breaks us. First, we take their blood, then we kill them. Always. His power overwhelms you because you never *killed* him. Take it all and it will become yours."

So his whole plan hinged on that. Baliel had to break the wards so that they could kill God. Once the final ward fell, so too did the limitations. Anyone could free him. Anyone could kill him.

It had been a long time since she had lingered this close to the Deathless God. His presence felt enormous, as though he were leaning over her shoulder. As though he were breathing against her neck. Selene could feel his strength waiting to rush through her, and her fingers itched to carve herself. To split her flesh and release it.

"I'm not a cruel man, Selene. I raised you—and love you— and only want the best for you." Cesare's voice was warm, and she tried not to believe him. It was difficult because he clearly believed it himself. "Kill the Deathless God and his powers will be yours alone, and together we will save Rome."

She shook her head, closing her eyes against the coaxing words. It was almost tempting.

Cesare saw her waver and continued speaking, that terrible charisma a force all its own. "With me as Primus and you as my sword, we'll do it together. Can you picture it, Selene?"

And the dreadful thing was, she could. It was a beautiful future, but one that would be built on a despicable act. And clearly he underestimated how she felt about Jules or he wouldn't waste his breath.

"You know I want it too, uncle. I've only ever wanted to make you proud."

"And I am."

Her lashes darkened her vision as they lowered, unable to hold his burning gaze. "All right," she said, and let him believe that she was weak-willed enough to do it.

Pressing her teeth together, Selene remembered her father's terror when she'd seen him here that day. What she was about to do was a death sentence. But it was the only choice she wanted to make.

She almost pitied Cesare, because fool that he was—blinded by power—he didn't realize that Baliel was playing his own game.

But Baliel wasn't here. *She was.*

Selene lunged for the spear, wrapping her hands around the shaft. It was at once familiar and so different. She could hold it properly now, and the studs pressed into her palms as she yanked it free.

Cesare's expression contorted. "What have you done?"

She backed up, shifting her stance so he understood she *would* fight him.

A breath stirred her hair. There was a slight movement, caught in the mirror of golden blood beneath her feet. Then an immense hand grasped her neck. *Dio Immortale.* His fingers were over her windpipe. She couldn't *breathe.* He would crush her spine.

Cesare darted closer. Grasping the spear, he shoved it back into the stirring god, cruelly twisting it as though to pierce his heart. Selene felt no change in the air, even as God's immense hand slackened on her neck. She fell, limp and useless, to the blood-soaked stone and her shoulder made a loud crunch. Dislocated. Gulping down burning breaths, she struggled to push herself up.

Cesare knelt in front of her and a tear slid down his cheek as he reached for her face. "Selene—"

She slapped his hand away. "Don't touch me."

His dark eyes were sorrowful as he watched her crawl away. But it was just residual. Like muscle memory. He'd already decided to kill her. As soon as he realized she was no longer his creature, he'd decided with that same aloof certainty he'd embodied when condemning her father.

Angling his wrist in a gesture Selene had made a thousand times, Cesare said, "Soon enough the last of the wards will have fallen. We'll know when Baliel arrives." He looked up at the Deathless God, his eyes flat as a snake's. She saw neither disappointment nor frustration on his face at the fact he had not struck a killing blow. Only terrible patience that was quite unlike him.

"There must be a thousand other ways," she said softly. "You don't have to do this."

Cesare pressed his lips into a sad smile. "Oh, but I do. For the Vatican, for our *Rome*."

Around Selene the chamber faded into a blur. Her throat still burned with the phantom grip of the Deathless God. She had to get up. Refused to die on her knees.

The vast double doors swung open and Sparrow strode through, her familial sword in hand.

Cesare did not take his eyes off Selene. "About time you got here."

CHAPTER FORTY

"Sorry I'm late," Sparrow drawled.

Betrayal flared hot in Selene's chest, though she had no idea why; she had never considered Sparrow an ally, had she? But watching him stride into the *Cor Cordium*, her breath felt tight in her lungs, an ache not entirely attached to her grief. As foolish as it seemed now, she had.

Cesare's expression melted into something ugly when his eyes landed on Sparrow, a wolfish snarl drawing his lips back from his teeth.

A wicked grin stole across her face as she realized . . . Sparrow was here for her. His lips pressed into a return smile as he circled away from her, forcing Cesare to split his attention between the two of them.

Cesare drew back his sleeves to reveal his many tattoos. Using the Primus's ring—with its concealed razor spike—he dashed a cut down one row of sigils and then another, triggering his magic. She could only imagine how many words of power he had drawn on.

Sparrow turned in place, hands pushed into his pockets. "Wow, I never got to see in here before. You know, what with the wards and all. Am I the first to come?" Sparrow indicated the Deathless

God with Selene's sheathed sword, then tugged his hair in an ir-reverent salute. "God, nice to meet ya."

Cesare made a sound not wholly human. Selene felt a tremor of fear through her blood. Surely—*surely*—he wasn't going to un-leash? She'd never seen him waver in the mastery of his own power. She'd always found him admirable. And yet . . . she watched him—wary.

Sparrow closed with Cesare, his only weapon her sheathed sword. The handicap did not slow him, and he struck Cesare a bone-quaking blow across the chest. If it had been a naked blade, her uncle would be dead. But of course she'd locked her blade at the Carnival Masquerade and had not had the opportunity to un-lock it since.

"I take it you're the one responsible for the wards falling?"

"In a manner," Cesare replied, eyes dark as he swept low to take Sparrow's feet from under him, snarling in aggravation when the other man effortlessly twisted his body to avoid it. "But not entirely."

"Why?"

Cesare laughed, straightening up. "Why do you think I'd an-swer your questions, Sparrow? After today you're nothing."

Sparrow raised one shoulder. "I've been nothing before, it's not that bad."

"Then you'll be dead."

Sparrow chuckled, not looking the least bit worried. "Oh? Show me."

He was buying her time.

The two clashed with brutal efficiency. After the first few ex-perimental parries, neither one wasted a movement. Sparrow was at a disadvantage with the sheathed blade, but the ring of it against Cesare's sword filled the echoing chamber.

At last the black around the edges of her vision started to recede and Selene got her feet under her, leaning heavily on a column. Sparrow caught her eye as he slammed his boot into Cesare's chest and used the moment to throw Selene her sword, so it arced through the air between them.

She lunged, snatching it from the air.

Sparrow grinned. "What good it'll do you. Even I couldn't draw the damn thing."

She unsheathed the blade and tossed away the scabbard. "Not strong enough, Sparrow."

"Where's Jules?" She heard the edge of concern in his deep voice.

The question was a gut punch. The ache of her dislocated shoulder. The bruising of her windpipe. All of it paled to the violent hues of grief. She bit her lower lip so it wouldn't tremble, teeth pressing hard enough to split it.

Cesare was no longer looking at Sparrow. His eyes bored into her.

With the arrival of her sword, she'd become infinitely more dangerous to him. Even broken. Even hopeless.

Finally, softly, "Dead."

Sparrow's face twisted—a toxic mixture of sorrow and anger. Then he pointed a steady finger at Selene. "This is the last time I let you live, exorcist. This was for Jules. Tomorrow we're enemies."

With that, he left. And a glimmer of hope left with him. Alone again.

Cesare shifted, circling Selene. "I see you're making friends."

She leveled her blade. "Who needs friends when I have family like *you*?"

There would be no more taking Cesare by surprise. Sparrow's presence in the *Cor Cordium* meant only one thing: the final ward had fallen. But to get to God, first he'd have to go through her.

Selene felt the temptation to tap her magic—she could feel the dark pull as clearly as the imprint of God's fingers on her throat. But she resisted, shifting into a fighting stance. To survive she'd need to bring her best.

"Fight me, *uncle*."

She was familiar with Cesare's every expression and didn't miss the fleeting pain on his face. When it hardened to determination, she recognized that too.

Cesare was ready for her, his eyes flaring as dark lines extended from his sockets and across his face. The seconds between quiet and violence ignited the air, so by the time they crashed together there was no oxygen left. Only heat and rage.

Selene sliced the air with her sword—intending to bisect him from shoulder to hip—but he folded away with the grace of a dancer. Every one of his smooth movements was bolstered by his magic.

Her blade had belonged to her father once, and it was strong. Which was lucky, because the next flurry of blows would have broken lesser blades, and lesser exorcists, too.

Cesare had forged his own sword and it had inches on hers. Giving him the advantage of reach.

But she was fast.

She delivered a handful of blows that landed. Even though they didn't cut deep.

His expression tightening with fury, Cesare came back harder, aiming for her knees. A miss. Then he slammed the flat of his blade across her shoulders. Her chin smacked stone and split, dribbling blood down her chest.

She shook off the shock, ignoring the stars that crowded at the edges of her vision.

He was getting faster and the foreign look in his eyes made him a stranger. The thought wormed inside her mind, undermining her next parry. He slipped beneath her guard. She skipped backward, the blade whistling beside her ear.

When Cesare triggered more magic, oppressive silence swallowed her. Her hearing snapped back in time to catch the shred of ligaments as he lengthened, shoulders widening until he was even more snake-hipped than usual.

He had more than two feet on her now.

Breath snagging, she reassessed the odds. She'd be lucky to make a hit. His reach was ridiculous.

"Come, Selene," he taunted. "Give me everything you've got."

Everything.

If she triggered her magic this close to God, she'd burn like a moth flown straight for the flame. She could taste blood. Panting, she wiped her chin with her sleeve. Her throat was sticky with it. "I don't need magic to beat you. Just a sword."

He chuckled, reminding her more of a demon in this moment than the man she had known.

When next he came for her, his blows chipped away at her strength. And his increased reach caged her in. Her muscles trembled with effort each time their blades met. She was covered with as many cuts as she'd given him. Deep slashes on her forearms, shallower ones on her ribs and thighs. She read his intentions and it kept her alive.

He shifted. A low swing. She leaped, and the second she did she knew he had her. She'd fallen for his feint like a novice.

A smile tipped the corner of his mouth and he slammed the pommel of his sword into her gut.

The stone cracked where she landed, and her ribs were in

equally bad shape. She slid across the stone floor, gasping for breath. It was nothing compared to the ache of betrayal. Part of her still thought this wasn't him. But it was—only a side of him she'd never seen.

Or—perhaps—never wanted to.

He killed your father, she reminded herself. *And now he'll kill you.*

Cesare strolled closer. "Do you give up, Selene?" He lifted her chin with his blade.

She snarled. Blood was the only taste she could remember. Pain racked her body. Even her heart seemed to stutter and slow.

He slid the blade behind her ear to rest on her neck in an executioner's pose.

She couldn't make herself move. The cold stone beneath her numb fingers injected ice into her veins. It was more than just Cesare causing this toxic listlessness to radiate into her limbs, like venom threading through her body. It was the knowledge that she had *nothing left.* Her world had been built on a foundation of the Deathless God. But it had been a lie.

Now her world tipped on its axis. Without Jules there was no up. During the last few days, he'd made himself vital to her. Like sight or breath. Now, without *Dio Immortale*, what was left to believe in?

Jules, her mind supplied. *And Father.*

Jules's words from her father's study came back to her. *You have control.* He believed her power was her own. Cesare had always, *always* warned her it was not. But who was he to her now?

Her enemy.

And Jules—he was dead. But he was still the most important piece of her heart. She could hear his deep, assured voice as he told her to embrace her power. He knew what the Deathless God was, and still he wanted her to know her power was her own. If there was anyone in all the world she could trust, it was him. He wanted her to own it.

Cesare sighed softly. "Goodbye, my darling girl."

She looked at the Deathless God. He would be the last thing she'd see. Of *course* he had forsaken her. She'd returned the great spear to its place between his ribs, ensuring he'd never know peace.

She closed her eyes, chest heaving. She was exhausted. Nothing she did now would be enough.

Cesare would kill her, but she couldn't fight another moment.

As though Sparrow's grief had taken root inside her, fighting no longer felt worth it.

I'm sorry, Jules. The sudden absence of Cesare's blade against her neck became her entire world. She pictured him drawing back his arm.

When it bit, she'd die.

All she felt was resigned.

But as the hairs on the back of her neck prickled and the cool air brushed her skin a moment ahead of the blade, her fingers curled against the stone of their own accord. As though mind and body were separate entities, and her body was not done living.

With none of her usual grace her body flung itself away. Only desperate survival remained.

Tumbling violently, Selene's body screamed with pain that darkened the world around the edges. *Dio*, death had to be better than this. But she didn't need God—she had his son.

Frustration twisted Cesare's face into something ugly as she staggered to her feet. "You're not done yet?" Cesare sighed indulgently, but a muscle in his jaw twitched.

She smiled a vicious, bloody smile. "Not yet."

Cesare submerged a hand into God's gold blood and licked it off his fingers.

Sacrilege. "Traitor!" she snarled.

He didn't seem to hear. Rolling his shoulders, Cesare stretched his arms as though pushing against the world. Muscles corded beneath smooth skin and dark raised veins spiderwebbed over the backs of his hands. More gruesome still, a second pair of arms unfolded from beneath the first. He stretched his fingers experimentally. "Now *this*—this is power."

His voice sounded wrong. Resonant and deep; even deeper than it usually was when he was tapped into his magic. Selene felt a sudden spike of fear that he'd lose himself.

As their battle resumed, the force of bodies and blades colliding shook the entire chamber. Plaster dust drifted down, settling on her shoulders.

She was bruised and broken, bleeding from a thousand cuts. Enough blood slopped to the floor that she was afraid her magic wouldn't work if—*when*—she needed it.

Opposite her, Cesare remained whole. Unbruised. Untouched.

He reached out with a lazy hand, manifesting a shadowy whip that wrapped around one of the alabaster columns, uprooting it like a tree, and flung it across the chamber at Selene.

She threw herself to the floor, sharp chips of marble slicing her cheeks as she pressed herself flat beneath its vast shadow.

But it was too little, too late.

Then there was a flicker of movement and a figure with burning gold eyes caught the column with a crack like thunder, arresting it effortlessly with one hand.

CHAPTER FORTY-ONE

Crack. The ring of metal nails through wood was distant. It didn't concern Jules. *Crack.*

He towered over Rome, but it was a Rome he didn't recognize. The Vatican was smooth and pale, instead of the thing bent on violence and martial primacy it had become.

And he *wasn't Jules.*

Looking at his hands, he saw that gold blood ran through his veins, his fingers were tanned and strong, his nails pale moons. These were not *his* hands. And this was not Selene's Rome. What little remained of Jules's mind was consumed by the Deathless God's memories. Smoke rose in billows that blackened the sky as, all around, Rome burned, fires licking toward the sky. Below him, the steady pace of life accelerated as fear spread like a plague through the winding streets.

Jules—*not Jules*—stepped from the edge of the roof, and by the time he landed with force on the broad flagstones below, any tattered remnants of his mind inside the memory were gone. The stones ruptured beneath his feet, but he barely felt it through bones that were built to withstand so much more and muscles like corded steel.

Turning, he caught his reflection in the paintwork of a shiny black car. A crown of briars was twined in his hair, the soft petals of pink roses standing out against dark curls. Wicked curved thorns protruded through his hair. This pale imitation was all he had left to show for his rightful place.

Rightful place? The thought flickered and was gone, replaced entirely by *now* as a frisson of energy licked up his spine. He pivoted, facing the one he knew would come.

And, sure enough, the Kairos woman stepped from the shadows beneath Bernini's colonnade. She was as beautiful now as she had ever looked in his bed. He could see the threads of chaos spreading from the tips of her fingers, extending into the city.

His heart broke and he turned his head away, not wanting her to see pain steal across his face. "I missed you this morning," he said softly, rubbing the pad of his thumb over his lower lip. "When I woke up you were gone."

She smiled, flashing pearlescent teeth. "Places to be, cities to burn. You know how it is, Arius."

A wordless hiss escaped his lips at her use of his name. Stolen now that she was no longer beneath him, tangled in his sheets.

Her amusement died. "Apologies, my king." She shifted, drawing something from beneath her coat, and set it atop her own raven hair, smiling slightly. A smile reserved for the cat that got the cream. "But aren't you missing something?"

The silver diadem was the wrought-metal version of the briars that twisted in his hair, and to see it stolen like she'd stolen his name made him angry. In the moments of quiet between her revealing his stolen crown and the moment their fight began, he saw it play out.

The way she would draw her weapon of choice, the spear of her family, from thin air and they would clash all across this holy place, a place humans valued and that should be respected. But he did not choose to destroy this city, though destroy it he would. Finally his love would kill him, slamming the spear into his chest, splitting his ribs for her satisfaction. But not before he exorcised her, sending her home. He would wound her soul so she could not return. Not for perhaps another two hundred years. Time enough for his father to decide on a plan. To protect these small, strange creatures. This . . . *humanity*.

Yes, he would die. But death was something he could live with.

"Kill me if you can, my love."

"Your wish, my command," she purred, hand striking out, punching through the fabric of reality as charcoal smoke coalesced around her wrist and she yanked the spear of her blood from the other side. "Anything for my *uncrowned king*."

Valeria!

Agony. Yearning. Despair.

Beneath his own emotions, Jules could feel the same from the Deathless God.

Please . . . let me die.

Pain was the first thing Jules knew as he was ripped out of the Deathless God's memories and into his own head. Agony shot up his arm from his hand.

There was a loud crack and he slipped, his feet hitting a hard surface before he fell to his knees, hanging by one arm.

He screamed, agonizing pain shaking him out of his half-sleep.

Kian was the first thing he saw, his expression as wild as his flame-hued hair as he hacked through the chains around Jules's wrist, the sound ringing like a hammer. A bloody spike had been discarded on the stones beside him, and Jules raised a hand to his face. A gaping hole had been carved through his palm.

Dreading what he'd find, he looked up. But his other arm was only bound by chains to the crossbeams behind him. They hadn't had time to drive in the second nail.

"Kian . . ."

As the chain broke beneath Kian's assault, Jules fell to the cobbled stones. The winter sun hung low over the rooftops now, stretching Jules's shadow beneath his feet as he tried and failed to stand.

The wordless presence of the Deathless God was impossible to ignore. A sharp pain behind his eyes spread into a raging headache. The immense weight of God's mind against his own affected his entire body. It was like an enormous hand grasped his chest, tightening its fingers by the inch. He slid back into a sitting position, too tired to hold himself up.

Kian dropped down beside him. "I've got you. Let's get out of here."

Jules's head lolled and he saw feet. He trailed the feet to the legs, tossed akimbo in the unmistakable repose of death. Kian had killed someone to get to him. "He said I wouldn't die. I don't think he *let* me die."

"What?" Kian asked.

Jules squeezed his eyes shut.

"No time, boyo. We're walking." Kian slapped his cheeks. "That crazy blond shorty and the tall scary one are covering our retreat."

Jules tried to push himself up, but his legs were weak.

"Who are . . . you," Jules began hoarsely, "to call anyone *shorty*?"

The ache in his skull made everything seem slightly dimmer than it had before. Why did the Deathless God want to hurt him? Before the question fully formed, he knew the answer: God was suffering.

It echoed through him, through his ligaments and joints, filling

Jules and . . . and emptying him of everything else. The Deathless God's suffering was *his* now.

Kian pulled him up, an arm around his waist to force him on.

Jules stiffened, fighting Kian's guiding hand. "No."

Kian shot him an aggrieved look, tightening his hand on his arm. "Move. You're not going back there."

"I have to go—"

"I won't let you die again."

"Again?"

Kian swallowed audibly. "I thought I was too late, Jules . . ."

Jules finally pulled his eyes up to look at him, reaching up a hand to roughly cup his cheek, bringing his face close so he could press his forehead to Kian's. "You weren't."

Kian gave Jules's forehead a bump. "Not through lack of trying."

Jules winced but a grin stole across his face. "Gotta keep you on your toes."

"If you wanted me any more on my toes, I'd need pointe shoes." Kian laughed, but the sound was strained and he looked toward Bernini's colonnade. "Please, Jules . . . we need to run."

Jules shook his head again. "Selene—"

"Sparrow's here. He's taken Selene her sword. Like you wanted. So *let's go.*"

Jules gripped Kian's neck as he struggled around to face the Vatican. "I have to free my father."

Jules followed the Deathless God's pain and Kian grudgingly joined him. But he didn't let Jules think for a second that he agreed with the plan. Only fear for Selene kept Jules moving, and he only knew the way because he was drawn by the Deathless God's suffering.

Rushing in—his usual strategy—would only get him killed.

Worse, it could get Selene killed. If Cesare was anything like her, he was formidable.

They passed through a familiar five-pointed corridor. A memory that felt as distant as Ostrava returned; he'd seen a map in Matteo Alleva's notebook that morning. Matteo had painstakingly re-created the halls of the Vatican, the *Cor Cordium* and stairs, hidden within the dome of St. Peter's. *Inside the walls.*

He knew where he had to go.

When he arrived at the silent Vatican necropolis, he wished very much that Selene were there with him. The dark ironwork gate blocked the entrance. Beyond it, the damp stone and carved skeletons atop their tombs gave him pause. Ignoring his prickling neck, Jules examined the lock.

"This is what they have guarding their dead?" Kian wondered aloud, grabbing the lock and then dropping it with a noisy clang. "Looks to me like they're asking to be robbed, boyo."

Jules laughed. He slid the knife into the lock and with his eyes closed, and with Kian's narration in his ears, he unlocked the gate.

An image pressed itself to his consciousness.

A hand. Selene. Her slender, breakable neck beneath his fingers.

. . . the intent to kill . . .

He had to hurry.

At the far end of the tomb, Jules saw a destroyed altar to some forgotten god. It had been rebuilt to the Deathless God, but Jules could see the charred remains of the past. Resting atop it was a cross. He reached to touch it, fingers trailing over it before he yanked his hand back, breath coming short and sharp as an oily wrongness seemed to coalesce, coating the hand he'd used to reach close.

Without needing to be told, or knowing how he knew it, Jules was certain that these bones were Elysian. They'd been plucked out of one of his own kind. He had to wonder what they would do if they caught him again. Would they cut him to pieces? Use his strong bones for weapons? For blood or for magic? Would they unwind his eyes in cruel experiments to learn how his very flesh might best serve the Vatican? Only then would they let him die.

He considered the Deathless God, and thought grimly, *Maybe not even then.* He curled trembling fingers into a fist.

The mosaic of blue lapis, red glass, and gold behind the altar was beautiful, but Jules had no respect left for beauty when it served only the Vatican. Beyond it were the stairs he needed. He smashed the mosaic with his elbow.

That putrid scent blew from within the catacombs once more and Jules held himself in place, his hand rising to cover his nose. As his eyes adjusted to the dark, he saw the way the stone was being eaten away as if by acid. The steady drip-drip of golden blood was leaching through the floor and destroying the foundation of this corrupt place.

Jules tore his eyes away. The stairs spiraled up and out of sight.

Kian stopped, his complexion ashen.

Jules hesitated, impatience making his voice rough. "What?"

"I can't go with you."

"Stop joking around—"

"Jules, I can't go near him. I wouldn't be able to refuse his commands."

Of course . . . before Kian was Jules's best friend, he had been his father's. Jules remembered the terrible voice in his mind begging for death. Would Jules have been able to refuse that request if he loved him?

Pulling himself through the gap he'd made in the mosaic, Jules crouched to look back at Kian. His face looked pale and small.

He didn't want to leave him. Reaching past the shattered tile, he scrubbed fingers through Kian's flame-like hair. "Thank you for coming back for me."

Kian grinned. "It's my job to get your ass out of trouble. One might even say it's my raison d'être."

Jules laughed, crossing his arms on his knees. "Don't make me that, boyo. Too much responsibility for me."

"Responsibility or culpability?" Kian's expression became somber. "Be careful, Jules. He may be your father, but he doesn't know that. And even if he did . . . he's been suffering a long time."

Jules nodded, then stood to go up the stairs. "I already know. I'm afraid his mind's broken."

CHAPTER FORTY-TWO

Selene looked at Jules with ravenous, disbelieving eyes. He was ashen. Bruises marred the skin beneath his fever-bright eyes, as though pressed in by cruel thumbs. Beneath his skin, blood flowed like liquid gold. But he was *alive*.

He cocked his head, as though unsure how he came to be there, and pushed the column away. It crashed through the wall, sending up a plume of dust and debris.

Emotion flooded up her throat, so suffocating she thought she might be choking on blood from some ruptured organ—perhaps a stray rib piercing through her lung. Instead, when he touched her cheek a sob spilled from her.

He caressed her lower lip with his thumb. "I'm here."

Her joy at seeing Jules shattered as cold terror filled her. He was alive but the power raging through his veins would destroy him. And it only worsened with his proximity to the Deathless God.

"You have to go!" She grasped his hands, propelling him into motion as Cesare rounded the spill of fallen columns.

Cesare was too close to being fully unleashed and deep shadows spilled from his eye sockets. Upon seeing Jules, those dark eyes flickered with confusion.

Boots slipping on damaged marble, Selene tried to move him. He didn't budge.

"Jules, you really have to go!" she begged, barely recognizing her own voice.

He shook his head. "I can't leave my father or the suffering will just begin again." His clouded eyes flicked up to the Deathless God. "Nothing's completely new, Selene. Sometimes it's just a shadow of the past."

She reached for his bloodless cheek. He felt cold to the touch. "I don't understand."

Cesare snarled, "You're harder to kill than you look, boy." His resonant voice echoed unnaturally. Raising both arms over his head, Cesare drew a pair of curved blades from a coil of dark smoke over his shoulder. Pleased, he turned them over in his hands. Selene had never seen him exhibit such a skill before. In truth, she wasn't sure *any* exorcist could do what he'd just done. It was a demon's skill.

Leveling a blade at Selene, he gazed along its length. "Ready? I'll give you one last chance to tap your magic." Cesare was skating on the edge of humanity, and Selene wasn't sure this was a state from which he'd ever return.

Worse, if Cesare let his power consume him, he would be nigh unstoppable. She had no intention of following him to hell.

Jules stared at Cesare, his eyes beautiful, gold, and blank. Threading her fingers with his, Selene tried again to make Jules move. Using her own thumbnail, Selene sliced a gash across her knuckles, carving into *strength*. Still he was immovable. Then he seemed to shudder, shaking his head as his hand tightened around hers.

Cesare chuckled, and that was all the warning they had.

He came at them in a flurry, landing blow after blow against Selene's sword as she threw herself between Jules and Cesare, barely managing to block both his blades.

One sliced her bicep, severing a tendon that dropped her sword hand uselessly to her side. She caught her blade before it hit the ground and deflected Cesare's second blade before it could gut her.

With his third arm he casually reached for the floor and tossed a handful of dust and marble shards at her eyes. She cried out, falling back as he swung again, drawing a line across her belly that was blessedly shallow but screamed through her nerves. Cesare roared at the near miss, less lucid and more animalistic by the moment.

In her blurry peripheral vision, Jules's boot planted itself in the middle of Cesare's chest, kicking him back. Cesare slammed through a colonnade and right through the travertine wall, exposing a flight of ancient stairs.

Jules's gaze was filled with more concern than flame. His expression cleared, and she recognized some of the Jules she knew returning. "You can't go on like this," he said quietly. "You'll die." He pressed his palm to her stomach, the other touching her spine.

Solemn and concerned. Afraid. But *himself* again.

She was frightened too, but *not* of dying. She was afraid of unleashing her power and unraveling her soul until it was a frayed, unrecognizable thing. She didn't want to become worse than the worst demon, hungering only for blood and chaos.

Cesare groaned and untangled himself from the debris. Jules's head snapped his way and a second pair of gold eyes opened beneath his first.

Incontrovertible proof he was a demon.

Selene didn't care. Here, where her father had written his own death warrant, the two most important men in her life squared up. She couldn't live in stasis. She had to adapt to survive. Falling to her knees, she laid out her limp arm as though on an altar. Knife in hand, she whittled into bone, triggering her runes. *Speed, strength, resilience, foresight, precognition, fire.* More than she had ever dared trigger in one go.

When the flames trickled over her skin, she felt the full power of God—her *Dio Immortale*—fill her up, running hot and liquid through her veins, scalding her center like wildfire. She felt herself hollowed out, and there was more raw power than there was Selene.

She smiled. Her fight with Cesare had lasted a second and a day. A *lifetime*. But soon it would be over. Jules seemed to sense the enormity of what she'd done. He eased back. Cesare's movements were erratic and strange, chilling her blood. She didn't think she imagined the flicker of fear that burned in his skull.

"I love you still, uncle," she breathed.

Cesare stretched his arms, preparing to fight her at her most deadly.

Her senses were assaulted by a wave of sensation—the blood rushing in Jules's veins, the heavy thud of his heart as it hammered itself against his ribs, the soft scrape of Cesare's breath through bared teeth. She could even hear her own threads snapping and breaking, untethering her from who she was and who she knew she could be until she was nothing but raw power. *Dio*, it felt good. Why had she ever resisted?

Tipping her head back, she laughed, the sound pealing out like Ave Maria. Overloud and wrong in this usually quiet place.

She pressed a palm to her stomach where Jules's hand had been and felt the skin knit as though the wound was nothing. Not even Lucia, specialized as she was, could have hoped for more. Without looking at Jules, with what little she could summon of her own self in this moment, she whispered, "If I am undone by this, promise you'll finish it. I want you to do it, Jules. I don't want anyone else to kill me."

And though his expression twisted, his eyes were as hard as flint as he lowered his chin in a nod. "I'll do it."

"Promise me."

"I promise."

Satisfied, she redirected her attention to her uncle. "Do you want to see how much of a pathetic shade you really are, Cesare? Because for that you need to see the light."

She thrust out a hand and a pillar of flame coiled from her palm, hissing and snapping with the head of a snake. The arm Cesare had destroyed hung limp and bleeding from her shoulder. With a thought she healed it.

First, tendons formed with the taut resilience of a strung bow. Then muscles wrapped around the bone. Finally the flesh she'd mutilated for power knitted and healed. Snatching her fallen sword, she held it.

"I am the light."

The Deathless God spoke through her.

CHAPTER FORTY-THREE

J ules knew instinctively that his power was a chrysalid not yet ready to unfurl. If he used it, he might destroy more than he could save. He was quiescent. Selene, on the other hand, was vital. Like life itself distilled. And as though jealous of that, the Imperium Bellum was becoming something less. His power swelled, lashing at the room around him, tearing chunks out of the stone and ripping up slabs of floor in disintegrating waves, destroying everything it touched. More powerful, more unhinged.

Jules watched Selene hungrily, eyes drawn to her as though he was a firefly battering itself against a lantern and she was the light inside. He would willingly die smashing his body to that light if he had to, just to be close to her.

Overhead, the dome creaked with the moan of a dying animal. One that had dragged itself somewhere quiet to die alone. He couldn't worry about the architecture—even as it threatened to collapse in on them—Selene was battling for her life.

Cesare was siphoning his power from the Deathless God, drawing on it greedily like he might never get enough.

Jules stared at the captive god. A fiery thread connected him and the spear, showing him where to strike for a killing blow like the ones he'd always been able to see on the battlefield. All it would take was a shift in the spear's angle, a slight twist, and an upward thrust, and God would be released from his suffering.

Humanity's God.

And *his* father.

With an almost hysterical urge to laugh, Jules considered the quandary before him. Patricide or deicide, which was the greater sin?

He recalled Baliel's words from the masquerade. *He will not die,* he'd said. *I won't let him.*

Baliel was wrong, because Selene was too far gone.

If Jules waited, she would die.

To save Selene, he would need to kill the Deathless God himself.

Like a frisson of distant lightning, Jules could feel the faintest flutter of Baliel's presence on the furthest edge of his senses. He was somewhere in the Vatican and moving toward them, but he wasn't close enough.

"*Dieu Immortel,*" he breathed. "I'm sorry."

He didn't hear his words through his own ears—he heard them magnified via his father's power and, distantly, through Selene.

Through their connection here in this strange chamber.

Through God's blood and his own and the borrowed blood in her veins.

Following that thread of power he'd always been able to see, Jules reached for the spear. He experienced Selene's moment of surprise and grief as he grasped the spear and threw all his strength into driving it home.

There were so many reasons he wanted to do this—so that Selene would not burn herself out, so that Cesare couldn't grow so strong he could overwhelm her, so that they'd have a chance of surviving this and killing Cesare. But he also wanted to release the Deathless God from his suffering. Though it hurt to know Baliel was so near and he would never have the chance to save him.

As the spear broke ribs, splitting God open and spilling a waterfall of golden blood to the floor, a pair of hands closed over his own. Delicate pianist's fingers with a will of iron behind them. Selene was nearly sobbing in pain as she leaned her shoulder against his. "Wait! We can free him."

Through the faint connection, he could feel her desire to atone. To finish what her father started. To thwart Cesare. But most of all she wanted this because it was *right*.

Because what the Vatican had done was so horribly wrong.

He stumbled back with one of Selene's hands on his chest. She grasped the shaft with her other hand and pulled, dragging it from her God's body with one final vicious yank before flinging it away. The spear embedded itself a foot into the wall. A sound like the cracking of thick lake ice resonated around the space as fissures appeared in the stone.

Then the Deathless God stirred.

Terrible eyes opened, revealing no hint of sclera, only burning, roiling gold in first one pair, then a second.

Agony twisted the handsome face as his back arched and the skin of his stomach stitched back together. Muscles rippled, bunching, as he wrenched an enormous limb from the crucifix, pulling twelve-inch nails loose as his chains fell.

The ground shook when he dropped to the floor, his ankles buckling so he collapsed to his knees. Jules pushed Selene behind him. The Deathless God cocked his head and flames licked over his long limbs. The same magic Baliel had used at the masquerade seemed to manifest clothes from flame. Even though they were almost identical to Jules's, they weren't quite right, as though made from a secondhand description.

Standing, he pulled iron nails from his flesh as he strode past them, the four burning eyes utterly intent on Cesare. When he reached the Imperium Bellum, he grasped Cesare in veined hands and threw him through the chamber wall.

Unhurriedly the Deathless God followed.

Selene and Jules shared a look and scrambled through the hole after them, emerging in time to see the Deathless God tearing each of Cesare's arms out by the root—the way a child might pluck off dragonfly wings—in the gold lantern light of a Vatican courtyard.

A high, uncanny sound tumbled from him as he tore out the last arm, throwing it hard enough to behead a statue. The Deathless God was giggling, taking insane glee in dismembering Cesare.

Finally, the Deathless God slammed Cesare into the stone by his shoulders. Once. Twice. When the Deathless God dropped him on the fractured stone, the Imperium Bellum was utterly still.

Moonlight trickled through cypresses, illuminating the Deathless God—*Arius*, Jules recalled—but there was no light of recognition in the Deathless God's eyes when they settled on Jules. Only the pain of madness. Only the sort of emptiness left behind by infinite losses.

Something that was not quite hatred twisted his expression as he approached.

When their eyes met, his brows crumpled predatorily. He might snarl or tear Jules's throat out with his teeth. Neither would shock him.

Jules stepped in front of Selene.

She was fading. Shadows crackled around her eyes where power had burned her sockets black. It was as though her body could barely hold it all, and flickering gold lit her veins as though burning her from the inside, and Jules had the awful realization that it might be too late for her as well. A shadowy serpent twined around her bicep, the needles of its ribs slicing her skin to ribbons.

She had pushed it too far in her final stand against Cesare while he agonized over his choice to kill his father.

The Deathless God raised a hand, as though to grasp Jules's throat in his fist, and a figure coalesced out of the darkness behind the fallen god.

Baliel seemed to sharpen around the edges and his youthful body changed—limbs lengthening, hair burning with blue fire. With terribly sad eyes, he looked from Jules to his son, bearing witness to the lack of recognition there. His blue eyes were dark with grief as he took in all Arius had lost. His grief was for Jules, too.

Between blinks, he was beside his son. Equal in size. He laid an enormous palm on his shoulder, the touch triggering a change in the captive God. The Deathless God's eyes cleared and his perfect lips parted as if to speak.

Breath stuttering, Jules took an unsteady step forward. But Selene's fragile weight against him held him back. Her breath was strained, whistling in a way that was deeply wrong. Still, he couldn't look away from the man who had been God. Baliel's blue flames engulfed them, their forms flickering. Jules bit the inside of his cheek.

The coiling flame on Selene's sword was quenched by an explosive wave of energy like a collapsing star. She buckled. He caught her beneath her knees and cradled her against his chest.

Baliel shifted, and for a moment his hand reached toward Jules from the flames.

I'm proud of you. Baliel's voice was indistinguishable from the crackling of the blue flames, and it might have been inside his mind. Jules tore his eyes away as Baliel and his father disappeared within the blinding fire. When the flame died, nothing remained but ashen footprints.

Jules dragged in a breath, relief and sadness warring for primacy.

Selene's power was still a roiling, burning thing inside her, not yet emptied out after so many years. Her cheek rested heavy against his collarbone. Heavy as death. And in her cold, still body only the core of his father's power burned hot.

EPILOGUE

On the marble inlay floor, Selene bent her head, both hands on her sword. The light in the chapel dimmed to red as an unseen choir sang from the nave. Her knees were already beginning to ache from the pose.

"Cry not as we farewell our departed. Rage instead. Rage, rage against time itself for taking him from us."

"*Vale*," Selene said softly.

"*Vale, saevus defensor et servus Dei.*"

Farewell, cruel defender and servant of God.

"*Vale.*"

Her heart broke as she dipped her chin at the body laid out on gold and cream tasseled silk. She looked right past the others— Caterina with her gun on the marble, hands atop it as she bowed almost to the floor, Gabriel with his knives—to the still face of the Exorcist Primus.

She squeezed her eyes shut. *Vale, Cesare.*

He wouldn't get a funeral like this or any funeral at all. After God rose again, his shadow had been widely disavowed by the rest of the Vatican leadership. The Imperium Politikos and all Cesare's lieutenants. The entire hierarchy had turned against him. Despite what he'd done to her, and what he'd tried to take, she could not hate him. He had been her teacher. Her only remaining family.

And it ached bone-deep to witness another pillar of her world discredited.

First her father, who had not deserved it. Now her uncle, who had.

The fresh wound ached the most.

She missed Jules's presence at her side more than anything right now. And she itched to be outside his cell with her hand on her gun. Being away from him made her insides squirm with the unknown of it all. What could be happening to him when she wasn't there?

The last time they'd been separated *he died*.

No matter how many times Selene told herself that Jules had not, in fact, died, her truth persisted. She'd lost him. Finding him again only took away *some* of the sting. She forced herself to remain still, ignoring the scream of aching muscles and bruised knees, her ribs which had been cracked and mended by Lucia, but still seemed to remember.

Adriano de Sanctis found Selene later, pulling her aside. "Don't look so worried. He's been pardoned." Selene bit her lip, holding in her questions. "Cesare's last official action was condemning a man to death, and so, naturally, it has become paramount to absolutely everybody that that man must live." He smiled slightly, but his eyes were full of the same grief she felt.

"Is it official?"

"Close enough."

The knots in her chest only loosened an inch—she wouldn't feel better until Jules was free. She cast a cool glance toward Ambrose, who stood nearby. "It's remarkable how quickly rats abandon a sinking ship."

Adriano nodded. "Nobody recalls how enthusiastically they supported him now. To hear them speak of it, the Imperium Bellum worked alone with nobody the wiser."

And that was how history would remember. A new dogma was already being written. The tale of the Imperium Bellum, Cesare Alleva, the Shadow of God, who broke all the rules and forced God away. All while the Exorcist Primus's body was still warm.

Their corporeal god had chosen to save them, and sacrificed himself, leaving his body in their charge. Or so the stories said. He was a warrior god and his rage at having his eternal rest disturbed had destroyed Cesare. Then he'd turned his back on humanity forever.

More lies. Lies upon lies, wrapping this place like a shroud.

Adriano saw the way her lip curled and he chuckled. "You know, your father used to wear that exact expression when he was particularly disappointed in others." He touched his own incisor. "His lip would snag on this tooth right here, just like yours is doing now."

Selene schooled her expression, pressing her lips together.

Adriano drew a book from his pocket and handed it to her. "I think this is yours."

It was her father's notebook, seized the morning she and Jules were arrested.

She pressed it between her palms. "I never thought I'd see it again."

His smile didn't reach his eyes. "And maybe you shouldn't."

She thought about that later as she walked through the Vatican gardens, after finally having been released from her duty. Nobody was sorry to see her go. She had thought the Alleva name could not lose any more of its luster, but she'd been wrong. Now she was the last Alleva, and all Rome expected her to be just as much of a disappointment.

At least Matteo and Cesare started out right, they said. *She's been rotten from the start.*

She curled her fingers around her father's notebook, smoothing her thumb over the raised leather. Why shouldn't she have it? What more was there to know? Seven years after the fact, she'd finished what her father had started. The words on these pages were history now.

A movement in her peripheral vision had her drawing her sword an inch, but then hands wrapped around her waist. Selene knew those hands. She let go of her sword, reaching back for Jules as his lips found the hollow of her throat and he stumbled with her into a small pencil pine. She laughed, inhaling the spicy scent of her own body wash from his skin.

"I'm a free man again." His hair was wet, dripping down his cheeks. "An official pardon."

She turned to face him. "So I hear."

Her relief was so intense it might almost be considered pain.

She pulled his head down, kissing him with all the fury she'd bottled up at seeing him imprisoned.

Jules groaned against her mouth, pulling her an impossible inch tighter to his body. She could feel his heart thundering through the thin fabric.

Her hand twisted in his shirt. "Idiot. You'll freeze."

He stole another kiss, sighing against her lips. "Worth it."

She took his hand, pulling him back toward her rooms, trying not to let him see her smile. He grinned broadly, lifting her hand to brush a kiss against her wrist.

The day after the Exorcist Primus's funeral, Gabriel was found dead in the frosted shade of a large cypress. It did not make any official reports. Selene wasn't sure when each new wound would stop hurting—she hadn't even really *liked* Gabriel.

A day later, two more bodies were found. Once they'd been identified—by their teeth, apparently—it got around that they were in the execution arm of the Vatican. Caterina had knocked lightly on their door late at night to impart the news.

Selene knew better than most that Cesare kept his own counsel. Even when he had condemned Jules to death, he had kept his reasons secret beyond a tight circle of his most loyal lieutenants. Gabriel. Ambrose. The executioners.

After Caterina left, Selene told Jules what she'd learned. He paled and she suspected she knew what he was thinking—that the people who knew about him were turning up dead.

"I'm sure it's a coincidence."

He shook his head. "No such thing."

The hammering of fists on the door to Selene's rooms made them both snap their heads up. Selene's gun was in her hand before she knew it.

When she eased the door open, Florentina tumbled in, tears streaking her face. She looked between Selene and Jules, then threw herself against his chest and sobbed big, racking sobs. But when she spoke, her words were for Selene. "I'm so scared. They're coming for me next. Please . . . Selene. Help me."

Selene and Jules shared a look.

As Jules ushered Florentina through to the sunroom, where there was a steaming pot of tea waiting, Selene noticed a large parchment envelope that had been pushed beneath the door. She only opened it after Florentina had fallen asleep. Wordlessly she handed it to Jules.

"This is bizarre," Jules said, turning the page over. "Do they really not know?"

Selene carded her fingers through her hair. "I don't know. And . . . I don't know who to ask."

The letter of pardon had arrived, but it was addressed to Eliot D'Alessandro. As far as the current Vatican leadership were concerned, Jules Lacroix didn't exist.

Cesare had kept his secrets close.

Jules dropped the letter onto the table. "This means I'm not really safe at all."

Selene shook her head wordlessly, but she couldn't deny it. Without a pardon in his name, he was at risk.

Picking it up, she frowned as she looked closer at the thick wax seal at the bottom. "What . . . what's this emblem?"

"Didn't you hear?" Florentina raked blond hair off her face as she leaned in the doorway, coming to sit on the arm of Selene's chair. "They've recalled the College."

"What does that mean?" Jules asked.

"It means the College is in charge," Florentina answered.

A chill unrelated to the temperature trickled down Selene's spine. "Only until they select a new Exorcist Primus," she interjected. "It won't be long."

Florentina shook her head, her eyes wide and her mouth pressed into a worried line. "No. They say they won't choose before they investigate what happened. They hung a decree on the doors of St. Peter's barely an hour ago. They intend to root out the corruption in the Vatican."

Selene went to her window. In the square below stood a figure. Extremum Filum.

She shivered.

As though he felt her eyes on him, the Filum turned and looked up at her. She resisted the impulse to pull away and held still, her hand trembling on the curtain. Selene felt the charge in the air as they looked at each other, though their eyes didn't meet. They could not. Because the man had an eyeless gunmetal mask on his face that would never come off.

With the Exorcist Primus dead, they were back.

It was late—or maybe early—when Jules woke with a start. The embers of the fire were burning low, and with a quiet groan he pushed himself off the brocaded chaise and tossed another log on the fire.

It was quiet and he wasn't sure what had woken him.

Florentina was asleep in his place in the bed, and he scowled at her as he knelt beside Selene. She murmured as he brushed gentle fingers against the bruises on her back and ribs. He pulled her hair off her shoulder and moved the silken strap of her camisole aside so he could press a light kiss to her warm skin. Even battered and bruised with that haunted look in her eyes, she was perfect to him.

She was *always* perfect to him.

His fingertips trailed along the vertebrae at the back of her neck, over the tiny tattoos. "I won't run again," he breathed, so quietly it barely stirred the still.

She didn't wake so he regretfully moved away, drawn back to the fire by its dancing light. He turned the small folded note between his fingers, then tossed it into the flames.

Written in Sparrow's distinctive hand, it had been waiting for him when he was released from the Vatican cells.

*The Vatican is already devouring itself, and it will
only get worse.
St. Peter's is more dangerous now than ever.
Especially for you.
Leave tonight.*

Sparrow

Jules watched the note catch alight, its edges blackening and curling.

He wouldn't run. Not again.

ACKNOWLEDGMENTS

Years have passed since *Cruel Is the Light* began as a delightful dream. A thousand tiny moments—flashpoints of good luck and great timing—have led to this book arriving in your hands now. It would not have been possible without the love and support of my family and friends and everyone who believed in me and this book.

To my incredible agent, Josh Adams, for being my champion ever since I first heard your even-keeled voice on the other end of the telephone line. Whenever you step in, I always feel as though everything will be all right—and attribute that to your big dad energy. Thanks also to Tracey Adams and Anna Munger for all your work behind the scenes. I'm so lucky to be a part of the Adams Literary family.

To Christabel McKinley, who handled everything UK and Australia, and everyone at David Higham Associates. Lizzy, Caroline, and all who had a part to play. Christabel, when we met in London and spent a whole day drinking tea and visiting bookshops, I knew you'd become a good friend as well as a great agent.

It was something of a global team effort to sculpt *Cruel Is the Light* into the book it is today, and I'm so lucky to have enthusiastic editors across three continents and on both sides of the Atlantic and Pacific Oceans. The multiple time zones may have been a logistical nightmare, but everything else more than made up for it.

To Melanie Nolan, my insightful editor at Knopf: I'll be forever grateful for your editorial vision, and one thought in particular drove an edit I love—the chapters in question are the way they were always meant to be now, thanks to your vision. Thanks also to the amazing Random House Children's team, who have worked with me on *Cruel*: Dana Carey, Casey Moses, Ken Crossland, Melinda Ackell, Alison Kolani, Natalia Dextre, and Jake Eldred.

And to the Penguin Random House Audio/Listening Library team who produced the astounding audiobook of *Cruel Is the Light*, special thanks to Kirby Crosbie, also to Rebecca Waugh, Emily Parliament, Kristen Capano, and Desiree Johnson.

To Anthea Townsend, my wonderful editor at Penguin UK. Your enthusiasm for this book has been apparent from our very first call. It was brilliant meeting you in London; thanks for treating me to a very special—and rather Selene-coded—afternoon tea at the Corinthia (*with* champagne, which is how all afternoon teas ought to be!). And thank you for championing this book. A special thanks to Ben Hughes, the art director behind my beautiful cover, and to everyone at Puffin/Penguin UK who helped me make *Cruel* the book I wanted it to be. To Libby Thornton, Shreeta Shah, Andrea Kearney, Afua Antwi, Sara Jafari, Chessanie Vincent, Sarah Doyle, Naomi Green, Adam Webling, Harriet Venn, Carmen McCullough, Ruth Knowles, Jane Tait, and Eleanor Updegraff.

To Zoe Walton and Mary Verney, my fantastic editors at Penguin Australia, thank you for being my enthusiastic home team. Every time I get an email from either one of you, I get a little boost of endorphins because you've been nothing but wonderful throughout this whole process. And thank you for all the adorable Penguin packages you've sent me. They're always a delight! And to Bec Diep, Maddy Taplin, Georgie Martin, Angela Duke, Adelaide Jensen, Hannah Armstrong, Debbie McGowan, and everyone on the sales and marketing teams, thank you all for being such brilliant cheerleaders and enthusiastic supporters for me and this book. I'm so lucky to have landed with you for my debut.

To Mona Finden, my incredible cover artist, for always seeing Jules and Selene so clearly. In my experience, a cover is not always *the book*, but in this case it certainly is. You captured the spirit of my story and truly realized my characters in your art. Thank you, always.

To Virginia Allyn, the artist behind the incredible map of the Deathless God's Rome and sinister Vatican. Thank you for drawing until your hand hurt. You created a masterpiece—one that I'll always treasure.

To Emily Thiede and Lauren Blackwood, my brilliant Pitch Wars mentors turned dear friends. Thank you for selecting *Cruel* out of a slush pile of hundreds and falling in love with it. Emily, I know *that* line in Chapter 2 was what sealed the deal for you. I hope readers fall in love with Jules as hard and fast as you did. And Lauren, thank you for being a steady hand during the ups and downs; I always love getting your perspective and advice.

Being part of the final Pitch Wars class was a huge milestone for me and *Cruel*. I met so many brilliant writers through the mentorship program and I wouldn't be here without it.

To Mikayla Bridge, who has been ride or die since the start. So happy to have been on this journey together—and now we're both 2025 debuts! And to fellow Pitch Wars mentees and other writer friends: Kelly Mancaruso, Sian Gilbert, Cait Jacobs, Clare Osongco, P. H. Low, Keshe Chow, Jules Arbeaux, Mallory Jones, K. A. Cobell, Morgan Watchorn, Kelly Andrews, Jihyun Jun, Kalie Holford, Maria Medina, Megan Scott, Shana Targosz, Crystal Seitz, Roanne Lau, Pascale Lacelle, Kristina Mancaruso, M. K. Lobb, Amber Chen, Ed Crocker, A. S. Webb, Christine Arnold, Megan Davidhizar, Alyssa Villaire, Emily Charlotte, and Natalie Sue, to name just a few. Thanks for your support, advice, and friendship; for helping me shape this story; and (for many of you) riding this roller coaster with me on the way to publication with your own debuts.

And to the authors who are ahead of me who lent a hand, answered questions, and gave advice and support in ways big and small: Jay Kristoff, Vanessa Len, Emily J. Taylor, Amie Kaufman, Maiya Ibrahim, Ayana Gray, Eliza Chan, Bea Fitzgerald, Rosie Talbott, Saara El-Arifi, Diana Urban, Dahlia Adler, Tess Sharpe, Gigi Griffis, Brenda Drake, Katt Dunn, Kate Dylan, Helen Corcoran, Keely Parrack, Lillie Lainoff, Miel Moreland, Meredith Tate, Frances White, Kate Armstrong, and more.

Thank you to those who checked the Latin, French, and Italian found in the pages of this book. To Lena Uesbeck, my best friend and Latin expert, with whom I once sat in on a Latin class at a German university. I had the unique and terrifying privilege of watching you translate entire passages of Latin in *minutes*. Thank you for explaining nominative, dative, accusative, genitive, ablative and vocative cases to me—I did not understand at all! And thanks for using your knowledge to create this vital phrase: *Deus, desiderium meum in Jules Lacroix averte*. I'm sure your professors would be so proud! To Cindy R. X. He and Penn Cole, who helped with French endearments, and to Holly Gramazio, who helped with Italian ones.

To the GH crew: Katt, Paul, Tim, and honorary member, Miles.

Importantly, to my family—my father, Nick, the journalist, who likes to claim I inherited his writing talent and has always been so proud of me and this book; my mother, Amanda, the artist, from whom I certainly inherited any artistic talent I have, who is always as excited as I am when something good happens for this book; my black-and-white and perfect border collie, Indy; and

Frances, Brianna, and Molly. Thank you all for your love and support. This book wouldn't be here without you.

And last but not least, to the readers who have picked up *Cruel Is the Light*—my heartfelt thanks for reading. I'm beyond excited to share this story with you and hope that Jules, Selene, Sparrow, and the rest force their way cruelly into your hearts as they have done mine.